THE SEA SISTERS SWIMMING CLUB

An unputdownable romance about sisterhood
and second chances

SUE MCDONAGH

Choc Lit
A JOFFE BOOKS COMPANY

Choc Lit
A Joffe Books company
www.choc-lit.com

This edition first published in Great Britain in 2023

© Sue McDonagh

Cover design by Berni Stevens Cover Design

Original art by Sue McDonagh

ISBN: 978-1-78189-587-0

*To the Cardiac Department of University Hospital of Wales,
Cardiff, without whom I probably wouldn't still be here.*

CHAPTER ONE

'You should be *daaanciing*, ye-ah!'

Sequins of sweat spangled through the disco lights as Fran Doherty flicked her hair to the deafening music. Bellowing the lyrics off-key, she gave it all she had. Out there on the light-changing dance floor, she was still in her twenties and not, gulp, in her fiftieth year.

Tonight was cause for celebrating. And what a cracking job they'd done, assisting in a protracted operation to nail the serial rapist who had been terrorizing the city for weeks. Weeks of double shifts and meticulous legwork. They'd all be looking forward to payday this month. The long hours and stressful investigations had finally paid off.

'So when are you actually retiring, Sarge? Maybe then we'll have shift nights off in *normal* places and not have to listen to all this seventies rubbish!' Gavin, her senior police constable, bawled over the music, his teeth gleaming against his youthful skin, his muscular shoulders gyrating to the beat.

'Are you trying to get rid of me? I am *never* retiring!' Fran twirled away, windmilling her arms left and right in a mangled version of the dance made famous by John Travolta all those years ago. *Saturday Night Fever*. She remembered dancing to it with her mum in the kitchen. Shimmying back towards Gavin, she grinned as he eye-rolled her and yelled over the music, 'And "rubbish"? I'll have you know, young man, *this* is the legendary Bee Gees!'

Her shift. She looked around at them. Their faces bright in the whirling kaleidoscope of lights and colour. Six of them, all under thirty, apart from Gavin and he was only a few years older. A tight-knit crew who'd do anything for one another. She'd honed them, bawled them out, straightened their dodgy paperwork and wiped their figurative arses. The nearest thing she had to a family, although she'd never admit it aloud.

She massaged the base of her neck as her throat constricted strangely. Her breath felt harsh, as if she'd just run up a steep hill. It had to have been the chips with the meal that evening. Or maybe she *was* getting old. Nah. Perish the thought. Fifty wasn't old. Everyone said it was the new . . . whatever it was. Who cared.

Though lately she'd felt every day of that nearly half a century. Like the soft bulge that had appeared around her middle. She ran regularly and cut out the tea break bickies, but the bloody thing would not budge. Everything seemed so much more difficult lately, except for a new ability to fall asleep midway through a shift. But never at bedtime.

The strange squeezing feeling in her chest had come on earlier that evening. If it wasn't for all the ribbing from the guys about how ancient she was now, she'd have cancelled.

Her chest flared now with a sudden sharp pain that subsided as quickly as it had arrived. Almost as quickly. She rubbed her chest with the heel of her palm.

It was heartburn. Of course it was. She hadn't had it for a while but shift work messed up regular eating. She wished she'd put some indigestion tablets in her bag.

The room tilted dizzily just as the next familiar song boomed out, and she staggered slightly. That was weird. It couldn't be the wine. She'd only had a single glass with the meal. She loved to dance, so she always stayed on cola or plain water. Put it in a big glass with lots of ice and a slice and nobody knew it wasn't alcoholic. Not that she cared what other people thought. Her body seemed to sway to the beat without her. *Heartburn*, she told herself firmly.

'C'mon — you're not sitting this one out,' she shouted, still kneading her breastbone as she saw them all heading for their table. 'It's a classic!'

'What fresh hell is this?' Gavin stopped and faced her, head on one side, listening. He frowned. She laughed at his expression.

'It's "Oops Up Side Your Head". The rowing song.' She rolled her eyes at their mystified expressions. 'Honestly, I swear I have socks older than you lot. You have to sit on the floor and pretend to row. Follow everyone else. And give me a hand to get down there too, I can hardly move in this stupid dress.'

'I'm wearing Armani!' Gavin grumbled, lowering them both gingerly onto the filthy floor. Trust him not to have gone for a seventies-vibe outfit. Fran leaned forward, preparing to fake-row in the oddest and most un-PC dance craze from the past ever, while someone stood at the front pretending to whip them as if they were galley slaves. She looked down at her long, muscular legs stretched out before her, the sequinned mini-dress charity shop purchase riding up her thighs, and smiled back over the last twenty-five years of her career.

The tightness in her chest exploded without warning into agonizing pain. Spasms staked her to the floor. Her eyes clamped shut. *God! What the hell?* Hunched forward, wrapping her arms around herself, she howled in helpless pain.

Heart — galloping. Jumping. Stopped. Bounced.

Lungs — Tight. Squeezed.

'*Oops upside yer head . . .*'

Can't. Breathe.

'*. . . say oops . . .*'

'Get on with it, Fran!' Gavin yelled over her shoulder. 'This was your idea!'

Pushed. Crumpled. Shoved. Eyes. Squeezed. Shut. Struggle. To. Breathe.

'Oi! You can't just sit there! Fran?' A hand on her shoulder. 'What's up? You okay?'

They lifted her to her feet. The music pounded. Her pulse drowned it. Opening her eyes made the room swim.

She shut them.

'I'm f-fine.' Her legs buckled. 'Fine.' Gasped. Scared. She was *never* scared. 'Fine,' she repeated.

'You don't look fine.' Gavin lowered her onto a bench seat. He squatted before her and frowned up at her. She was dimly aware through clenched eyelids that he was taking her pulse. She heard the word 'ambulance'.

'What are you . . . my m-mother?' Fran tried to glare at him but her eyes stayed shut. Voice a whisper. 'Can't . . . get my . . . b-breath . . .' She rubbed her sternum. 'S'probably . . . indigestion . . .'

CHAPTER TWO

Wyn's mobile buzzed in the pocket of his overalls just as the delivery driver disappeared out of the gates of Y Hen Ysgol — the Old School. He glanced at the screen, eyeing the heap of newly delivered rolls of insulation that he needed to move before it rained, and clicked accept.

'Hi, Tash.'

'Wyn! It's Tash.' She said it every time despite surely knowing that her name was visible with each call. 'I'm really sorry to ask you, but I've got a puncture and AJ is at work and . . .'

'Oh dear. You've got breakdown cover, haven't you?'

'Uh, I did have, but, um, I cancelled it. It was so expensive! I'm sorry to be such a nuisance.'

Wyn breathed out a long, silent sigh. 'Where are you?' She told him and he calculated in his head how long it would take him to get there, get Tash mobile again and get back. So that was his afternoon taken up. He looked up at the leaden sky.

'Look, I have to get this stuff under cover. I'll be there as soon as I can, okay?'

'Okay.' She made a long, teary-sounding sniff. 'Thank you, Wyn. I've always been able to rely on you. I'm sorry to be such a pest.'

'Don't worry about it. I'll see you later.' He ended the call and decided to throw a tarp over the insulation instead. It would take him ages to move it. It still took him nearly an hour to gather his tools and get the van on the road.

Why was Tasha penny-pinching over breakdown insurance? She'd surely had enough money out of their divorce. Although knowing her spending habits, she'd probably bought a designer dress with it.

The police car flashed him as he was halfway there, bowling along the long coast road. He pulled over into a rutted lay-by. His wing mirrors showed the policeman strutting towards him and his heart sank.

'Mr Morgan.'

'PC James.' Otherwise known as AJ to Wyn's ex-wife, Tasha. And PC Knobhead to Wyn.

'We've had a report of stolen goods being transported in a white van. Open up, please.'

Wyn climbed down and strolled to the back doors of his van, mentally totting up what was in there and how much of a nuisance the man would make of himself. He watched, silently fuming as the policeman made a point of inspecting everything he could find.

'Where are you off to in such a hurry?' He photographed the serial number of a disc cutter, as Wyn gritted his teeth.

'I'm going to help a friend with car trouble,' he said.

'Really? Well, aren't you just the knight in shining armour, Mr Morgan.' PC James sneered. Wyn refused to rise to the bait.

'I do what I can.'

The policeman made him show his lights and indicators and laboriously inspected his tyres — letting him go with a warning on those, which Wyn knew was entirely spurious — before waving him away in a manner that suggested Wyn had wasted his time.

Driving away at snail's speed so as not to give the policeman another reason to stop him, Wyn seethed. As if it wasn't bad enough that Tasha had left him, she'd picked that total dickhead.

By the time he found Tasha and her immobilized car, he'd worked himself into a snarling fury. Tasha winced as she saw his face and he was instantly contrite.

'Wassup?'

'I met your charming husband on the way here.' Wyn took the space-saver wheel out of the boot, loosened the wheel nuts and jacked the car up. Tasha shrank back.

'Oh God — you didn't tell him where you were going, did you?'

'Of course I didn't.' He grunted as he heaved the wheel off. Things like this were difficult now. Things he'd taken for granted.

'Can I help?' Tasha stepped forward.

'Why do you stay with him, Tash?' Ignoring her offer of assistance, he hefted the wheel awkwardly into the boot of her car.

'He's okay.'

'He's a bully.'

'No, it's me. I'm so silly at times. *You* know what I can be like. Isn't that why you used to work away so much?' She gave a tinkling laugh that didn't fool Wyn in the slightest. He clenched his jaw. She'd defend the man to save losing face.

'Why does he hate me so much?' Wyn glanced at her over his shoulder as he fitted the spare. 'He got what he wanted. He got you.' He saw her give a tiny, mute shrug. Would he ever know, he wondered. 'It makes life bloody difficult.'

'Sorry.' She hung her head. 'I do appreciate this.'

'Mmph. And for goodness' sake, sort out some break-down insurance. I can't keep coming out and doing this.'

They both knew he would. 'Thanks, Wyn.'

'And get that puncture fixed asap.'

'I will.' He watched her fold her high-heeled, slim legs into her smart black BMW, her nails still perfect, hair immaculate, and he looked down at himself. Dusty in old overalls, driving a battered van, living in a building site. Damaged goods. Not the man he once was — what did he have to offer her? No wonder she'd left him.

He lifted his good arm to wave as she speeded away and realized he hadn't even asked her where she was going or what she was doing out there in the middle of nowhere. She sold new houses on posh developments. He hoped that didn't mean another rash of identikit homes here, on this beautiful rural landscape of West Wales.

He stared over the multicoloured fields to the slice of grey sea, dark beneath a lowering sky that entirely suited his mood.

CHAPTER THREE

'Fran!' Gavin's shout followed the increasingly long presses on the doorbell. Fran eyed the door from her spot on the sofa, her thumb hovering over the pause button on the TV remote. She sighed. Gavin was a lovely young man, but his energy and sheer youth right now only underlined how old and worn out she felt.

'Sarge, I know you're in there. I can hear *Homes Under the Hammer*.' His voice took on a wheedling tone. 'Come on. We . . . I . . . We just want to know that you're okay. Not dead or anything. None of us have seen you for *ages*.'

None of them *had* seen her for ages. She'd made sure of that. Her parents had collected her from hospital in mid-February after the six-week stay during which her body had been reassembled after the complications of the surprise heart attack.

It was now April and her entire life had been turned on its head.

In the beginning, sporting a horrific, livid scar from neck to navel — a legacy from the open-heart surgery to fix the valves that had apparently simply flapped apart — she'd still felt like one of them. A warrior, with her battle scar. But still a police sergeant. Still in charge. They'd updated her on

9

cases they'd worked on, and the latest station gossip. Asked her opinion.

It had felt, newly home, as if she were on a very long period of leave. Just an extended holiday. A couple of weeks of convalescence had been overseen by parents who made no secret of the fact that they were keen to get back to their overseas adventures in their bus-sized motor home — and to top it all, were positively relieved at the prospect of her retirement from the police.

'Let's face it, darling,' her mother had said, smoothing back Fran's curly auburn hair as if she were still five years old, 'we never understood why you even wanted to *do* such an awful job. You should have stayed at that lovely gallery. You were so happy there. Much more suitable.'

More suitable for them, Fran grumbled inside. How was it that you reverted back to being fourteen when you saw your parents, whatever age you were? She was grateful that they'd returned to look after her — really, she was, even though they'd completely failed to appreciate her lovely, no-expense-spared apartment, and instead regaled her with constant tales of travelling the world while apparently spending no money at all, living in lay-bys and vineyards and eating from roadside stalls.

She'd asked them once what they did about fresh water, and they'd just shrugged and said they managed, and there was always wine. Fran had hoped they were joking. She didn't like to think about how they managed things like hygiene.

'I mean, you do seem to have a very skewed idea about people now,' her mother carried on. 'You're so suspicious of everyone. It's not good for you. And after all these years, you're still on your own, when everyone else has a grown-up family. What have you got out of it, really?'

'A whopping pension,' Fran replied firmly, 'and a flat in a prime spot in the city. The world is my lobster.'

Her mother sniffed. 'Let's hope so.'

And eventually, in a flurry of hugs and tears that Fran found horribly embarrassing, they'd left. She'd heaved a sigh of relief, telling herself that everything would return to normal, refusing to acknowledge the unaccustomed silence. She could watch her favourite TV programmes without their running commentary, for one thing.

Then at work, the 'chat' with her boss about her future in the police. The utter horror of handing back her warrant card. Lastly, that dreadful, awful, farewell dinner at a quiet country pub to mark the occasion.

If she'd ever thought about retirement — and ageing coppers counted the days down as it got closer and closer — she'd visualized a big celebration. She *loved* a party. She *was* the Dancing Queen, and no party was complete unless she'd been invited. She'd imagined dancing, loud music, outrageous cocktails and the promise of embarking on a new adventure — whatever shape it may take.

She'd always thought she'd go out with a bang.

Instead, the quietly tame evening had seen her out on a bleat. Not so much a door closing as a window slamming gently in her face. Over the polite dinner, Fran did her best to sound positive and jokey about being a retiree, on 'that colossal pension'. Cruises? Visit the world and convalesce at the same time? Of course, why not? She'd forced a laugh.

She couldn't imagine anything more hellish.

The evening of her retirement she'd looked around at the young men and women from her shift — and felt completely alien. She didn't belong. Their lives were galloping onwards and hers had stalled. Conversation was stilted and she had no idea what the joke was when spontaneous laughter broke out. She thought longingly of her TV and the movie package she'd yet to work through.

Overnight, it seemed, she'd morphed into a police pensioner. How had this happened? She groaned inwardly. There'd be invites from Headquarters for the annual garden party with her wearing a ditsy frock while pretending to all the real oldies that she was enjoying doing nothing. Nothing useful, anyway. Washed up, hopeless, finished. Useless. The whole idea was ghastly.

That dinner marked her retirement as finally official, and her shift stopped telling her things. Work-based things, anyway. They stopped asking for advice.

And worse — was it worse? She still couldn't decide — they had a new sergeant. A new *woman* sergeant. So she, Fran, wasn't their 'mum' anymore. She chastised herself for thinking the words. It was unworthy of her. She'd championed women's rights in the police for years and she was not a jealous person. Usually.

But rather than trying to unravel her feelings of loneliness, it was so much easier to stay away from everyone. That way she didn't even have to try to work out how to wear a brave face. The 'I'm fine, thanks, making the best of it. No, really, I'm living the dream, everyone should have a heart attack' face. It wasn't hiding, she told herself. Nobody liked a misery around the place. *She* didn't even like herself. She blew out a long and irritated sigh.

'Fran, if I don't hear you tell me you're okay, I'm breaking this door down.'

Gavin was persistent enough to carry out his threat, she knew that.

'I've taught you too well, Grasshopper.' Sweeping the multipack chocolate bar wrappers behind a cushion — online shopping really did sabotage her half-hearted attempts to diet — she rocked herself off the sofa without using her arms to push her up as she'd been instructed. Sliding back the bolts, she turned the key in the lock and pulled the door open.

'Good morning, Gavin. Of course I'm not dead, you arse. Did you think I'd done a Bridget Jones and been half eaten by Alsatians or something? And I'm not your sergeant. Not anymore.' Her stomach somersaulted as the words hung in the air. She hoped her tart tone disguised her nervous swallow.

'Same old grumpy Fran then.' Gavin's face split into a relieved grin. 'And of course you'll always be our Sarge. I brought salted caramel muffins . . .' He held out a paper bag. She saw his gaze scanning the flat over her shoulder and snorted.

'Do you want to come in and check that I'm looking after myself?'

'If you're offering . . .' Gavin stepped through the open door, and Fran shut it behind him, not sure whether she was pleased to see him or exasperated. She stalked to the kitchen.

'I'll put the kettle on then, shall I?'

'Are you allowed to lift that?' Following her like a puppy, Gavin hovered nearby.

'I'm not an *invalid*, Gavin.' Fran filled the kettle and flicked the switch. 'Get the big coffee pot down, if you would. I'm not supposed to reach up. And mention that again and I'll stab you with this spoon.'

'So, erm, how have you been? You're looking good!' Gavin leaned against the worktop, watching her, his hands drumming against his long, jeaned legs.

'I'm looking *fat*.' Fran pursed her lips. 'I'm on a diet,' she lied. People had gifted her vast boxes of luxury chocolates and other goodies, and sick of hospital food, she'd devoured the lot. The softness around her middle was now a fully fledged spare tyre. Her eyes strayed guiltily to the multipack chocolate wrapper peeking out from beneath the sofa cushion.

'So, you don't want these, then . . .' Gavin dangled the paper bag of muffins between thumb and forefinger.

'I didn't say that.' She rolled her eyes at him. 'So. What is it you want, Gav?'

'Milk, two sugars, same as . . . oh. Sorry, you mean, why am I here? Well, apart from wondering how you really are, I've got a proposition for you. A bit of R and R.'

'Rest and recuperation? I'm doing okay here, thank you.'

Gavin shuffled his feet and looked out of the window.

Fran narrowed her eyes. 'What?'

'Are you, though? Okay? Look, I don't mean to be blunt—'

'Then say nothing.' Fran lined up the handles of the mugs one way then the other while she waited for the kettle to boil.

'—but I know you're not getting out, and you're supposed to be walking twice a day. At least.'

'Oh my God. First you're my mother and now you're my doctor. I've already started cardiac rehab classes, as it happens.' Even though they seemed to be full of people twice her age and bored her to tears . . .

He narrowed his eyes at her and continued, 'That's good, but let's face it, this place isn't really conducive to taking a stroll. Your lungs would be full of diesel fumes by the end of the street — if you haven't already been run over by a souped-up pizza-delivering e-bike.' As if to underline his message, a cacophony of vehicle horns sounded outside. Even through the triple glazing, it was loud. Fran pretended to ignore it.

'I'm used to it.' She poured boiling water over the fresh coffee and stirred carefully, determined not to meet his eye. Beneath his scrutiny, she felt old. He was right, of course. Apart from the glacially slow cardiac rehab classes, she wasn't going out. She had everything she needed delivered, although it took her an eternity to put it all away — she was so slow. She even had to sit down while she did it. 'And Gav, while I appreciate you popping round, I don't need a carer. I'm doing okay.'

'Well, the thing is — you'd be doing me a favour.'

'You'd have done better if you'd started with that line. I was starting to feel really ramshackle.'

Gavin laughed. He spread his fingers and rubbed his palms together rapidly. 'I'm not sure where to start with this.' His hands smacked together as if he'd come to a decision. 'Mum and Dad are retiring and doing Route 66 by motorbike. And then the Rockies.' Fran opened and shut her mouth. His parents must be older than her, and they clearly had a lot more energy than she did. She compressed her lips, trying not to feel envious.

'They're planning to be away until the end of the year, and the thing is . . .' He flicked a glance at her as she opened her mouth to urge him to get to the point. He hurried on, 'They could really do with someone to look after their house while they're away. It's an insurance thing.'

14

'No.' Fran stirred the cafetière slowly, making sure the grounds were all under the water. It was decaffeinated these days, but it could still taste good if she took her time over it. 'Till the end of the year? No. God, no. Definitely not. What makes you think I'd want to sit in someone's house for all that time? That's a hell of a commitment. I might hate it! And what about my place here? I'd have exactly the same issue with my insurance.'

'One, it's newly renovated, absolutely gorgeous and practically *on* a fabulous beach.' His voice lingered on every vowel of 'fabulous' and Fran was reminded of his Welsh roots. 'You won't hate it, I promise you. And you don't have to stay there the whole time. You could maybe stay for the summer though . . .'

'Abroad?' Fran said, hopefully.

'West Wales.'

'Nearly abroad then.' Fran tried to conjure up a map in her head of West Wales and failed.

'Straight down the M4, and then a few country roads,' Gavin said, reading her mind as usual. 'It's a lovely drive. Honestly.'

'Summer in a middle-of-nowhere Welsh village.' Fran pushed back her overlong hair. She needed a trim. 'Don't you have your own language or something? Will I need lessons?'

Gavin puffed out a sigh, rolling his eyes at her. 'It's not Outer Mongolia. It's Britain. Everyone speaks English there too, y'know.' He put his mobile in her hand, open to his photos. 'Look. Keep scrolling. This is the house.' Fran peered at the colourful photos. A white stone cottage, with roses clambering over the front door and . . . some other flowering things she didn't have a clue about. And there was the sea behind it, turquoise and twinkling. The sea . . . She frowned.

'That's a big garden. I don't know anything about gardening. And I'm in no fit state to walk a dog. Or a horse or whatever other creature they might have. I'm a city girl.'

'No animals. Why would you think they have animals? And they have a gardener. You don't have to worry about a thing. You can have your groceries delivered if you don't want to shop. Although there is a shop. And a pub. And the locals are really friendly.'

'A thriving metropolis then.' Fran lifted a corner of her mouth to show she was teasing him. It did look inviting, she supposed. Even though it wasn't abroad. And the thought of strolling along a golden beach in Wales, the salty air tousling her auburn curls, was a more appealing prospect than dodging the multitudinous electric scooters on a city high street.

She carried on scrolling, enlarging the photos of the rooms and trying not to be impressed by the state-of-the-art kitchen and the plush master bedroom. 'And you grew up here? You lucky thing.'

'It wasn't this posh when I was a kid.' Gavin laughed. 'But it *was* a great village to grow up in. It's called Llanbryn. It means "church and hill", more or less.'

'I suppose I could do a month. Maybe two. See how it went.' Fran inspected the interiors minutely and pursed her lips as she thought. She tried out the village name. 'Clan what?'

'Bryn.'

'*ClanBrinn*,' she repeated, phonetically.

'That's it. You're a local already.'

Fran pursed her lips in a twisted smile. 'Yeah, right. But I wouldn't be happy about leaving my place empty.'

'Ah. That's number two in my plan.' He swallowed and Fran watched him thoughtfully. What was coming next? 'You remember I was telling you about selling our place?'

'Mmm.' Fran squinted at him. Somewhere in the distant recesses of her mind she remembered him telling her that. Her brain didn't seem to hold on to information the way it used to. Guiltily, she thought, it was all about *her* these days. Her hospital appointments, check-ups, the scar, fear, memories . . . *Stop it.* She tuned in to Gavin again.

'Ye-es . . .'

'We got the price we wanted . . .'

'That's great!' She frowned at him, sensing his hesitation. 'Isn't it?'

'Yes. Yes! Totally. But the house we wanted has fallen through, and our buyer wants to move in straight away . . . We don't want to lose the sale, but the alternative is renting . . .'

Fran grasped the situation instantly.

'. . . and wasting all that money . . . whereas you both could move in here for nothing while you're house-hunting, be close to work and kill two birds with one stone?'

Gavin fidgeted, blushing. 'Yeah . . . Course, Mum and Dad's will be empty but it's a long way to commute! Sorry. Forget it. It's a bloody cheek of me to suggest it . . . and obviously we'd pay you . . .' He tailed off, watching her.

'Would I be paying for my stay at your parents?'

'God, no. You're caretaking. They should be paying *you*!'

She nodded, drumming her fingers. Her stomach tingled with — what? Anticipation? Apprehension? The words *What if?* echoed in her mind. What if she needed a doctor? The hospital? How far away was it from civilization?

'There are doctors in Wales too . . .' Gavin smiled gently at her.

'Ah . . .' Fran groaned inwardly. She hadn't meant to say it aloud. Now she looked like an old worrywart. And not that long ago, she'd been a woman of action. Leading the charge. She cleared her throat. 'When are your parents leaving?'

'Early May.'

'They've left it late to get someone to look after the place.' Although that would give her time to finish the course of after-surgery warfarin along with the twice-weekly blood tests.

Gavin fiddled with the settings on her toaster. She reached over to reset them.

'They weren't going to bother. It's so quiet there, nobody gets broken into. Nil crime rate. But it's a condition on the house insurance that it's not empty all that time. And I thought of you. Well, to be fair, it was Ally's idea.'

Ally, Gavin's wife, was a pretty, level-headed nurse from the local hospital. Fran had liked her the minute she met her. She had a terrific sense of fun and Gavin adored her. Fran privately thought that babies would be next on their agenda.

'And if I want to come back here? Where will you go?'

Gavin shrugged. 'Well, we'd move out. We'd have to be flexible, all of us, I suppose. I mean, Mum and Dad might have to come home for some reason, although they wouldn't mind you still being there, there's plenty of room. Don't worry about us. Police accommodation is still available.'

'I see. You've obviously thought it through. And I have a spare room, as you know, even if it's tiny, so it would do you both in a pinch if I did have to come back here.' Fran stared into her mug, mulling the idea over. Almost to herself, she added, 'And I'm driving again.' Her stomach fluttered. 'Gives me time to practise some longer trips.'

Fran tried to sound upbeat about driving. She wouldn't admit to Gavin that her single trip to the local shops had been at the pace of a very elderly snail. She'd driven like someone who'd never even seen a car before. Like the drivers she despised, dithering and juddering below the speed limit.

How had she become this anxious old lady? It was as if the world had sped up around her. Her stomach lurched again. All the way to Wales? By herself? She squared her shoulders, then rubbed her sternum as the long scar pulled painfully. She felt the strange lumps and bumps beneath her fingers where she'd been wired together.

While part of her mind was saying no, a sneakier part conjured up the scent of the salty sea. She saw herself taking exhilarating breezy walks, dabbling her toes in sun-kissed shallows. An abrupt longing to escape the grime and fumes of the city flooded through her. The satellite movie package had long since exhausted its appeal. Surely, with practice, her driving skills would return to her. Wouldn't they?

Gavin watched her over his coffee mug. 'Shall I get them to ring you so you can ask them any questions?'

Fran tipped her head from side to side. 'Erm, I'm not sure. Not yet. They're very trusting, having a complete stranger staying in the house. I'm not sure I'd like it. I need to think about it.'

'They've packed all their personal stuff away and put it in storage. Just in case of flooding or something. It's peace of mind for them that they have a police sergeant staying in their house.'

'Even though there's a zero crime rate. And I'm retired.' Fran lifted her eyebrows at him as she sipped her coffee. 'And what could I do about flooding?'

'Aw, you know what old, er, older people are like.'

'At your age, Gavin, everyone seems old. Give me a day to think it over. I promise to let you know one way or the other by tomorrow evening.' Fran led the way into the sitting room. 'Come on then. Bring the muffins and give us all the gossip.'

Gavin wrapped his hands around his mug and smiled at her. 'Some things never change.'

They chatted for at least an hour. Beside his casual youth and fitness, she felt aged and doughy. It didn't stop her enjoying a muffin though.

The flat seemed to echo and feel empty when he'd gone. Fran washed up at the kitchen sink, staring thoughtfully out of the window at the rooftops and chimneys of the grey city. The doorbell rang again and she opened it absent-mindedly, thinking Gavin had forgotten something.

It wasn't Gavin.

'Ryan!' Astonished, she stared at him. They'd hung out together almost a year ago. At her age, she refused to call him a boyfriend, and in any case, he'd simply drifted away after a few months and she'd been so busy at work that she'd barely noticed he was missing. She'd since heard rumours about his two-timing and realized what a lucky escape she'd had. His handsome face was uncharacteristically unshaven. Her eyes drifted from his crumpled clothing to the trolley suitcase. She raised her eyebrows.

'Going on holiday?'

'Oh, ha ha. You gonna let me in?'

'Um . . .' He barged past her. Clutching her chest protectively, she backed away as his trolley case ran over her foot. 'Ouch. No, I'm fine, don't worry. I have another one just like it.' Rubbing her foot against her opposite calf, she closed the door. 'To what do I owe this unexpected pleasure, Ryan?'

Eyebrows raised, she watched him slump onto her sofa and pick up the remote. She tried again, louder this time.

'Ryan, you haven't been by or near me for more than six months. I've had a heart attack and major surgery, there's been zilch from you and now you show up like *this*?'

'Yeah, I heard you'd been a bit unwell.' He stared at the television, channel flicking.

'A *bit* unwell?' Fran felt her jaw sag. 'I had nine units of blood to replace what I lost on two gastric bleeds, which needed a barbaric procedure to fix. I have a thirteen-inch scar from neck to navel.'

His mouth turned down in disgust. She suddenly remembered that he'd always been squeamish.

She continued slowly and with relish, 'They hacked open my sternum, Ryan, took my heart out and repaired it. My chest is held together with wire. That is more than being "a bit unwell".'

'But you're okay now though, hun?' he persisted in a breezy tone, looking everywhere but at her. 'And look, I can be here to look after you now. All the time!' He patted the seat beside him. Fran's legs were aching just standing up but she held on to the back of an armchair, staring down at him. Her brain whirred.

'Ryan, what the fuck is going on?'

'I've left her.' Swivelling her way, he held his arms out. 'At last.'

Fran ignored the open arms. Frowning, she stepped back, in case he hadn't quite got the message. Slowly she repeated his words.

'You've *just* left her . . .' She glared at him. 'This will be the wife you told me you'd broken up with last year . . . ?'

His eyes slid towards her and away. 'Oh, er, we got back together and um . . .'

'She's finally realized what a snake you are and thrown you out, hasn't she?'

He slumped forward, resting his elbows on his knees. 'No! Yes. Well. She might have . . .' He ran his hands through his black hair, leaving it standing up in tufts. Fran remembered running her own hands through it in passionate moments. Guilt drenched her.

'God, you lying, faithless pig.' Hands on her hips, she glowered at him. Between shift work and perceptions of her job, it was virtually impossible to meet potential partners. Men from civvy street were either creepily fascinated by the idea of handcuffs and shagging a copper, or scared off. Or criminal. Or dodgy. It was a minefield. It was easier to look for a partner within the confines of the job. Other coppers. And from that small pool, accepting baggage was one thing, finding the single men among them was completely another. She'd always been so careful. And she'd thought Ryan, a detective at the same division, was a good bet. How wrong she'd been.

'Get out.'

'But Fran! You're the one I love the most. Honest, Fran. I can't live without you, hun! Let me stay, please?'

'You're a weasel. Fuck off.'

He barely paused for breath, but she saw his features rearrange into a sly expression, which took her aback. 'You invited me in, Fran. Exactly how are you going to throw me out?'

Fran blinked and her pulse pounded. What a scumbag. What had she ever seen in him? As an active copper she would have twisted his arm up his back and slammed him through the door, hurling his suitcase after him. Now she was having trouble even standing for very long and a light shove would send her to the floor. Fear clawed tentacles into her stomach.

She took a deep breath and lied, pinning a broad smile on. 'Well, if you're determined to stay, it will be handy to have you here. Because the district nurse will be here any minute, to check the dressings on my scar. It's infected just at the bottom here—' she pointed at her stomach — 'and

I need help squeezing out the pus and re-dressing it.' She watched the colour drain out of his face. 'It's pretty yucky. And it's going to take weeks to heal . . . so it'll be lovely to have someone here to help me, won't it?' She hooked a finger in the neck of her T-shirt and pulled it down, revealing the puffy, still-raw, puckered scar.

Ryan sat bolt upright, holding his hand over his mouth.

'Best not get too close to me either, *hun*. It's really quite smelly . . .'

He jumped to his feet and was at the door in a single bound. She stepped back smartly.

'Goodbye, Ryan,' she said, the door already closing behind him.

He turned on his heel and snarled at her. 'I only came here because I knew you'd still be single. There's not an ounce of real woman in you. You're just cop all the way through.'

Fran slammed the door in his face and leaned on it, breathing heavily, feeling her heart bouncing. Sliding all the locks home with shaking hands, she backed away from the door, sagging onto the arm of the sofa, staring at the door as if Ryan might materialize through it.

His expression of utter revulsion together with his parting words reverberated in her head and, even as she dismissed them, they dug their barbs in and brought blood to the surface. She'd lied about the pus and infection — there was no problem with her scar, other than how it looked and what it represented. How would anyone be able to look at her now without that terrible reaction? She needed to get away. The phone appeared in her hand as if by magic.

'Gavin? I've thought about it. I'll do it. Send me your parents' number and I'll give them a call. And thank you to Ally for thinking of me.' It was a new beginning and she was going to make the most of it. No worrying about who would see the terrible scar. She'd be alone and man-free in middle-of-nowhere West Wales.

CHAPTER FOUR

The pub had been a mistake, Wyn decided. He'd spent the morning working on the old school, then he'd popped down late afternoon to April and Ken's cottage to fit new locks to the front and back doors. They were off for a year, apparently, on a motorbike trip of a lifetime, and had found someone to house-sit for them. Which was when the snag of the lost keys had arisen. Like everyone else in the village, they never locked their doors, and had turned the place upside down looking for the errant keys.

Having tidied up after himself, he'd then walked next door to Elin, the neighbour.

'New keys for Tŷ Gwylan, Mrs Pritchard.' He handed over the bunch of new keys.

'Thank you, Wyn.' She smiled up at him. 'Good timing too — I've just signed for a delivery for the house-sitter, so I'll go and put it away now. Can I get you anything? Cold beer?'

'No, thanks, Mrs P. I'm planning an early dinner over at the Mermaid, couple of cold ones and an early night. Lots to do up at the old school, as usual.'

'Right you are, Wyn. Thanks again.'

Strolling the few hundred yards to the only pub in the village, he perused the menu over a perfectly pulled pint of draught bitter. Ordering a fillet steak, rare, a large salad and chips, he instantly regretted his table for one by the window as Tasha and AJ sauntered in.

He should've gone for takeaway fish and chips instead of sitting there on his lonesome while his ex and PC Knobhead smooched in front of him. Why had they come here? There was a pub near them, couldn't they go there? He'd cancel his order.

No. Why should he? He'd got there first, they should go. He caught himself sounding like a petulant child. Draining his beer, he got up to order another, resolutely avoiding Tash's eye.

'I'll bring it to your table, Wyn,' said the girl behind the bar.

'That's okay.' Wyn rested an elbow on the counter. 'I'll wait here.'

Without missing a beat, the girl glanced over his shoulder and said, casually, 'Would you rather eat in the Front Bar?'

'Oh God, aye.' Wyn jerked upright, almost knocking over the beer she'd just pulled for him.

'We don't normally, like, but if you don't mind them playing darts round you . . .' She waved him through behind the counter, which meant he didn't even have to return past Tasha and the Knob. Following the barmaid, he ducked beneath the doorways, sniffing appreciatively at the delicious aromas as they passed the kitchen and stairs into the Front Bar. 'I'll set a place for you. It won't be long now.'

'Thanks, lovely.'

The Front Bar occupied a much smaller space than the restaurant but was stone-flagged where the restaurant was carpeted. Wyn remembered this room from years back, yellow with cigarette smoke, full of big men with rough knuckles and kindness in their hearts.

A game of cards or dominoes would always be in play, their dogs beneath the tables, usually with a bone or scraps from the kitchen. Dai the Milk's black lab used to lie under the table and break wind silently before slinking stealthily to an adjacent table, leaving the men blaming one another for the noxious stench.

The walls had reverberated with impromptu hymn singing on rugby internationals, and he himself had been plied with beer after scoring the winning tries for numerous games. Jukeboxes or piped music would have been given very short shrift. A radio was occasionally allowed, and a battered TV to watch the sport on.

The Front Bar these days was sanitized — clean and smoke-free, although the inevitable smelly dog could still be found lurking under the table, hoovering up fallen pork scratchings. He knew most of the customers there, exchanging easy banter and news as he waited for his food to arrive. Nobody seemed surprised by his appearance behind the counter as he made his way to a table.

'Well, look at you, blue-eyed boy then,' said someone, nodding at Wyn's loaded plate as it passed him. 'What'd you do to deserve that then? Mrs B would have me shot if I ate in 'ere.'

'I'm special.' Wyn winked at him, slicing into his perfectly cooked steak with deep appreciation.

'Aye, lad. That you are. Some people don't know where their bread's buttered.' The speaker inclined his head pointedly in the direction of the restaurant, raising his glass to Wyn.

'Cheers, butty,' Wyn said, using the colloquial Welsh term for 'mate'. He lifted his glass in a returned salute and nodded at the dartboard. 'Crack on, lads. Don't mind me.'

The evening passed pleasantly to a backdrop of groans and cheers from the darts game, and rumbled conversation that Wyn occasionally joined in with. The food made its way from Wyn's belly to his toes, and he stretched his long legs out luxuriantly under the table, connecting with something soft and furry as he did so. A pair of indignant bushy eyebrows appeared beside his thigh. Wyn reached down to scratch the wiry brown and white hair under the dog's chin.

'Oh, hello, Scruff! Sorry, matey, I haven't left you anything. I didn't know you were there!' Wyn lifted the tiny bit of gristle and offered it to the dog, who sniffed it politely and carried on staring at him. Wyn looked around for Scruff's owner, Phil. Maybe he was in the gents. He got up and ordered a packet of pork scratchings at the bar.

'Don't tell me you're still hungry, Wyn?' The landlady, known to all as Mrs B, looked him up and down. 'We've got sticky toffee pudding.'

'Yes to the pudding, but the scratchings are for Scruff. I kicked him under the table, poor little beggar.'

'Hmm. Phil's not here, which means he's come in by himself. Again. I hope Phil's okay. Hang on . . .' She disappeared into the kitchen. Wyn looked down to see the shaggy little dog sitting at his feet, eyeing him hopefully.

'We're sorting it, lad,' Wyn told him, seeing the little dog's tail thump as if he understood every word.

Mrs B returned with a dog bowl containing a wedge of steak pie with the top pastry removed. Scruff tucked in ravenously, his tail wagging.

'That's two of you,' she said, giving the little dog a pat, 'eating in the bar. Don't tell anyone, they'll all expect it!'

'Not if we 'ave to eat it off the floor, like.' A deep voice boomed with perfect timing and was greeted with a volley of laughter.

'Anyone seen Phil lately?' Wyn asked, looking around.

'I saw him in the shop yesterday,' said someone. 'Or was it the day before?'

'I'll pop over and see if he's okay,' Wyn said. Mrs B shoved a package at him as he left, Scruff trotting alongside. 'What's this?'

'Bit of grub for Phil. He probably won't accept it, but just in case,' she said briskly, turning on her heel and returning behind the bar.

Phil, a sprightly eighty-something, lived in a pretty, whitewashed cottage halfway up the hill. The garden was showing signs of needing a tidy but was otherwise okay. Phil insisted on doing everything himself and got quite crabby with Wyn when he offered to help. His two children visited regularly and he always looked clean-shaven and spruce. It was very unusual for him not to be with his dog.

Scruff scampered round to the open back door with Wyn in hot pursuit.

'Phil? Hello? It's Wyn — you okay?' He stepped inside. 'I've brought Scruff back — just wondered if you were all right, butty?'

'Aaah! Scruff, lad, where you been?' A querulous moan reached him. 'Wyn! Bugger, I'm in 'ere.' Phil groaned and Wyn followed the voice into the little front room where he then stood, looking round him. 'I can't bloody get up, Wyn. Sorry, mate, I've made a bit of a mess here, lad . . .'

Wyn stepped further into the room to see the old man crumpled on the floor, one leg twisted around his chair.

'Oh, Phil, mate!' He squatted beside him, twitching a blanket off the back of the sofa and pulling it over him. 'Don't worry about a bit of mess. I've seen worse on nights out with the lads. What hurts?'

'I think I've broke me hip, lad.' He compressed his lips. 'Hurts like buggery. I did try to get up, but . . .'

'Let's get you an ambulance.' Wyn picked up the phone, only just out of poor Phil's reach. 'I don't want to make anything worse by trying to move you.'

'Don't let them put me in a home! What will happen to Scruff?' Tears tracked down Phil's lined face.

'One thing at a time, Phil, let's get you sorted, mate. Hello? Ambulance, please.' Wyn hung up after giving the details. 'Phil, they won't be long, they said. A quiet night, thank goodness! I can't give you a drink in case they need to operate, but I can wet your lips. Let's get you a bit more comfortable if we can.'

'M'daughter's number's in the kitchen, Wyn, if you could let her know.'

'I'll do it now.'

Phil's daughter was a sensible woman who said she'd meet her father at the hospital and ring her brother. She told Wyn where to look for pyjamas and toiletries.

'Right, Phil, your daughter's on the way to the hospital, so I'd better get you sorted out with pyjamas and whatnot.' Wyn kept up a cheery monologue as he went round the house with a holdall, locating the things he thought Phil would need. His own hospital stays weren't that far behind him, prompting his memory about what was useful. Phil's bedroom was as spick and span as his garden, if sparsely furnished. The stairs were steep as hell though. Wyn had to duck and place his feet sideways to negotiate them. He wondered how Phil would manage if he needed surgery.

The paramedics turned up surprisingly quickly and agreed with Phil's assessment, and the old man's colour returned a little as a painkiller took effect. He was lifted efficiently onto a stretcher and towards the waiting ambulance.

'What about Scruff?' Inside the ambulance, Phil struggled to get up, suddenly agitated.

Wyn looked down at the little dog, who'd followed them out and was intent on getting into the ambulance with his master. He reached down and scooped him up like a rugby ball, tucking him under his arm. 'Don't worry about him. I'll hang on to him for now. He'll be fine. You concentrate on getting better, Phil, okay?'

He smiled reassuringly at the old man as the ambulance doors closed, and watched it out of sight. Inside, he scrubbed the rug Phil had been lying on, leaving it draped to dry in the sunny back porch. Locating a lead on a hook behind the back door, he clipped it to the little dog's collar, checked the cottage was secure and pocketed the key as the daughter apparently had one already.

'Now then, young man,' he told Scruff. 'Much as I'd love to keep you, I know just the place for you to stay for a bit.' He ambled the few hundred yards to the pub, back into the bar, and met Mrs B's eye. Rapidly he brought her up to speed.

Her first words were, as he knew they would be, 'And little Scruff?'

'I wondered if you'd look after him for a little while . . .' He'd barely finished his sentence before Mrs B was down on her haunches and Scruff had his front paws on her knees, licking her face. He'd known exactly where to go for help, Wyn thought.

'Of course! He needs feeding up, poor little fella, don't you, *cariad*?'

Wyn left the food parcel on the counter that had been intended for Phil, and with the pleasant sensation of a job well done, strolled out of the pub — straight into Tasha and PC Knobhead having a blazing row in the car park.

CHAPTER FIVE

The weeks before she was to leave passed in a flurry of lists. Fran's tastes ran to minimalist and she was rigorously tidy, so there wasn't much to pack away to make room for Gavin and Ally's stay.

Gavin sat beside her on a few drives, under Fran's lame guise of needing him to carry stuff.

'You must think I'm really feeble,' she said on their first outing, as she hesitated to pull out of a junction. The world barged towards her at speed and her hands were sticky on the wheel. He was silent for a moment, staring ahead through the windscreen.

'I think you're amazing, Sar — Fran.' Fran heard him stutter over what to call her and the corner of her mouth lifted. Habit was hard to shake off. Gavin flicked a glance at her before continuing. 'You looked after me when I was a wet-behind-the-ears, pain-in-the-arse probationer. You taught me so much. I owe you, big time. We all do. Here I am, about to be promoted. I'd never have passed my exam if you hadn't pushed me.'

Fran blinked back tears. 'Naaah.' She looked at him sideways. 'You're just hoping I'll peg out among the sand dunes, having left you the flat in my will.'

'And there's that too,' deadpanned Gavin without missing a beat. Their laughter drove the tension from the car and Fran finally began to relax.

He and Ally helped with anything that she needed to put into storage, bringing their own brand of brisk fun. The flat felt silent and empty in their absence. Fran found herself almost wishing that they were all staying there together. She knew the flat would be in good hands.

Over the coming days, her car was serviced and she bought maps of Wales. Long phone conversations with April and Ken, Gavin's jolly and upbeat parents, left her reassured that they were prepared for her stay. April and Ken were planning to visit a poorly relative en route to their adventure, meaning they would be leaving earlier than planned and be gone before she arrived. She would collect the house keys from the neighbour, Mrs Pritchard.

The day before she was due to leave, she attended hospital for her cardiac follow-up. Despite feeling well and fit, just being at the hospital made her pulse accelerate. She was scanned and monitored and eventually called in to see the consultant.

'Very good,' he announced, checking her sternum for unwanted movement or noises as she turned her head to one side and then the other. 'You can do whatever you like now. Dig the garden, go to the gym, drive, swim, whatever. Have a few glasses of wine, no need to go mad, just enjoy yourself. Just take everything slowly and be sensible.'

'I'm going to the coast for a few months. Maybe more. West Wales.' It felt good to tell him that. That she wasn't somehow letting life slip past her. Sitting about watching TV. That their faith in her recovery wasn't misplaced. She wasn't sure why she felt the need to do that. Surely to them she was just another number.

'Perfect. Keep up with the walking, a couple of times a day, keeping your heart rate in the target range just as you have been. Ring us if you've any concerns.'

Feeling guilty as she hadn't done nearly as much walking as she'd been told to, Fran envisaged herself strolling in the sunshine along the sand dunes that she'd seen in photos of the village. Stomping along the coastal paths. She bought herself a pair of walking boots and some woolly socks from one of the big outdoor specialists on the way home. They seemed so much at odds with her sparkly party dresses and tops, already packed into storage. Like outdoor fancy dress.

On the morning she left, the sun shone, and Fran handed over the flat keys to Gavin and Ally.

'Enjoy!' She hugged them both tightly.

'Oo-er. Hugging. This is a first.' Gavin grinned at her as she quickly released him. 'It's only Wales, Sarge. Not the end of the world.'

She laughed, holding back tears. 'Shut it, you.'

Still, the familiar title gave her confidence and she didn't correct him for once. She could do this, being away from home. Being someone new — a new persona, exposed without her uniform as camouflage. By herself. With nobody who knew her. Nobody who knew that she would put a brave face on everything and insist that nothing was wrong, even if she was hanging by the thinnest thread. Despite her shaky smile, her throat constricted. 'It's a big deal to this decrepit old lady.'

'You'll never be decrepit. You'll come back a new woman! Give my love to Llanbryn!' Waiting while she set the satnav, they waved her to the end of the road. She was on her own. The beginning of an adventure, she told herself firmly, even as she felt the damp trickle of nerves between her shoulder blades.

At the first motorway services out of London, and desperate for a real, caffeinated coffee, she bought a peppermint tea instead and took some deep and calming breaths at an outside table, tipping her face to the sun. The M25 had been a nightmare but then, she reasoned, it always was.

She sent a text to Gavin — *Nothing to it!* — and smiled at his replied row of thumbs-up emojis. Only another hour to the next services. And then the next . . . She didn't care how long it took. She'd even earmarked one or two Travelodge hotels on the motorway that she could overnight in if she felt the need.

As it turned out, she didn't need her emergency stopover plans. Her confidence returned gradually, and even though she drove *much* more slowly than usual, her knuckles darkened to their more normal pink by the time she saw the sign that read *Croeso i Gymru*, and beneath, *Welcome to Wales*. There was a symbolic red dragon above the words.

Fran was impressed. A land of dragons, with its own language — and still in the United Kingdom. The soaring suspension bridge impressed her further, and she glanced right along the great river to see its older sister spanning the two lands. As she drove towards the undulating dark hills of Wales, the water reflected the pink-and-blue sky between the pale-green struts of the vast bridge.

A bubble of anticipation grew as the motorway wound past an astonishing fairy-tale castle, perched high on a forested mountain.

Stopping at the services revealed a new world of overheard accents. People called one another 'butt' and 'butty'. The words 'by here' peppered the conversation randomly, as in, '*Is that your bag/jacket/coat by here?*' It was baffling, as was the phrase, '*I'll be there now in a minute.*' Whatever that meant. Either you were there now, or in a minute. It couldn't be both.

Everything else looked exactly the same as home. Although the road signs, in this strange and mysterious language that seemed to be made up of mostly consonants, reinforced the awareness that she was in another country.

Leaving the motorway at its end, at the last services near Carmarthen, the well-maintained dual carriageway eventually narrowed to country lanes, and Fran's already slow speed became almost glacial.

Trees outnumbered houses the further west she travelled. Sheep replaced people. Tangled hedgerows whipped at her wing mirrors and pavements disappeared altogether. The traffic thinned considerably, and with it the radio station signal. She couldn't remember the last shop she'd seen.

The day was long, but as the sun finally fell out of the early May sky, it felt like the end of civilization. The car headlights came on automatically and she shivered, suddenly stupidly homesick for streetlights and rows of neon-lit takeaway shops.

A glance at the satnav showed there wasn't far to go. Yawning, she lowered the window for a gulp of fresh air. A colossal tractor, towing a vast trailer full of manure, rumbled past her in the opposite direction, filling her car with the rich and pungent pong of the countryside. Despite the terrible whiff, she laughed. *And Gavin thought this was an improvement on the traffic fumes of the city!*

The lanes twisted towards the sea, and there was an unmistakeable tang of salt in the air. Stunted trees leaned into the road, their trunks contorted by coastal gales. Verges abundant with tall grasses and greenery studded with wild-flowers threatened to scrape her small hatchback on both sides. She was forced to creep around the bends, expecting to confront another tractor. Her eyes watered with yawning and she longed for her own bed. This was a ridiculous idea. What on earth had she been thinking?

By the time the headlights illuminated the signs for Llanbryn, her shoulders were hunched around her ears. She was relieved that the satnav had found the village, as despite practising she couldn't remember how to pronounce the name of it if she had to ask directions. What was with all the double Ls? Gavin had made some clicking noise at the beginning that eluded her.

The name of the house was even worse. Tŷ Gwylan . . . Despite Gavin repeating it several times it still looked as if it didn't have enough vowels and nothing would persuade her otherwise.

She'd tried to pronounce it but couldn't seem to get past the first two letters. Were they pronounced *tie* or *tee*? Gwylan meant either 'seagulls' or 'seashells' but she couldn't remember which it was now. She hoped Gavin hadn't been kidding about everyone speaking English. At least there were a few streetlights on the empty lanes.

Set back on a sharp corner was a tiny church, the unusual bell tower illuminated. Houses painted white, with purple-grey slate roofs, cascaded downhill as if they'd been shaken out of a box. Drystone walls flanked the lane, interspersed with clipped garden hedges. Tall, arching trees on both sides met overhead and plunged the narrow lane into gloom.

But there, at the end of the road, the dark sea sparkled beneath a huge moon. It was like a fairy tale. Her jaw dropped. For a moment she felt like an adventurer, a visitor to a foreign land.

Relief swept over her. She'd finally arrived. She'd done it, all that way, on her own. Even as she thought it, her mind swept back to the Fran who'd busted a nightclub not that long ago for drugs and people-smuggling. And here she was, awarding herself a pat on the back for driving from one side of the UK to the other. Talk about baby steps.

Having delivered her safely, the satnav had given up, but she'd pored over Google Maps enough times to know it was left on the corner, towards the Mermaid Inn. At least she could pronounce that if she had to ask.

Spotting the illuminated sign for the pub, she carefully negotiated the tight turn. The full beam of her headlights fell on a group of two men and a woman, entangled together in what looked very much like a scrap. In the middle of the road.

'What the actual fu . . . ?' Fran stamped on the brakes. She expected this back home, not in this supposedly idyllic rural village. Her mind took a snapshot of the scene. A giant of a man in a pale-blue short-sleeved shirt gripped a shorter man at arm's length by the clothing at his throat. The shorter man, barely on tiptoes, flailed his arms and legs towards his assailant, who evaded them easily, the corded muscles on his bicep bulging.

A slight, dark-haired woman tugged at the tall man's unoccupied arm. They all looked old enough to know better.

The three of them stared at her, blinded by the lights, frozen in surprise. It was a reflexive reaction to get out of the car and use the words she knew so well.

'Oi! Police! Pack it in!'

The tall man relaxed his grip a little. The shorter man squeaked immediately, 'Help! Assault police! Arrest this man!'

He was *police*? Adrenaline boiled in Fran's stomach and her fingers scrabbled automatically and uselessly for the radio and tools on the utility belt that she was so accustomed to wearing. She suddenly realized how vulnerable she was now. And she had a massive fresh scar down the middle of her breastbone, so she was not about to get involved in a tussle. Not that she fancied her chances with this huge man. Nobody — luckily — was paying her any attention.

The tall man snarled into the short man's face. 'Shut up, AJ, you arse. You're lucky I'm *not* assaulting you after what you just did.'

Fran hesitated, taking stock. At the moment, they couldn't see her behind the headlights, so she had the advantage. But she couldn't just walk away if a fellow officer was being assaulted, whatever it was he'd been accused of. Staying firmly where she was, she cleared her throat.

'Okay, guys, maybe let's just calm this down, shall we? Take five, tell me what's happened.'

'He assaulted me! Arrest him!' AJ gasped, still on tiptoes courtesy of the tall man's giant fist beneath his chin.

'Wyn! Leave it!' The woman pulled at the tall man's arm. 'Please, Wyn! You'll only make it worse.' Wyn's eyes slanted towards the woman, and Fran saw indecision cross his features.

Somebody came out of the pub and shouted in a tone of astonishment, 'It's Wyn!' This was followed by a chorus of rich Welsh accents as more people spilled from the pub.

'Wyn? No, really? He usually stops the fights, he don't start them, mun! What's going on, Wyn, butty?'

'What the bloody hell's going on here?' The crowd parted for a burly man with an air of authority. Wyn released AJ with reluctance. Fran winced as the man crumpled to the ground. Nobody moved to help him. Staggering to his feet, he puffed his chest out, pointing his finger at Wyn.

'He assaulted me! That's assault on police, that is.' His voice was scratchy and he massaged his throat. 'Bar him, landlord!'

'Hmm. What a way to end a nice meal out for the two of you.' The landlord heaved a sigh. 'So, are you injured then? Do you need an ambulance?' The burly landlord eyed him sternly for a long moment as AJ's mouth worked in silence.

Finally, AJ managed a disgruntled tut and a 'No.' He left off his neck massage for a moment to point at Wyn with a quavering finger. 'But he, he . . .'

The landlord turned to the crowd. 'Fun's over. Now bugger off, the lot of you.'

The woman transferred her attention to AJ, grabbing at his coat. 'Please, Alix. Just take me home.'

'She saw it!' Shaking the woman off, AJ swivelled his pointing finger at Fran. 'And she's police. She said so. She'll give a statement!'

Fran had from force of habit stepped forward, and now felt the interested eyes of the crowd turn towards her. A growing part of her wished she'd kept her mouth shut and stayed where she was. Things didn't seem quite as cut and dried as she'd first assumed. She stuck her chin out. 'I'll say what I saw, of course.'

'And technically, it's assault just laying hands on someone!' AJ persisted, pushing his chest out.

'Yeah, well, you oughta know . . .' somebody said from the crowd, eliciting a rumble of assenting murmurs.

'I'm with Wyn,' yelled someone else, followed by another and another.

'Me too!' another said. 'And I wasn't even here, tell the missus!' Laughter greeted this pronouncement.

'Wyn wasn't here either!' There was laughter. Fran noticed that even the landlord allowed a small smile to curve his mouth. There was no love lost here for the police, by the looks of it. Or perhaps just for this particular police officer . . .

A man in the crowd said, 'Want a lift home, Wyn, mate?'

'No, don't worry, thanks, butt,' said Wyn. 'I'll walk.' Lifting a palm-forward hand the size of a dinner plate, he rounded on the hapless policeman. 'If you want to nick me, you know where I live.'

His gaze swept over Fran and rested there. Unable to decide whether his glare was in disgust or disappointment, she met his eye squarely, taking in the lean, chiselled jawline, generous mouth and sharp cheekbones framing deep-set eyes.

Annoyed with herself for admitting he was a bit of all right — startlingly handsome even, if you liked the rugged, outdoor look — she also noted, as he turned away, the deeply puckered, disfiguring scars rising from his elbow into his short sleeve. She turned to address the policeman in, she realized belatedly, almost the same mode as Wyn had addressed her.

'Okay, well, I'm staying in . . .' She coughed in an attempt to disguise her inability to pronounce the Welsh version of the name. 'Tie, tee . . . um, Seagull House, er, Cottage . . .' She jerked a thumb in what she hoped was the general direction. 'If you need me to give a statement.'

Climbing back into her still-running car, she drove what turned out to be only a hundred or so yards around the corner to the cottage with a helpfully illuminated nameplate and turned the engine off. Sitting in the driver's seat, she stared towards the cottage, feeling uncomfortably as if she'd ducked the issue. She hadn't given her name or her real address. It didn't sit well with her to let a fellow officer down. She was pondering on her motives for that as light spilled from the adjacent cottage, framing a diminutive woman Fran could only describe as round. Like a currant bun.

'Hello! I'm Elin,' she called. 'Welcome to Llanbryn.' With a beaming smile, her snowy-white hair cut and styled in a smooth bob that made Fran feel travel-stained and grubby, Elin held up a set of keys and jingled them.

Fran reflected that her recent introduction to the village hadn't been much of a welcome, but climbing out of the car, she settled for, 'Hello! I'm sorry it's so late. Don't you want to see some ID?' She showed her driving licence anyway, once again lamenting the loss of her warrant card. Elin squinted at it.

'Oh, I suppose I should have. But April and Ken told me all about you and showed me photos, so I knew it was you.' She handed over the keys with their attached seagull ornament. Unable to decide whether the idea of this woman having her photo and 'knowing all about her' was a bit stalkerish, Fran allowed herself to be satisfied that she'd apparently at least got the meaning of the cottage correct earlier, even if she couldn't pronounce it.

'How was your drive? Those narrow lanes are a bit of a bugger, aren't they?' Elin's accent was more pronounced on the last few words, and Fran smiled, pushing away her anxieties about the incident outside the pub. This was more like the Welsh welcome Gavin had led her to expect. 'Would you like a cup of tea?'

'I should go and unpack . . .' Fran gestured towards her car, securely locked in the driveway.

'I've been baking all day,' Elin continued, as if she hadn't heard Fran. 'A whole pile of Welsh cakes and a nice bara brith.'

'Barbara's breath? Sorry, what?' Fran gave up, sending a lingering glance back at her car. 'And Welsh cakes? How are they different to English cakes?'

Elin laughed, holding the door wide. 'Barbara's breath . . . hehehe, never heard that one before!'

Beyond her, and entirely at odds with Elin's immaculate appearance, Fran could see a pile of mismatched shoes and wellies, left where they'd been shaken off. A jacket or two, a scarf and some knitted items topped the jumble. 'Come and see for yourself. If you like them, you can take them with you.'

Fran hesitated, trying not to judge the messy hallway, wanting only to get into Seagull Cottage and subside into a tired heap. Catching the fragrant scent of fresh baking as she stood at the open doorway, her shoulders dropped. 'Thank you. That would be most welcome. I've, um, left my handbag in the car. I should go and get it.'

'Oh, you don't need to worry about that. You could leave it out there with the doors wide open and it would be perfectly safe.' Elin turned to lead the way into the spacious kitchen. 'April and Ken had the devil of a job to find all the keys for the cottage. I don't think they've locked a door for years — they've had them all changed for you.'

Fran nodded slowly and silently. In her opinion, leaving a house unlocked was just *inviting* burglars in. Her own flat was alarmed to the hilt. She felt uneasy, lost, without her bag containing her phone and her bank cards. 'I just need to let them know I've arrived safely. Back in a mo.' She jerked her thumb over her shoulder and backed out of the front door, scurrying to the car. Reunited with her worldly goods and back in the cottage, she smiled widely at Elin. 'Sorry. Force of habit. Lovely kitchen.'

'Thank you. Tetley, Earl Grey or peppermint? I have some redbush—'

'Oh gosh, so much choice!' Fran interrupted her firmly. 'Earl Grey, please. Black, no sugar. Thank you so much, that will be lovely.' She looked around her. The floor was flagged, and a scrubbed pine table that would fetch a fortune in the shops near her was strewn with books on cooking and gardening. A wing chair in one corner, reupholstered in a bold fabric, was piled with cushions, cardigans and orphan socks. A vast dresser was laden with colourful mugs, plates — and a colossal serving bowl that seemed to serve as Elin's filing system, overflowing as it was with mail, flyers, till receipts and pens. Fran itched to empty and sort the entire kitchen. But despite the clutter, it was clean enough.

Elin busied herself with pretty flowered cups and saucers. She placed a matching milk jug and sugar bowl on the table, along with cake tins and plates. It was like being transported back to a bygone era of having high tea in the parlour with the best china, Fran thought. Her mind drifted back to the incident earlier. She frowned, absent-mindedly rattling her cup in the saucer. She was appalled when Elin jumped up to stir the pot.

'Oh, sorry, I wasn't being impatient! I was just, um . . .' She stared at the cup, willing herself to take her hands away and relax, for goodness' sake.

Elin poured the golden liquid from the pot, pulling a large flat tin towards her.

'Bara brith? Or Welsh cakes? Or both?' Taking the lid off, she tipped the tin towards Fran, who to her relief saw a perfectly normal oblong fruit cake and a pile of what looked like small, flat scones, both nestling in a nest of greaseproof paper.

'Oh my goodness. They look amazing. I have no idea which is which, so . . . both, please, I think. Thank you!' Taking a bite out of the flat disc of sugar-sprinkled cake, she licked her lips with an enormous smile on her face. 'Mmm, this is delicious!' She lifted it to eye level and peered at the golden crumb, bursting with sultanas. 'It's so moist — I thought it was going to be dry and I'd have to lie . . .'

Elin burst into laughter, her billowing bosom jiggling along. 'I knew I was going to like you. That's a Welsh cake. Haven't you been to Wales before?'

Fran shook her head. 'No. It's shameful, isn't it? Where I live, it's easier to get on a plane and fly somewhere than drive all this way.'

'So why didn't you?' Elin sipped her tea, levelling a shrewd, bright-blue gaze at Fran.

Fran turned the question over in her head. Why had she chosen Wales over the Med? It wasn't as if she couldn't have afforded to spend a month in the sun.

'I think,' she began hesitantly, following the grain of the pine table with her fingertip, 'it feels safe here. It can be very anonymous to be alone in a foreign hotel. There's a link here — I mean, I know Gavin quite well—'

'Such a sweet little boy,' Elin interrupted with a smile.

Fran grinned at the idea of Gavin as a little boy. 'I'm sure. He used to work with me.' The words 'used to' seemed strange and unfamiliar in her mouth, especially as earlier she'd had no hesitation identifying herself as police. Had that been habit? Or a reluctance to admit that she was now nobody. Nobody special. She frowned. 'And I *was* thinking that at least I knew the language, in the event of any—' she whirled her hands in front of her — 'health complications, if you know what I mean.'

Elin sliced her cake into quarters and buttered it. Her eyes were sympathetic. 'Have you had heart issues for a long time?'

So she knew about the heart attack. It was almost a relief not to have to explain herself. Fran felt, weirdly, as if she ought to apologize for it. As if being much younger than the typical heart attack sufferer, and not being overweight and unfit, meant that she was somehow attention-seeking. Being a drama queen.

'If I had, I was keeping it a secret from myself.' Fran laughed ruefully. It was still a mystery to her. The cardiac team had all but shrugged their shoulders and informed her that these things happen. Could be stress. Or genetic, they'd said. It hadn't been very reassuring. Did that mean it could happen again? That shrug again. 'The doctor in casualty asked me how long I'd had a heart murmur and I said those immortal words, "I haven't got a heart murmur."'

'Next thing, they told me I'd had a heart attack, that there was damage — only surgery would fix it, and could someone bring a bag in as I'd be in hospital for a few weeks. I had two heart valves repaired. Luckily, my arteries were fine, so no stents. Just . . . major open-heart surgery.' She stared sightlessly around the room, remembering the consultant breaking the news to her. 'The doctor thought I was bonkers, I'm sure. He said, "Tell me what were you doing leading up to the pain that brought you in." I said I'd been dancing to "Oops Up Side Your Head". I was still wearing the sequinned mini-dress I'd been wearing in the disco, and it kept riding up my legs until it was more like a top than a dress. I felt like a complete tart.'

'I love that song.' Elin mimed the rowing dance perfectly and unexpectedly, and Fran laughed with delight.

'That's the one! My guys were like, "What the hell is this?" Kids, huh?'

'It's a favourite at the summer beach party here.'

'You have parties?' Fran sat up straight and then slouched a little, rubbing at the lumpy scar that pulled and reminded her constantly of its presence. 'And there was me thinking it was a sleepy little seaside village.'

'It might be little,' Elin said with raised eyebrows, her eyes crinkling with humour, 'but it's far from sleepy.' She sipped her tea and pulled a face, getting up to put the cup in the microwave. 'These cups and saucers are pretty but they don't hold the heat. Shall I do yours too?'

'Mm, please.' Fran held out her cup. 'They are pretty though.'

'Mugs next time, I think.' Setting the newly hot tea down before them, Elin sat opposite. 'I probably should have made a fresh pot, but if you have the technology, why not use it?'

Fran heard herself say, 'Actually, I don't know why I said it was sleepy. I drove straight into a punch-up outside the pub as I arrived.'

Elin cocked an expressive eye at her. 'That's very unusual. Barty, the landlord, keeps a tight rein on things over there. It's a nice, proper country pub. The food is excellent. I often go.'

'It did break up pretty quickly when he came out.' Fran hesitated, wondering how much to tell and how far it would have gone had she not driven into it. Perhaps Elin could shed some light. 'There was a very tall man right in the middle of it. Huge guy. Strange name, I'm sure it can't actually be short for Winifred but it did sound like that . . .'

Elin pealed with laughter. 'It's Wyn.' She spelled it aloud. 'Short for Wyndham but nobody ever calls him that. I expect he was breaking up the fight.'

'Um, well, no, actually. He seemed to be the cause of it.' Fran watched Elin closely as her eyebrows shot up.

'Goodness me. That's not Wyn, not at all. Maybe it was someone else, dear. Our Wyn is a gentleman, in all senses of the word.'

'Perhaps I did get it wrong.' Fran knew she hadn't, she'd heard it called out several times, even if she hadn't known

43

how it was spelled. 'I nearly ran them over — they were in the middle of the road.'

'Who else was in this fight?'

'Apparently a policeman called AJ? Alex? And there was a younger woman, dark hair.'

'Ah.' Elin's lips clamped together and she nodded. 'That would explain it.' Fran waited to see if she might elucidate, but Elin clicked the lid onto the cakes and stood up. 'Well, now. The rest are for you. It's late and you must be exhausted from driving all this way. From London!'

'I am, rather.' Fran yawned, smothering it with her hand. She clapped both her hands over her mouth. 'I'm so sorry — I'm not used to it!' she mumbled through her fingers, as Elin laughed.

'Don't apologize. I'm glad to have met you. You'll need a few days to recover and get into the swing of the place. That bit of a punch-up — it's just a kerfuffle. Don't pay any attention to it. It'll all blow over, you'll see. Here are my mobile and landline numbers.' She passed a printed card to Fran. 'There's barely any mobile signal here, you'll discover. Everyone has internet though, and we all communicate via WhatsApp and a village Facebook hub.'

'Wow.' Fran was astonished.

'It's the twenty-first century here too, you know.'

'Yes. Sorry.'

'I'm only teasing you, lovely.' Elin's eyes creased in humour. 'Come on, I'll show you around next door.'

'Oh, thank you, that's very kind. And thank you for the tea and cake.'

'It's what neighbours are for, my lovely. And *croeso i Gymru.*'

'Pardon?'

'It means "welcome to Wales". We can practise it later.' Elin shepherded her gently out of the kitchen, carrying the cake tin.

The evening air was sharp after the warmth of the snug house. She breathed in the salty tang. Fran wondered how much Welsh she was actually expected to learn, and whether Seagull Cottage would be as 'lived in' as Elin's. With her head on one side, she listened as Elin showed her which of the keys was which.

'I can hear the sea!' Fran's stomach jolted. How close would it come to the cottage?

'Tide's in.' Elin nodded. 'And you'll be able to see it from your balcony.'

'There's a *balcony*?' Fran turned the key and pushed open the door. She didn't mind *looking* at the sea.

It was an upside-down house. Gavin hadn't mentioned that, had he? They walked into a spacious, stone-tiled hall-way that opened right up to the pale oak roof joists. The effect was airy and impressive. Fran fell in love instantly.

'Two bedrooms off here.' Elin pointed. 'Do I sound like an estate agent?' She smiled. 'Kitchen is upstairs. Lounge has a view over the beach.'

'Wow.' Fran gazed across the pale carpet, huge bed and blonde furniture to the French doors. Through muslin drapes, she could see a neatly tended garden, sparkling with loops of warm-white fairy lights. Leaving her wheeled suitcase on the stone tiles of the hallway in case the wheels muddied that pristine cream carpet, Fran went to investigate upstairs.

The kitchen was stunning. Sterile, in sharp contrast to Elin's warm but cluttered cottage. Fran breathed a sigh of relief. Much more her style. Deep-blue painted cupboards and marble worktops contrasted with blonde-stone flooring and white walls. A wicker basket bearing a card addressed to Fran sat on the counter, a bottle of red wine poking out of one end and a bottle of white at the other.

'This arrived for you earlier. I've put some of the things in the fridge here, look.' Elin opened the enormous American-style refrigerator and pointed at the variety of cheeses, terrines and other goodies.

'Oh my goodness!' Fran picked out one or two, reading the labels. 'How kind. What a shame I wasn't able to meet them.'

Returning to the basket, the little card read *Croeso i Gymru — Welcome to Wales! A few local tasters to get you started. Hope you enjoy your visit. Diolch yn fawr — many thanks, April and Ken X.*

Everything in the basket bore a sticker from a Welsh company. Fran could see teabags, bread, biscuits, chutney and more, all nestled in shredded tissue paper.

'They're lovely neighbours. I hope they're having some wonderful adventures.' Elin nodded. She tapped a card that hung on a key rack. 'This is your Wi-Fi code. I expect you'll want to let people know you've arrived safely. And useful numbers are on here.' She pointed to a printed and laminated list taped to the back of the door. 'Now, will you need help bringing anything upstairs?'

'No, everything can stay down there. Thanks so much.' Wincing inside that an old lady had offered to help *her* carry things, Fran gazed around her. It was all so calm and stylish. Tranquil, she thought. And some stunning artwork.

'Okay, if you're sure . . .' Elin regarded her thoughtfully. 'My number is on that list, but just knock if you need anything. You're here to recuperate and build your strength up, remember. Rest now, and don't overdo it.'

'I will, thank you,' Fran said, meaning it. She was more tired than she wanted to admit. She barely suppressed a yawn as she waved goodbye to her new neighbour. Connected to the internet, she sent texts to Gavin to confirm safe arrival and to April and Ken to thank them for the food parcel, sank into one of the comfy linen-covered sofas with the TV remote in her hand and was asleep within seconds. She hadn't even managed to switch it on.

CHAPTER SIX

Stomping towards home over a beach lit by the bright disc of the moon, Wyn's thoughts strayed back to the fracas that evening. He shook his head, mad with himself for losing control. He was no better than that smarmy uniformed shithead Tasha had upped and left him for.

And that woman, appearing out of nowhere in her car like that, turning out to be yet another copper and offering to give a statement, of all things! As soon as she'd started mangling the name of April and Ken's cottage, he'd realized that, of course, she was their house-sitter. Although, the little voice in his head reminded him, rather pretty. If you liked your women tall and leggy, with long, curly red hair that blew across her face in the breeze. And watchful eyes.

But she'd only seen what she'd wanted to see. Made a snap decision that he was the bad guy. Coppers. They all stuck together, didn't they?

Veering right on a whim, he crossed the dunes, jogged across the beach to where the tide had turned and stripped his clothes off, leaving them in a heap just before the dry sand became wet.

He ran into the sea, knees high and out to the side in a rocking motion to clear the wavelets. He could do this. It was just him and the sea. It was where he'd always belonged, before . . . He pushed the dreadful thoughts away with an effort. *It was just water, just as it always had been. Only . . . dark. Don't think about the blackness. Think about the clear, softness of the salty sea in daylight, lifting, buoying, calming . . .*

Throwing his arms forward, he dived beneath the frill of pure-white surf lacing the indigo, moonlit sea. The dark chill closed over his head, and instantly the treacherous images returned to terrorize him. Reliving the terrible, nightmarish, thick blackness, the pain, the appalling fear of imminent death that crippled his thoughts, his breathing, his whole being.

Clawing his way to the surface in panic, he flailed his way back to the shore. Flopping forward, he rested his hands on his knees, dragging oxygen into tortured lungs. His ears rang and stars sprinkled his vision. He glared at the ocean, the colour of a mussel shell, lapping gently at his toes, innocent and playful. He dried himself on his T-shirt and pulled on his jeans.

'I'll be back,' he told the sea, as he turned towards home. 'You won't beat me. Just watch.'

* * *

The following morning, he battled awkwardly with the lawnmower in the garden shed of Tŷ Gwylan. There were no signs of life from inside the house. Either the woman was still asleep, she was an early bird and had gone out, or she was in the house ignoring him. He couldn't really blame her if she was. She hadn't exactly had a warm welcome. He didn't really want to bump into her anyway, after last night.

Her yell made him jump. He whirled around, banging his ankle against a stack of paint tins. Tousle-haired, she was in turquoise pyjamas adorned with brilliant-orange bird of paradise flowers. She looked furious. And thoroughly gorgeous, his brain told him treacherously.

'Argh!' she yelled at him. 'Go away! Get out! Who are you? What do you want?'

'I don't want anything.' Wyn yanked the mower finally free of clutter and emerged into the light. 'I'm gardening.'

'What? *What?*' Fran glared at him and then wrapped her arms around her body as if she'd remembered she was still in her nightwear. 'Oh, for goodness' sake. But you were at the pub last night — and *you* assaulted that policeman!' She combed her fingers through her hair, creating a bird's nest. 'I don't think you should be here.' The colour drained from her face and she swayed.

'Are you okay?' Wyn's actions were swifter than his words. He moved a little wooden stool closer and, with one hand under her elbow, guided her onto it. She flopped forward, the curly mass of red hair tumbling over her face.

'Sorry,' she mumbled from beneath the dishevelled mop. 'Recent surgery. Heart attack.'

'Do you need anything? Pills? A spray or something?' He hovered nearby, feeling awkward and guilty for startling her. She shook her head, breathing more deeply.

'I just need a minute. Thank you.'

'I'm sorry I scared you,' he said, staring down at her, feeling helpless. So — was this convalescence for her? And she'd waded into their punch-up last night . . . He blinked with respect, despite himself. He decided not to tell her that he'd been round the day before changing the locks. It might sound a bit suspicious, even though April and Ken had actually asked him to do it. She might think he'd kept a key. God, he was starting to feel guilty and he hadn't even done anything illegal!

Fran held a hand over her chest. He could see her concentrating on breathing slowly and calmly. After a minute she looked up at him. Her green-blue eyes were caught by the sun. There were gold flecks in them.

'As if it's not bad enough being woken up at sparrow fart by the Dawn Warblers shouting right outside the window, or having the seagulls turning the chimney into an echo chamber . . .' She took a gulp of air. 'This has not turned out to be the sleepy rural idyll I was expecting. I think I've been mis-sold. I got more sleep in hospital!'

49

A bubble of laughter rattled in Wyn's chest. 'An echo chamber . . . Dawn Warblers?' He guffawed aloud, and to his surprise, so did Fran.

'Yes! Bloody crowd of people — women, I think — with their car doors slamming and all bloody bellowing at one another at five this morning.' She paused for breath. 'And do the gulls stick their heads down the chimney for extra amplification or something?' Fran glared up at him and his mouth dried as he looked down into her face, her pink lips, her extraordinary green-blue eyes speckled with amber chips, framed by that mad chestnut halo of hair. 'But anyway,' she continued, clearly not letting him off the hook. 'You ought to knock.'

'I didn't want to wake you up,' he said weakly. He told himself that April and Ken knew when he was due and they'd always been early risers, so they'd been out there already with a mug of coffee for him. Nothing at all to do with hoping to avoid her.

'So you decided to scare me half to death instead. Well, if you wanted to give me a heart attack you're too late.' She burst into laughter at her own words. He wasn't sure whether he ought to laugh and hovered, feeling awkward. She looked perilously close to tears. 'So, last night . . .'

'What about it?' Wyn was instantly on his guard. 'It wasn't what you think, but you'd already made your mind up about me. You coppers all stick together. It doesn't matter what actually happened, or what I say.'

'I said I'd give a statement about I saw.' She gave him a sharp look. 'Here's your chance. What did actually happen?'

He frowned at her. 'Is this a stitch-up?'

'Up to you.' She shrugged. 'No skin off my nose, I'm just a visitor. But I like to know what I'm getting into.' She hesitated, squinting at him thoughtfully. Wyn waited in silence. In the stand-off, she flapped a hand. 'Come on then. Get it over with.' A smile hovered over the corner of her mouth. 'Confession is good for the soul, y'know.'

'I'm sure the Inquisition used the same phrase.'

'You never know, I might be able to help . . .' There was another long silence that he had no intention of filling. He was taken aback when she said, 'God, I need a coffee. Do you want one?'

'Er, oh, yes, please, if you're sure?' He wasn't at all sure that he wanted coffee, or even if she should be making it, but at least it stopped her questions for now and got her out of the garden. 'Or I can make it, if you'd prefer?'

'I'm okay now, thank you. It . . .' She waved an approximate hand at her chest. 'It just needs a minute to catch up. I'm still learning to work it.' She laughed shortly. 'It's fine now. Bloody thing. How do you like your coffee?'

'White, one sugar, please. And, um, I'll crack on here, shall I?' He plugged the lawnmower into the outdoor socket that he'd installed and, feeling her eyes burning into his back, pushed the mower in careful stripes along the lawn.

* * *

Feeling horribly aware that she was still in her pyjamas, Fran glided back into the house with all the sangfroid she could muster and climbed the stairs to set the coffee machine to work.

She'd seen the hulking shape in the dark shed and it had scared her more than she wanted to admit. She felt so vulnerable these days. It was difficult to imagine ever being normal again.

Also, she really hadn't had the restful night she'd hoped for. The cottage creaked and sighed, sending her into a wide-eyed state of anxiety that someone was in the house. Freaked out by the sound of the sea together with the dense blackness outside the windows, her imagination went into overdrive that the sea would rise up, engulfing the cottage and her along with it.

It was never fully dark at home. Streetlights, neon signs, cars — there was always something to illuminate the streets. The city had its wildlife, of course. She was used to hearing the strange, high-pitched barks of foxes as they strolled bold as brass along the pavement. The silence and darkness of the country was unnerving. She'd faced situations in work that would terrify other people, and yet here, she was scared of the dark. It was ridiculous, she told herself — but it hadn't stopped her sleeping facing the door.

She was furious and dismayed at her terror. Losing her warrant card was like losing a force field. For God's sake, she'd spent half her life chasing lawbreakers, arresting violent men twice her size and dealing with vicious women intent on gouging her eyes out. And she'd gone all feeble and helpless in a sleepy village about an unexpected visit from the *gardener*.

Then she'd remembered that it was also the Wyn who Elin next door — and most of the pub, apparently — regarded as a gentleman, which went some way to settling her nerves. And he'd been kind enough when she'd humiliatingly nearly fainted.

On top of that, last night's fight had whirled repeatedly on a loop through her mind. She'd have thought nothing of a simple scrap between a couple of blokes in the pub, but twenty-five years of policing placed her automatically on a policeman's side. But — and it was the 'but' that kept her awake — there were plenty of clues signalling things weren't as they'd seemed. Why did she care? Was she simply clinging onto an idea that she was still somehow useful? Or was she meddling to fill her otherwise empty life? The thought led her down another rabbit hole of what on earth she was going to *do* with her life once she was back to 'normal'.

She'd barely drifted off to sleep when the racket outside had jolted her awake. Slamming car doors accompanied called greetings and cheery voices.

'Morning!'

'Nice bathers, are they new?'

'Have you actually *brushed* your hair this morning?'

Gales of laughter had reached Fran's ears. She'd eased open one bleary eye and checked the time. Five thirty! What the hell? Sheer exhaustion sent her back to sleep before Wyn had appeared to terrify her in the garden.

Trekking downstairs, she pulled sweatpants and a hoodie out of her case and over her pyjamas. A comb made her tangled hair worse, so she gave up and piled it on top of her head instead.

Back upstairs, her stomach rumbled. She noticed that she'd already recorded more steps on her watch than she would have at home. Gavin would be proud. She put two slices of bread into the toaster for her breakfast and then added two more for Wyn. She'd worked in a predominately male environment for years and couldn't remember a time when food had been refused.

A swift root through the many cupboards unearthed a tray. She considered a milk jug and sugar bowl as Elin had, and decided on just mugs, pre-sugared. And she'd pre-butter the toast too. It wasn't a tea party. He was working. And so, in her own way, was she. Carrying the loaded tray downstairs made her heart pound. She really wasn't convinced about this upside-down house thing when it came to taking things outside. One trip on the stairs would smash the lot.

The scent of newly mown grass filled the air and she inhaled deeply. It was the smell of new beginnings, she'd always thought. Wyn was making precise, meticulous stripes along the lawn and nodded to show that he'd seen her. Fran bit into her toast, watching him.

She'd never had a gardener. She'd never had a garden, come to that. The whole idea of having *staff* to do what you should surely be doing yourself made her feel uncomfortable.

It had taken her ages to decide recently that she needed a cleaner in her flat, but seeing the dust bunnies building up in corners that she couldn't get to had finally nudged her to action.

That was different though. Temporary. She was recuperating. She got tired. Wasn't gardening something people did on Sundays to keep themselves fit? Along with visits to garden centres. Whatever happened in those. She had no idea.

She chewed thoughtfully. Wyn looked pretty fit to her, despite the apparent injury to his left arm. She'd munched her way through almost all her toast by the time he joined her.

'Hope your coffee's not cold,' she said. 'I can nuke it in the microwave if it is.'

'It's fine. Thank you.'

'I made you some toast.'

'Oh.' He inspected his fingers, wiping them on his over-alls before lifting a slice. 'That was very kind of you. Thank you.'

Fran was determined to get a bit more information with-out sounding as if she were interrogating him. She'd been good at that, in her previous existence — the one that had given her status, friends and a kind of family. She hadn't properly appreciated any of them until she'd lost it all. 'Have you lived here all your life?'

He nodded, chewing. Hunched forward, he avoided her eyes and stared at the garden. He certainly didn't need a solicitor to prompt him to reply, 'no comment'.

'Is there a lot to do in the garden?'

There was another long pause and Fran gave up attempts to converse. She got to her feet to leave him to it.

Quite unexpectedly, he said, 'It depends on the time of the year.' Picking up another slice of toast, he stared at it thoughtfully before biting into it. 'The first lawn cut in early spring is a good time to check for any bald patches, re-seed if there are. Now it's about pruning the early flowering shrubs. The climbers are blooming and just need tidying up now and again.'

Fran sat down again, still holding her empty mug. 'What are the climbers?'

'Roses.' He eyed her, and after a pause added, 'The pretty pink flowers over the door.'

'Gotcha.'

'You don't garden at all?'

'I'm a city girl. I can murder a geranium.'

'It's a talent.' His wide mouth quirked up at the corners and those deep-set eyes crinkled. She could see in the daylight that they were dark blue, which was unusual. He seemed nice, when you cracked the crusty shell.

She felt irritated that he'd made a snap assumption about her, based on a job that she'd left. Despite her retirement, she still couldn't shake off the feeling that she was simply on a very long holiday. Her next words were out of her mouth as fast as she thought them and only a tiny part of her was sorry.

'I know why you didn't knock. You just wanted to get in, do the job and leave without having to speak to me, didn't you?'

'I, er . . .' He looked taken aback and then gave a tiny shrug. 'It's not so much *you* personally . . .' He caught a crumb on his bottom lip with his tongue, and Fran caught herself watching it. 'But you as a whole. All of you — singing from the same hymn sheet. Sticking together. Even when . . .' Brows lowering, his mouth closed.

Fran's irritation with herself rose. Considering that she was a skilled interviewer, she was making a crap job of it. He was determined not to like her, and she didn't care if he hated her when she was doing her *job*, but she wasn't, and he didn't even *know* her.

'How many handymen do you think I've nicked? For doing awful, ghastly, terrible crimes. I don't go around hating gardeners and workmen just because!'

She stopped speaking, horrified at herself. Renowned for her blunt attitude at work, she'd definitely sunk to new levels since her heart attack. It was as if her mouth bypassed her filter system completely. It was probably a good thing she'd retired. She'd have a whole raft of complaints against her by now. No wonder she didn't have any friends. She didn't like *herself* lately. How could she expect anyone else to like her?

His eyebrows rose into his battered khaki fedora and his face swivelled towards her, his expression incredulous.

'You think I'm — what, a casual, unskilled *labourer* or something?'

His shock was so palpable that she hesitated. 'What are you then?'

'I'm a commercial diver. Deep-sea diving.'

'Wow.' Her eyes widened. 'Okay. I wasn't expecting that. So — are you between dives? How long do you have to go away for? Isn't it really isolating?'

His dark eyes rested on her, the tell-tale crinkles at the corners betraying that he was playing her at her own game. 'Do I have to answer all of those questions or is there a particular one you wanted me to answer?'

She allowed herself a small smile. 'You can choose.'

'Yes, it's extremely isolating. Yes, you have to be very good at getting on with people as, yes, you are cooped up with them for long periods at a time.'

Fran blew out a long breath. 'That's something I couldn't do. I have zero tolerance with people, apparently.'

Wyn rubbed a finger over his bottom lip. 'With people you work with though?'

'Okay. That's a good point. I have—' she cleared her throat — 'I *had* all the patience in the world with my shift.' She changed the subject hurriedly. Why hadn't she told him she was retired? 'So — are you filling in time between dives now?'

'Nope. I've finished with all that now. It's a young man's game. Now the sea is my playground, not my office.' He said it lightly, as if he'd said it a million times, and Fran got the feeling that it had become a kind of cliché. Unfolding himself from the chair, he smiled politely at her. 'Well, thanks for the coffee and toast, but I must get on.'

'My pleasure.' As she collected the empty mugs and plates, she replayed the conversation in her head. *Singing from the same hymn sheet? Sticking together?* Something had happened to make him feel that way about the police. Either she was losing her touch, or she didn't really want to know. Because what could she do to put it right now? She was just any old member of the public now. *Impersonating a police officer*, her conscience reminded her.

Huffing, irritated at herself for allowing her thoughts to travel down the same dead-end rut, she loaded the dishwasher and got changed. She had plenty to be thankful for. A decent pension, a lovely house to live in for the whole summer if she wanted to. But it was harder than she'd imagined to shape her own day without work. Before, even her holidays had been activity-based. She'd hiked Machu Picchu and the Great Wall of China for charity.

She couldn't remember when she'd done nothing all day. Had no deadlines. All those times when they'd groaned about how busy they were and how desperate for a break, and now . . .

She refused to allow herself to slide into depression. She would make an excellent recovery and her life would start all over again. In a different direction. Somehow.

She could walk. She *would* walk. Track her steps and improve her count. She remembered in the early weeks after her surgery that just walking the few hundred metres to the end of the road and back had felt like a marathon. She could manage a mile or so now, but she was slow and often worn out afterwards. It was hard to imagine getting back to where she'd been pre-heart attack. Little and often, that's what she needed. This was just the right place to do it.

'I'm off then,' she called into the garden as a matter of courtesy. Wyn was on his haunches under a big shrub. He showed no signs of having heard her and she sloped out of the back door, feeling rather out of sorts.

* * *

Wyn heard Fran leave. He'd hunkered down, pretending to be busy beneath a flourishing hydrangea bush. The garden was well cared for but there was plenty to do in May. Even so, he'd somehow managed to make the job last at least twice as long as it merited. And he didn't really want to examine why.

Or why he hadn't had the manners to return her goodbye. It wouldn't have killed him, would it? She'd even made him coffee and toast. He could still see her in his mind, with her mad hair all piled up and wispy bits round her ears that the sun shone through.

Wincing, he remembered telling her much more than he intended to. Why had he done that? *Oh, look at me, the macho deep-sea diver* . . . Using a hand fork, he dug viciously in the soil, yanking tiny weeds out and hurling them into the green recycling bag at his elbow.

Although he prided himself on his many skills, these days he *had* become little more than a jack-of-all-trades. A stranger to the village, as Fran was, would have no idea that he wasn't the resident handyman. When had it taken over his life? He knew the answer to that one. When he and Tasha ended, so had his hopes and dreams. He'd been devastated. And it had made him gung-ho. Which was how he'd ended up like . . . like *this*.

She'd taken up with that . . . that jumped-up, pompous, bullying *arse* while he was away, risking his life to earn money to buy the things *she'd* insisted they needed — and that he only too willingly provided. He had all the money he could ever want now. Just not the woman.

He tugged up a deep-rooted dandelion with savage glee, flinging it into the recycling bag. Then felt guilty about depriving the bees.

He'd thought it was what Tash wanted. The hopes of a family, a life living happily into old age. When he thought about it, he should hate *women* really. Not just the represent-ative of a police force that had spawned the most two-faced, conniving, arrogant git ever to have strutted about in his too-tight uniform.

But, of course, he didn't hate women. He didn't even hate Tash, although there were some pretty good reasons to. He shook his head as if he could dislodge the incident with PC Alix James.

As if thinking about Tasha had conjured her up, a mes-sage arrived.

Hope you're okay. Thanks for last night. Sorry to be a nuisance but the washing machine has stopped working. Do you know anyone who fixes them? Or could you? Pretty please???

He glared at the phone. Why did Tash keep doing this? Of course, he could just block her . . . but he knew he wouldn't.

Because she needed him. Didn't she?

CHAPTER SEVEN

Stomping away from the cottage and trying not to feel irritated with Wyn, who hadn't even been arsed to return her goodbye, considering she'd made him toast and everything, Fran looked around her in the bright morning sunshine.

The turning circle at the end of the cul-de-sac led to a break in the fencing, bounding a sandy path dividing the sand dunes from the houses. A few steps along, she came to a well-trodden path crossing the dunes. Handy for a beach stroll, she decided. And she couldn't exactly get lost with the sea as a compass point.

A short stroll on what seemed to be the main path brought her to a row of shops facing the sea, fronted by a little scrubby green area, complete with picnic tables. The nearest in the row was a fish and chip takeaway with adjoining restaurant. Both closed, but promising to be open later, at 5 p.m.

The last shop seemed to be a typical beach emporium: shrimp nets and plastic beach balls hung from the bleached but gaily striped awning, and a metal rack of postcards clanked against the window in the breeze. The door was locked. A hand-scrawled note said *Gone to get boat, back later.* The note was attached with a scruffy sliver of sticky tape that seemed to have been used many times. Fran wondered how much later it would be. What a strange way to conduct a business. Although, as the place was deserted, maybe there wasn't that much business . . .

Seagulls cawed and cackled overhead, some of them perched possessively on the picnic tables in front of the shops. One eyeballed her, head on one side.

Close up, she was surprised at how big it was. She looked at the strong, curved yellow beak. It was nothing like city sparrows and pigeons. Hesitating about where to go, she walked onto the beach and turned left. She had no desire to return the way she'd come and risk bumping into Wyn again.

It wasn't long before her legs felt leaden and heavy, unused to the soft, dragging sand. She sank into a sheltered dip between the dunes, a little more than halfway across the beach, automatically checking her pulse with her smartwatch. Thumping along nicely at about eighty to ninety. She'd been told to limit it to about a hundred and fifteen, for the time being, during exercise. Would there ever be a time when she'd use it just to tell the time? She closed her eyes, and within moments was asleep.

She awoke, disorientated and still drowsy, an hour and a half later. Through sleep-heavy eyes, she watched a line of people trekking onto the beach. Silhouetted against the sun, burdened by huge holdalls and rucksacks, there were a dozen of them, in vastly oversized coats that reached almost to their ankles. Their voices reached her, laughter drifting over the sand, as they dumped their bags on the dry sand about a hundred feet away.

Stiff from her nap, she hugged her knees to her chest, and watched in amazement as they pulled the huge coats off and filled the holdalls with their many layers of clothing. In ragged groups they walked, jogged or ran to the water's edge in their swimsuits. Just their swimsuits. No wetsuits. All women and all shapes and sizes. From thin to voluptuously curvy.

A paddle? Did you need to strip off to a swimsuit to do that? Couldn't you just roll your trousers up? Her jaw dropped as they walked straight into the shimmering sea, their voices shrill and laughing. Some inched in, shoulders hunched. Others dipped below the water, emerging shaking their heads like dogs.

Their shrieks and giggles reached her, and suddenly, Fran was six. She knew she was six because it was on the badge she was wearing. At her birthday party. On some beach that she couldn't remember.

All her friends paddling in the sea or swimming.

From the unfamiliar beach, she watched through tears . . .

The picture faded.

And right here, in front of her, these women were having fun. Jumping the sparkling waves and laughing. Fearless. Like the children in that long-ago memory.

Fran watched them with a mixture of deep-seated dread and envy. Her mother's terror of water had infected her so that, somehow, Fran had gone through her entire adult life as a non-swimmer. The only one at police training college to leave without a life-saving certificate. Staying resolutely in the shallow end of hotel swimming pools when shamed into it on holidays, but always near the lifeguard or the side of the pool. Swim-up bars were a nightmare.

Splashing and dancing, the women lifted their arms to the sun that gilded the sea into molten gold. Their laughter drifted towards her. Fran scrambled awkwardly to her feet, feeling stiff, cold and angry without really knowing why.

When she arrived back at Seagull Cottage, the garden resembled a photo from a Sunday supplement. She'd have said a gardening magazine if she'd ever read one. Perfect contrasting stripes covered the lawn, and everything seemed neatly tidied up in a way that she couldn't identify what had been done. She peered around for Wyn, in case he was hiding in the shed again. She wondered whether she was supposed to have paid him and decided she needed to check with Ken and April. She took a photo on her phone and sent it to Gavin and Ally on their WhatsApp.

Living the dream, she wrote, adding several smiling emojis.

Glad you're enjoying yourself! Gavin replied. *Some of us have to work, y'know.* He accompanied his words with a photo of his in tray, overflowing with files.

Fran tapped on her screen. *You know you love it. Stop slacking and get on with it.*

Gavin sent back a cartoon naked bottom and she laughed, before tapping, *So much for your promise of a quiet rural idyll!*

Oh?

Got time for a quick chat?

In response to her question, the phone rang in her hand.

'What's up, Sarge? You okay?'

'I'm fine, Gavin, yes,' Fran began. 'Just that I drove straight into a punch-up when I arrived and—'

'You did *what?*' There was no mistaking Gavin's shocked tone. 'A fight? Tell me you didn't get involved . . .'

'Ah, well, see . . .'

'You're not in the hospital, are you? I knew I should have video-called —'

'Gavin. Calm down. I didn't hit anybody and nobody hit me. Listen.' She related the tale in an official and succinct manner. Gavin punctuated the tale with satisfactory tuts and hums but didn't interrupt.

When Fran ground to a halt, he said in a stern voice, 'Did you forget you'd retired?'

Fran grinned at the phone. He was so predictable. The most reliable young man she'd ever met. 'The thing I wanted to ask you about, is this Wyn. Do you know him?'

'Wyn? Of course! *Everyone* knows Wyn. Not only because he's possibly the biggest man alive and no normal person would want to be in a fight with him because all he needs to do is give you a bit of a shove and you'd go down like a sack of spuds, and let me tell you, he was the best rugby centre ever and nobody could stop him in a tackle . . .'

Fran stared at the phone in surprise, hearing Gavin sucking in a long breath before continuing, 'But he's also the mildest bloke you'd ever wish to meet. I've *never* heard of him starting a fight. Ever! Even on the pitch he'd be the one breaking up the handbags!'

Fran frowned. Handbags? Pitch? Rugby? It was mystifying. '*Okaaaay* — so this policeman then . . .'

'AJ? Never heard of him. There was a woman, you said?'

'Yes. Slim, dark hair, nicely dressed, quite a bit younger, possibly? Pretty — she was hanging on Wyn's arm, trying to stop him and—'

'Oh.' Gavin groaned. 'That sounds like Tasha. Wyn's wife. Ex-wife. She ran off with—'

'Don't tell me. A copper?'

'Mmm.' Gavin blew out a sigh. 'How did you leave it?'

'I left the scene without giving him my contact details.'

There was a silence for a moment and then Gavin laughed. 'So you can't be done for impersonating a police officer then . . .'

'Don't!' Fran laughed too. 'I'm not proud of myself. I had a sleepless night worrying about it. I just had a gut feeling about something not being quite as it seemed, and Wyn turned up in the garden first thing, so I—'

'He what?'

'Apparently he's the gardener?'

'Really? But . . . he's a commercial diver! Or he was last I saw him.'

'He has a really terrible scar on his left arm . . .'

'Oh. I don't know anything about that. Poor guy. I hope he's okay.'

'I tried to talk to him today. He doesn't give much away.'

'That's Wyn. Strong and silent. Always has been.'

'Hmm. Well, he doesn't like me.'

'Hello? He thinks you're a cop and a cop ran off with his missus. Anyway, why do you care?'

Fran tried out a laugh. 'You know me. Hate bullies and injustice.'

'That's definitely not Wyn's style. Sounds to me like you might need to keep an eye on this AJ though. Trust you to drive into the only punch-up the village has had off the rugby field in years!' Gavin tutted. 'Everything okay otherwise?'

'It's lovely, thank you. Very picturesque.'

'It is that.' Gavin sighed.

Fran said into the pause, 'Obviously this is still your home, Gav. You and Ally are welcome to come down for a break whenever.'

'Thanks, Fran. Seems a bit wrong somehow . . .'

'Bah,' Fran snorted. 'Of course it isn't. Have a word with Ally. Any time.'

They chatted about this and that, and when the call ended Fran felt a little lost. Severed from the life she knew.

Her cardiologist's words about enjoying herself ringing in her ears, she poured herself a glass of wine and sipped it while she mixed half a pack of fresh pasta with a carbonara sauce she'd bought from the Marks & Spencer at the services on the way there. Pre-heart attack, she'd loved to cook. These days, she didn't seem to have the energy to stand and do all the chopping and slicing. Even using shortcuts like ready-made sauces seemed to take too long. She set the table on the balcony, unpacked one of the fat novels she'd brought along and ate, read and watched the sun drop into the sea.

It was an effort to stay awake long enough to load the dishwasher and clean up the kitchen, and it was still before nine when she snuggled up in the comfortable bed with her book.

CHAPTER EIGHT

Bang! Slam! Laughter . . .

'Morning, ladies!'

'Looking very colourful today in your new bobble hat!'

'I knitted it myself!'

Fran groaned, hands over her ears, as the voices called to one another. Five thirty again. Couldn't these people sleep? Well, neither could she, now.

She stretched carefully and padded upstairs to the kitchen to get the coffee on. Lemon rays of dawn sunshine patterned and warmed the pale walls and weathered-oak floor of the lounge. She couldn't help noticing how much earlier the sun seemed to rise compared to London.

Feeling like an advert for life by the sea, she popped her morning pills while the coffee brewed and the sourdough bread she'd brought with her browned in the toaster. Adding the jar of marmalade from the welcome basket, she balanced everything carefully on a tray and took it onto the balcony, planning to eat outside.

Within moments, she'd retreated into the house to fetch a sweater from downstairs and a couple of throws. It might look warm, she thought, but this was Wales and not the Costa Brava. Stepping back onto the balcony, she looked down in surprise. The plate was empty. Her toast had disappeared. What the hell? Scanning the dunes ahead, she peered over the balcony, fully expecting to see somebody munching her breakfast in the garden, but there was not a soul in sight. No sound but the incessant mocking cackle of gulls.

Bloody hell, she texted Gavin, along with a photo of her empty plate. *You've seriously mis-sold this place to me, I've just been robbed!*

Whaaaaaaaaat??? He must be on the early shift.

Suspect appears to be feathered variety! She couldn't find a seagull emoji so used an eagle instead.

Argh! Don't feed the gulls — the whole village will hate you!

I didn't feed it on purpose! Maybe I need an instruction manual for this village.

Gavin sent a row of laughing emojis. *Everyone says hi and hopes you're okay.*

Fran visualized them all sitting in the briefing room and a wave of nostalgia swept over her. She sent back a thumbs-up and a smile. It was a long way from how she felt, but those little illustrations had saved her making a fool of herself with rambling self-pity several times recently.

And stay away from fights! Gavin replied.

* * *

Down to only four slices of her favourite sourdough, Fran toasted and buttered afresh. A gull perched on the balcony rail and regarded her speculatively.

'You, my cheeky friend, can bugger off. This is mine.' All the same, she didn't fancy her chances and was ready to abandon the toast if it swooped, whatever Gavin said about feeding them.

The sun rose into a cloudless blue sky and Fran decided it was time to have a bit of an explore in the village. She found some shopping bags neatly stashed in the cupboard beneath the sink, and wandered slowly along the sandy path behind the dunes. The row of shops popped into view a little further on.

Two old couples, muffled in walking jackets and with sticks, cupped hot drinks at one of the picnic tables. They all faced the beach, and Fran's gaze followed theirs towards a large orange truck parked on a sort of informal roundabout between shops and beach. Three men unloaded barriers and signage.

'It's the triathlon,' one of the old men supplied without being asked, glancing up at her. He pronounced every syllable plus a few more, so it came out like *tri-ath-er-long*. 'We're doing it this year, ain't we, Walter?'

'Oh aye,' wheezed Walter, who had to be over eighty.

'I'd like to see you two in a pair o' them budgie smugglers!' one of the elderly ladies said, smiling mischievously up at Fran, who couldn't help smiling back.

'Ooh, you wouldn't be able to keep yer 'ands off us, girls.' Walter's eyes disappeared beneath his wrinkled smile. Gales of laughter, punctuated by explosive coughing and more laughter, accompanied Fran to the beach shop.

A row of bells above the door announced her arrival and, used to vast, anonymous supermarkets, she slipped inside almost apologetically as the few customers inside looked up to see who'd entered.

Despite the sun-bleached buckets and spades hanging outside, the shop was well stocked and a scent of baking made her stomach rumble. She'd brought some basics with her — Earl Grey loose tea together with her favourite cherry-coloured infuser teapot, some salad, and there was pasta left over from the previous night. She was hoping for fresh local fish and shellfish, plus fruit and veg. If there was maybe some nice, artisan bread, that would be a miracle, but she doubted it. Maybe it was time to have a crack at making her own.

She was pleasantly surprised to see an entire central aisle packed with curry spices and pastes, speciality rice and flatbreads, and chutneys.

'I know. Impressive, isn't it?'

Fran jumped as the woman beside her spoke. Had she spoken aloud?

'I'm Caitlin.' She smiled, and held out a hand. 'And you're . . . ?'

'I'm Fran. I'm house-sitting for the summer.' She shook the proffered hand and returned the smile. 'I must admit, I thought I was going to see rows of tins of little sausages in baked beans.'

'Like you had when you were camping, as a kid?'

'Yes!'

'Here you go.' Caitlin reached out and dropped a tin into Fran's hand with a grin. Dark-haired, her eyes made even bluer by her outdoor tan and freckles, Fran judged her to be in her forties, and imagined her with horses, or some other outdoorsy job. 'The shop does a roaring trade from the campsite across the road. The locals like it too. Geraint here, who owns the shop, does a good job keeping us stocked up. If there's anything you need, just ask him. If he doesn't have it, he'll know where to get it.'

'Good to know. Thanks!' The doorbells chimed a new arrival, and Fran looked up with everyone else. A tower of boxes appeared above a pair of bowed legs and disappeared behind the counter. The delivery man was red-faced and sweating profusely by the third delivery, and returned twice more.

'Stocking up for the triathlon,' Caitlin murmured to Fran.

'Is it a big event?'

'Compared to the London Marathon? No. For a little seaside village . . . mmm, well . . .' Caitlin held a tin of coconut milk upside down and stared at the label. She muttered, 'Any . . . minute . . . now . . .' Her head jerked up like a meerkat. 'Oh, aye. Here we go . . .'

A tall, lean man sprinted from behind the counter. Fran caught a glimpse of a furious expression and wild, sticky-up hair before he crashed out of the doorway.

'That was Geraint, that was.' Caitlin nodded, craning her neck to follow his progress.

'Blimey. He's speedy. Is he competing?'

Caitlin chuckled. 'Not. A. Chance.'

The voices outside rose to a crescendo. Fran took her cue from Caitlin and both of them moved towards the window, pretending to peruse items for their shopping baskets. Geraint, sleeves rolled up, hands on hips and head pushed forward, looked livid, even from this distance. He was equally matched in stature by the other man, whose hands were lifted in supplication.

A tiny, elderly lady in the shop tutted at the young woman behind the counter. '*Duw, duw.* There'll be blood one of these days, you mark my words. I'll have half a dozen of those nice corned beef pasties, Bethan, my lovely.'

'Righto, Mrs Rees-Morgan.' Behind the counter, Bethan, her bright-pink hair piled up above a number of mismatched earrings and a tattoo that twirled down one side of her slender neck, wielded the tongs with dexterity and the chunky golden pasties slipped into several brown paper bags. 'So is Mr Rees-Morgan feeling better now then?'

'Oh no. These are for me! Got to keep your strength up, you know!'

Fran listened to this exchange with half an ear as it played out in the reflection of the shop window. She made a note to herself to tell it to Gavin, and ask what '*duw, duw*' meant. The men outside squared up to each other. Their voices carried on the still air.

'Why do you have to do this today?' Geraint demanded, his hands punctuating his words. 'The bloody thing isn't until Saturday. Today's only bloody Thursday!'

'I can't just magic up all the barriers for the entire course on the day it starts, for God's sake, you idiot!'

'You should've let me know!'

'You had an email! Like everyone else! Everyone knows when it's on but you — *you* have to make a bloody scene about it.'

'I'm here all year round and you turn up once in a blue moon and lord it over everyone!'

'Oh, give over, you tart. You make a fortune out of all the visitors.'

'I have to buy in all that crap they like, don't I? All them drinks and protein bars taking up the space for my usual customers.'

'Fine. I'll sell it then.'

'You bloody won't!' Geraint snarled, now inches away from the other man. 'Stealing my income? And you're blocking my shop. My driver can't deliver or turn round properly!'

'He's already delivered and I'm not blocking your bloody shop! And your bloody driver can't bloody drive properly, can he, if he can't get round there! No offence, Ianto, mun.'

Ianto, evidently the perspiring delivery driver, shrugged and cracked open a can of pop, leaning against his cab. 'None taken, Dyl.' He took a Mars bar out of his pocket and sank his teeth into it, watching the scuffle with relish.

It went on and on. Bloody this and effing that. Their faces pushed together, fingers poked in chests, legs splayed. Fran's eyebrows rose into her hairline. Did everyone in this village shout and argue with one another? Was there something in the air? She added the word 'mun' to her mental list to ask Gavin about.

Should she maybe intervene? How bad was it likely to get? And she could just imagine what Gavin would say if she . . .

As she thought about it, Geraint's fist shot out and struck Dyl a glancing blow. He staggered backwards, holding his face. Throwing caution to the wind, Fran strode outside, leaving her basket in the doorway.

Caitlin called after her, 'Fran, er, you should know that . . . uh . . . oh.' Her voice petered out as Fran strode on.

* * *

Wyn was already up that morning when the Surf Shack and the Coffee Pot called with their plumbing drama. It happened frequently as both premises were shoehorned into a gap between ancient dwellings with plumbing to match. But it was a big weekend for both businesses, so he was there promptly to fix it.

The two girls from the Coffee Pot were busy in their tiny kitchen, making brownies and muffins by the trayload. They also delivered to locals and surrounding cafés. Wyn admired them enormously. In the summer, they employed a bevy of cheerful students who cooked, served or delivered, depending on their skills. If there was somewhere bigger in the village for them to move into, he was sure they'd make a really good go of it. In the meantime, if he could help even a little by keeping their temperamental plumbing and electricity in order, then he would.

'Mwah, you're a darlin', Wyn.' Delyth handed him a coffee — cappuccino, chocolate sprinkles, one sugar — and two brownies joined together, warm from the oven, in a brown paper bag printed with their *The Coffee Pot* logo. 'Send us your bill!'

The Surf Shack also teemed with activity. Stand-up paddle boards for hire were racked outside, along with a selection of bodyboards and surfboards, despite there being no surf whatsoever on that section of coastline. The shop had been started up two generations ago and remained in the family, now employing brother and sister, and when occasion demanded, as with this weekend, Mum and Dad.

The shop did a roaring trade in surf wear, thanks to the sharp eye of the daughter, Ffion, who also sold her own hoodie designs and jewellery. Her brother, Cai, was a photographer, specializing in wave photography while he actually surfed them. His images graced the pages of magazines and surfing competitions, and on a much smaller but no less stunning scale, prints and greetings cards for the shop.

Although the Llanbryn Triathlon frazzled the nerves of the residents at times, it also brought much-needed cash and motivation to the village, which always rose to the occasion with bunting, fresh licks of paint and tidied-up gardens. They might moan, but they were proud of their village.

'Plumbing sorted, I'll pop the bill in later,' Wyn said, sticking his head round the door. Ffion was perched on a stepladder, pinning up a string of bunting. 'Want a hand with that?'

Ffion glanced down at him and wobbled precariously. 'Thanks, Wyn. Are you sure?'

Wyn saw the sympathy in her expression as she tried not to look at his bad arm. 'Of course!'

'Then, yes, please, if you've got time. Cai's put the boards out and swanned off somewhere.'

'No problem,' Wyn said, holding the ladder steady for her. 'Just tell me what you want doing.'

During the next hour, he manhandled boxes in between drinking his coffee and munching his brownies. He was slow and awkward nowadays, and it drove him mad, but as long as he took his time, he could manage. His legs and back were still strong. Up and down the ladder, he'd heard and seen the steady stream of caravans and camper vans as they passed on their way to the campsite for the weekend.

He'd already seen Dyl arriving in the hire van that contained the first lot of barriers and signage, so when he spotted Ianto's delivery truck trundle past, he anticipated the usual fracas.

Ffion had seen it too. 'Time you were off!' She flashed a quick grin at him as she steamed a colourful sweatshirt to display in the window. Geraint and Dyl were well known for their incendiary tempers.

Collecting his tool bag, he strolled out, knowing that it would take a while for the punch-up to develop. If he stopped it before it started, they just bided their time and it happened later. Enjoying the sunshine, he paused to retrieve secateurs from his bag and snip back the hedge that was overgrowing the stile from the car park to the surf shop and coffee house. He heard the rumpus outside the beach shop before he saw it, which didn't surprise him. Another thing that didn't surprise him was that policewoman, Fran, in the middle of it.

He quickened his step, hearing her pointing out to the driver that the truck unloading the barriers was, in fact, parked illegally, and suggesting that it was moved. She was, to be fair, quite right, but what she didn't know was that the illegal parking was merely the tip of the iceberg as far as the two men were concerned.

She had stayed out of reach of the punches already flying between Geraint and Dyl, he was relieved to see. Wyn waited until they'd run out of steam before he reached in and separated them.

'Now, then.' He used the same tone he'd used for decades to break up brawls on the rugby pitch. It worked now, just as it had then. Geraint and Dyl stopped beating lumps out of each other instantly. 'Pack this lark up or I'll tell your mother!' He hoisted each man upright by their collars.

He'd swear they waited for him to end these incidents. First, it meant that they'd made their point without coming to any serious harm, and second it saved face for them as each was prevented from claiming victory.

'Enough now,' Wyn growled, releasing his grip and glaring at them. 'Every year we have this! Go and have a word with yourselves.'

'Sorry, Wyn,' panted Geraint, his head low, blotting the blood from his nose with his sleeve.

'Sorry, Wyn.' Chest heaving, Dyl rubbed his chin and looked at his bloody hand before wiping it on his tracksuit trousers.

'Ianto, you useless—' Flicking his glance briefly at Fran, Wyn tempered his language to the delivery driver, currently excavating his teeth with a fingernail of one hand while holding an unwrapped Snickers bar in the other. 'Stop stuffing your face and move that heap of shit. You're perfectly capable of reversing it. I've seen you do it.'

'Sorry, Wyn,' said Ianto, staring thoughtfully at his snack before pushing it whole into his mouth and chomping, eyes bulging.

'Right, Ianto. Now you've had your sugar rush, shall we get this road cleared?'

He'd known the two brothers since they were born and was used to their warring, but it was embarrassing to have someone from outside the village seeing this ludicrous pantomime.

She'd be thinking it was like the Wild West — two punch-ups in short order, and him in the middle of them both. Not that this had been much of a fight. More of a scuffle.

He caught himself. What did he care what she thought? And they did not need her poking her police nose into village business, adding two and two and making five.

Brave of her though, he conceded, turning to her. While he was trying to decide what to say, she raked him with a cool, thoughtful look and spun purposefully on her heel. He watched her go, trying not to admire the swing of her hips in those jeans.

* * *

Brothers, Fran realized, on her way back into the shop. They were brothers. That explained a lot. She'd watched, feeling invisible. It was old-fashioned policing at its best and she applauded it. Wyn had turned the full beam of his blue eyes her way and she'd returned it steadily, noticing the broken nose that did nothing to mar his good looks.

Her thoughts drifted back to the fight outside the pub. What *had* happened? If she was going to be called on to make a statement, she wanted to know.

'Well. That was brave.' Caitlin regarded her with interest. 'I was about to tell you they were brothers but you were off.' She sighed. 'It was like something out of *Braveheart*.'

'Me?'

'Oh, er, yes, course.'

'You meant him, didn't you? Wyn?'

'Uh-huh.' Caitlin smiled, gazing back out of the window.

75

'Hmm.' Fran frowned, watching the scene outside. Wyn was seeing Ianto back in his truck and Geraint was helping cable-tie the event signage to the barriers. Apart from the preponderance of blood, it was as if nothing had happened. 'So . . . is Geraint that horrible to the event visitors?'

'Nah.' Caitlin shook her head. 'He loves it. Just gets in a bit of a state about it disrupting his routine.'

'Oh.' It made no sense at all to Fran, recalling the note about being closed due to boat collecting. And Wyn's glare had clearly said *nothing to see here*, so it would seem that this was a familiar domestic quarrel.

Wyn was well liked, judging by Caitlin's smile and the testimonies from both Elin and Gavin. Even the two warring brothers allowed him to stop their fight with little resistance.

She picked up her abandoned basket. Caitlin peered into it.

'What are you going to make with that?'

Fran stared at the contents. A sachet of Thai red curry paste, a tin of beans and mini sausages, and a yoghurt. 'I have no idea.'

'Fancy coming to a cooking class tonight? It's at the village hall, just up by the church here.' She waved a hand. Fran hesitated. Did she? She could already cook . . . even though she'd stalled lately.

'It's pizza,' Caitlin continued. 'We're cooking it in a pizza oven outside. There'll be wine. It's fun. Not serious. Great way to meet some more people, especially if you're going to be here for a while.'

Considering a solitary evening in the cottage followed by another sleepless night, Fran decided with a nod. 'I think you had me at wine. How much is it and what do I need?'

'It's twenty quid and includes the ingredients, wine and tuition.' Caitlin led her to the counter, where Bethan unpacked the boxes Ianto had delivered. She looked up.

'Cooking class? Here you go.' She handed over a printed sheet. 'Pick what you're making. I've still got most of the stuff.'

Fran ran her eyes down the list and burst into laughter. 'Sex on the Beach? Isn't that a cocktail?'

Caitlin laughed too. 'I'm making that one. Prawns and pineapple.'

'Erm, I think I'll go for . . . Pop My Pizza Cherry? No, maybe Crazy Cow is more me . . .' She was, she thought, the opposite of crazy. She was sensible, measured and responsible. And maybe it was time to be someone different for a change.

Caitlin peered at it. 'What's in it? Er — hot chilli beef, hot this and hot the other. You'd have to be crazy to eat it.'

'I like a bit of hot,' Fran said with a grin. Caitlin sniggered. Fran liked her more all the time.

Bethan ran a decorated turquoise fingernail down her list. 'Here you go. Weighed flour and yeast sachet in one bag here, enough to make two pizzas.' She took a pack from under the counter. 'The Crazy Cow topper bag is in the chiller. Minced beef, jalapenos, chilli peppers, mozzarella. Everything else you need will be at the hall, all in the price.'

'This is a brilliant idea,' Fran said, following Caitlin to the refrigerated cabinet and collecting the specified items. 'I've never actually made pizza from scratch.' She paid for her shopping and peeped outside just as Geraint barrelled through the front door.

'A'right, ladies?' He nodded at Fran's purchases as he breezed towards the back of the shop, showing no signs of having seen her outside earlier. 'Pizza tonight then? I'll see you up there later!'

'Is he the teacher?' Fran whispered to Caitlin.

'No. He'll be up with everyone else to eat the pizzas. And he brings the wine.'

'Huh?'

'He's got a booze licence. It's a community thing that we do before the triathlon. We make pizzas, everyone brings something else to eat with it. Pastas, salads, quiches, cake, whatever. It's lush. A bit of a party.'

'Don't the pub mind?'

'Hell no. Keeps us out of the way. They'll be rammed tonight. There'll be hordes of campers and VWs arriving today and tomorrow and they all need feeding. The queues for the chippie will be down to the sea.'

'Chips and pub grub? Aren't they all honed athletes then?'

Caitlin eyed her, straight-faced. 'Some of them,' she said, twitching an eyebrow. 'Shall I meet you there or shall I come and get you?'

'I think I can find it. There's only one church, isn't there? I passed it on the way here.'

'Yep. The hall is round the back. See you at six.'

'Okay. Thank you!' Fran found herself addressing Caitlin's back. The woman was a whirlwind.

But Fran had a plan. Time to put it into action.

CHAPTER NINE

Fran stowed her shopping in the enormous refrigerator, sat down for a drink of water to let her heart rate settle and then strolled to the pub before Gavin's warnings about getting involved and impersonating the police sounded any louder inside her head.

It was a picturesque, whitewashed stone building, thatched and well kept, adorned with flourishing hanging baskets and planters among the picnic tables on the forecourt. The entrance door was propped open and Fran wandered inside, looking around. As her eyes adjusted to the lower light she could see that the stone flagging at the entrance was clean, the carpet vacuumed, tables and pumps on the bar polished to a shine, and there were vases of fresh flowers in the deep sills. It was as well maintained inside as out, which boded well for the menu.

The air of welcome was repeated in the broad smiles of the staff who bustled back and forth, all wearing black polo shirts and trousers with a smart black apron. A young woman, setting out menus and straightening chairs, hailed her.

'Good morning! Coffee? It's a little early for lunch but it won't be long now.'

'I'd love a coffee, please. Black Americano. Do you do decaf?'

'Of course.' The woman whipped out her order pad. 'Anything else? We have fresh scones, Welsh cakes and toasted teacakes . . . ?'

Fran's mouth watered but she could feel her spare tyre wobbling over the waistband of her jeans, plus she still had Elin's baked donations back at the cottage. 'Sounds delicious, but not for me today, thank you. And, um, is the landlord around, please?'

'Yep, I'll give him a shout now. Is he expecting you?'

'No.' Fran shook her head and smiled, to show that she wasn't a threat, and the girl hurried away. Fran picked up a menu. The choices looked delicious, and had quite a lot of healthy options too. She wondered if that was because of the competitors for the event.

'Good morning — can I help you?' Fran whirled to face the burly landlord. His smile fell a little. 'Have we met?'

'Good morning — we sort of met the other night. A couple of nights ago?' She couldn't think what day it was. It felt as if she'd been there for ages already. 'In the car park around closing time . . .' Fran watched his mystified expression clear. 'The, er, altercation, between Wyn and the policeman.'

'Oh. That.' His eye-roll included his eyebrows and he finished it looking over his shoulder at the bar, as if that was where he'd rather be. 'Best forgotten, probably. Okay? Right then . . .' Fran caught an echo of Wyn's *nothing to see here*.

'Mm,' she murmured, noncommittally, standing her ground. 'I was just wondering whether you have CCTV that looks over the car park? Only—' she foresaw him about to shake his head and hurried on — 'Wyn was insistent that he hadn't assaulted the policeman, and video footage would help to prove that, if charges were brought against him.'

The landlord ran the tip of his tongue over his bottom lip and frowned.

'Look, Miss . . . ?'

'Fran. Francis Doherty.' She held her hand out and he shook it.

'Bart Morris. Everyone calls me Barty.'

'Pleased to meet you.' Fran nodded, and moved on smoothly before he could remember that she'd announced herself as police and ask to see her warrant card. Her stomach jolted. It was so out of character for her to brazenly lie like this and she licked her lips, dry with nerves. 'So, everyone tells me that Wyn is a good bloke, and that the fight was very out of character. And . . . it got me thinking.' She shrugged and fixed him with what she hoped was a disarming smile.

His eyes narrowed. 'Yes?'

'About what really happened before I arrived.'

'Uh-huh?'

Fran swallowed. He was giving nothing away. And why should he? She was a stranger to the village. 'I was wondering what might be on the CCTV. That might be helpful.'

'You obviously know that there are rules about who sees it.'

Fran chewed her lip. She did — only people on the actual footage could see it — but she'd been hoping that he didn't, and that she could bluff it. Her coffee arrived, along with two little homemade cookies.

'That's a lovely touch,' she said, staring at the cookies pointedly and diverting attention from her quest for a moment. 'Your menu looks delicious. I'll be in for lunch sometime soon.'

Barty regarded her steadily for a long moment as she sipped her coffee with averted eyes. Eventually he said, 'Of course, Wyn can apply to see the footage, as you know. I'm sure it will be helpful. To him.'

'If I see him, I'll let him know,' Fran said with a nod, understanding him perfectly.

'As will I. And er,' Barty continued in a rush, 'you never know who might have videoed it from their phones. People do, don't they? It would be worth Wyn asking about. Just saying, like.'

'Thank you,' Fran said, with a smile. She took her coffee to a table by the window and sat facing the door. From her vantage point, she people-watched. The pub ran smoothly, the staff were courteous and efficient and her coffee was excellent. It felt like a job well done, even though she hadn't actually done anything.

* * *

Fran arrived early that evening at the village hall, with her Crazy Cow ingredients and a pinny she'd found in the kitchen of Seagull Cottage. She'd strolled up there that afternoon just to be sure she knew where she was going, and had spent an interesting hour or so wandering through the church and graveyard. To her surprise, it turned out to date right back to the sixth century. She'd stood and read the printed posters with interest. Apparently lepers could watch the priest taking the service through a tiny window aperture right at the back. How terribly sad their lives must have been. Her mind wandered back to her discoveries as she stood waiting for everyone in the doorway of the hall.

'Hi, Fran! Oh, you all right?' Fran jumped as Caitlin came into view, heading up a group of about a dozen people.

'Yes! Just thinking about lepers.' Fran waved a hand at the church as Caitlin's brow creased.

'*Okaaay*. As one does.' Caitlin turned to the small crowd behind her. 'This is Fran, everyone! She's staying in the village for the summer.'

'Hi, Fran!' they chorused, smiling.

'Are you enjoying your stay?'

'Where are you from?'

'Have you been to Wales before?'

Fran did her best to answer the barrage of questions. She couldn't help comparing it to a city welcome, where people would have nodded politely and felt it discourteous to interrogate the newcomer. Where people sat on trains and didn't even look at one another for an entire journey, in preference to their phones. She'd only been there a few days but she definitely preferred the Welsh welcome, she decided. Even if it was a bit full-on.

The double doors to the village hall were thrown open from inside.

'*Noswaith dda*!' Elin beamed from within. 'Hello, Fran. How lovely to see you here. That was "good evening", for you.'

'Hello! I'm so glad you translated,' Fran said, somehow not surprised to find Elin already there. 'What's Welsh for "pizza"?'

'*Pitsa*.' Elin shrugged, with a grin. 'There you are. Fluent already. Come in, come in, lovely to see you all.' Fran caught more unintelligible phrases. It was intriguing, this idea of a foreign country within a country.

The village hall was equipped with a kitchen, two ovens and hobs, plus cupboards rammed with crockery, pots, pans and cutlery. Rows of tables were covered with gaily patterned oil cloths, and the centre table at the front bore what Fran assumed were the communal ingredients. She sidled to a table and was delighted when Caitlin joined her.

'Seeing as you're a pizza virgin,' she said in a loud whisper. There was laughter from the other participants.

'Are you a virgin yet, Walter?' Two old men were sharing a table and jostling each other's elbows, their lined faces split into broad grins.

'I'm working on it.' Walter's friend laughed wheezily and Fran recognized them from earlier that day outside the little row of shops, teasing each other about the triathlon.

'I can see I'll have to split you two up,' Elin called out to more laughter. 'Right. Hand washing first, please. No nose picking or bum scratching allowed afterwards, so get it over and done with now.' The good-humoured banter continued as they filed to the two bathrooms.

'Was Elin a primary school teacher, by any chance?' Fran asked Caitlin.

'What gave it away? Most of us were her pupils — and I don't think many of us have grown up since!' Caitlin laughed and elbowed Fran playfully out of the way to beat her to the nearest empty sink.

'Oi!' Fran's jaw dropped for a second and then she gently hip-bumped Caitlin aside just as she'd pressed the liquid soap dispenser, catching the perfumed pink dollop neatly in her own hand instead. 'Muhahaha. You snooze, you lose.'

Caitlin tipped her head back and laughed. 'I knew I was going to like you.' Fran felt a warm and fuzzy feeling of belonging that took her by surprise.

Elin was an excellent and entertaining teacher. Once the dough was made and set to rise, she divided the group. Some made the tomato base, others cooked their toppings, and another group lugged tables and chairs outside. Geraint, from the shop, turned up during all this activity, bringing with him a crate of wine, the neon-haired Bethan and a little boy of about five. Fran wondered whether they were a family and quickly decided it wasn't important. She wasn't undercover here, working out who belonged to who. The little boy seemed to be known by everyone as he wandered from table to table proclaiming himself pizza judge.

'Fingers to yourself, young Rhodri.' Elin's schoolteacher voice ensured that the little boy's hands stayed away from the pizzas. 'I'm just going out to check the ovens.' She bustled out of the double doors.

'I'm *hungry!*' Rhodri wailed. Fran knew how he felt. She was starving. She hoped the ovens were hot. She was going to eat these huge pizzas all by herself at this rate. Bethan produced a little bag of sliced apples and Rhodri sat on a chair to eat them, his legs swinging.

'Have you got children?' Caitlin asked, fishing bits of leftover pineapple out of the tin and eating them.

'Me? No. You?'

'Uh-huh. Two. Grown up. More grown up than me. Daughter's about to go to uni, son studying pharmacy. Don't know where they get their brains from.' She laughed, affection in her eyes.

Fran looked back at the little boy. She'd never had that hankering for children that so many women had. Although she *had* mothered her young shift, she remembered, not that they were children. She'd found herself wondering how she could have got to nearly fifty and still be single. What did that say about her? Was she really that picky? And if she was, why shouldn't she be? She had no intention of sharing her life with just anyone to avoid being single.

She frowned. She was in a beautiful cottage by the sea. It could be so romantic and she had nobody to share it with. But she'd never met anyone she *wanted* to share her life with. It had always felt as if she'd had to change too much, compromise too much. What did that say about her? The doors swung open, dissipating her pity party for one, and Elin bustled in, directing operations.

'The pizza ovens have been fired up, so let's get this show on the road!' A cheer greeted her words. 'If you could bring out your pizzas — on the baking paper, please — we'll get them cooked! Mind they don't slide off.' She hooked the double doors back and Fran filed out with the others into a waiting crowd of people.

She stared around in wonder. Several big gazebos had been erected since her arrival, draped with dozens of fairy lights. One sheltered long trestle tables covered in oil cloths and already groaning with food, the others were filled with round tables and chairs. In front of the gazebos stood three pizza ovens, tended by two men and a woman. Placing her offerings on the table marked *Meat*, Fran could feel the intense heat shimmering from the burning wood.

'Hello. Again. What's yours?' Fran looked up at the now familiar deep voice of Wyn. Once again in short sleeves, he managed to look manly but incongruous in his pinny. His muscular chest stretched the plain navy T-shirt he wore beneath, and those fissuring, deep scars could be seen more clearly, rising up his left arm from the elbow. As she stared at it, she became more aware of her own scar, hitching up her top to cover it. Would she ever be able to bare it as brazenly as he did his?

Nerves made her mouthy, and biting back the urge to reply to his question with *Mine's a gin and tonic*, she settled for, 'I'm a Crazy Cow.' She felt her face heating up. It was the pizza oven, she told herself. Obviously.

'Of course you are.' Wyn's dancing eyes met hers silently for a long moment before he shook semolina over the metal surface of what looked like a long shovel and slid one of her pizzas onto it. 'I'll call them out when they're done.'

'Good thing I didn't make the Sex on the Beach then,' Fran heard herself blurt, when she'd actually, totally meant to let him know about the CCTV footage. Appalled at her brazenness, she looked around for Caitlin on the fish table and stomped over the grass towards her without looking back. 'Wine, Caitlin?'

'God, yes. Is yours in?'

Fran spluttered with laughter. 'How could making pizza sound so smutty? Is it the sea air?' Grabbing two paper tumblers of red, they bagged themselves a couple of chairs and went to see what food there was. Fran was astonished at the range. 'I won't be able to eat any pizza after this lot,' she muttered, surveying her loaded plate.

'That's the plan,' said Elin, piling potato salad onto her plate. 'Share and share alike.'

Fran had time only to take a gulp of wine and a bite of the most delicious sausage pie when she heard Wyn's deep voice boom, 'Crazy Cow!'

Caitlin laughed so hard that wine came out of her nose. 'That's you, that is.' She smirked. 'Off you go.' Fran cringed for a moment. Taking a deep breath, she got to her feet. She felt like an idiot, the stranger among all these people.

Then she looked around again at all their smiling faces, and realized she'd had a great time that evening. She'd forgotten herself for a couple of hours and laughed more than she had since the heart attack. The ridiculous pizza name had been chosen in a moment of bravado, a sudden urge to be seen in a different way. And she could totally pull it off. Wasn't she the Dancing Queen? She turned around, waved to the crowd with jazz hands and swaggered to collect her pizza, high-stepping model style, hands on swaying hips.

'Work it, Frannie!' yelled Caitlin, clapping to her steps. 'Work it, work it . . .' Her shout and clap were taken up and chorused until Fran reached Wyn. She dropped one hip and looked up at him under her eyelashes.

'One Kerraaazy Cow to collect,' she said in a terrible American accent. 'Please.'

Wyn contemplated her, his expression unreadable. But was that maybe a teeny-weeny dimple now appearing beside his inscrutable mouth?

'Well done,' he said in a neutral tone, handing her the cooked pizza on a wooden board. 'Looks good. Take it to the cutting table, and bring the board back, please.' Fran glowed for a second until she realized that, of course, she wouldn't be the only Crazy Cow to be called out by Wyn that night. She'd just happened to be the first. She hoped she'd set a precedent for craziness though, she thought, hiding a grin.

She muttered a thank you to Wyn, feeling more than a bit silly, and bore her creation away to be sliced into wedges. Taking two slices dripping with melted cheese, she returned to her seat, now squeezed between many people, all talking at once.

'Yer done good, kid.' Caitlin winked and nudged her companionably. Fran felt her earlier warm glow return. As she sipped her wine and ate her way through the variety of delicious food on her plate, she felt as if she'd lived there for ever. If there'd been an estate agent in the village, she'd be diverting to its shop window on the way back to the cottage.

Banter and hilarity greeted the names of each pizza, and she watched old Walter hamming up his voyage over the grass to collect his 'Slow, Comfortable Screw'. She hadn't seen that one on the list and suspected he'd made it up, which made it even funnier.

Caitlin knew everyone there, and everyone made a point of greeting her. Fran watched, returning the smiles that came her way. She couldn't help contrasting it with the anonymity of her city life. It was possible to spend day after day without speaking to anyone there. Fran had thought her friends were the people she worked with, but since she'd retired, nobody had so much as even texted . . .

She sipped her wine thoughtfully. It had been shockingly easy to lose touch with people she'd considered friends. To fall out of easy conversation and to realize that only the job glued them together. Not friends, merely work colleagues. Once the common ground of battling the bad guys fell away, there was apparently nothing.

She thought about it. They used to all go to pubs together — and just talk about the job. Maybe sport or films. But never personal stuff. Not really. Nobody brought their partners to shift socials. It was too awkward to try and involve them and the partners resented the closeness that the team shared.

The wives had eyed her, Fran, as if she were trying to steal their husbands. And it was true that there were men who were 'over the side'. The job was stressful and it was often difficult to share feelings with partners back home, so Fran could understand how liaisons were made. She had managed to avoid those complications by never committing. The disappointment of yet another man who'd lied to her about his marital status, combined with shift work and the pressures of the job itself, meant that she'd become accustomed to the idea that she'd be single for ever.

And now — well, who would want her, scarred and feeble? Old before her time. She was destined to be alone, just as Ryan forecast. She cast an eye around the crowd at the table, seeing that Elin and Caitlin were without men. Fran hadn't felt sorry for them, so why was she dwelling on it? She didn't even *want* a man in her life — especially if the duplicitous Ryan was anything to go by.

Friends would be good though. Someone to share with. Even though she acknowledged that she didn't share well.

88

Sharing had to be done on her terms. Intrinsically, after all this time, she was a loner and probably preferred it that way.

With the last pizzas cooked and eaten, and food running out, people began to drift away, several with bottles of wine bought from Geraint's crates. Bethan and little Rhodri had left much earlier, and only older children remained, huddled together over their mobile phones. The party was winding up and people were stacking chairs, plates and dishes. Fran got to her feet, trying not to yawn. It had been a long day though, and she thought she wouldn't have trouble sleeping tonight.

Elin — where *did* the woman get her energy? — seemed to be coordinating the clear-up. Summoning up her last shreds of energy, Fran marched over to her. 'Right, what can I do?'

Elin handed her a roll of black bin liners and another of small green bags and held out a box of latex gloves. 'Rubbish,' she said succinctly. 'Non-recyclable in black bags, and food in the green ones. The wooden cutlery can go on the pizza ovens that are still burning.'

'Okay. I know my place.' Fran grinned, taking a pair of gloves and unravelling a black bag.

A wave of laughter marked the group that was dismantling the gazebos and stacking the chairs. Wyn was among them. Not that she was watching or anything.

She found an empty bowl and swept all the used cutlery she could find into it, marching across to the pizza ovens before they petered out. There weren't any oven gloves to open the oven door with, so she popped them down the chimney two or three at a time instead. A satisfying lick of flame leaped up as they caught.

'Shall I help with that?' The now familiar deep voice behind her made her spine tingle right up to her ears. In a moment, Wyn had the oven door open with one gloved hand and had swept all the cutlery in with the other. Her face flamed. What was wrong with how she'd been doing it? It had been slow but oddly gratifying. Was he one of those overbearing blokes who couldn't bear to see a woman doing something different to how he'd do it?

Resisting the urge to retort with a teenage roll of her eyes and a *Whatever*, she muttered instead, 'Thank you,' through clenched teeth, which even to her own ears sounded childish and grouchy. She swept away with her black bin liner to continue the clearing up.

He could find out about the CCTV himself, she thought, instantly reprimanding herself for how petty that sounded. Of course she would tell him. Unless he'd already worked it out for himself, that is.

'Gotta go, Fran.' Caitlin hurried towards her, pink-faced and smiling. 'It's been lovely to meet you today.'

'I've really enjoyed it, thank you for inviting me!'

'Catch you on the Hub!' Caitlin called as she darted away. Fran watched her go, blinking. The Hub? Elin had mentioned that, hadn't she?

'I so enjoyed this evening, Elin,' she told her neighbour as she waited for her to lock up. 'Is it a regular thing? Anything else I could get involved with? I know I won't be here for long but I'm not very good at doing nothing.'

'I'm glad you enjoyed it. Everything's on the Hub.'

'And that's, um . . .'

'Facebook.' Elin glanced at her. 'Message me when you get home and I'll send you the link. I suppose you're *on* Facebook?'

'Well, no, actually. I've never really wanted to be. Y'know, you arrest someone and next thing is you've got a load of hate mail on your profile. That sort of thing.'

'Make a name up then.' Elin made it sound like the easiest thing in the world. 'You could just set up an account to use here.'

'That's a brilliant idea.' She brightened up. 'Yes, I'll do that. I can be Fake Fran Facebooker for the summer.'

They hadn't gone far when she heard footsteps behind. 'Would you ladies like to walk me home?'

Fran whirled to see Wyn, still in his T-shirt and seemingly oblivious to the cooling evening air. She felt her face flame as it had beside the pizza oven. Elin was quicker off the mark.

'Good evening, Wyn. You did an excellent job of the pizzas tonight. Whatever would we do without you?'

Wyn smiled and Fran gaped up at him. Deep dimples appeared either side of his mouth, his teeth were white and even and the cliché about the sun coming out came to mind. 'You're most welcome, Mrs Pritchard.' He strolled easily beside them, shortening his considerable stride to keep pace.

Elin kept up a stream of chit-chat with him as they made their way down the hill, and Fran contented herself with listening. When they reached Elin's cottage, she was impressed that he waited until Elin was inside the front door. She began to tell him what she'd found out today when he cut her dead.

'Goodnight.'

She glared at him. Well, fine. If that's the way he wanted to play it. She turned on her heel and let herself inside the cottage, not looking to see whether he was there or not. Infuriating man. Well, he was big enough. Let him fight his own battles.

* * *

She was one of those annoying women who had to do it her way, Wyn decided, watching her sashay away from him to her front door. Seeing her laboriously putting one piece of wooden cutlery at a time down the pizza chimney, he'd gone over to help. It was just a waste of time, that was all, and he had oven gloves.

It was absolutely nothing whatsoever to do with the fact that — he felt the corners of his mouth curling upwards as he remembered her playing to the crowd on her way to collect her pizzas — dammit, he liked her. Even if she *was* a copper. He'd seen her hesitation as he'd called out the ridiculous name — possibly louder than he should have — but it was as if in that split second she'd wavered between ignoring him or going with it. And he liked her for going with it.

Having seen the ladies home — well, Mrs Pritchard *had* been his primary school teacher, and even at his age, he'd never managed to call her Elin — he decided on a whim to visit the crowded pub for a pint and to see how the triathlon arrangements were coming along. Dyl spotted him and lifted a hand.

'Pint?'

'Just a half, please. My body's a temple . . .'

'Ancient ruin, you mean?'

Wyn grinned. Only Dyl could get away with a crack like that. 'Careful. I won't be so quick to rescue you from your brother next time . . .'

'Dunno what you mean! I was clearly winning.' Dyl's mouth compressed into a self-deprecating smile as he signalled the bar for a pint anyway and handed it over to Wyn.

'Cheers, mate.' Wyn held the pint to the light. 'I can't believe you're still feuding after all these years.' He took a long and appreciative sip. 'Over a running jacket.'

Dyl had the grace to look abashed. 'What can I say? It was only a bit of sweat.'

'I heard he picked his expensive, saved-up-for jacket — brand new and unworn by him — *off the floor* after you'd borrowed it without asking, and sweat actually *ran out of it*.'

Dyl spluttered a laugh into his pint. 'He said, "Who's pissed in my new jacket?" He was bigger than me then so I looked all innocent, but it was the beginning of the end really.'

Wyn surveyed Dyl over his glass. 'Sounds like you deserve a pasting. I might just leave you to it next time.'

'Argh, no! He'll make mincemeat of me!' Dyl pulled a face, pretending to be scared, and they were silent for a moment, looking around at the noisy crowd.

'So, how's it all going?' Wyn said eventually, wondering how Scruff was doing and looking around to see if he could spot him. 'Need a hand with anything?'

'We're pretty much on target, thanks. It's all good.' Dyl nodded. 'Forecast is looking fine too. Should be a good weekend.'

Wyn nodded slowly. 'Yep. I'll be there. That's what counts.'

'Aye,' Dyl said, raising his pint in a salute with a perceptive expression.

They chatted easily about this and that as other people joined and left the conversation until the barman called time. Among the flurry of orders for the last round, Wyn took his leave.

'See you over the weekend, mate.'

His departure was accompanied by a volley of calls and waves, and he'd almost gone when the landlord hailed him.

'Wyn, mate.'

Wyn turned to face him, squaring his shoulders. It would be a nuisance if Barty was to ban him after the other night, this being the only pub in the village. 'Barty. Look, I'm sorry about the other night.'

'You've got friends in high places.'

'I . . . what?'

Barty closed the gap until they were inches apart and lowered his voice. 'Your lady copper mate came in today to see me. She wanted to see the CCTV.'

'She's no mate of mine.'

Barty cut across him. 'Well, GDPR means she can't see it, but you can ask to. And I'm telling you now, it would be worth your while.' He looked around like a comedy spy, and added, 'Between you and me, I'd have punched his lights out. Has he been round to nick you?'

'No. What did *she* want to see it for?' Wyn frowned. Interfering woman.

'She, er, had a hunch that there was more to it than she'd seen. She was very . . . uh, circumspect, I'd call it. But on your side, I'd say.'

'Oh.' Wyn was taken aback. 'Well. There's a surprise.'

'So pop by when it's quiet and I can show you the footage. Okay?' Barty shrugged his eyebrows knowingly. 'Unless you've got time now? It's going to be a busy weekend.'

Wyn nodded decisively. What exactly did he have to rush home for? 'Yeah, I have, as it happens.' The landlord beckoned him behind the counter.

'So, Scruff's ruling the roost at home,' Barty told him. 'Phil's getting regular updates about him.'

'How's Phil doing?'

'He'll be staying with his daughter till he's back on his feet. Scruff will be as round as a pound by the time he gets him back.' He laughed affectionately. 'Bloody dog. He's even sleeping on our bed!'

Wyn grinned. 'Scruff knows where his bread's buttered, I reckon.' There seemed to be a labyrinth of narrow stone corridors before it opened into an office. Sitting in a worn and tatty swivel chair, Barty waggled his computer mouse to make the computer screen live, and brought up the footage from the other day.

Both men recoiled and grunted in disgust as they watched the incident unfold. The screen, though grainy, clearly showed Wyn reaching out to grip the policeman by the collar of his shirt, just as the headlights from Fran's car fell on the group.

'He came that close to a pasting,' Barty murmured. 'Perhaps a good thing your lady friend showed up.'

'Maybe. Maybe not.' Wyn glared at the screen. What the hell did Tasha see in that bully? She was doing her best to pull Wyn off him, for goodness' sake. 'I almost hope he does come after me.' Several colourful adjectives queued behind his teeth, but Barty's expression told him that both men felt the same about the policeman.

'I'll email a copy to you, Wyn.'

'Thanks, mate.'

'Thank Fran. She's on the ball.'

'Indeed!' Wyn stared at him, his mind whirling. He picked himself up and left, calling to the landlord's back, 'Thanks, Barty — good luck with the weekend!'

CHAPTER TEN

Slam. Bang. Laughter. 5.30 a.m.

'Morning!'

'Gorgeous, innit?'

'Bluddy luvly.'

'I've brought cake!'

'You can come again, missus.'

Fran gritted her teeth. She wanted to run out there and shove that cake where the sun didn't shine. Pummelling the pillow, she squeezed her eyes shut. She was exhausted after the long day she'd had yesterday, and her body was telling her it needed rest.

She didn't surface until mid-morning. There was a big crease down one side of her face when she looked in the mirror. God, she was looking old. Without the energy to wrestle the seagulls off her breakfast, she ate her last two slices of sourdough inside rather than on the balcony.

The sun was shining and the blue sky cloudless. She'd stroll along the path beside the dunes for a bit, see where it went. Get some muscle back in her flabby body. Do a bit of shopping and avoid men having fights. Then maybe think about having a pub lunch.

No. She hated eating alone in public. Maybe fish and chips instead. Her cardiology team had said nothing about diet at all. It was all about being normal and sensible. She could do sensible, she thought, pushing aside the memory of intervening in two fights in as many days while sporting a half-healed breastbone . . . Walking out of the front door, she felt the soft flesh under her chin wobble in time with her expanding belly. She sighed. A sensible salad in the garden it was then.

Her watch reminded her to slow down and let her heart, currently galloping along in the high nineties, catch up. She glared at it.

'Yes, thank you,' she told it. 'I *know* what a weakling I still am. You don't have to keep telling me.' All the same, she slowed right down until she was almost walking on the spot. She watched her pulse drop to a more sedate seventy-something, one beat at a time. Breathing slowly and rhythmically, she forced herself to stroll, not march as she usually did. She looked at the tiny wildflowers pushing up through the inhospitable dunes and wished she'd bought a pocket guide to identify them. Maybe Elin would have one she could borrow.

She'd thought about bringing out the large-scale Ordnance Survey map she'd purchased, but even she could work out that as long as she followed the coast she'd return to this beach. Even if she could manage such a long walk that it rendered her 'lost', which she doubted. Remembering what hard work it had been walking in the sand, she stayed on the path, arriving in due course at a clutch of houses marking the other end of the beach. Fran read the sign plate. *Oxton*. Why couldn't her village have a simple name like that? Interesting though. Two villages sharing a beach.

She wandered around, admiring the tiny, well-kept hamlet, reaching a building site set just back from the beach. The entire roof was being replaced on what looked like a Victorian village school. What used to be the playground was now covered in piles of building materials and machinery, and the sound of hammering and drilling drifted out from inside, along with a tinny radio.

Fran thought it would look amazing when it was finished. Her own flat was in a converted Victorian warehouse and she loved the period details. As she wondered whether it might be destined to be several houses together or possibly a small hotel, she caught sight of a now familiar tall figure in navy-blue overalls, lifting a sheet of some building material. Despite his obvious strength, he looked awkward and ungainly, one arm doing most of the work. Another man took the weight of the board from above without comment and Wyn turned away to collect the next one.

Fran ducked away and scuttled out of sight before he could see her. She was a bit shocked and wondered again what terrible accident had befallen him. He'd avoided her question about whether he was between jobs, she remembered. Poor man. Reduced to working on a building site despite not really being capable of doing so, and odd jobs.

Ambling back along the coast path, she realized that she was starving. And rapidly running out of energy. A glance at her watch told her that she would have managed her step target for the day by the time she got back to the cottage. The idea of an afternoon in the garden appealed. Reading one of the novels she'd brought with her. She *was* meant to be convalescent.

She stopped off at the beach shop and bought a loaf of wholemeal bread and a Thai red curry vegan pasty, on the basis that vegan was healthy, wasn't it? And better for her than fish and chips, surely. Bethan was sporting a tie-dyed harem-trousers-and-T-shirt outfit that included an emerald-green scarf in her pink hair.

'Hello, it's Crazy Cow!' she exclaimed, with a smile. Fran was taken aback for a moment and then laughed.

'It seemed like a good idea at the time,' she said, flashing her bank card over the gadget on the counter. 'The pizza night was great. I enjoyed it.'

'Good to hear. You watching the triathlon tomorrow?'

Fran hadn't really thought about it, past the fracas of the previous day. She'd planned to simply stay out of the way. 'Erm . . .'

'It's an awesome day.' Bethan stared out of the window at the portable railings and banners. 'Makes me cry.'

'Ah,' said Fran, bemused and doing her best to sound as if she were keeping up.

'All that effort . . .' Bethan shook her head, her eyes misty. 'Amazing.'

'Sounds like I shouldn't miss it.' Fran nodded, stepping backwards slowly with every intention of missing it.

'Plus, we're stocked up to here—' Bethan lifted a hand to her chest 'with pasties for the day. Good time to stock your freezer.'

'Okay!' Fran said, breezily. 'Good to know. I'll check this one out, and, um, I might be back!' She jerked a thumb over her shoulder to indicate she was leaving and sidled out before Bethan could burst into tears over the triathlon.

She thought about it as she made her way back to the cottage. She ran, or she used to, for fitness, and because it energized her afterwards. It kept her weight down and made her feel strong. She ran alone though, as she did everything, and it had never occurred to her to enter a competition, although she'd occasionally caught bits of the London Marathon on the telly.

Fitting in regular runs with other people was always tricky with shift work, and she'd inevitably been the one to drop out. Running was — or at least had been — *her* thing. She'd never seen it as a group activity. And she loathed crowds. One of the advantages of shift work was that you never had to share your activities with a bunch of strangers. The gym was always empty, and you didn't have to shop at weekends or go to the cinema in the evenings.

She'd always seen it as a perk of the job. Another example, she realized now, of 'them and us'.

Now that she was one of 'them', being so much on her own was rapidly losing its appeal.

* * *

It wasn't long before she was ensconced in the garden with a fat thriller, a glass of elderflower cordial with ice, and her pasty, which proved to be delicious. If they were all like this, she'd definitely be stocking up. The sun beat down and she nipped inside for sun lotion, a hat and a light scarf to protect her scar. As she was heading back to the garden with her supplies, she heard the familiar sound of banging car doors and raised voices. She listened for a long moment.

'Hiya!'

'Gotta be done, innit?'

'Did you bring lunch?'

'Ooh, new board?'

'I brought cake . . .'

'God, I'm caked out from this morning.'

'I'll eat yours then.'

'You bluddy won't, missus.'

It was the Dawn Warblers for the second time that day!

She rushed out to peer over the garden fence. Half a dozen of them, in those ludicrous oversized coats even though it was so warm, carrying huge holdalls and chattering loudly to one another.

'Hello!' she called, waving. She'd have a polite word, just to let them know how annoying it was so early in the mornings.

'Hello!' Louder this time. All sorts of beach paraphernalia appeared out of the cars, which were parked in the turning circle at the end of the cottages. Which wasn't a car park. There was a big enough car park right by the beach, why didn't they go there?

'*Oi!*' Several heads turned her way and she took her opportunity. 'Ah. Hello. Is it you lot who park up here at five in the morning?'

Their eyes swivelled towards one another. *Guilty as charged, yer honour.*

'Erm . . .'

'It is, isn't it? You've woken me up every single morning with your racket. Car doors slamming, shouting at one another. Laughing at the tops of your voices. Don't you have any consideration? I'm meant to be convalescing!' Silence descended on the gathering.

'Hi, Fran, hi! God, I'm so sorry.' Carrying a paddle, Caitlin appeared from behind some kind of enormous surf board, propped it carefully against her car and came towards her.

'Oh. Caitlin! Um, hi . . .' Fran ran a hand through her hair. 'Um . . .'

'I don't think we realized how loud we were. I'm really sorry . . .'

'Er, oh, no problem. Maybe I'll, er, buy some earplugs or something. Aha hahaa. Er, sorry to have um, y'know . . . Anyway, er, things to do, hahaa . . .' Her mirthless laugh echoed hollowly in her own ears and she retreated backwards with a lifted hand until she got to the French doors where she slammed the door on herself and flipped the curtains shut.

Oh, well done, Fran. Just alienated the only person you've actually had fun with. She couldn't go out there again. The garden was off-limits now. For ever. She couldn't risk meeting their undoubtedly accusing eyes as they filed silently past. Whatever must they think of her?

She peered through the curtains until she was sure they'd gone and then crept out to snatch her novel, taking it upstairs to the chair on the balcony instead. At least she'd be able to see them coming from up there.

Oh, she really could be a pompous ass at times. She watched them as they straggled down the beach, their voices lifting again as soon as they thought they were out of earshot. The edge of the sea twinkled and shimmered in the sunlight. There were little islands of people, families, on the beach, digging, kicking a ball about, eating picnics, sheltered behind their windbreaks. Several large, coloured buoys had appeared out to sea, and inflatable boats sped back and forth between them. To the right she could see a row of barriers snaking up from the beach and along the road. Sunlight glinted off the many camper vans and caravans in the campsite set back from the beach. Already she could see what a busy day tomorrow was going to be.

She dragged her eyes back to the novel. The thriller was good, but it couldn't compete with the warmth of the sun and her persistent weariness. It seemed hours later that she opened her eyes. She went to check the turning circle. There were no cars parked there. She cringed, imagining them all jeering at her as they passed, asleep on the balcony with her mouth undoubtedly gaping open.

Well. She could hide away and avoid everybody, or she could tough it out. And they *had* made a racket. Maybe they felt as bad as she did. She recognized some of them from the pizza party, she was sure, and they'd all been pleasant, chatty women. She'd create an account on Facebook and make a breezy best of it.

Setting up the account was dead easy — except for the fake name. Maybe she could be Trinity from *The Matrix*. Or Jean Grey from *X-Men*. She laughed at herself sheepishly. Who did she think she was? She typed *Crazy Cow* into the box and sent a link to the new account to Elin next door.

Check your settings, Elin returned. *Your privacy is wide open.*

It was? *Where are they?*

I'm in. Come over.

Fran picked up her laptop and hurried round. She laughed at herself, getting social media lessons from someone two decades older. She knocked on the door.

'Door's open!' Elin called. Fran went in, finding Elin at the kitchen table where they'd had their first cup of tea. It seemed ages ago. She was already on her laptop.

'G and T?' she asked, without looking up. 'Sun's already over the yardarm.'

'Oh!' Fran was a bit taken aback at the idea of drinking in the afternoon and then relented. Why not? She wasn't driving anywhere, and she'd already had enough of her own holier-than-thou attitude. 'Okay then. Shall I make it?'

'Go on then. It's all over there or in the fridge. I just need to finish this.' Elin indicated with a nod of her head and Fran collected a gin in a posh bottle with a label she'd never heard of from the dresser. She opened the fridge to find several little cans of tonic water and a lemon.

'Weak, strong or pub measure?'

'As it comes,' Elin replied absently, her fingers flying over the keyboard. Fran made two weak gin and tonics, sliced lemon into them and added ice from the extremely well-stocked freezer. The drinks fizzed invitingly as she transported them to the table.

'Not bad,' Elin said, sipping hers. 'Apart from there being no gin in it.' Fran got up and obligingly brought back the gin bottle, placing it on the table by Elin's glass. 'Right, all done,' Elin said, clicking save and sitting back in her chair with a smile. She added a generous slosh of gin to her drink and smacked her lips together as she slurped it. 'That's better. Right.'

Opening another tab on her browser, she turned the screen round so that Fran could see. 'Here are all your settings.' Patiently, she talked Fran through what information to add or leave out, and by the time they were on the second gin and tonic, Fran had joined the village hub and had five friends, one of whom was the local vicar. None of them were Caitlin.

Emboldened by the gin, she said, 'I made a bit of a cock-up this afternoon.'

'Not Wyn again. I saw it was his day for the garden.'

'Oh. That was the day before yesterday's cock-up.' Fran winced. 'He scared the pants off me by appearing in the garden unannounced, and I, er, had a bit of a shout at him. Before I knew who he was. I thought he was a bad guy hiding in the shed.'

'He's a big boy. He can cope, I'm sure.' Elin shrugged. 'Next?'

Fran told her about the Dawn Warblers, which made Elin laugh. 'I wouldn't worry about it. Some of them are up for milking hours before they get here so forget it's so early. If it's any consolation, they probably feel bad about waking you up.' She sipped her drink, then got up and brought back some crisps. 'Don't you have disputes with neighbours in the city?'

Fran thought about it. 'I've been to some humdingers when I was in the job. Neighbours threatening to kill one another over a barking dog, or spilled recycling, an overhanging tree. Dog poo. Domestics are rife. Sometimes with machetes.' She grimaced, remembering. 'But the block I live in is terribly genteel. You almost need an appointment to speak to one another.'

'I've never seen a machete involved, but here in the country it can get pretty heated, and we have axes as general garden tools. Boundaries and footpaths, noise, wife-swapping, horse poo, dog poo, dogging — it all makes for an interesting life.'

'Wife swapping? *Dogging*? Really?'

'Of course.'

Fran was beginning to get the measure of Elin and wasn't entirely sure that she wasn't being teased. Elin carried on, 'The swimmers are having a moonlight dip tonight — it's a full moon, the Flower Moon — and then a few drinks around the firepit. They call it a dip-and-sip. I'm going down too . . .'

'To swim?'

'Goodness me, no. To have a drink and a natter. They're nice girls.' Fran felt even more guilty for her outburst. 'Come on down and bring a bottle if you want to. Maybe some nibbles. That'll smooth it all over.'

'What time?'

'It's dark enough to see the moon by about ten so they'll turn up for around nine thirty. You'll probably hear them. Unless they're all creeping about in silence after you bollocked them.'

'They're swimming in the sea *three times* today?' Fran was incredulous.

'Triple-dipping. Although I think most of them paddle-boarded and sunbathed this afternoon.'

Fran sat up straight. 'Okay. I'll come down. I really liked Caitlin. So much fun. I don't want to fall out with her.'

'Lovely girl.' Elin nodded. 'Another gin?'

'Much as I'd love one, I'd better not, thanks. Got to look after the ticker.' She pushed herself to her feet. 'Thanks, Elin. You're very wise.'

'I'm very *old*.' Elin grinned. 'See you later.'

CHAPTER ELEVEN

Fran nipped round to the little shop and bought salty snacks, chocolates and some little cakes in a pack, as cake seemed to form a large part of the swimmers' dawn conversations. The shop had been transformed since her last visit and was now an athlete's emporium, packed with protein powders, bars and sports drink powders and complete with athletic types browsing the shelves ready for the next day. She felt guilty and chubby with her nutritionally empty basket and shuffled quickly to the counter.

'Mm,' said Bethan loudly, holding the cakes up and peering at them. 'These are new. They look nice. Let me know what they're like.'

By *nice*, Fran heard, *These are fattening. Should you be eating them?*

'They're not for me,' she mumbled, paid quickly, grabbed her calorie-laden haul and scuttled out of the shop. She clock-watched until nine, her ears straining for the sounds of the Dawn Warblers. She piled a warm sweater, scarf, jacket and her walking boots by the front door, ready to leave. Lurking behind the door at nine forty-five, she began to think they'd changed their minds and jumped out of her skin when the doorbell rang.

'You must've frightened the pants off them,' Elin said, blinding her with her head torch. 'They sneaked past like a line of church mice over twenty minutes ago. You ready?'

'Ye-es.'

'Come on then. We'll have a paddle on the way.'

'We'll *what*?' Locking the door, Fran whirled to stare at her neighbour. 'I thought you said . . .'

'We're not *swimming*. We're paddling. Come on.'

Picking up the bag of goodies, Fran tailed Elin across the dunes, seeing the circle of bags, boots and those huge trademark coats in little heaps. 'Leave your stuff there. No one will touch it while we're in the sea.'

'Okay.' Fran's voice was a squeak and she cleared her throat. She'd been a rufty-tufty police sergeant for years and years and there was *nothing* she couldn't handle. Except the water. And leaving her handbag behind.

Elin sat to take her shoes and socks off, and rolled up her trousers. After a long moment, Fran reluctantly did the same, tucking her socks into her boots and placing them just so. Her handbag stayed with her.

The sea was close. No more than twenty paces on the cold sand to reach it. It hissed and shushed onto the beach, a multilayered sound with a background resonance that never stopped. A moonlit frill gilded the tiny waves that inched towards Fran's white toes. She looked up, seeing only the pom-pom-hatted heads of the swimmers about thirty feet away as they bobbed on the undulating surface like seagulls. Floating with them were multicoloured lanterns, reflecting in the blue-green water.

'What are those lights?'

'That's their tow floats. They put bike lights inside them before inflating them. Safe and pretty.' Elin lifted an arm in greeting, her head torch acting as a miniature lighthouse, and Fran saw the glittering arcs of saltwater droplets as they waved back. Their laughs carried across the darkening sea, and Fran found herself waving to them too. Saluting their bravery in that moonlit sea.

Mesmerized by them, she tore her gaze away to follow Elin into the glassy shallows. The water licked at her toes, her ankles, her calves . . .

'Holy shit!' she yelled. 'It's freezing! How in the name of God do they *do* it?' Her shoulders up to her ears, she wrapped her hands around her upper arms and jogged on the spot. 'Ouch! My feet have frozen!' Laughter drifted towards them.

Someone's call of 'It's okay once you're in!' was greeted with much hilarity by the other swimmers. A pair of legs waved momentarily above the water as somebody did a handstand. Elin strolled along the shallows, kicking sparkling arcs of water as she went. 'It's gorgeous, isn't it?'

Fran narrowed her eyes. She didn't want to be a party pooper, but it was bloody bitter. How did anyone get used to it? If she didn't drown in it, she'd die of hypothermia.

'Come and have a little walk. You'll get used to it, honestly.' Elin turned and walked away from her. Fran's gaze daisy-chained from her intrepid neighbour, to the swimmers, and lastly her heart rate. It was normal. Thumping away in its nice new sinus rhythm. And her feet didn't seem quite so cold now. Or maybe they'd just gone numb.

Grumbling to herself, she stomped after Elin, hopping over any stray, breakaway wavelets. Glancing out to sea, she saw a lone swimmer moving across the bay, trailing another floating lantern.

'That'll be someone getting a swim in before tomorrow,' Elin said, the beam of her head torch swinging first one way then the other. She tutted. 'Should be resting.'

'Wow. He makes that look so easy.' Fran couldn't help but be impressed. He seemed to be made of the same stuff as the sea. His arms cycled, leaving a faint silver ripple behind him. The swimmers had turned to look too, several of them lifting their arms high and whooping their encouragement. 'Woohoo!'

'He can't hear them, all the way out there,' Elin said. 'Wyn used to win the swim every year at the triathlon, you know.'

'Used to?'

Elin nodded, wading in the deeper shallows while Fran tippy-toed on the beach side. 'Not since his accident. Poor man.' Silence followed her words and it was clear that she wasn't going to say more on the matter.

'Tell me what happens at the triathlon.' Fran was becoming intrigued. It sounded as if it consumed the entire village.

Elin explained that the event comprised swimming, cycling and running, in that order. She looked out to sea. The swimmer was returning across the bay now. 'He shouldn't really swim by himself. Very naughty.' She stomped away.

Fran's gaze followed the ripples of the moon's bright reflections and she stood still to watch the crowd of swimmers, shaking her head in disbelief at their laughter. They were all mad. They had to be. Crowd hysteria, surely, brought on by the glacial temperature of the water.

Elin stopped to wait for Fran to catch up and then continued at a steady pace. 'Is this speed okay for you?'

'Yes. Thank you for thinking of me. This is fine, but I find walking on the soft sand really hard work.' Fran was about to add, *I'm like an old lady after a hundred yards*, but a sidelong glance at her neighbour showed her that Elin was in far better shape than she was. 'How do you keep so fit, Elin?'

Elin shrugged. 'Probably the burlesque dancing.'

'The . . . the *what*?'

'Burlesque. You know . . .' Elin shimmied her substantial bosom and turned to Fran with a grin on her face. 'It's all on the Hub.'

'Wow.' Fran gazed at her companion with respect. So, not just jam making and knitting in this village then. She resolved to have a proper look at this Hub thing now she had an account. Looking over her shoulder, she saw the swimmer wade out of the sea, sleek and glossy as a seal in his wetsuit. How amazing that must feel.

Caitlin's swimmers were out of the sea and dried off when Fran and Elin arrived back at the dunes. Huddled into their huge coats and colourful hats, they were grouped around a driftwood fire in a wide metal bowl wedged into the sand with some big beach stones. Fran had never felt more of an outsider, a city girl among beach dwellers. She was grateful for Elin's bridging presence.

'Hi!' Standing before them, she took a deep breath and decided to tackle it head on. She chewed her lip, her eyes flicking round to each of them as they gazed up at her. 'I'm so sorry that I went off at you earlier. I'm just a grouch.' She brandished the wine bottle from her carrier bag. 'I brought a bottle of apology with me though. And snacks . . .' She shook the remainder of her goodies onto a mat in the middle of the group, where she could see other offerings. 'I didn't bring glasses though. Drat. I can go and get some from the house . . .'

'We don't need glasses! It's what mugs are for. No breakages in the sand.' Caitlin grinned over at her. 'And we're sorry too. You were well within your rights to bollock us. A bottle of apology though . . . that's funny.' She laughed, and Fran was relieved that the laughter rippled around the group. 'Cake makes anyone welcome. Sit yourself down. You're giving us neck ache.' She opened Fran's bottle, sloshed a generous measure into a spare mug and handed it to Fran. 'Meet the Sea Sisters.'

'Great name,' Fran said, lifting the mug in salute. 'Cheers, ladies. Nice to meet you.'

Fran's wine was shared out, along with several other bottles and various cakes. The firepit licked orange tongues into the dark-velvet chill. Fran felt warm and peaceful out there in the dark dunes, the only noise the sound of the surf, the only light the moon, stars and fire.

The conversation ricocheted from one subject to another at lightning speed. These ladies clearly knew one another very well, slipping in and out of one another's chats and laughing easily. Elin seemed conversant with all of them, and Fran could sense the respect in which they held her. Fran herself was quite content to listen and learn.

When the talk lulled, she said, 'You ladies are awesome. It's so cold in there! How do you do it?'

'I've been swimming here since I was a kid,' said one lady, staring into the fire. She had to be in her late fifties, Fran guessed, perhaps older, but her skin was smooth and her features strong.

'Me too,' said another. 'I used to lifeguard here.'

'Well. It seemed like a good idea at the time,' said the older woman whose bleached-blonde hair peeped from her bobble hat, her mouth twitching up at the corner. 'I screamed the place down on my first dip . . .'

'Your language was shocking, Wendy. Shocking.' The speaker grinned.

'Was? It still is!'

'I learn a dozen new words off Wendy . . .'

'. . . every time she swims.'

'Mostly about tits . . .' mused Caitlin, a glint in her eye.

'Well, let's be honest, you couldn't miss Wendy's tits.'

'Oi! They're my built-in flotation devices!' Wendy folded her arms beneath her substantial breasts and hoisted them upwards, to much laughter.

'We all saw them tonight. Full moons!'

'Naah, that was Lila's arse . . .'

'I thought she was wearing white bathers!'

Fran listened, barely aware that her mouth had been curved into a smile for ages as she followed their banter. These women were brave, funny, ribald and kind. It was a completely different type of flavour to the meetings between her mostly male workmates.

'So, do you swim, Fran?' Caitlin asked, casually.

The smile fell from Fran's face. They were all looking at her. Should she laugh it off? If she said she swam, wouldn't they wonder why she didn't join them?

'Well, I, er . . .' she began, and fizzled out, staring into the fire.

'Fran's had recent open-heart surgery, so maybe the shock of the cold sea isn't a great idea for her,' Elin said, after a pause that seemed to go on for ever. Fran sent her a grateful glance, hearing the murmurs of assent and *oh my*

110

Gods rippling around the group. But she hated lying. You had to remember what you'd said, and then you avoided people in case you dropped yourself in it later. And she liked these ladies. Lying wasn't an option.

'That is true, Elin.' She nodded. 'But I, er . . .' She cleared her throat. 'I can't swim. And I'm scared to death of the water.' She waited for the derision that must surely follow.

'Oh my God, that must be awful!' said Wendy. 'I can't imagine my life without these swims. They've been a lifesaver.'

'For me too,' said Lila. 'I'd be a wreck without my regular swims.'

'And me. It's therapy. I forget everything when I'm out there.'

'I'm so sorry I brought it up, Fran. It didn't even occur to me that you might not be able to swim. Did something happen to bring this fear on?' Caitlin's kind eyes rested on Fran's. 'But only if you want to talk about it. You don't have to.'

'Well, it sounds stupid, really, because something happened when I was a little kid, and nobody will talk about it, and my whole life has been blighted by my mother's fear of the water. And I feel like I should be old enough to shake it off, but somehow I can't. And I don't even *know* what it is I'm scared of after all these years! So it's been easier to avoid it.' In the end, it was a relief to get it out there. Fran felt her entire body become boneless.

'Aw, bless you, *cariad*. And you just a *dwt*,' someone murmured.

Fran's eyes slid towards Elin's for a translation.

'*Cariad* is our wonderful Welsh word for "darling", "dear" or "loved one", and we use it for everyone we care about, including our animals,' Elin supplied. '*Dwt*, or *dwtty*, just means "little".'

'Aw. That's rather lovely.' Fran swallowed a lump in her throat, feeling buoyed up by these women who she didn't even know. And who earlier that day she'd shrieked at.

'And *cwtch* is another Welsh word you *have* to know,' put in Wendy. 'The English might hug, but only the Welsh can *cwtch*.'

'We'll get you back in the water.' Caitlin nodded firmly, her eyes kind and earnest. She ruined the effect by cackling with laughter as she topped Fran's glass up with a wobbly slosh of white wine. 'Whether you want to or not.'

'Oh. Thank you.' Fran's stomach went into freefall with terror. 'That will be nice . . . As long as you're not all going to try to drown me for yelling at you.' They laughed.

'Tempting . . .' Caitlin raised her glass at her with a sly grin.

Fran laughed even though the very word 'drown' made her feel a bit sick. But hope pierced her panic. At her age, it was time to conquer this fear. After what she'd been through recently, could anything really be that bad? And from what she'd seen of this bunch, she might actually have some fun doing it.

Caitlin had carried on talking to her crew while Fran was absorbed in her anxieties. 'We talked about meeting at the Coffee Pot for six tomorrow morning. Who's in? They make the absolute best brownies and blondies.'

'I'm drooling already.' Wendy licked her lips.

'And as long as you eat them outside and standing up, there's no calories in them. Fact.' Caitlin's eyes sparkled in the flickering firelight. 'We can take our coffees away and go for a perv at the merch before it all starts.'

'A what?' Feeling smug that she knew where the Coffee Pot was, although the bit that she'd seen had looked tiny, Fran sat forward, tucking her hands between her knees against the evening chill. She could see the allure of those big coats now. 'Hang on — six o'clock? In the morning? Don't any of you sleep? Why so early?'

'Merch. Merchandise.' Caitlin nodded sagely. 'There'll be trade stands setting up from dawn. All sorts of stuff. Some end-of-line they want to get rid of, all sorts. Get there early, get the best stuff before someone else does. Although some of it is for *real* swimmers.'

'Aren't *you* all real swimmers?' Fran was perplexed.

The ladies all pealed with laughter, their voices competing together.

112

'We don't actually *swim*.'

'I bloody do.'

'I'm not wasting good nattering time with actual swimming.'

'I've never known *anyone* stand in the water chatting for as long as you do.'

'I can't talk — *unless* I'm in the sea.' Fran saw hands reaching out towards the speaker for a brief moment of reassurance.

'Did you know that if your thighs touch,' said Wendy, into the lull, 'you're one step closer to being a mermaid?' Laughter greeted her pronouncement.

'I'm having that on a T-shirt!'

'We *swimble*,' Caitlin cut across them with a grin. 'Like a stroll, a wander, a bimble, only in the sea.'

'Ah,' said Fran, nodding sagely as if she completely understood. Which she didn't. But she was, to her surprise, looking forward to her early-morning coffee and cake the next day. She'd been woken up at five thirty every morning since she'd arrived. She might as well get up and do something. It was good to have a purpose again.

* * *

Whether it was the wine, the cold air or the company of the swimmers, Fran couldn't decide, but she had the best night's sleep since she'd arrived. Saturday morning, the racket of the Dawn Warblers was as nothing compared to the megaphones from the beach. Elin had said she'd catch up with her later, so, dressing warmly, Fran strolled along the beach path and was stunned to see the transformation. A red carpet rolled down to the beach from the parking area, topped by a towering red inflatable arch. Bunting fluttered from every barrier. The weak morning sun glinted from the hundreds of cars and vans in the huge car park, which was lined with sign-written gazebos. Tall feather flags followed the path of the marked course, flapping noisily in the breeze.

All of the shops were open. The chip shop was doing a roaring trade in teas and coffees, and judging by the number of people walking about with pasties halfway to their mouths, so was the beach shop. Her stomach rumbled.

Arriving at the Coffee Pot, also festooned with bunting, she didn't have to look far to see Caitlin and her Sea Sisters halfway along the queue that had already formed. They beckoned her over.

'What do you want? We'll order yours,' Caitlin hissed, looking over her shoulder at the queue behind.

'Americano and a brownie, please,' Fran replied promptly. 'No milk, no sugar. Can I pay you now?'

'I'll use my card. Pay me after.'

Fran mooched over to the surf shop. Admiring the colourful window display, she caught sight of her reflection. In her baggy beige walking trousers and navy-blue fleece zipped to the neck, she didn't look as smart, practical and outdoorsy as she'd hoped. She looked shapeless and drab. She supposed this was what happened after twenty-five years of wearing a uniform. She had party clothes and gym clothes, but her daytime wardrobe was definitely uninspired.

Scanning the Coffee Pot queue, she saw skinny jeans, sheepskin boots and shorts, cropped jeans and beach-type sandals, hoodies, thick jackets and the ubiquitous bright woolly hats with oversized pom-poms. Caitlin dangled a paper bag and a takeaway coffee before her.

'Here you go. A fiver.'

'Cheers.' Fran retrieved a five-pound note from her fleece and handed it over.

'Wassup?'

'Oh, nothing. I was just thinking that I maybe need a makeover or something . . .'

'Really? You've had an actual heart attack and you're worrying about your look?' Caitlin considered her, head cocked to one side. 'Although that's probably progress, isn't it?' Fran was still mulling it over as Caitlin hailed the rest of her crew. 'Come on, ladies, let's make some space here. Time to shop.'

Swept away by the group, Fran listened to her new friends discussing the merits of five-millimetre neoprene versus three-millimetre for gloves and boots, how easy those leggings would be to put on when you're cold and wet, and whether it was really worth squashing your boobs into a zipped neoprene vest for a little bit of extra warmth in the winter.

It was a world away from her real life. Around her, the village had awoken from its sleepy persona. The pub was busily dispensing hot drinks and breakfasts, and she could smell a barbecue on the air. Her chocolate brownie was, as Caitlin had promised, delicious. And Caitlin had been quite right with her observation about progress, now that Fran came to think about it. She hadn't checked her pulse once this morning. Or even thought about it until now. Maybe she *was* moving on.

Men and women of all ages and shapes passed her wearing skintight all-in-one shorts-and-vest outfits, many pinning numbers to one another's backs or writing on their honed biceps. They were like warriors, preparing for battle. One stand was consistently busy.

'That's Registration,' Wendy told her. 'And once they've done that, they need to get their bikes into Transition, over there, by the red arch. The competition is a mile, give or take, in the sea, twenty-two on the bike, and finishes off with a six-mile run across the beach.'

Fran thought she could have easily managed the six-mile run, pre-heart attack, but maybe not after a twenty-two-mile bike ride, and she wouldn't even *go* into the sea, let alone swim for a whole mile. All these people, pitting themselves against the elements and one another. There was an almost carnival atmosphere. Many of them had families with them and carried babies and toddlers on their shoulders or beneath brawny, wetsuited arms.

Wyn was chatting to people around the stands. Fran wasn't surprised. Having been a top competitor here for years, he probably knew just about everyone. He looked up suddenly and met her gaze as if he knew she was there. She felt the blood rush to her face. He lifted his hand in a brisk wave and she waved back with the hand holding the half-full cup of coffee so that it sloshed over her sleeve.

Patting her pockets for a tissue, she muttered, 'Oh God, I am an idiot!' Flicking a quick look back, she saw a petite woman approach him. Her sleek, dark bob made Fran run her fingers through her own windblown locks in an attempt to tame them. In skinny jeans, pale, knee-length sheepskin boots and a thick, oversized sweater, the woman looked expensively dressed in a way that Fran couldn't explain. She rested a small hand briefly on his sinewy forearm, and Fran could see, even from a distance, that his attention was wholly on her. It was the woman she'd seen on that very first night, tugging at his arm in a very different way to this.

'I see Tasha still hangs around Wyn,' Caitlin muttered, raising an eyebrow. 'She wants to make her mind up, that one. I don't know what she sees in that . . .' She cleared her throat and took a deep breath, continuing brightly and more loudly, 'So, Fran. Have you brought bathers with you?'

'Bathers?' Fran still stared at the woman with Wyn. He seemed very attentive. Either they were very civilized or he was still in love with her. How sad that would be. Caitlin cleared her throat pointedly and Fran snapped to attention. 'What are bathers?'

'A swimsuit. A costume. Bathers. Don't they call them bathers in England?'

'I've never heard them called that.' Fran shrugged. 'I've got a swimsuit for sunbathing. Will that do?'

'Probably. It's just that they're on sale over there.'

'Okay. I like a bargain.' Fran allowed herself to be towed away by Caitlin, putting the enigma that was Wyn out of her mind. She was quite enjoying a rummage through the sales bins on the stand until a thought occurred to her.

'Erm, when you asked if I'd brought a swimsuit with me, you didn't mean here, now? Today?' Her stomach began to squeeze the brownie and coffee back the way it had gone in . . .

'Yeah, I've got some armbands on me. We'll blow 'em up now and chuck you in the sea for the newcomers' race.' Caitlin rolled her eyes. 'Of course not *today*, you eejit.'

After a split second, laughter burst from Fran's nose, nearly bringing the coffee and brownie with it. It had been a long time since someone had teased her so mercilessly. As a shift sergeant, she saw herself as the buffer between her shift and the upper ranks. Which meant that she wasn't quite one of the blokes, or one of the officer ranks. And while she might enjoy a bit of ribbing from the guys every now and again, they didn't quite include her in their own jokes. She'd always been apart. Mindful of her position.

She was getting a taste here of what it was like to live without hierarchy. A normal life. She felt as if she'd been in this village for ages already.

Her thoughts flashed back to Gavin. She wondered whether he missed living here and then dismissed her thoughts. Young people needed to explore and find their own way, where they were tested and grew. Llanbryn was a sleepy hamlet by the sea, and if you didn't count all these fit competitors who were, she presumed, visitors, she hadn't yet seen any young inhabitants, apart from children and pink-haired Bethan from the shop.

Thinking about her job coincided with her eyeline falling upon another man in Lycra, contorting himself to apply Vaseline or whatever it was. He seemed familiar. When he stood up straight, pushing his chest out, she recognized him as the policeman who she'd seen squaring up to Wyn, and she frowned.

Tasha was back, fiddling with something in the boot of their car. The policeman handed her the tub of cream and she took over the anointing, for all the world like the dutiful wife.

CHAPTER TWELVE

The starter horn sounded.

Lining the beach at the water's edge, Fran screamed encouragement and clapped along with Caitlin, her friends and all the other spectators as the mass of black neoprene hurled itself into the sea. The water churned with arms and frothed with kicking legs as the swimmers battled for positions. Shouts for various names carried across the sand.

'Oh my God! How can they see where they're going?' Fran yelled at Caitlin.

'I don't think they can,' Caitlin replied, before shrieking, 'Come on!'

'Are you supporting anyone?' Fran squinted at the swimmers. They all looked the same to her.

'Just some of the villagers,' Caitlin said, her eyes fixed on the sea.

'Mrs Roberts' grandson is out the front. There's a little group of them.' Elin materialized alongside with a pair of binoculars. 'Looks like two of them together, and then another three.'

'How long will it take them?' Fran had no idea who anyone was, and realized there was no point in asking. She wished she had binoculars too though. Not that she'd be able to identify them even if she *could* see them.

'Around thirty minutes, maybe less, for the best ones,' Elin said from behind her binoculars. Fran watched her. She wouldn't have been surprised to discover that Elin had been a competitor in the past — she was so knowledgeable.

'I'd need a calendar, not a stopwatch,' said Wendy.

'We should do this, next year,' said a woman who Fran judged to be about Caitlin's age, thoughtfully.

'By *we*, you mean *you*, Cora, I hope.' Wendy shaded her eyes with her hand as she watched the race progress.

'I'd do it if I didn't have to do all that other stuff,' Caitlin said. 'All that cycling and running. Pity they don't do a team version. Wendy, you could use your e-bike.'

Fran listened to them with a smile as she watched the swimmers. She thought she understood what Cora meant. Whenever she'd watched the London Marathon, she'd found herself wondering whether she could do it. And maybe she could have, if she'd trained hard enough and hadn't had a heart attack. But the water — it was an alien environment for her. If you stopped running, well, you walked or fell over. If you stopped swimming . . . she swallowed.

'Ooh, ooh, the Roberts lad is coming in first . . .' Elin gave a running commentary via her binoculars. 'Come on, we need to get to Transition.'

Caught up in the excitement, Fran followed her neighbour and squeezed herself among the homemade banners, supporters on tiptoe and toddlers in pushchairs so she could see the area where all the bikes were corralled. Yellow-vested marshals lined the route. She strained to see the competitors leaving the sea, blowing their noses with one hand and reaching behind to pull wetsuit zips down with the other. How the hell did they have the energy to run like that after swimming for a mile, she wondered. And it was uphill. Surely their legs must feel like jelly.

'Yay! Keep going!' Her palms stung from clapping. She was astonished to find tears pricking at her eyes and remembered Bethan's words about how she always cried. There was something heroic about the competitors. She could imagine Wyn doing this, and as she wondered what he must feel about being a spectator now, she saw Tasha clapping with enthusiasm as her husband passed them.

The competitors, stripped down to what looked like swimsuits to Fran, grabbed their bicycles and leaped on them, pedalling off up the hill out of the village.

'Don't they get cold?'

'Not for long, the speed they're going,' Elin told her.

'How long is this bit?'

'About an hour and a half. It's pretty hilly.'

'Time to get another coffee, I think,' said Caitlin. 'Want us to bring you one back, Elin?'

'If you would, my lovely, yes please.' Elin remained glued to her binoculars and the remaining swimmers as Caitlin and Fran regrouped with the other girls.

'Elin knows nearly all the competitors,' Caitlin told Fran as they walked. 'The older ones, anyway. She taught games at the village school here for years. We thought she was never going to retire.'

'I haven't seen a school here. Only a building site on the other side of the beach.'

'Yes, it closed a few years back. All the kids are bussed to a super-school about ten miles away. That's what they call them now. It's a shame, really. It was lovely when the village school was here. A great way to keep the community together, know what I mean?'

Fran didn't, as she'd never had children, but she could imagine. 'What happened to it?'

'Oh, Wyn bought it. He's been doing it up ever since. Big project. I mean, unless you particularly want a house with a dozen teeny toilets . . .' Caitlin chuckled.

'Wyn *owns* that enormous place?' Fran stopped in her tracks. 'I saw it yesterday! I saw him working on it and thought . . .' Her voice trailed away.

'You thought he was a builder?' Caitlin raised her eyebrows at her.

'I did, yeah.' Fran stared back, aghast. 'I mean, he was working in my garden!' She frowned. No wonder he'd been cross that she'd called him a labourer. 'So, why does he — I mean, he must be loaded to afford that place, so . . . ?'

'Cos he loves it here. Americano again?'

'Only if it's decaf. I've had my one caffeinated coffee for the day. Here, let me go and get them and I'll buy yours and Elin's. More brownies?'

'Nope, saving myself for the bacon butties.'

* * *

Before long, the cyclists returned and Fran watched in increasing admiration as the competitors seamlessly shrugged off their bikes, donned running shoes and continued to pound down to the sea and continue loping along the long beach. She fired off a few photos to send to Gavin, wishing she'd remembered to take some before. There was no signal there, of course, so she'd have to remember to send them later.

'How do they run like that in their swimsuits?' Fran murmured to Caitlin and the other swimmers. 'I can barely *walk* along that beach. One way.'

'No idea,' said Wendy. 'I'd have knocked myself out after a hundred yards.'

'And everyone else,' one of the girls retorted.

There was laughter as Wendy blew her a kiss and replied mildly, 'You're just jealous. If you've got it, flaunt it.'

When the last runner was out of sight, Caitlin said, rubbing her hands together, 'Who's for a bacon butty?' Their response was unanimous.

'I'd love one,' said Fran. 'My stomach has been rumbling for ages. But I'm wrecked already. I need a sit down, sorry. Can I give you the money instead? Brown sauce, please, if they have it,' she added to Caitlin's instant nod, digging cash out of her purse.

Caitlin and a couple of the other girls whose names she'd forgotten headed off with their list, back to the car park, leaving Fran with Elin. Elin had a tiny, pack-away picnic blanket in her pocket, and she flicked it open, laying it on the sand.

'Can you get down there okay?' she asked Fran.

'Yeah. Getting back up is a different matter.' Fran snorted a laugh, settling herself beside Elin. 'That word, *butty*,' she said, into the companionable silence. 'I've heard people calling each other butt or butty here — and I'm guessing it's nothing to do with the bacon variety . . .'

Elin shook her head. 'No. It's from the mines, in the Valleys, but you hear it all over, really. The miners worked in pairs, one more experienced than the other. They were known as *butties*.'

'Aha!' Fran nodded. 'I thought I might have been mishearing it as *buddy*! And what would someone mean when they talk about handbags on a pitch?'

Elin laughed. 'Handbags is when there's a bit of a scrap between teams in rugby. It's nothing serious, a lot of pushing and some fisticuffs.'

Fran thought about the scrap outside the shop. 'I get it. One more. It sounded like "doo doo" . . .'

'*Duw* means "God". It's a sort of "goodness me". You have a good ear. You'll be bilingual by the time you leave.' Elin cocked an eye at Fran. 'The first words out of the mouths of all the babies in Wales is "Hiyaaa!"'

She exaggerated the accent so well that Fran laughed out loud, and several people nearby laughed along with them. Fran was reminded again how much friendlier it was compared to home.

'Even my own great-grandchildren do it!' Elin said, with a tut. 'Speaking of which, you'll be able to hear it for yourself. I'm having the family over for a picnic lunch party in the garden tomorrow afternoon. It would be lovely if you came round.'

Fran opened her mouth to say no, thank you. She wasn't family, wouldn't know anybody, she'd be the only

122

Englishwoman there, she'd have to explain that she'd had a heart attack and that's why she wasn't working, and no, she wasn't married and didn't have a boyfriend or children . . . But Elin had phrased it in such a way that it would be rude to refuse. She didn't have to stay long, just enough to satisfy courtesy. And if all else failed, she'd just have to plead medical reasons and scuttle off back to Seagull Cottage.

'Thank you, that sounds lovely,' she said, with a smile. 'What time and what can I bring?'

'That's very kind of you, but you don't need to bring anything, there will be plenty. Just bring yourself. Any time from twelve thirty will be fine.'

'I can manage that, thank you,' Fran said, interpreting that as twelve thirty exactly and wondering what on earth she was going to make at such short notice and with only the little beach shop available. After all, Elin was a pensioner — she couldn't just rock up and eat the old lady's food.

She could drive to the nearest supermarket, of course, wherever that was. But one, she was already dog-tired after the early start and activity of the day, and two, she found herself curiously reluctant to go elsewhere. There was something almost womb-like about the village. She felt safe, as if she were on an island completely away from the rush and bustle of the city. Also, she told herself, it was important to support these little village shops, or they'd disappear. And anyway, she liked cooking. She'd cooked for the shift often enough, and nobody ever went home hungry, she was sure of that. It would be a challenge. As long as she paced herself, she'd be fine.

The bacon rolls returned with Caitlin and the others, who flung themselves onto the sand with enviable flexibility and handed them out.

'Wyn was cooking, so they should be top-notch,' Caitlin told them. 'We asked him to cut all the fat off for us . . .'

'He's such a sweetie, isn't he?' one of the girls said, and the others agreed. Fran remained silent. The man was a mystery to her.

As the competitors thundered past on the return leg, flinging themselves exhaustedly beneath the huge inflatable finishing arch, Fran clapped and cheered as rapturously as the others and caught Wyn glaring at her from the other side of the finish line. His eyes were like lasers and she almost jumped. What had she done now? She hadn't even spoken to him! She glared back, refusing to be intimidated, and then wondered whether Caitlin had said something about her thinking he was a builder. Oh well. Whatever. She'd dealt with bigger idiots than him in her time.

Elin called her goodbyes, and Fran sat with the swimming girls for a little longer, feeling warm and sleepy. Eventually, they could stand her capacious yawning no longer.

'Go and have a nanna nap, Frannie.'

'I'm not even a mama, let alone a nanna.'

They laughed at her grouchy tone, and she allowed herself a smile. She'd go home via the beach shop and hope for inspiration for Elin's garden picnic.

'Bye, ladies.' She clambered to her feet, collecting her bag containing the new swimsuit. 'It's been a fun day, thank you all.'

'Now we know where you live, we'll knock you up for that swim.' Caitlin grinned up at her.

'Argh. Sounds like a threat . . .' They laughed again, and despite the familiar terrified lurch in the pit of her stomach, Fran felt something else. These women made her feel as if anything were possible.

Her body felt a hundred years old and fifty stone as she dragged herself up the slight, sandy incline to the shop. As she pushed the door open, she had a brainwave. Frittata, of course. She did those really well. There was bound to be the basics: eggs, cheese, potatoes. She would add to it and make a couple of different ones.

Thanking Gavin's parents in her head for buying a house so close to the shop, Fran lurched tiredly through the front door of the cottage, carrying two plastic carriers filled with groceries. She felt utterly drained. Running on empty.

She stared up at the first floor to the kitchen and wanted to cry. Why couldn't the kitchen be downstairs, like normal houses? She'd totally overdone it, getting up so early and rushing about all over the place. Would she ever be normal again? It felt as if she'd been unplugged. As if everything inside her body had seeped out and nothing was working her bones. Not an ounce of energy left.

Sagging onto the second step of the beautiful oak stairs, she slumped forward. Catching her head in her hands, she collapsed into helpless sobs.

CHAPTER THIRTEEN

Wyn strode down the path to Fran's cottage. He had to say his piece. Every single time he got anywhere near her today he'd been distracted by someone wanting something. He spotted her in the crowd earlier, but with the sun in his eyes he wasn't sure whether she'd seen him.

As he stood indecisively at the slightly open door, the sound of weeping came to him. He nudged the door without entering and said into the hallway, 'Hello? Fran?'

The sobbing continued and he peered inside. 'I saw the door open and I, oh . . .'

Fran was slumped on the stairs, elbows on her knees, auburn curls tangled through her fingers. He couldn't decide whether he should throw the door open so that he couldn't be accused of breaking and entering, or close it to protect her privacy. He stepped inside and closed it. 'Whatever's wrong?' He squatted before her. 'Can I help?'

'I . . . I . . . I'm so *tiiiired* . . .' she wailed, still behind the curtain of hair.

In a flash of understanding, Wyn knew exactly what had happened. She'd overexerted herself. He'd spotted her all over the village that morning. Tall and red-haired, she was hard to miss. She gave a mighty sniff. Crossing the few steps to the bathroom to the right of the hallway, he brought back a toilet roll and tore off a long section, offering it beneath the hair.

'Th'nk you.' She blew loudly. 'I d-don't think I'll ever be normal again,' she stammered brokenly. 'What did I do to deserve this?' Her tear-stained, pale face appeared through the hair and then dropped back into her hands.

'Fran, you've just overdone it,' Wyn said, hoping he was right. 'You'll be fine in the morning after you've had a good night's sleep.' Her head nodded. He sighed. She was virtually asleep where she sat. What on earth should he do?

'Fran? Fran — wake up. C'mon, butty, you need to go to bed.' Her eyes opened blearily.

'I need to go to bed,' she repeated. 'I'm so *tiiiired*.' The sobs began again. 'And I have to make frit-ta-ta-tat-taaaa!' she ended, on a long hiccupping wail.

'Whatever that is, it can wait until tomorrow. You need your bed.' Wyn had lost count of the number of rugby mates he'd put to bed over the years, worse for wear, their girl-friends or wives rolling their eyes. He set his jaw. This was no different — except that Fran was unlikely to pee in a wardrobe in the middle of the night.

Poised to lift her bodily and put her on her bed, he hesitated mid-bend and straightened up, his hands hanging loosely. He was an uninvited man, in her space . . . and he didn't really know her, so . . . hmm. No.

'Fran, wake up — do you need to take any tablets?'

'No.' She shook her head. 'Done 'em all.'

'Do you feel okay? Should I ring the doctor or some-body? Do you need someone to sit with you?'

Pushing back her hair, she lifted her head. Her unfo-cused eyes drooping, she said, 'No, 'm okay, thank you. Jus'. Need. Bed.'

'Can you get up?'

Nodding, she stumbled to her feet and blindly staggered towards the bedroom, ricocheting off the doorway. He put his hands out to steady her but she managed to wobble to the bed on her own, flopping onto it. He bent to unlace her boots and pulled them off. She rolled untidily beneath the duvet and he decided it was good enough. Stepping back into the hallway, he pulled her door to, and seconds later, a noise like a Siberian tractor drifted towards him. He listened for a moment or two and then closed the front door quietly behind him.

Their conversation could wait.

* * *

Fran sprang out of bed the following morning, mystified to find herself still in yesterday's clothes. Had there been a party last night? If so, it must've been a good one as she couldn't remember a thing. She had no hangover though. In the shower she sang the words to 'Oh, What a Beautiful Mornin'', and was energetically lathering her hair when she remembered Wyn's visit. Shampoo ran into her eyes.

'Oh!' Well. At least he hadn't been a total pervert and put her to bed or anything ghastly like that. He hadn't, had he? She'd still had all her clothes on, so . . .

She'd dressed, taken the shopping upstairs and was assembling the ingredients for her frittata before her memory returned fully. She'd noticed her memory failing several times since surgery and sincerely hoped it was a temporary side effect. And, she admitted, yesterday had been a lesson that it was time she learned. For her peace of mind, she rang her cardiac support nurse after breakfast.

'Give yourself a chance, Fran! You've had major surgery, and your heart needs time to get stronger. How do you feel now?'

'I feel awesome!' Fran admitted. The nurse laughed.

'Well, there's your answer. You're still healing. I'm giving you permission to slow down. Let go a bit — you're not being lazy, you're healing. Hope you're having a lovely time there?'

'I am, thanks,' Fran said, happy to realize that she was telling the truth. 'House is stunning, I'm right on the beach and the people are so friendly.'

'Just what you need. Now take it easy!' She rang off, and Fran, much reassured, sat at the table, slicing and assembling the ingredients for a potato and pepper frittata with a sweet-corn and chili salsa. The electric oven took longer than hers and she walked back and forth fretting that it might turn out like cardboard. It was satisfying to have a task to complete and she thoroughly enjoyed her morning.

Her heart behaved impeccably throughout, and taking her cue from that, she made herself a decaf coffee and sat on the balcony in the sunshine with her novel. She'd give the steps a miss for that day. Relief flooded through her and she realized how stressful she found the constant monitoring and how much she'd been pushing herself.

At 12.28 p.m., Fran bore her perfectly browned offering plus a bottle of wine round to Elin's. The front door was open and Fran called through, assailed by a sudden piercing memory of Wyn doing the exact same thing through her door. Oh dear. She'd almost fainted on him in the garden and now she'd fallen asleep in front of him.

A young woman in a pair of tiny cut-off denim shorts appeared in the hallway, a solemn baby on her hip. She eyed Fran's offerings. 'Hi!'

'Can I put these in the fridge, please?'

'If you can find a space . . .'

Fran's jaw dropped at the array of bottles — alcoholic and non-alcoholic — in the kitchen. The fridge was bulging and the worktops and table were groaning with food. Now feeling rather silly about her assumption that there wouldn't be enough, she found a sliver of shelf space in which to squeeze her frittata, left her bottle with all the others and followed the girl into the garden. Chairs and tables had been arranged in the pretty space, paper lanterns strung from one side to the other, and a generous assortment of glasses and bottles set out on a long table near the doors.

'Gran!' called the girl. 'Fran's here!' Elin detached herself from setting baskets of cutlery on each table. Wearing a long, flowing cotton dress and wide-brimmed straw hat among the flowers in the garden, she looked as if she'd stepped out of an Impressionist painting. Blooming. Generous. Motherly.

'Fran!' She leaned forward and left a light kiss on Fran's cheek. 'How lovely. And on time too.'

'Thank you for inviting me.' Fran looked around admiringly. 'It's so pretty! It reminds me of that John Singer Sargent painting, *Carnation, Lily, Lily, Rose*.'

'Thank you, lovely! I love that painting too.'

'He captures the light beautifully in it, doesn't he?' Fran nodded earnestly, her mind filled with the painting as it over-laid Elin's garden. 'I saw it at the Tate years ago. It's stunning. To think it was all painted outside. Amazing.'

Tall purple flowers nodded among a kaleidoscope of colour. Fran's horticultural knowledge stopped at daffodils, and she said so.

'I live in a flat in a city with a tiny balcony, and not a pot in sight. This—' she waved her hand around the garden — 'is wonderful. But it looks like it must be very hard work.'

'You just need to loosen your grip,' Elin said, her eyes roaming the garden and then resting on her thoughtfully. 'Let go a bit. Weeds are flowers that might be in the wrong place. But if they look okay, then just leave them where they are.'

'That sounds like my idea of gardening.' Fran nodded. She'd just heard the phrase 'let go a bit' from two completely separate people. It was a sign, surely. 'I don't have a clue. I'm glad Wyn is calling regularly so I can't wreck next door's.'

Elin smiled. 'It might be just what you need. No better way of getting close to Earth, a bit of gardening.'

'I'd be terrified of killing something.'

'Plants are pretty tough, you know. A bit like babies. Love them and feed them and they grow like weeds.' Elin laughed lightly. 'But ignore me. I'm being bossy, as usual. You're here to convalesce, not dig the garden!'

'So, what can I do to help?' Fran was happy to change the subject as she knew as much about babies as she did about gardening.

'Would you like to put the napkins and cutlery out, please? I'm expecting everyone any minute.' Elin passed over artfully colour-coordinated packs of floral and checked paper napkins, and showed Fran what she wanted. Busying herself in a corner, Fran was happy to be given a job. She could hear people arriving, and the sound of kissing and laughter. The girl who'd welcomed her in appeared with a large gin glass, adorned with a bright paper umbrella and a slice of lime, in one hand and the baby in the other.

'G and T for you, Gran said.' She set the glass on the table beside her, and casually dumped the baby on Fran's lap. 'Could you take Arthur for a minute? Just need to . . .'

'What? Me? I can't! I don't know how to . . . oh, okay . . .'

The girl whirled away and Fran found herself eye to eye with the frowning baby.

'Hello, Arthur,' she said after a pause. 'I'm from next door.' The baby fixed her with an owlish glare. Fran stared back, unnerved. Was she holding him right? She couldn't remember the last time she'd held a baby.

Arthur poked a damp, miniature finger into Fran's mouth and gripped her lips but otherwise seemed placid enough, and she carefully redistributed him to a more comfortable position on her lap and tried, unsuccessfully, to reach the gin and tonic. Arthur wobbled precariously and she clutched him, gripping more firmly around his solid middle with both hands. From his unblinking gaze, there was no sign that he'd been bothered by his near-departure from his perch.

'Whoa. That was close.' She looked over at the increasing gathering near the back doors to see if anyone had noticed. Although there were several other babies and toddlers, there was no sign of the girl, and Fran wondered if Arthur had in fact belonged to her in the first place. Was she participating in an involuntary game of Pass the Baby? Her stomach rumbled.

It felt like hours before she felt brave enough to slide one arm around to clutch the child and swivel around to glug at her gin and tonic. Guests filtered into the garden, holding plates of food. A bunch of little boys hurtled across the lawn, struck fighting poses, howled war cries and hurtled back, to a parental chorus of 'Oi, what did I tell you?' and 'Can't you lot walk anywhere?'

She was regretting choosing such an out-of-the-way corner. She could be stuck with this baby until he was walking.

'Couldn't you just cry a bit? Maybe someone would come and get you. And please blink. You're making my eyes hurt.' Arthur had to be the most placid baby ever, fixing her with his blue gaze as she spoke. Emboldened, she carried on chatting to him, trying to avoid those probing, icky fingers in her mouth.

'I made a terrible arse of myself yesterday, Arthur,' she said, rapidly running out of things to say about flowers and dicky birds. 'Not that I could help it. I've had a heart attack, you know, and yes, I know I'm very young for it, thank you for noticing. I can't imagine what Wyn thought of me. Although it's not as if he even likes me . . . so he ' A shadow loomed over them.

'Hello, Arthur! Are you being a good boy?' Arthur treated Wyn to his solemn glare and hid his face in Fran's neck. Wyn laughed and Fran felt absurdly gratified. 'Hello. You're okay now, Fran?'

Fran opened her mouth with no idea what to say and felt a warm dampness spread over her thighs. She lifted Arthur up and his face wreathed in smiles. 'Yeugh. He's leaking! Oh, yuk . . .'

Wyn took Arthur one-handed, or so it seemed to Fran. Swinging him over his shoulder, he said, 'We'd better find you a clean nappy, I think, young man!' He strode across the lawn towards the cottage, the baby tiny over his broad shoulder. Fran was dismissed and she wasn't at all sure how she felt about that. That baby had been her responsibility. She stared down at the wet patch spreading across her cotton trousers. She'd have to go home and change.

Elin materialized in Wyn's wake with a cloth and handed it to her. 'Oops! It'll soon dry in this heat. Come on, let's get you another gin and tonic. You're a natural with him though, he doesn't take to everyone.'

Her, a natural! Who knew? Dabbing at her trousers, Fran beamed as she followed Elin. And what was a bit of baby wee in a party full of babies? It made her one of them. Let it go, as Elin and her rehab nurse had said.

'Are you ready for food?' Elin asked over her shoulder.

'I am!' Fran said, seeing loaded plates everywhere and sniffing the delicious mix of aromas. 'I'm starving. I just need to, er, wash my hands . . .' Elin showed her to the downstairs cloakroom and Fran checked her appearance in the mirror there. Just in case the baby had left sticky marks on her, obviously. Not at all for Wyn's benefit.

'Let me introduce you to some of my wonderful family,' Elin said, escorting Fran and her now loaded plate back out to the garden, and placing her in a chair in the centre of a large, chatty group. 'Everyone, my new neighbour, Fran. She's house-sitting for the whole summer.'

Fran held her breath until Elin moved away, relieved that she hadn't mentioned her heart attack or made any jokes about *being careful what you say — she's police, ho ho,* as she'd heart-sinkingly heard on so many occasions, along with *she's got her handcuffs in her handbag, so watch yourselves.*

'Hi, lovely to meet you all! Elin's been brilliant since I turned up. She's even got me on Facebook and I never thought that would happen.'

'Oh, Mum's fully embraced twenty-first century technology,' said a tall, lean George Clooney clone. 'Her blogs are hilarious.'

'I'll look out for them,' said Elin, tucking into her plate of food and wishing that somebody else was also eating. In the way she'd come to expect though, questions were fired her way about where she lived, what she thought of Wales, had she been before, and as ever, banter ricocheted from each topic in that soft, lilting accent. Coughing with laughter at one tale, she excused herself to top up her drink and ran straight into Wyn, who held a now dry Arthur hooked into the crook of his elbow. He put a hand out to steady her as she bounced off him.

'Bloody hell, man.' Fran glared up at him. 'Could you not look where I'm going?'

He stared at her for a moment and then boomed a laugh.

'Let me top you up.' He took the glass from her surprised fingers. 'What is it?'

'G and T. A weak one. Not an Elin one.' She followed him as he carved a path through the throng. 'I can do it, actually. You don't have to—'

'Fine. I was just trying to be friendly.' He handed the glass back and they stared at each other. Arthur stared at them too. Fran felt her face flame. She squeezed past his bulk, trying not to notice how his proximity made her skin prickle and her stomach bounce, and shovelled ice cubes halfway up the glass. As she sloshed in the gin, she heard his voice, from somewhere above her head, 'You should put that in before the ice, really. Otherwise you can't gauge how strong it is.'

Fran rounded on him with a snort. 'Are you still here?'

One eyebrow shot up. He bent his head and said, quietly, close to her ear, 'Yes. I need to speak with you.'

Her skin quivered with goose pimples. 'What about?'

'Er, well, er, I think I owe you an apology.' He looked around him. 'Could we go somewhere a bit quieter?'

'An apology? For what . . . ?' Fran trailed off, running out of breath hurrying after his back as he searched for an unoccupied spot. They ended up in the front garden. Fran perched on the low wall and Wyn followed suit, which put him at a more comfortable height for conversation.

'I see you've still got Arthur.'

'This is Tomos.'

'Oh! They all look the same to me. Is he yours?'

'Nope.' He shrugged as if it were perfectly normal to be handed a baby at a party and twitched the baby's cotton sun hat over his face. Tomos yanked it off and flung it. 'I'm not playing that game, young man. Wear it or you'll frazzle and I'll be in big trouble.'

Fran stooped to pick it up at the same time as he did and they knocked heads.

'Ouch!' She rubbed her head. Tomos gurgled, then looked at her expectantly. 'Ouch!' she said again, flicking her hair. Tomos chuckled and Wyn took the opportunity to pop the baby's sun hat on again.

'Finally found my calling in life.' Fran laughed. 'Baby entertainer.'

They sat in the sunshine, making Tomos giggle until he finally fell asleep and Wyn said, pointing at her empty glass, 'That seems to have evaporated. Want a refill?'

'Not yet. I want to know what you lured me out here to say.'

'It's about the thing outside the pub that night.'

'Your assault on police.'

'You *would* say that.'

'Apparently, we coppers are all the same.'

He heaved a sigh. 'Yes. And *I* said *that*. But that's before I knew that you'd been over to the pub.'

'You've lost me.'

'You went to see Barty and asked about the CCTV.'

'Ah. That.'

'Yes.'

'Have you seen it? *Does* it help?'

'It does actually. So, thank you.' He cleared his throat. 'I, er, I was wrong about you. And I apologize.'

'That's okay. I was wrong about you too.' Thinking back over the incident, she added, 'So, has he contacted you? The policeman? AJ?'

'No. And yes. Not directly. He's not been round to nick me, if that's what you meant. He's making a nuisance of himself instead.'

'In what way?'

'He's breathalysed me twice, once in the afternoon outside somebody's house where I was about to unblock the sink. And he stop-searched the van for the millionth time.

Very "surprised" to find nothing but my tools and associated crap. Sorry, *clutter*.'

'You can report him to Professional Standards for harassment.'

Wyn heaved a sigh. 'I think that would just make things worse.'

'Things?'

'You're interviewing me again.'

Fran laughed. 'Okay. Shall we start again? My name is Fran. I'm a newly retired police sergeant.'

'Retired? So you lied about being a cop?'

'Yep. Sorry. Turns out I'm better at being a pretend cop than being an ordinary civvy.'

'Ah. I think I might know where you're coming from there.'

'And, um, my turn to thank you for yesterday afternoon. And, er, either I was dreaming, or—'

'You dreamed about me?'

'That would be a nightmare.' She slid a grin his way. 'I remember letting myself into the cottage and then . . .'

'You fell asleep on the stairs.'

'Oh God, really? I have absolutely no memory of it. I've never been so tired . . . It was like someone had switched me off.'

'Yeah, I just wanted to be sure you were okay. Look, I'm sorry if I overstepped the mark. I swear to you I did nothing . . . you put yourself to bed. I took your boots off. But that was all. I didn't even touch the duvet. Nothing. At all. Erm.'

'No, really, I think I'd remember.' Blood flamed in her face. 'I mean, er . . .'

'No problem. Recovering from surgery takes it out of you. But you will improve. It just takes time.'

'That's what my cardiac nurse said this morning.' Fran sighed. 'I'm not very good at being patient.'

'You don't always have a choice. See it as character-building.'

'Sounds like you're speaking from experience.'

'I am.' Careful not to wake the sleeping Tomos, he hitched up the sleeve of his shirt and Fran caught her breath at the terrible disfigurement. Where his right bicep was muscular and solid, his left arm, from the elbow and extending into his shoulder as far as she could see, was frankly hideous. Withered, puckered and twisted. She put a hand to her mouth as her stomach turned to water, imagining what he'd been through.

'*Shiiit*. What the hell happened?'

'Crane fell on me at work.' He stared at it and then looked away. Fran wondered if he, like her, relived the incident every time he saw the scars. What a terrible reminder. Poor man.

'God.' She shuddered, imagining the horror of it and trying not to. 'And I thought mine was bad.' She hitched down the round neck of her T-shirt without a second thought. Compared to his terrible disfigurement, hers seemed minor. 'It goes right down to my belly button. My sternum is wired together.'

He winced satisfactorily, peering at it. 'Ouch. It's healing well though.'

'I think it's hideous. It's lumpy. Bits stick out of it. Like a pig's back. I still can't get used to it.' She clapped a hand over her mouth. *For God's sake, Fran, talk about oversharing. Bits stick out of it like a pig's back? That was gross. Jeez. Nobody needed to know that!*

He reached out a hand and placed it briefly on her forearm. His hand was warm, dry and rough, and her stomach fizzed. Really, she was far too old and sensible to be feeling this silly and girly about his nearness. 'Survivor's scars. You won't even notice that in a few months. They're dissolving stitches. Get some Bio-Oil, it's brilliant — and it'll be faded in no time. You think you're never going to come to terms with it, and then, little by little, you stop noticing and it's almost gone. Your body is amazing at healing itself. Trust me.'

In that moment of sharing, she did trust him. Connected by their scars, by pain, terror. There was a world of experience to talk about there, but they'd just managed to encapsulate it. For the second time that day, Fran felt tension seep away from her. They sat together in the sunshine, and she felt peaceful. No need to carry on some inane small talk for the sake of it. After a pause, she looked at the peacefully sleeping Tomos.

'You seem very at home with babies. Do you have a family?'

'We tried.'

'I'm sorry. That must be tough if you want kids.'

'Mmm. Apparently, I didn't "show much empathy" at the time.'

Fran fidgeted, looking at this colossal man, his huge, capable hands cradling the sleeping baby. She'd probably been short on empathy about kids in the past too. Her shift had been young and mostly single, apart from Gavin. Babies hadn't featured much in their day-to-day lives, if at all. It had all been about parties, living, adventures. She hoped he and Ally's dreams of a family would happen for them, now that she knew them so well, and understood their longings.

She was silent for a while before saying, 'Is that true, or did you hide it well?'

He stared at her. 'Very perceptive, Mrs Ex-Cop. I was as devastated as she was.' He cleared his throat. 'I think I wanted kids more than she did.'

Fran sipped at her drink. '*Ms* Ex-Cop. At least you committed. I've never even managed to do that.'

'Really? Why ever not?'

'Have you any idea how weird blokes are around policewomen?'

'Ah.' He nodded, pursing his wide mouth. 'Let me guess. *Have you got your handcuffs? Do you do kissograms?*'

'Yep. And worse.' She snorted at a memory. '"Can I try on your uniform?" was a new low . . .'

Wyn laughed. 'So — now?'

'Sworn off men, obviously. You?'

'Yeah. Sworn off men too.'

They laughed. He looked at her empty glass.

'Another drink?'

She shook her head. 'I'm up for pud. They looked delicious.'

'I'll get them. Any preferences?' He transferred the still-sleeping Tomos to Fran and their skin touched, sending tingles through Fran.

'Anything with chocolate, cream and bad for you.'

'Gotcha.'

Tomos woke up at the change of position and glared at Fran in a suspicious and distrustful way. Wyn returned bearing two dishes heaped with a variety of desserts to find her giggling helplessly at the baby's expression.

'That's his judgy look,' he said. 'He does it to me too.'

'He's hilarious. I can't look at him without laughing. He's appalled by me. Just like all my blokes.'

'More fool them.'

Fran shot a glance at him, not knowing what to make of that comment. They both stared at the baby for a moment. Changing the subject briskly, she said, 'Show me how to hold this baby so I can eat my pudding before it melts.'

'The trick is to appear confident. They can smell your fear, babies.' Wyn laid Tomos so that his head was against Fran's neck, and put her hand on the baby's back. Nestling in, Tomos's eyes closed instantly. 'He might dribble a bit but it all washes off.'

'Nice.' Fran made a disgusted face although, secretly, the baby felt somehow just right, moulded into her shoulder. She peered into her brimming pudding bowl, anchoring Tomos with her forearm. 'You've short-changed me. I can see a gap.'

Wyn dug into his bowl with a grin. 'Get on with it or I'll finish yours off too.'

'Not a chance. You forget I've worked with men for more than twenty-five years. I'm a past master at guarding my food.'

They ate in a silence, punctuated by the odd appreciative 'mm', until Fran sat up straight with a groan and pushed the bowl away. 'My eyes are bigger than my belly.'

'Waste not, want not.' Wyn stacked her dish on top of his empty one and polished off her leftovers.

'Ew.' Fran wrinkled her nose. 'That's gross. You don't even know me.'

Wyn snorted a laugh, his shoulders rising and falling with the sound. He put a hand over his mouth.

'It's the rugby player in me,' he said around a spoonful of trifle. 'And there's a lot of me to fill. You get used to taking your chances where you can.'

Fran remembered him at the old school, hefting a sheet of insulation board. Even with his injury, he was massively strong. She could just imagine the quantity of food he could put away. 'So, you own a school.'

'Mm.' He swallowed, nodding. 'Were you there the other day? I thought I saw you.' He cocked an eyebrow at her with a mischievous slant to his mouth. 'Were you spying on me for your new police pal?'

'Why? Have you been naughty again?'

'Me? I'm Mr Goody-Two-Shoes, me. Ask anyone.'

'I have, actually.'

Wyn bellowed a laugh. 'And?'

'I think Gavin, my senior PC, is one of your groupies.'

'Gav? April and Ken's lad?' Wyn nodded, his mouth lifting at one side, which Fran could see created a fetching dimple in his lean face. 'I taught him to play rugby. How's he doing?'

'He's in my flat, while they house-hunt.'

'That's handy.'

'Yep. He's passed his sergeant's exam and he's doing his inspector's next. Awaiting promotion.'

Wyn whistled and waved his spoon. 'Good man. Send my regards.'

'So what are your plans for the schoolhouse? It's pretty huge, isn't it?'

'Originally, it was meant to be a house for me and Tasha. Space for the indoor pool she always wanted, plus a spa and gym.'

'Wow.'

'Yeah.' He rested his elbows on his knees and stared at his feet. 'Anyway. Life is never how you imagine, is it?'

'You can say that again.' Fran nodded, chewing her bottom lip. 'So, now?'

'I'm just going through the motions, to be honest with you.'

'Is it habitable? I mean, are you living in it?'

'A bit of it is. I have a kind of studio kitchen, bedsit and bathroom. It's perfectly adequate for me.' He shrugged. 'Plenty to keep me busy.' He stared into space for a moment, and then added, slowly, 'I meant what I said earlier. About the thing outside the pub with me and that knob . . .' He cleared his throat. 'That PC James. Now I've seen the CCTV I can see how easy it was for you to decide what was happening. It takes guts to look beyond the beliefs you've held for most of your life.' He rubbed his chin. 'It would have been easy to assume. So, thanks for not.'

'Well, to be fair, I did assume — to begin with. It's kind of what you have to do, assess the situation and—' she made speech marks with her fingers — '"prevent loss or damage to life and property".'

'Tough job.'

'I loved it. Every day different. Everyone has a story. People go through things that change them. It's easy to forget that.'

'Amen to that.' He slapped his hands on his knees and unfolded himself with a groan from the low wall. 'Good to chat. Maybe we could—' His mobile chirruped in his shirt pocket. Frowning at the screen, he turned away to answer it.

'Hi — yes, no. No, I can't, I've had a drink. No, Tasha. Look, surely it can wait, couldn't you . . . ?'

Fran turned away, curious and a bit embarrassed. Still clutching Tomos, she rose carefully to her feet. Collecting the stacked dishes in one hand, she contemplated the glasses and decided not to risk juggling them along with the baby, and quietly returned to the cottage to locate the child's keeper.

Would he have done Tasha's bidding — whatever it was — despite his couple of beers, had she not been there? Did he see her as the perpetual keeper of the law, even in retirement? She relinquished Tomos to a cooing aunty in the kitchen and helped out the other women with the washing-up and bins, making chit-chat as her mind travelled back over her conversation with Wyn.

Just what had he been about to say that had begun, *Maybe we could . . .* ?

Because at that point, following on from their nice, matey chat, she would've said yes. Now, though . . .

She'd slammed the door on complicated relationships a long time ago. After all this time, she was beginning to wonder whether she could even cope with a relationship. Other people's needs and nose hair. Did that make her selfish?

Obviously, said her inner voice. *You're all take and no give, you are.*

In Elin's welcoming cottage, among her family, she wondered, as she always did around strangers, how many were really happy with their lots, and if they were, what was the secret? What did they sacrifice of themselves to a relation-ship? What compromises?

Fran didn't think she'd ever compromised. She'd always retained the high ground in a relationship. The control, if you wanted to be picky about it. Was that so bad? Most women had little control over their lives as far as she could see. Once they had children, that seemed to be it. From what she'd seen, their lives became submerged in a dreary welter of caring for others while nobody cared about them. A jaded viewpoint, maybe?

Drying a large serving dish, she stared thoughtfully into the garden. A gang of children tore at speed round the lawn, hurling plastic projectiles at one another. A group of men refereed, joining in and mending the flying things, and as

Fran's gaze travelled across the garden, she saw a table full of women laughing, chatting and drinking. Several bottles of prosecco and wine sat empty between them. Only one held a baby and that was fast asleep. It was strange how people separated into genders so readily the older they got.

If she'd ever been among a gathering of non-police women at a police function, all they seemed to do was complain about their men. They'd suddenly be aware of her listening to their conversation, remembering that she worked with their men, and become uncomfortable and secretive. Perhaps she saw different facets of their men, and couldn't always recognize them as described by their partners. Those men were her workmates, her backups, all in it together, them and us. Often flawed, scared, helpless, exasperated. Loyal to one another. Admittedly, she never had to go home with them afterwards.

Usually the sole woman in a man's world, she'd found it difficult to align herself with other women, simply becoming the odd one out among both genders.

So what was it she wanted from her life now? How did she see herself in ten years' time? Knitting in a rocking chair? Skiing down the Alps? Paddling a canoe down the Congo, maybe? Since her heart attack, she couldn't project a future at all. Every day seemed like a mountain to conquer, and the incident yesterday made her realize that she needed to be a whole lot nicer to her body and stop taking it for granted.

Stacking a set of prettily patterned plates, she decided that Wyn probably had no intention of asking her anywhere, and was simply relieved to find that she wasn't still ganging up on him in the accusation of assault.

Maybe we could . . . avoid each other from now on? That was no doubt what he'd wanted to say. Besides, he had enough on his plate with a school to do up, the entire village relying on his plumbing and electrical skills, and a needy ex-wife. Much too complicated for Fran. And life was about more than men, wasn't it? She needed to spend some time on her own needs. Allow herself to be selfish.

Full of food, gin and sunshine, she was once again overcome with tiredness. She went in search of Elin to say goodbye.

'Thank you, Elin, it's been a lovely afternoon.'

'Oh, thank *you*! Your frittata was delicious, you must give me the recipe.' Elin rose and kissed her cheek. 'Glad to see that you and Wyn have hit it off,' she whispered in Fran's ear. 'I said he was a gentleman, didn't I?'

'Aah — mm! You did!' Fran nodded, aghast that Elin was matchmaking and hoping Wyn wasn't still in the front garden. 'See you soon, Elin. Bye everyone!' She raised a hand and felt quite guilty that some people had remembered her name, despite her not remembering any of theirs.

She got to the front door with her backward-facing waves before colliding yet again with Wyn, poised to duck inside.

'Oops — oh, Fran! Are you going? Sorry, I was hoping to catch you.'

'Yes, ha ha, off for another marathon sleep before I pass out, you know me!' Fran ducked beneath his arm and scarpered, squeezing her eyes shut with embarrassment. He'd think she was bonkers now. But she was rubbish at relationships. Selfish, impatient, bossy. She was too old to change now. And the whole idea of sex, with this horrific zip from neck to navel?

She couldn't bear the idea of anyone seeing her naked, bifurcated by her livid, lumpy scar. It had been bad enough buying a bra after surgery, even though the ladies in the store had been kindness itself. Plus, imagining herself being under the village microscope while she tried a new relationship on for size filled her with horror.

She'd enjoy this summer by the sea, enrol in all the classes, get herself fit again and get back to her life. Whatever direction it took. And with no complicated men in it.

CHAPTER FOURTEEN

She was bonkers, Wyn decided, watching her neat hips and swingy red hair flounce away for the second time since he'd met her. Had he read their chat this afternoon all wrong? They'd got to know each other some more, ascertained they were both single — which was always useful to know and saved making a fool of yourself — and he was about to suggest that they hook up for a coffee somewhere, sometime, and then, *boof,* she'd had a personality transplant and rushed off.

Standing in the middle of Elin's garden party and oblivious to the children rushing around him and people chatting, he cast his mind back for some clues. He'd never been brilliant with women, preferring the uncomplicated company of men, but since Tasha had left he seemed to have more women friends, and enjoyed the particular nuances of their conversations. From being furious and uncomprehending that his wife had left him, he'd begun to understand, following conversations with women friends, why it might have happened.

He would never forgive PC Knobhead for stealing her away, dazzling her with bright lights and baubles and all the things he'd never acknowledged that she needed. Hadn't he indulged her requests for bigger, brighter and better though, by giving up the teacher training he'd loved to pursue commercial diving? She was never going to be happy on his teacher's pay, in the little two-up two-down on the edge of a suburb, which was all they'd been able to afford then. Maybe if they'd had children . . .

His brain tuned in to what his eyes were looking at: dads with babies on their laps and sugar-high kids charging about. Mums gathered together, laughing, adding to the collection of empty prosecco bottles. Would he and Tasha have been like that? He could see himself in the dad role, but could he see Tasha among the other mums, happy and joking in a seaside garden, pawed by sticky children and managing to mop up spills, vomit and nappies without seemingly pausing for breath? He shook his head ruefully. Tasha would have had kittens about spoiling her designer outfit.

Elin appeared beside him. 'Penny for them, Wyn?'

He smiled down at her. 'Great party, Mrs P. You have a lovely family.'

'I have a very big family,' Elin said, settling herself on a chair beside him, her gaze travelling around her garden. 'And I love them all. Even the ones I don't like.' She grinned up at him and he laughed. 'So, you and Fran then?'

He shook his head. 'I think that's a non-starter. She just cut me dead, and I thought we were getting on okay.'

Elin was silent for a long moment. 'I think Fran has a lot to think about at the moment. Heart attack, forced into retirement from a job she loved, health all over the place — and the first thing she sees you doing is having a punch-up with the local copper . . . no wonder she's steering clear. She probably doesn't know if she's coming or going, poor lamb.'

'But she knows I wasn't . . . I didn't actually . . .' Wyn began. 'Oh God, and I found her yesterday sobbing her heart out on the stairs because she'd overdone it.' He slumped forward, resting his elbows on his knees. 'You're right, Mrs P. I hadn't really thought about that.'

'Just take it slowly. She seems a nice girl. Anyone who puts up with having Arthur dumped on her all afternoon has to be nice.'

Wyn laughed. 'She was chuntering away to him when I found her earlier. I think she'd hypnotized him.'

'Well, good for her. His mother probably never gets off her mobile long enough to speak to him.' Elin's tone was crisp, and Wyn was instantly transported back to his schooldays. 'Hmm, listen to me, I'm like an old woman complaining about the "youth of today". If you're at a loose end, Wyn, I could do with some muscle to help me wind this party up. Time they all went home. Some of us need a nap, y'know.'

Wyn did as he was told. He very much doubted that she needed a nap, but you didn't argue with Mrs Pritchard, even when you were six foot five and nearly fifty.

CHAPTER FIFTEEN

The knock on Fran's door for a swim came in the shape of a WhatsApp message from Caitlin a few days later.

Tomorrow, 7 a.m., outside yours — tide is halfway in, sea is forecast as flat and sun will shine. Bring loose, warm clothes to change into, hat/gloves, towel, hot drink, something yummy to eat for afterwards.

Fran managed a brief *Okay* with trembling fingers and spent half the day deciding what clothes to take, what to eat and how to make a hot drink on the beach — and the other half visiting the loo. Her stomach was an internal Vesuvius and she began to wonder whether she'd even get to the water's edge without needing to rush back for the toilet.

She visualized herself frolicking in the sparkling water with the Sea Sisters, laughing merrily before scampering up the beach, glowing with good health, to sit with the ladies and sip her hot drink as they exchanged banter. Her inner voice nearly wet itself laughing.

'What?' she told it. 'Shut up. It could happen!'

To distract herself, she joined the village Facebook hub and enrolled in Pilates, sewing and craft classes, some of which would occupy the long, solitary evenings. There was textile art the following evening, which she'd always fancied.

At six forty-five the next morning, she was waiting at the cottage door, after a sleepless night worrying that she'd over-sleep. The swimsuit she'd bought at the triathlon stalls was plain black, but with a high neck at the front that completely covered her scar. It was actually pretty slinky, she'd decided, admiring her reflection, despite the churning in her stomach. She had the rucksack she'd brought with her for walks, con-taining a T-shirt, underwear and towel, a teabag and mug, plus her stainless-steel bottle containing boiling water.

She'd struggled with the 'something yummy' and decided on a banana. Healthy and full of energy. A hat and gloves joined the rest of the items, although she couldn't imagine needing them. It was nowhere near cold enough to wear a woolly hat, for goodness' sake.

Slam, bang, 'Morning!'

'Ready for it, Fran?'

'Loving the hair colour, Wendy!'

'Morning, ladies,' Fran hailed them shakily from her doorway. Five of them. All around forty to sixty, she guessed, so she fitted right in. Caitlin, Wendy — her hair dyed a brilliant flame red — Cora, Lila and another lady she hadn't met yet. Fran's nerveless fingers clutched the holdall as she stepped through the front door and locked it behind her. First problem — where to put the key? There was a little zipped pocket on the inside of the bag and she tucked it in there.

Her brain told her in its sly voice, *Now it'll fall into the sand and be gone for ever. Or stolen. The cottage will be broken into, all your possessions stolen, the walls will be daubed with filthy slogans and you'll have to explain to April, Ken and Gavin that you're not nearly as trustworthy as they'd imagined. Fancy going into the sea and leaving everything on the beach, unattended! Asking for it.*

'Shut up,' she told the voice, silently but firmly, even though, privately, she agreed.

Her knees turned to jelly and she seemed to have for-gotten how to swallow as she brought up the rear of the little convoy. Barely listening to the banter of the other ladies as they stowed their gear into their bags, she changed in silence. She set her watch to Outdoor Swim so that she could keep an eye on her pulse rate, trying not to notice that her hands shook already.

'Come on then, Fran, let's go.' Caitlin carried a net bag of brightly coloured plastic balls and Fran inspected them, her arms wrapped around her body. 'First off,' Caitlin continued, as they strolled towards the sea, 'nice bathers. And you're not going to learn to swim today, so you can stop panicking.'

Fran felt her shoulders sag with relief, and at the same time was aware of her disappointment. She looked enquiringly at her friend.

'Today,' announced Caitlin, 'is just for play!' Sprinting away from Fran, she dropped the bag closer to the water's edge and emptied the balls onto the sand, kicking them backwards to the girls.

'Oh God, I can't run — I'll knock meself out!' panted Wendy, her red hair sunlit into crimson. Holding her considerable chest with both hands, she aimed a kick at the nearest ball and missed. 'Stupid thing!' She bent to pick it up and the breeze rolled it away. Colourful swear words peppered the air and Fran laughed as the ball settled enticingly close to her. She picked it up.

'To me, Fran, to me!' Caitlin yelled, dancing about with her hands in the air, her feet splashing in the shallows. Fran underarmed it in a high lob and Caitlin performed a dramatic dive after it, falling with a splash into the water. The ball returned to Fran on a tiny wave, and as she bent to retrieve it, one of the other girls barrelled past, whipping it away from her with a laugh. She threw it back to Caitlin and Wendy, and Fran found herself playing piggy in the middle, with all the balls from Caitlin's bag in play.

Fran couldn't pinpoint the moment when she realized she was in the sea just past her knees. She was too busy having fun. As she stared down at herself, a ball bounced off her head. She laughed aloud.

'You rotters!'

'You're so *English*, Frannie!' Caitlin cackled. 'Whaddya think of our Welsh sea then?'

Fran grinned back at her. 'I think it's *bluddee luvlee*!' she shouted, imitating their accents. She picked up a passing ball and hurled it at Caitlin. It missed her completely and Caitlin howled with laughter.

Scrabbling for a footing, Fran was caught off balance. She toppled headlong into the water. Jumbled thoughts crashed together:

The girls will laugh at me.

I'm so clumsy.

It's only water . . .

I'm going to die.

Her fists thrashed the water as she fought to stand, her eyes squeezed shut, her heart pounding in the dark cavern of her terror.

'It's okay, Fran, you're okay!' They stood her up and she gasped, coughing, throat raw, willing herself not to cry.

She would never be like them. She might as well give up now. It had been just a moment, in a scant couple of feet of water, and she'd lost it.

Caitlin was made of sterner stuff though.

'Splash your face, you have snot everywhere,' she commanded, and Fran, holding back her tears, did as she was told. 'Now blow your nose. Good girl.' Caitlin clapped. 'I bet you wouldn't have done that ten minutes ago. At least you went in, *and* you looked as if you were enjoying yourself.'

Fran nodded, surprised. It was all true.

Caitlin nodded firmly. 'Okay. Let's finish on a positive note, shall we? Time for my hot choccy! Make sure you've got all the balls, ladies!'

'Now there's a sentence you don't hear every day,' said Wendy nearby. Fran smiled shakily, touched that two of the ladies took an arm each as she waded out of the sea.

'It's surprising how wobbly you can feel, coming out,' said Cora. 'I went flat on my face coming out of the sea once.'

'Oh, well you're a fine one to be helping someone else then, Cora!'

'You're clumsier than I am. I didn't see you catch the ball once!'

'That's because you can't throw straight, woman.'

Despite their gentle ribbing, Fran felt their arms firmly linked around hers and was comforted. Tears lurked just behind her stiff smile. She wanted to curl up in a ball away from everyone and wail with self-pity. Her throat was sore. She was a failure.

Had she really thought that, buoyed up by their positivity, she'd instantly overcome her terrors and bound fearlessly into the sea? Was she really that stupid? And yet, she reminded herself, as Caitlin had pointed out, she'd managed ten minutes or so in the sea. The actual sea! She glanced over her shoulder at the dancing, sparkling waves, and that long submerged memory bubbled into her mind . . . and faded away again, like a dream in the morning.

'Well,' Caitlin said, as they sat in the sunshine, sheltered from the wind by the dunes and sipping their hot drinks. 'Good start, Fran. Probably not as bad as you thought, I'd say. Definitely something to work with.'

Fran eyed her. Not as bad? It had been awful. Every fibre of her being felt ashamed. She wanted to run away and hide. She sighed.

'Thanks for being here for me this morning, ladies. Without you, I couldn't have even gone in the little way I did, and I'm sorry if I spoiled your swim. But . . .'

'. . . but maybe you need a bit more expert help than we can provide,' finished Caitlin.

'Yeah,' Fran agreed on a long exhalation. That got her off the hook. She could enjoy their company for the rest of her stay and not feel obliged to join them in the sea.

'And I know exactly where we're going to get it,' Caitlin wound up triumphantly, to Fran's consternation. 'Elin was our games teacher! She'll do it.'

'Oh. Excellent.' Fran gawped at her. But even as her heart drummed, minute bubbles of excitement rose and popped too. The tiny glimpse of the freedom of the sea had made her greedy for more. Surely she could overcome this. She'd survived a heart attack, after all. She'd arrested horrible, nasty bad guys, dealt with dead people and terrifying situations. She was tough. She could do anything. Couldn't she?

'Elin took us through our life-saving awards,' Wendy said, hugging her knees. 'Bloody hell, she was a brute. Like a sergeant major. Kick harder! Straighten your legs. Keep your head still! Stop talking! Ten more lengths and fifty push-ups afterwards!'

'She's joking,' Caitlin said quickly, frowning at Wendy.

'Only about the push-ups,' Wendy said gloomily. There was laughter, as there always was following anything Wendy said, and Fran saw her eyes crinkle with humour as the girls teased her.

'Did you ladies all grow up here?' she asked, making a face as she bit into her banana, already turning black from being bumped about in her bag. She was bringing cake next time.

'Quite a lot of us, I think,' said Caitlin, looking around at the faces.

'I don't know where any of my school friends are now,' Fran said, holding the slimy banana skin between her finger and thumb and wishing she'd brought a rubbish bag. 'My parents were what you'd call free spirits. I was never in one place long enough to put down roots.'

'What did your parents do?'

'They worked in films. Still do, occasionally.'

'Wow — but that's so exciting!' Cora's eyes widened. 'Do you know anyone famous?'

Fran laughed. 'Probably. People dropped by. I suppose I took it all for granted. They were quite normal. Mum's a make-up artist and Dad's a cameraman. They're both also

153

supporting actors when the opportunity arises. We didn't even live in a house for most of the time. We once lived on a barge in London.'

'Wow, that sounds brilliant!'

Fran thought about it. 'It was a nightmare, with Mum being terrified of water, wittering on about it and expecting me to fall in and drown at any minute. She used to make me wear a buoyancy jacket just to go outside.'

'And a lead, so they could reel you back if you fell in,' Caitlin said, straight-faced.

Fran stared at her for a moment and then laughed. 'Yeah. Bonkers. It was probably one of Dad's ideas. Maybe he thought it would be the perfect exposure therapy — or they were living there for free, which is more likely.'

'And they're still alive, your folks?'

'Yep, and very much kicking. They have a monster motor home and go round the world in it. Sort of retired but they'll do anything if they fancy it.'

'Wow, how exciting! Sounds amazing.'

'It does, doesn't it?' Fran said, cupping her mug. 'They came back to look after me when I came out of hospital.'

'Aw, that must've been nice, to spend some time with them.'

Fran grunted. 'Mm.' She was still mentally unpacking their time together after her surgery and wondering if she really knew her parents at all.

'Brexit's probably clipped their wings then . . .' the lady Fran didn't know said.

'Apparently not,' Fran told her. 'They spend a lot of time in the non-Schengen countries and back in the UK, and seem to know enough people to be able to park up on various country estates and drives, use the washing machine, that sort of thing.'

'So they're free spirits — and you joined the police,' Caitlin said succinctly.

Fran laughed. 'Yeah. Make of that what you will.'

'Sounds like typical youthful rebellion to me,' Wendy said. 'But enough psychoanalyzing poor Fran, I've got things to do!' She scrambled to her feet. 'I can't do the next couple of days. We'll check the tide and I'll post it up. Fran — if anyone can help you, Elin can. You're mistress of your own destiny. Okay?'

'Okay.' Fran nodded, getting up awkwardly and brushing the sand off. 'Thanks, Wendy.'

'I'll speak to Elin and be in touch, okay?' Caitlin picked up her holdall. 'And don't be downhearted. We'll sort it.'

Fran felt a lump in her throat as they went their separate ways. If she felt like a useless failure before, she felt like an even bigger one now. And the girls were so determined for her to succeed. If she had half of their determination she'd have swum the Bristol Channel by now. Glancing down at her watch, still recording her as if she were in the sea, she allowed herself a small smile. At least her watch had faith in her.

Well, she told herself — *even the longest journey starts with a single step*. And she'd taken that step. Putting the kettle on for a coffee later, she realized that she hadn't once worried about baring her scar to the girls as she'd got changed. Another baby step.

CHAPTER SIXTEEN

Wyn tapped on Elin's door late one afternoon about a week after her garden party. It was ajar as usual, and he called inside.

'Mrs P? It's Wyn. You wanted a job doing?'

'Come on in, Wyn.'

He trailed her voice into the kitchen, where she was stationed before a laptop, her fingers tapping busily on the keyboard.

'Sorry, lovely, won't be a sec . . . I just need to . . .' Elin turned her head towards him briefly but her eyes remained glued to the screen. Smiling at the sight of her focused like a teenager on her computer, he pulled up a chair and waited, his elbows on his knees, hands clasped loosely.

The last time he was here, he'd had that long chat with Fran. He hadn't seen her since. Not that he'd been avoiding her, he lied to himself. He'd been turning their conversation over and over in his mind and still arrived at no conclusion other than Elin's explanation. He'd thought she was lovely. Refreshingly genuine company. And he'd wondered since how he could retrieve their earlier ease.

He gazed around the cool kitchen and resolved to stop thinking about her. She'd be gone at the end of the summer anyway. And, he thought, it wasn't as if he didn't have enough to do. The roof of his school was now watertight, and he was doing well with the pointing on the old stone. Most of the windows were in now, except for the ones that hadn't fitted and needed to be remade. The building was well on the way to being weatherproof.

It was all going according to plan, albeit slowly, given the usual glitches that occurred with building projects. Except for one thing. It didn't feel like home. Just like a project. Should he sell it, maybe? Move away? Start afresh? That felt wrong too. As if he were running away. He was stuck. In limbo.

Elin gave a final decisive bash on the keyboard, hit save and closed the lid of the laptop.

'Wyn, I do apologize. Thank you so much for coming. Tea? G and T? Beer?'

He eyed her, a smile lifting one side of his mouth. 'Depends what you want me to do.'

'Have a beer, if you're not driving.'

'Are you trying to butter me up?'

'You must be thinking of someone else.' Elin placed a pint glass and a can of draught beer before him. 'I can't pour it without making a milkshake, so you'd better do it. I'm celebrating with a G and T.'

'Celebrating what?' Wyn tilted the glass and poured the beer slowly into it. Elin returned to the table with a vast round gin glass, full to the top with clear liquid, ice and a slice of lime, and chinked her glass with his.

'I'm doing a course.'

'Really? What have you chosen?'

'Art appreciation. After something Fran said recently, as it happens. I've spent my whole life being academic, and now I want to be—' she waved her arms about — 'more . . . bohemian. I want to know more about what I'm looking at when I go to galleries.'

'Well.' Wyn lifted his pint to her. 'I'll drink to that. Mrs P, you're amazing. You never let the grass grow under your feet, do you?' He lifted his glass towards her in a salute and

157

took a long swallow. The beer was chilled and slipped down his throat nicely. 'Always on the go, you are.'

'Mm. Got to be done, hasn't it? We're only here once. Now then.' She leaned forward. 'This is the reason I called you.'

'*Okaay*. I'm intrigued.' Wyn compared his own life. He was always on the go too, but was it a way of fending off the real decisions about his life? 'Want me to build you a study in the garden?'

'No — although that's a rather nice idea.' Elin sipped her drink with a thoughtful look in her eye. 'I've been asked to do something, and I *could* do it, but I'm not really going to have the time while I'm doing this course, and you'd do it so much better anyway.'

'You've lost me.'

Elin got up and opened her capacious larder, fishing out a family bag of crisps and cheesy nibbles. Opening them into a large, colourful ceramic bowl, she placed them on the table before him. Wyn wondered if his home would ever be this welcoming. His hand reached out seemingly of its own accord and scooped up the salty snacks. Chewing and sipping satisfied the inner man even as he continued his mute inquisition of Elin, who was wearing an expression of complete innocence.

Eventually, and clearly judging when he was appropriately full of beer and crisps, she broke the silence. 'It's a teaching job.'

'I haven't taught in—' he shrugged — 'years. As you know.'

'Swimming.'

Wyn sat back as if he'd been shot. He shook his head, folding his arms. 'No.'

'Wyn, you were the most promising young teacher I ever laid eyes on. You can do anything.'

'I can't do that.' Wyn spread his hands before him and was horrified to see that they were shaking. He clasped them together beneath the table. 'I can't. Please don't ask me.'

Elin got up and went to the fridge, bringing out another can of draught beer. She placed it before him. 'You can stand on the side, just like you always did. You don't even have to get into the water.'

She was calm and waited for him to come back to her. He was ten again, and she was giving him a pep talk about rugby. He rubbed a hand across the back of his neck, feeling the sweat there. Did she know about his fear of the water? How? He'd never told anyone. Nobody.

'You don't know what you're asking.'

'This is for someone who's been terrified of the water since they were very small. And that fear has been compounded by the mother since. As a consequence, no swimming ability or confidence around the water at all. You can help with that. You got generations of children swimming.'

Wyn nodded. 'I did, didn't I?' He stared at the beads of condensation collecting on the pint glass as his mind travelled back over the years. 'I loved it. Getting the kids to play, be frogs, bark like dogs. They didn't even know they were learning to swim.'

'That's what you need to do with this person,' Elin said, gently. 'Make it fun. Get them to lose the fear.'

'I don't know . . .'

'I do. You'll be brilliant.'

'I'm . . . scared.' He dipped his head, ashamed of the words as they left his lips.

'It's okay to be scared,' Elin said, patting his arm. 'This person is scared too. It's what you do with that fear that counts. It'll be good for both of you.'

'Hmmph.' No amount of beer could make Wyn's mouth feel moist after that.

'Do you still clean the Edwards's swimming pool?' Elin asked, with the studied, casual air he knew so well. Elin always had a plan. 'Perhaps they would let you borrow it? Only, I'd say that somewhere where you have some control, rather than the sea, would be the best way to start.'

Wyn grunted. 'Mm. Like I have any control over anything else in my life.'

159

Elin fixed him with a hard stare, and even at his age, he winced. 'Being sorry for yourself gets you nowhere, Wyn Morgan.'

He flung his hands up. 'Okay! I know when I'm beaten.' Hunkering forward, he crossed his ankle over one knee and pulled on it to stretch his leg muscles. 'But I chucked all my dive toys and stuff in the move.'

Predictably, Elin said, 'I'm sure I've still got a bagful. Let's go and have a look, shall we?' She was off the chair and out of the room before Wyn had even lumbered to his feet. He felt like Gandalf to her Frodo. How did she remain so nimble at her age, he wondered, ducking as he followed her up the narrow stairs of the cottage.

The spare room was rammed with what Wyn could only describe as 'stuff'. He pivoted in the centre of the space, taking in the loaded shelves, boxes with bulging lids and over-stuffed bags hanging on hooks. Elin seemed to know exactly where everything was though, and directed him to a clear box labelled *Pool* beneath several other boxes. Incapacitated and awkward as he was, it took him a while to free it from the teetering columns of storage.

Rummaging through the shapes that sank or floated, and wind-up toys that swam or quacked, they reminisced about classes they'd run and children they'd taught.

As Wyn kneeled on the floor, snatches of their conversation returned to him, and he said, slowly, 'So, how old is this child?'

'About your age, I'd guess.'

'What?' Wyn sat back on his heels. He shook his head and frowned at her.

'What?' Elin wide-eyed him. 'Does it make a difference? Adults have less confidence learning new skills than children, on the whole.' She shrugged. 'So it's the same approach. Maybe less barking like a dog . . .' She gave a wry grin. He gazed at her, exasperated. She'd drip-fed this whole thing at him and now it was a done deal, as far as she was concerned.

Years of ingrained respect for her inhibited him from saying what he thought. He huffed a long sigh.

'Do I know this person?'

'Undoubtedly,' Elin said, tipping her head to one side and narrowing her eyes. 'But you know I'm not going to tell you who it is, as I don't want you to have any preconceptions.'

'Oh, what? Mrs P!' Wyn ran a hand through his hair. 'Why the secrecy? Now I *am* suspicious!'

Elin chewed her lip and her gaze flicked around the room. Wyn noted her indecision. It was not like Elin to dither. 'We-ell — I just don't want you to think I have ulterior motives, or, well, erm . . .'

Wyn put his stern teacher voice on and was quite surprised that it was still lurking inside him. 'Tell me, or I'm not doing it. It's not fair to send me into the lion's den unprepared.'

'A good teacher is prepared for anything,' Elin quipped quickly.

Wyn raised his eyebrows and remained silent.

Eventually, Elin caved. 'Oh, okay. It's Fran.'

'Fran. Fran — retired cop, scared of nothing and nobody, rocks up to a punch-up outside a pub she doesn't know with a newly wired-up breastbone? That Fran? She's scared of water?'

'Yes. See, I said you'd have preconceptions.' Elin regarded him sternly. 'It's quite a sad story, actually.' She hesitated and then gave Wyn the gist of it.

'Hmm.' Wyn picked up a pink dive stick and waggled it as he thought. 'And you think she's going to overcome a deep-rooted fear chasing about after a few of these.'

'Well, no. Of course not. But you know how to build confidence. And she's keen.'

Wyn was silent for a long time. Fran would be the sort of person who'd need things proved to her. He couldn't see her as a 'whatever you say' type of learner. It would be a challenge . . . and despite his misgivings, he liked her. Perhaps it would be a chance to get to know her a bit better. And, somewhere buried deep down, he wondered selfishly if helping her might help him heal himself of his terrors too.

'I'm probably off my rocker for agreeing to this, but yes.'

'I'm pretty sure she'd pay you, Wyn, if that helps.'

'I'm sure that's something we could discuss,' Wyn said stiffly. 'I suppose I'd better coordinate the Edwards's pool and our schedules now.'

'I know the Edwards's pool is available this week,' Elin supplied instantly. 'I happened to see Gwynedd walking her cockapoos this morning, and she mentioned the new changing shed.'

Wyn gaped in astonishment and then bellowed a laugh, slapping a hand on his thigh. 'You told them I was already doing it?' He shook his head. 'Mrs P. You're a minx. You should have been in the diplomatic corps or something. What would you have done if I'd said no?'

Elin winked at him. 'I always like to look on the positive side,' she said enigmatically, nodding at the box of assorted pool toys. 'Shall we take this lot downstairs? There's some noodles, pull buoys and swim floats over there, and an inflatable flamingo . . .'

'What will I need that for?'

'Ice breaking?'

'The pool is heated . . .' Wyn laughed as he piled everything up and negotiated the stairs with the wobbly pink and yellow polystyrene noodles over his shoulder. 'I'd better go and write up my lesson plans.' He hesitated at the front door. 'You know she might not agree if she knows it's me and not you.'

'Fair point.' Elin tugged at her earlobe. 'Okay. I'll meet you there too, and then I'll just—' she clicked her fingers and twirled them — 'vamoose when it looks like it's all going swimmingly.'

'She won't fall for that.'

'Always with the negative waves! Go and write that lesson plan. I'll keep you posted.'

CHAPTER SEVENTEEN

The day dawned cold, cloudy and drizzly. Irritated and out of sorts since her failure to suddenly become a swimmer now that she'd decided to do it, Fran was restless. She'd been in Llanbryn for a fortnight now and, to her constant surprise, had settled into a pleasant routine. She walked twice, often three times a day, further and faster each time. She'd joined classes and met people. But there were no classes that day. Fran was enjoying them, even if her skills at sewing harked back to secondary school, which was the last time she'd attempted anything similar.

The textile class definitely appealed to her. More art-based, they didn't rely on her producing something wearable, and seemed to free her brain. She was noticing more these days. Shapes of wildflowers, how the leaves grew, colours. Her fingers twitched for a paintbrush, a mark maker of some sort. Art. Trawling the village Facebook hub in search of a distraction, she found it in the shape of the Art Hotel.

Curious, she clicked onto the website, delighted to see some really good examples of contemporary art. Situated on the Gower coast, and recently renovated from crumbling gentility to incorporate what had been the renowned Art Café, which had been destroyed by a huge storm, the whole

163

place looked stylish and amazing. She caught herself thinking guiltily: not at all what she'd originally expected of Wales.

It was exactly right for a trip out. She could go that morning. The knock on the door sounded as she was saving the details into her phone.

'Hello, Elin. Come in — coffee?'

'Thank you, lovely, but don't let me stop you doing something.' She stared pointedly at the phone in Fran's hand.

'Oh, you weren't — I was looking at the Art Hotel. Do you know it?'

'I haven't been since it was the Art Café. I've always wanted to go and somehow I never did.'

Fran's words tumbled out in a rush. 'Would you like to come with me, today? It takes less than an hour, according to Google Maps, so we could have lunch and a look round . . .' She stopped her headlong word assault. 'Sorry, you probably have plans, you're always so busy. Ignore me.'

'Not at all, and that fits in very nicely with something I've just applied for, as it happens.' Elin headed for the front door. 'I'll fetch my jacket and bag and see you back here in twenty minutes?'

'Lovely,' Fran said, tugging her fingers through her hair and already mentally changing her clothes. 'See you in a bit.' Halfway to closing the door, she called to Elin, 'Sorry, Elin, what was it you wanted?'

'I'll tell you on the way!' Elin bustled away into her cottage. She returned wearing a cornflower-blue cowl neck tunic over a pair of dark-wash jeans, topped off with a loosely draped patterned scarf.

'You look lovely!' Fran told her, taking in the carefully put-together details of the older woman's smart but casual outfit, right down to the tan ankle boots and coordinating bag.

'Thank you, my dear. As do you. Your hair is beautiful.'

Fran gave an involuntary glance at her own reflection in the full-length mirror near the front door as she stepped outside. Her jeans, fleece and trainers were perfectly functional, but seemed to lack any style or cohesion whatsoever. It was as if she were hiding inside them. But yes, she did have nice hair still. And her skin was good. That was something.

'Come on.' She grinned, pushing thoughts of clothes shopping out of her mind. She was surprised at how excited she was to go somewhere new. That was a good sign, she thought, remembering her crippling anxiety about driving to Wales. Time was healing. And they were going to see some art! 'We're Thelma and Louise on a road trip!'

'Without the mayhem and death, one hopes,' Elin said, straight-faced.

'Give it time,' Fran deadpanned. Elin laughed. The sat-nav located their position outside the village and Fran was prepared now for the crowded lanes, competing with over-grown hedges, tractors, ponies, loose sheep and dog walkers. Elin was a restful passenger who gazed calmly out of the win-dows and made no comment when Fran overshot a turning to the accompaniment of several swear words.

Once on the main roads though, they settled into chat-ting — Elin had a fund of anecdotes from her teaching days — and the journey passed quickly. Following the brown tourist signs for the Gower coast, Fran was gratified to find her driving skills returning, as she deftly negotiated the leafy suburbs and industrial estates of north Gower.

'Oh, it's so pretty!' Finally meeting the sea again, Fran's exclamation was involuntary. She'd been disappointed by the broad dual carriageway edging the coast, but as the road narrowed to a single lane, lined by tall pine trees, she could see two little islands, like teeth, jutting into the sea from the coast.

'That's the Mumbles, which gives the town its name,' Elin told her. 'It's said that, in Norman times, French sail-ors called the two islands *Mamelles*, meaning "breasts".' She shrugged. 'That's the story, anyway. Typical sailors, if you ask me.'

Fran laughed, turning right and driving up the main street. 'It's a busy place, isn't it?'

'Yes, plenty to see for a visit another time. There's a castle, a pier, shopping, a good restaurant along the front there . . .' Elin laughed ruefully. 'Sorry, I sound like a travelogue.'

'Not at all, it's great to have someone so knowledgeable with me. Do you get here often?'

'Not often, no. I have everything I need delivered these days. Thank goodness for the internet!' She turned towards Fran. 'It's kind of you to have invited me today. I don't get out of Llanbryn as often as I ought to, really. One can so easily become stuck in one's ways.'

'Aw, Elin.' Fran was quite surprised. Her neighbour always seemed so confident. 'I'm happy to drive you anywhere while I'm here, you only have to say.' Fran swallowed, remembering how nervous she'd been getting back behind the wheel and visualizing a glimpse of what it might be like to be buried in a small, out-of-the-way village and not able to drive. Getting about in London was a breeze by comparison — there was no end of public transport to choose from.

She pushed away the thought that barely anyone there spoke to you, you had to clutch your bag and be on the lookout for pickpockets on the Tube. That was the price you paid for city life, smart coffee shops, theatres and galleries. Even if she couldn't remember the last time she'd actually visited any of them.

It wasn't long before they reached the impressive wrought-iron gates of the Art Hotel, each pillar topped with a steel sculpture of a dragon. As Fran turned into the broad drive, she could see an airy orangery ranged along the front of the elegant Victorian hotel.

'Gosh. This is smart,' she muttered, peering at it. 'I feel distinctly underdressed. It sells itself as a seaside café with art!'

'You look perfectly fine, Fran,' Elin said. 'The Art Café *was* a seaside café. It was a lovely place to go, and not at all the greasy spoon type of café you might have imagined. It was bright and contemporary, and did the best cakes I've ever tasted in my life. I'm delighted that it survived, in whatever shape it is now. Fingers crossed the cakes are still good!'

166

'Right,' Fran said, reversing neatly into a space. 'Lead me to it. My stomach is rumbling.' She got out, stretching and looking about her as Elin gathered herself together. 'Those are interesting.' Fran pointed towards a collection of life-size horse sculptures grouped on the lawn and walked towards them for a better look. 'Goodness me. It's all driftwood. How clever.'

'Bathroom,' said Elin without preamble, bringing up the rear. 'And coffee. In that order.'

Smiling, Fran beeped the key fob to lock the car and they made their way into the Art Hotel entrance, following the clear signs into the extension that was marked as the Art Café.

With its blonde beams, black wooden-framed floor-to-ceiling glass, natural stone and rush textures and mixture of cool colours, the spacious orangery reminded Fran of the smart contemporary coastal eateries she'd seen on a visit to New Zealand. Display units along the same theme broke up the space into a variety of table sizes. The delicious aroma of freshly ground coffee hung in the air and chiller cabinets held a stunning variety of cakes and pastries.

'They've done this beautifully.' Elin's head bobbed in all directions. 'It's just like the old Art Café, with that huge window, but still somehow cosy and inviting. Very clever.'

'Oh my gosh,' Fran said, staring into the cake display. 'I can't decide. I might have to have cake for lunch too . . .'

'We could share,' Elin said.

'Share?' Fran was horrified.

Elin laughed. 'Cut two different ones in half and have half each. I'm not daft.'

They chose a gigantic, gooey lemon muffin and a towering, triple-layered jam and cream sponge and took a table near the huge panoramic windows. From their slightly elevated position, the view extended across the bay, and Fran sat gazing at it for a while. Elin took charge of slicing the cakes and pointed out where the original Art Café had been.

'They've done a good job of replacing it, as far as I can see,' Fran said. 'This cake though . . . Mmm.' She ate in silence, appreciating the tastes, and then looked around her.

'Do you know, I was so busy stuffing my face, I didn't even look for the art. I'm shocked at myself.'

Elin laughed, sending a small cloud of icing sugar puffing over her nose. She dabbed her face with a paper napkin and looked around her. 'I can see small things, ceramics and jewellery, in the display units. Is that the gallery, over there?'

Fran followed her gaze. How could she have missed it? It was a whitewall gallery, beautifully lit, and even from where she sat, she could see the glowing colours of the paintings hung there.

'I can't wait to have a look. But I'm not rushing this. It's heaven.' She nibbled a forkful of the moist sponge. 'By the way, what was it you came to tell me this morning, Elin?'

'Caitlin asked me to organize some swimming lessons for you, and I've done that.'

'Oh.' Fran put her fork down, the cake suddenly tasteless in her mouth. She recovered her manners. 'Erm, thank you, Elin.'

Sipping her coffee to disguise the feeling that her body was dissolving right there at the table, she stared sightlessly through the window, the fears of her childhood stacking up in her mind. That memory that hung just out of reach.

She shivered, becoming aware of what was before her eyes, and blinked reflectively. It was strange. She didn't have a problem *looking* at the sea. She could admire its vast blueness and the colours it reflected in the wet sand at sunrise. It was being in it that was the issue. And primarily, swimming in it.

But she had swum a width, once, when she was really little. She remembered how euphoric she was about getting a badge. Then, *something* . . . what had happened? And afterwards, all that time — no more swimming. It had dogged her life and it was time she nailed it. Did it matter that she couldn't remember what had happened? The more she strained for the memory, the more elusive it was.

After a pause, she said, 'So, when you say you've organized lessons, that sounds as if it's not you who'll be teaching me.'

168

Elin cocked her head to one side and fixed her with a bright-blue gaze. 'I will introduce you, but I think this teacher will be much better for you. I would have done it myself, but I've just enrolled in a course that will take up a lot of my time, and I don't like to give anything less than my best to something.'

'What course are you doing?' Fran clutched at the change of subject.

'Art appreciation.' Elin drained the last of her coffee. 'You piqued my interest talking about that painting at my party.'

Fran nodded. 'That sounds fascinating. I wanted to do history of art at university, but somehow I got funnelled into English as something more "useful". I didn't really mind — I loved English and English lit, but I always felt as if I'd missed out on the art.'

'What did you plan to do with your degree?'

'No idea. I think I did it to get away from home. I'd much rather have been working and earning.'

'So — what did you do afterwards?'

'Well. You'll probably think this is a terrible waste of an education. I got a job in the Tate Britain gallery.'

' The Tate? In London?'

'Yes.' Fran grinned. 'Don't get too excited. I worked behind the bar.'

Elin smiled. 'Every great dream begins with a dreamer.'

'I'd wangled my way into jobs there while I was at uni. Waiting at functions, bit of catering, runner on documentaries, anything I could, really. My parents were actually quite good at finding me those. They knew *everyone*.' Fran was silent for a moment, remembering. 'I've never really thought of that before.'

'So, what turned you towards a career in the police? It sounds as if you enjoyed your time in the art world.'

'I did. I loved it. I learned so much. I bombarded them with questions.' She laughed. 'I wanted to know about everything. Why were all the paintings the same at *that* time in history, what happened to make everything change *then*. When the museum was empty, I'd be the one with a magnifying glass on *The Execution of Lady Jane Grey*, with Fred the gallery steward telling me all about it. He was a retired teacher.' Fran tipped her head at Elin. 'I guess the learning never stops.'

'No, indeed.' Elin allowed a pause to settle. 'And the police? Forgive me for pursuing it, but it seems such an unlikely career after your background.'

'It does, doesn't it?' Fran stared through the huge windows. 'I think it was a combination of having no money, nowhere to properly live and needing a structure to my life. I couldn't live like my parents, in their chaos.' She huffed a mirthless laugh. 'While I was at uni, they took over my bedroom and turned it into a studio. They bought one of those Victorian day beds to replace my bed and that's where I slept when I came home. So when I wasn't there, they could use it for their models. Art classes.' She heard the bitterness in her voice.

'I've always wanted one of those day beds,' Elin said dreamily. 'They're very beautiful.' She glanced quickly at Fran and added hurriedly, 'But I'm sure they're not terribly comfortable.'

'No,' said Fran. 'They're not. It was like camping in your own house. Don't get me wrong, my folks were perfectly welcoming, but I always felt like they swept me further and further out the door.'

'Perhaps that was their intention.'

'Sorry?'

'Grown-up children can be reluctant to fly the nest and find their wings.'

'Did you kick your children out?' Fran didn't believe it for a minute, after seeing her among her family at the party. She was clearly held in high affection by all of them.

'Oh yes.'

'Oh.' Fran was silent, and if she admitted it, a bit shocked. After a while, she said, 'How did you do it?'

'Probably in a similar way to your parents, my dear. I knocked two of their bedrooms together and had an en suite put in.'

'Oh my God!' Fran laughed despite herself. 'That's a bit harsh, isn't it?'

Elin laughed too. 'Probably. But they all had lovely partners, and they were using me as a storeroom for all their junk while they "travelled", surfed, bummed about in bars . . .'

'Uh-oh . . . that sounds familiar.' Fran grimaced.

'Mmm. I'd asked them hundreds of times to sort their things out, and one day I judged that enough was enough and I took action.'

'What did they say?'

'They grumbled a bit and suddenly each of them became adults, bought or rented and settled down.'

'Wow.' Fran blinked. 'That's more or less what I did.'

'Works, doesn't it?' Elin smiled gently. 'Let's go and see what we can find in this gallery, shall we?'

'Good morning, ladies.' The blonde woman behind the desk smiled as they entered. 'I'm Lucy. Let me know if I can help at all.'

'Thank you.' Fran smiled back. 'It's a lovely gallery. Very nicely lit.'

'It is, isn't it? We're very proud of it.' Lucy pointed into the space. 'We have a new exhibition every two months — this one started last week.'

'It's done well already — I can see plenty of red dots!'

'Yes!' Lucy smiled. 'A really good start. Enjoy your browse, and just shout me if I can help at all.'

The paintings were vibrantly coloured, the confident brushstrokes capturing a wild and rugged coastline that Elin informed Fran was the Gower Peninsula.

'Gosh, the bits I've seen today look quite manicured compared to these,' Fran mused. 'I can see why they've sold so well. They make me feel as though I want to get an Ordnance Survey map and my walking boots and explore.'

'No reason why you couldn't do that,' Elin said. 'You can't get lost on a coast path.'

Fran laughed. 'Good point.' She left the main exhibition and stopped before an oil painting on canvas of a different scene altogether, a little over a foot square. After a moment, she realized she hadn't taken a breath. In the painting, a glowing red moon hung low in a sky of the darkest indigo, reflected in a deep-turquoise sea. A group of women swimmers stood in the sea, raising their arms to the moon. Completely naked, these were not stylized, impossibly thin model types. They were real women, with love handles, bingo wings, breasts and luscious big bottoms like peaches. The moonlight shimmered over their skin, illuminating them against the velvet dark sea.

Elin stepped alongside to see what she'd found. She chuckled. 'That reminds me of the other night at the full-moon dip.'

'It does, doesn't it?' Fran stared at it, unblinking. 'I love it. It's a real celebration of women's bodies.' She peered at the information card on the wall beside it. 'It's called *Beneath a Strawberry Moon*. What *is* a Strawberry Moon?' She threw an enquiring glance towards Lucy at the desk and was then horrified as she waddled towards them. She was hugely pregnant.

'This is one of my favourites,' Lucy began. 'A Strawberry Moon is—'

'Go and sit down again,' Fran said. 'Please. You're making me feel bad for getting you up. I'll come to you and you can tell me there.'

'I'm fine, really,' Lucy said, even as she trundled back to the desk. 'I'm not due for weeks!'

'Oh my goodness. Shouldn't you be on maternity leave?' Elin frowned and Lucy laughed.

'I *am* on maternity leave! I only popped in to collect something and *wham*, here I am working again! My boss is a slave driver, I tell you.'

'Really? In this day and age? That's shocking.' Fran tut-ted. 'Would you like me to have a word, or email and tell them how uncomfortable you are? I must say, that's made me view this place in a whole new light, it's—'

Lucy held her hand up. 'Oops, I'm sorry, let me stop you there. It was naughty of me to tease you. *I'm* the boss. Well, I'm one of them, anyway. I'm literally covering for the usual assistant while she visits the dentist for a temporary repair. I volunteered. I had to force her to go, and she'll be back any minute. And it's lovely to be in here. I do miss it. It's my other baby.' She smoothed her belly with a smile.

'So, a Strawberry Moon is a once-a-year, every-year event. Never on the same date, and it's something to do with the moon being at its closest point to Earth along its orbital path. It's supposed to be the month of strawberry picking. I've seen it in real life as the skies are so clear here. Sometimes it is that red. Amazing. You'll be keeping an eye out for it this year now. Fingers crossed there's no cloud cover.'

Fran gazed at the painting and found herself stepping nearer. She looked at the price. Reasonable, she judged.

'Are there any more paintings by this artist?'

Lucy shook her head. 'No, sadly. We don't get many. That one only came in yesterday.' She turned her head to look at the painting and then back at Fran. 'What does it say to you?'

Fran said, still looking at the painting, 'It says freedom. Friendship. Fun. And bravery.' She took a deep breath. 'And it's telling me to step out of my comfort zone—' she glanced at Lucy, whose eyes had never left her face — 'and learn to swim.'

'Gosh. Good for you.' Lucy nodded. 'I learned to ride a motorbike when I was nearly forty. It completely changed my life. I left my controlling husband, married the most wonderful man, along with his beautiful daughter, and now we're having the baby I never thought I'd have.' She nodded firmly. 'Grab life with both hands. That's my motto.'

'I had a heart attack a few months ago,' Fran said. 'Those words resonate with me too.'

'Oh my gosh, you poor thing! And you're so young!' Lucy's brown eyes rested sympathetically on hers.

'Yep. My whole life has changed. I have no idea what to do with myself.' Fran heard herself as if from a long way off. She couldn't seem to help offloading to this woman. 'I'm now a police pensioner.' She laughed. It still sounded wrong. She couldn't possibly be talking about herself.

'My husband is police. He's a bike instructor at the training school now. I don't think he's ever going to retire.'

'I used to say that.'

'It's like a family, isn't it? I bet you miss it horribly.'

Fran blew out a long sigh, swallowing the lump in her throat. 'I do, and I don't. I mean, I miss being the person I was, when I was in it. I don't quite know who I'm supposed to be now.'

Lucy nodded. 'Aw, bless you. It's bound to take some getting used to. Healing comes first though. Don't skip that.' She was incredibly easy to talk to. Fran was astonished at how loose-lipped she'd become. It was a while before she realized that Elin had taken herself away and was perusing ceramic jugs.

By the time they'd regrouped for lunch, Elin had bought a pair of turquoise enamel earrings that exactly set off her eyes. Fran had bought the painting, and offered her services to work at the gallery should Lucy ever need someone temporarily during the summer.

She was still talking about it all the way home, the painting carefully wrapped and stowed in the car. It was, she acknowledged, the first time she'd felt enthusiastic about something in ages.

Hanging in her flat, it would be a wonderful reminder of her summer here. Her stomach lurched strangely at the thought of her flat. It seemed very far away.

'Thank you for a wonderful day,' Elin said as Fran parked outside their cottages. 'I'll pop over with some dates for our swimming lessons asap.'

Her words stoppered Fran's flow of happiness instantly. 'Lovely,' she said, trying to mean it. 'I look forward to it.' Waving goodbye to her neighbour, she stomped up the stairs to the lounge, staring out to sea restlessly. It was sort of dinner time but she was still full from her Art Café lunch. She picked up one of her unfinished textile projects, staring at it with unseeing eyes.

All she could think about was the forthcoming swimming lessons. How would she cope with them? She'd laid her fears out now to these people she hardly knew — and pride wouldn't let her back down. Not an option. Stabbing herself with a needle for the third time, she picked up her laptop and sat at the table before the window with it. She ought to check up on Gavin and Ally. Somehow her fingers clicked her parents' number to video call. They wouldn't answer, of course. They never did.

'Hello, darling!' Her mother's pixelated features danced across the screen for a moment or two before settling. The view skewed sideways as she angled her iPad. 'Look, James, it's Fran! Fran, darling! How lovely — we're coming to see you!'

Fran grinned at them, noting their evening gin and tonics and dish of olives. She wondered where they were. 'I'm not there,' she said. 'I'm in Wales.'

'Yes, we know! We rang to see how you were — you're very naughty to have gone off like that and not told us. We would have worried, you know! But we spoke to your young man, Gavin. What a lovely accent he has. It's so Welsh!'

Fran blinked. This was going a bit fast for her.

'He *is* Welsh. But he's not my young man . . . he's—'

Her mum was unstoppable. 'Married to Ally, yes, I know, but one of your little gang, wasn't he?'

Fran gritted her teeth. Her little gang? Did her parents think she was still fourteen? 'Er, so, where exactly are you now, Mum?' She peered out of the window, almost expecting to see her parents right in front of her.

'Gavin told us about the campsite by you — and right on the beach! It sounds gorgeous, although it's more than we usually pay — well, we *don't* usually pay, haha — but Gavin said there wasn't room to park the MoHo outside your cottage.'

Fran breathed a sigh of relief. 'So, um, when . . . ?'

'And — oh, it sounds so romantic, darling! What a lovely idea. We can't wait to see it, and Gavin said there was a little sea swim group there too that you're in, so that will be lovely. We can swim together!'

'We can *what?*' Fran felt her jaw drop. Had she heard correctly? 'Mum, when did you—?'

'Here you go, talk to Dad for a minute, I'm just going to top us up.' Her mother vanished from view, to be replaced by her father's kind, handsome face, his silver hair too long, as ever.

'Hello, love. Looking well. How are you doing? How's that ticker doing?'

'Hi, Dad. I'm fine. Are you really coming all this way to see me? And did Mum say she's *swimming?*'

'Mmm, of course we are, yes. We realized that we've never visited Wales, so we thought, why not? Plenty of places to camp for free there, it's all on the apps if you know where to look, and there are quite a lot of people we know there, to our surprise, so we can—'

'Dad? Dad! What did Mum say about—?'

'They've been asking us to visit for years, but we've always headed abroad for the sun, so we thought, let's have a change, why not? What was that about your Mum?'

'Is she swimming?'

'Hello, darling, back again!' The screen whizzed around and Fran's mum appeared, full glass in hand, licking her fingers. 'Mmm, delicious olives. Farmer's market! What's that? Swimming? Yes! Love it. Can't wait to meet your girls!'

'But . . .' Fran clamped her mouth shut, took a deep breath and tried again. 'Mum — you stopped me going anywhere near the water when I was a kid! You used to throw a total epi about the sea!'

'What? Really? Oh, how silly. I don't remember that. No. Surely not.' She gave a light laugh.

'You did!' Fran could hear her voice rising. Along with her pulse rate. 'You . . . you . . .' She shook her head, unable to line the words up in her head and even more unable to articulate them aloud. *You blighted my childhood with your fears! My life!*

'You're not still paying attention to that, surely,' her mother said. 'But that's just silly! I had a bit of a thing then, but that's all it was. A thing. You surely haven't let it bother you all these years, have you. Mm?'

'I, er, no. No! Me? Course not. Haha.' Fran's ears rang, drowning out her mum's next words. She couldn't bear to tell her mother that she still couldn't swim.

'So we'll be down there in three weeks or so, I think.' Her mum waved an airy hand. 'It'll take us a while to get there. I've got the dates somewhere, but you know, everything changes by the minute here. Ferries, all that. I'll send them to you when I find them. See you soon, darling!'

'Bye, darling!' her dad said, and then Fran heard him say, 'You always hog the screen, Jean. I hardly had a minute to speak.'

'Oh, stop moaning. You need to be more assertive, that's all. Bye, darling. See you soon! Looking forward to it, *mwah-mwah!*'

'Bye, Mum. Bye, Dad. See you—'

The screen blanked with a noise like a submarine and Fran stared at the dark laptop. She got up, fetched a glass and emptied into it the last inch or so of a red wine from one of the bottles Ken and April had gifted her in their basket. It was so delicious, she'd been eking it out at a small glass a day with her dinner, savouring each mouthful.

Her phone pinged a text alert from Gavin.

Your parents called. They're so great, aren't they? I let them know where you were.

There it was, the unspoken disapproval that she hadn't told them herself. He, of course, was in touch with his parents — halfway round the world — almost daily.

Thank you, she typed back to Gavin. After a pause, she added, *They're coming to stay, in their MoHo, in a few weeks' time.*

You know they could stay with you, Fran. Mum and Dad said you have to treat it like your own home.

Fran gulped. The thought of it made her shudder. *Thanks, Gav. I think they prefer their van X.*

She took a swallow of her wine. Chocolately, blackcurranty and heady. Probably a good thing there was none left

177

now. The way she felt in the wake of that video call, she could have necked back an entire bottle. She pushed the barely touched glass aside. It would just make her maudlin. Her brain whirled, reliving the conversation. Her mother was not only swimming, she'd totally dismissed Fran's fears as 'silly'.

As she took deep breaths to calm her rising heart rate, her legs fidgeted. The sky was streaked with shades of mother of pearl and peach as the sun began its descent into the sea. She needed to walk.

CHAPTER EIGHTEEN

The lowering sun sent long shadows across the sand. Wyn stared at them as he stomped over the beach. Grey, or blue? Hard to tell. He put the tips of his fingers together and squinted through the diamond-shaped hole. Purple? Who knew. Who cared? He blew out a long and irritable huff, stopping to stare at the sea, mirroring the duck-egg-blue sky and same as ever. Reliable. It had always been his touchstone, the sea. Through his whole life.

But not now. And now, Elin, with all that confidence in him, thought he could teach Fran to swim. What if she got into trouble in the pool and he couldn't save her? And she drowned because he was a coward? Or he did such a shit job of teaching her that she never got over her fear of the water, and blamed him for ever?

He shook his head, irritable with his revolving and negative thoughts. He was a good teacher. He was. And Elin had faith in him. He'd do a good job. Like he always did.

The shorter figure bounced off him and he put his hands out to steady them.

'God's sake! You're like a bloody door!'

He recognized the cross voice. 'Hello, Fran. Are you okay?'

'Gah. Hello. Yes. Sorry.' Fran blew out a long and exasperated sigh. 'Just, cross. Really, really cross.' She glowered up at him through wayward tendrils of russet hair. He looked down into her face, the frown, the pink cheeks and pursed lips and was overcome with a totally alien urge to sweep her up and kiss her.

'What are you cross about?'

Fran huffed again, scuffing her boots into the sand. 'Bah.' She stuffed her hands into the pockets of her jacket. 'Bloody bah! Are your parents still alive?'

'What? My dad is.'

'Oh. I'm sorry.' Fran looked out to the sea and back at him. 'That didn't come out right. Sorry about your mum, I mean. God, shut up, Fran.' She rolled her eyes. 'Um, look — do you fancy a drink?'

He grinned. 'Hell yeah. I could kill for a beer.'

'Really? Bad day?' She smiled up at him suddenly. 'I'll tell you mine if you tell me yours . . . Or not. Whatever.'

'Deal. The Mermaid?'

'Where else?' They fell into step, side by side.

Wyn shoved his hands into his pockets to dispel the strange urge to take her hand in his. His stomach rumbled. 'Have you eaten?'

'Sort of. Elin and I went to the Art Café today. We ate our bodyweight in cake.'

'The Art Café? I've heard of it. Or the Art Hotel, as it is now.' Wyn looked down at her. 'What did you think of it?'

'Loved it. I've offered to work there if they need someone when the woman who runs — owns — it has her baby.'

'Really? I didn't realize that was your thing.'

'Yep, I used to work in a big London gallery, before I joined the police.'

'Did you enjoy it?'

'I did.'

'How come you didn't stay?'

Fran made such a long and mournful sigh that Wyn regretted asking. 'It's a long story. Parent stuff again.' They walked in silence for a while and then she said, 'You know when you've left school, and you're kind of wondering who you are and what you're going to do with the rest of your life . . .'

'Mmm . . .'

'Did you make your own decisions about what you did, or did your parents make suggestions that you ended up doing, even though it wasn't really what you wanted to do?'

'Does anyone really know what they want to do when they leave school?'

'Evasive.'

Wyn laughed. 'Is it? I've never really thought about it. I suppose I haven't done anything that rocked the boat. Defied expectations. Or at least, my folks never said they were disappointed in me.'

'You're lucky.' Her tone was gloomy.

'Yes. I guess I am.'

'Apart from losing your mum, of course. Sorry.'

'Mm. You said.' He held the door of the pub open for her and shepherded her into the restaurant. Midweek, it was quiet and there was no sign of Tasha or her knobhead husband. He indicated a table for two. 'This okay for you?'

'Fine, thanks.' Unzipping her jacket, she took the seat facing the door and picked up the menu. 'I thought I wasn't hungry, but looking at this lot . . .'

'I can recommend the steak.' Mainly as that was what he usually had.

'I'm going for the Thai green curry. What's half and half?'

Wyn grinned. 'Chips and rice. Don't you have that in Ingerland?'

'Never heard of it. Sounds dreadfully unhealthy. I'll have that.'

'Good girl. We'll make a Welshie of you yet. Laverbread and cockles next.'

The same girl as last time arrived to take their order, her eyes flicking towards Fran. It would be all over the village

181

by tonight, Wyn knew. They both asked for a pint of the guest bitter, to his surprise. Fran took an inch off the top of her beer.

'Mm, just what I needed.' She licked her lips. 'Go on then. What's up?'

'Boring really.'

'Try me.'

'Building supplies. Builders. Tiles bloody nicked off the roof. Shitty copper. Sorry.'

'Shitty copper? This is . . . what's his name?'

'AJ. Yes.' He glared at the pint before him. 'Turns up, smirks, says what did I expect, putting Welsh slate on a roof? Course the thieving shits have had it away, we'll never find it. Et cetera, et cetera. Lazy bas—' He sat back, squeezing the table top with both hands as if it were AJ's ears. 'Couldn't be bothered. I'm better off looking for it myself.'

'Oh bloody hell. Is it covered by insurance?'

'Yeah. Just takes time to arrive.'

'Is Welsh slate very desirable?'

'Oh, yes. Plus it was the original slate, and because it's Welsh slate and not the cheaper Chinese slate, they can be taken off the roof and reused, and shaped to fit. Sorry, this must be boring as hell for you.'

'Not at all, it's fascinating. I had no idea. Theft of roof tiles isn't something I've come across in the city.'

'Well, it's likely long gone by now. But I've put feelers out already and if I find out who's had them, I'll go round and get them back myself. And then I'll give 'em a bloody good pasting.'

'Doesn't sound like your style. I thought you were the peacekeeping type.'

'I am.' He took a deep swallow of beer. 'Usually.'

'Did they take the tiles off the actual roof?'

'No. They waited until I'd spent days taking them off the roof and put them into neat little piles. All they had to do was load them up. And I slept right through it. Bastards. They were obviously watching. Or someone was.'

'You've not got CCTV, I guess?'

'Nah. But funny you should mention that. I've ordered a system. I know it's like slamming the door after the horse has bolted. But they won't be lucky second time around.' Their food arrived and Wyn was glad of the distraction. The steak made his mouth water. Knife poised over it, he cocked his head at her. 'So that's my tale of woe. What's yours?'

'This—' she stared at her plate — 'is huge. I am never going to eat it all. There's, like, a family portion of chips here!'

'You'll cope. You need feeding up.' He waved his fork. 'Story.'

She laughed, tipping her plate towards him and moving most of her chips onto his steak. 'I really don't need feeding up. Here you go. You'll only eat it off my plate otherwise, I'm sure.'

'Cheers. Stop procrastinating. Story.'

'Hmm. Okay. When I was little, I swam a width in the pool. I remember being so overjoyed. I was going to get a badge! And something must have happened, because afterwards, my mother was paranoid about going in the water, or even letting me anywhere near it.' She chewed thoughtfully.

Wyn was still. His heart beat faster. He forced himself to breathe and chew slowly.

'This is delicious. Really good.' She nodded at her plate. 'But I have no idea what the thing was that happened. Obviously it was something awful, something kind of "drowny", but nobody will tell me. I don't know if it was me, her or someone else.' She ate in silence for a while. 'So, as a result of my mother's fears when I was a kid, I can't swim.' She met his gaze. 'It's stupid, isn't it?'

'Why is it?'

'Well. *Everyone* can swim.'

'Not true.' He shook his head. 'I bet if you took a poll round this pub there would be a good many people who can't or don't. So, what happened tonight?'

'My parents are coming down for a visit.'

'That's nice.' She did another one of those long sighs. 'It isn't?' He signalled for more beers.

'In their motor home. They've booked into the camp-site.' She nodded her head in that direction. 'And Mum tells me, in this call, all tra-la-la and couldn't-care-lessy, that she's looking forward to going for a swim. With my swimming friends.'

Wyn was silent for a beat, listening for more. 'So . . .'

'And, when I mention that *she* was the one who stopped *me* swimming all those years ago, she says I'm being silly!' She glared at her food and then up at him. 'You're a commercial diver. I bet you think I'm silly too.'

He blinked. 'Not in the least.' *If only you knew* . . .

Their fresh beers arrived. 'I don't know how I feel about her now. Like I've been duped somehow. How is it that I've hung onto my fears — the groundless fears that she's instilled in me — and she's not only shaken hers off but completely dismissed mine?'

Wyn didn't know what to say. Should he mention that Elin had asked him to teach her? It seemed a bit late in the day now. On the other hand, how bad would it look if he'd said nothing until the actual lesson? He'd have to tell her. Before it went any further.

'And, uhhh . . .' She put her head in her hands, hidden behind the curtain of hair. 'I . . . oh God. She mentioned about us swimming together! And I can't. Not. At. All. Not just, can't swim very well, but a total non-swimmer. What am I going to do?'

'Have you ever tried having lessons?'

'Yes. Sort of. Shift work doesn't help. I went to one class but it wasn't really for total non-swimmers like me. It was for the ones who go up and down without ever getting their hair wet. They weren't having full-on snot-and-tears meltdowns like me.' She shrugged. 'I just got used to making excuses. And by coincidence—' she shredded a paper napkin — 'Elin has arranged for me to have swimming lessons here with someone. Someone she says is perfect for it.'

'Ah.' He swallowed, seizing his chance. 'That'll be me then.'

She laughed. 'Sure it is.'

He laughed too. 'No, really. It's me. I'm your teacher. Elin asked me.'

She glared at him and laughed again. 'You're kidding me. You? But, but, you're . . . Flippin' 'eck, you're the gardener, the pizza cooker, the plumber, electrician, punch-up referee and *vet* for all I know . . . Is there anyone else in this village except you?'

He shrugged. 'Sorry.'

'Are you really a swimming teacher?'

He nodded, chewing. 'Uh-huh. Fully qualified. I've taught hundreds of kids to swim. A few adults. Not much difference, except that the adults argue back.'

'I feel like an idiot now.'

'Why?'

'Telling you all that stuff about my mum. You must think I'm so feeble, hanging on to all this for so long.'

'Fran, believe me, I really don't. Fear is a physical thing as well as psychological. And it's how the human race has survived — fear of danger keeps us all safe. Otherwise we'd all be throwing ourselves off cliffs hoping we could fly. The good thing is, you've made the decision to do something about it.'

'Hmm. Good point.' Placing her knife and fork tidily together on the plate, she sat back, her eyes narrowed. 'Now you know I'm a nut job, are you still going to teach me?'

'Full-on snot-and-tears meltdowns?'

'Probably.'

He nodded. 'I like a challenge.'

She grinned. 'I want to be swimming before my mum gets here.'

'Swimming — in what way exactly? If we break it into measurable steps, it's a whole lot easier to tick off.'

'Okay.' She narrowed her eyes. 'Keeping myself upright and afloat, in my depth. Going along would be a bonus. Stylish would be utterly awesome.'

'Quantifiable outcomes.' He nodded. 'Apart from "stylish", which is a matter of opinion.' He laughed at her expression. 'When are they coming?'

'Few weeks . . . whatever that means, could be three or even four . . . dates are not their strong point.'

'Bring it on. You'll have to work your butt off, mind.'

Her mouth set mutinously. 'I'm up for it. You're not the only one who likes a challenge. Right. Pudding? To celebrate?'

They clinked glasses together. Both decided on sticky toffee pudding, Wyn's with custard and Fran's with cream. Telling him her tightly held secret seemed to open the floodgates, although it could also have been the effects of the second beer, and they chatted and laughed easily over their desserts. It was dark by the time they left the pub, and he walked her to her door.

'See you in the pool. I'll sort out times and days.'

'Okay. And, um — thanks, Wyn.' She smiled up at him. He wondered whether to kiss her cheek. He wanted to. 'Oh, and Elin has my mobile number. Night!' She gave a little wave and let herself in. 'And thanks again!'

Wyn strode home, listening to the sea whispering on the sand. If he could help her master her fears, perhaps he could deal with his own. *One thing at a time*, he told himself. *One thing at a time. Baby steps.*

CHAPTER NINETEEN

Fran couldn't decide whether she was excited or terrified. Neither could her heart, which drummed a tattoo in her chest as she waited for Wyn in Elin's kitchen, the day of her first lesson. It was only two days since their meal together. Fiddling with the high neck of the swimsuit she wore beneath her zip hoodie and walking trousers, she tried to breathe slowly and evenly.

'Oh bum. I've forgotten my underwear!' She whirled out of the front door into her cottage, located what she needed and stuffed them quickly into her pocket as she saw Wyn on the garden path. 'Morning!'

'*Bore da*! That's "good morning" in Welsh.'

'Uh-huh. Is my lesson going to be bilingual?' Her pulse threatened to jump out of her throat with nerves.

'Do you want it to be? Two birds with one stone?'

Her gaze travelled down his body, from the red rugby shirt, to the white shorts. Shorts being the appropriate word — there was a considerable quantity of muscular leg revealed beneath them and she blinked. She was pretty sure the players in the few rugby games she'd seen hadn't worn shorts this skimpy though. These days, they were much longer and looser. Wyn's had to be ancient. A nod to yesteryear.

'No. One thing at a time, please.' She took a deep breath. 'Nice shorts . . . Did I miss the memo? I thought we were swimming today?'

'Yeah, I know, I look like I'm about to run onto the rugby pitch, but I couldn't find my teaching kit. I was quite surprised to find these! They've got to be twenty-five years old.' He squeezed his thumbs into his waistband and breathed in, beaming. 'Still fit me too!'

'Really?' That was debatable. Closing her sagging jaw, she wrenched her gaze away, retreating into Elin's kitchen and stuffing her underwear into her rucksack. 'Wyn's here!' she announced unnecessarily, as Wyn blocked the light behind her. 'Are we all ready then?' She threaded her arms through her rucksack.

Elin glanced from one to the other, her eyes rolling briefly at Wyn's attire. 'Did you brush the cobwebs off those? You don't need me there. Off you go.'

In the corner of her eye, Fran saw Wyn's body clench. 'What? But you . . .'

'Come back and tell me how it went,' Elin said, opening her laptop. 'See you later!'

Dismissed, Fran and Wyn filed outside into the sunshine.

'Was she your teacher too?' Fran asked him as she climbed into the cab of his van, predictably covered in a fine layer of dust and sand and strewn with bits of invoices and sweet wrappers. She buckled her seat belt.

'Yeah. How can you tell?'

'No reason,' she said, straight-faced. 'Where are we going?'

'The Edwards's farm. Up the hill, just out of the village.'

'They have a pool, presumably. I'm not being thrown into a cattle trough or anything.'

'Yep. Posh one too — heated, with a cover!' As he drove carefully up the narrow lane, he told her how the pool was used for parties as well as lessons, and that payment was often made using the village's informal barter system. Wyn, with his assortment of maintenance skills, was well in credit, he said. Even so, Fran made it clear that she expected to pay for both the pool hire and for his time.

'It's really good of you to agree to this, Wyn. I don't expect you to do it for nothing.' She frowned at him. He said nothing, running a finger around the collar of his jersey and through his hair.

Gwynedd Edwards must have spotted them on her drive and bustled out to let them through into the garden. Her eyebrows rose into her steel-grey hair as her gaze landed on Wyn, carrying a bag of wobbling polystyrene tubes in rainbow colours.

'Good Lord, Wyn. You'll give an old lady a heart attack in those shorts, boy. It's not my birthday. Couldn't you find a pair to fit you?' She cleared her throat with a harrumph.

Fran smothered a laugh at the ludicrousness of the enormous Wyn being called a boy, and his mystified frown as he stared down at the offending garment. Gwynedd held out a thin but strong hand and pumped Fran's with enthusiasm. '*Bore da*! I'm Gwynedd, and you must be Fran. I've heard such a lot about you. What an amazing recovery — and so young for a heart attack!' She beckoned them to follow. 'Come along.'

She kept up a flow of words and Fran hurried to keep up with her rapid stride, wondering if, and what, the entire village knew about her. She blamed the classes. They did such a friendly line in interrogation though. She could have learned a lot from them, back in the day.

The glass structure housing the pool was attached to the back of the farmhouse. It would grace a small leisure centre.

'My goodness.' Fran gawped. 'This is huge! When you said there was a cover, I thought you meant like a blanket thing . . .'

Gwynedd laughed. 'It's marvellous, isn't it? Keeps me fit.' She held the door open for them and Fran breathed in a familiar smell. Chlorine. Her stomach bucked. Gwynedd showed her to the little wooden changing room. 'Shoes off here, please! Now, everything is cleaned and checked, so you don't have to worry about hygiene. But obviously, no weeing in the pool please or—' she glared at them both fiercely in turn — 'anything else.' She exited the pool as if she'd been shot from a gun.

'*Anything else?*' Fran repeated. Holding her trainers in one hand, she levelled a glare at the top of Wyn's head where he bent over his bag of wobbly tubes. She could see the tips of his ears turning red. 'Like what? What does she think we're going to do in here? Oh my God, is there one of those old posters in here that says "No running, jumping, bombing or *petting*"?'

His shoulders shook. He looked up and wiped the tears from his eyes.

'*Duw, duw*, sorry, she really is priceless.' He laughed aloud and Fran couldn't help joining in. 'Dear me, *no weeing in the pool*? How old does she think we are?' His almost silent, wheezing laugh was like that cartoon dog from years ago. What was it? Muttley. Dick Dastardly and Muttley. It was completely contagious. 'Are these shorts really that bad?'

'Let's just say there's not much left to the imagination . . . but at least it's taking my mind off the swimming.' Fran wept with laughter, holding on to the wall of the changing room, as Wyn wheezed with helpless mirth. 'Oh dear . . .'

'Oh no! I'm so sorry. I might have to actually buy a full-length mirror. I only saw myself in the reflection in the van. Which is filthy . . .' He wiped his eyes with the hem of his rugby shirt and Fran caught a glimpse of a well-maintained set of abs, even cruelly pinched as they were by the waistband of his vintage shorts.

'I'm sorry. This is getting us nowhere.' He shook himself, clearly trying not to descend into laughter again. 'Sorry. So unprofessional of me. Go and get changed while I sort the pool out.'

Fran was still giggling as she stripped off her hoodie. It was nerves, she knew. She'd had many awful, inappropriate bouts of helpless laughter prompted by tense situations in her job. She wrapped her bath towel tightly around herself, and sipped from her water bottle. It did nothing to dispel the dryness in her mouth as she stepped onto the poolside.

There was nowhere to hide in a swimsuit. The thought of him seeing her in it was outdoing the fear of swimming. Almost.

CHAPTER TWENTY

Wyn dipped his plastic-sleeved lesson plan into the pool and stuck it to the wall, as he had a million times before. He knew it by heart. Relieved to see that Gwynedd had roped the pool off halfway as he'd asked, he threw a couple of kickboards and some of the polystyrene tubes into the pool, leaving the others on the side.

Spotting the pink plastic flamingo at the bottom of the bag, he pulled it out and, on a whim, blew into it. Anything to distract him from the jumble of fears in his head. *What if, what if, what if* . . . His head was spinning by the time the pink bird was inflated, and not just from blowing.

She emerged from the little wooden hut in a black swim-suit and clutching a bath towel around her. Her limbs were lean and smooth, and it was hard to imagine that she'd ever had a heart attack. Her long hair was tied back in a ponytail. She combed her fingers through it repeatedly.

'I suppose I should've brought a hat or something. Not that I own one. I hadn't thought about it.' She grinned at the pink flamingo under his arm and he gave it a pat.

'This is, um—' he scrolled rapidly through his brain, trying to think of names beginning with F apart from hers, and could only come up with — 'Fanny,' he said. 'Fanny the, er, Flamingo.' Oh, what? First the terrible shorts, and now inappropriate body part naming . . . He cleared his throat. 'Yes. Right. Okay. So.' He mentally shook himself, grappling for some vestige of professionalism. 'Tell me what you want to achieve, Fran.'

'I want to learn to swim,' Fran replied promptly. 'Not just "not drown". Proper swimming. You can be hard on me. I won't cry.'

He laughed. She was being brave, he knew. If it were that easy, she'd have got over her fears decades ago.

'Shall we sit on the poolside here? It's the shallow end. Only eighteen inches. And nice and warm.' He would be able to gauge the level of her confidence right at the beginning. He sat down first, ensuring that he didn't shy away from using his bad arm as a prop, and let his bare legs drop into the water. He plucked at his thick rugby shirt, feeling hot, but decided to keep it on as he had no intention of getting into the pool. Nothing at all to do with not wanting to bare his scars in full.

In the corner of his eye, he saw Fran hesitate fractionally before wriggling out of her towel and joining him, about two metres away. He could see she was also awkward about using her arms to sit. She pointed her toes and slid them in slowly, hesitantly, one foot at a time, stirring the water slowly. Not too bad. Something to build on. Some people couldn't even do that.

'Fanny can sit here.' He dangled the bird's ridiculous floppy legs over the poolside between them and was cheered to see her small smile.

'Health and safety first. What have the doctors told you about exercising since your surgery?'

She shrugged, staring at the flamingo between them and not at the water. 'I can do whatever I like. Just take it slowly.'

He nodded. 'We'll keep it nice and calm. No excitement. I can see you have a smartwatch — so you can keep an eye on your pulse.' She nodded. He stirred his feet in circles, watching the swirls. Clean, clear water. Nothing like the dark, drowning depths of . . . 'So, talk to me about water.'

She shrugged. 'If I can't remember what I'm so scared of, why am I scared? I've dealt with dead bodies, been beaten up, seen terrible, awful things. It's ludicrous that I'm so terrified of bloody water.' Her laugh was high-pitched and her mouth wobbled as she fought back tears. Lifting her feet out of the pool she hugged her knees, a tight ball of tension. He wanted to soothe her, smooth her fears away. He kept his voice low, careful not to belittle her.

'Not at all. Our minds hang on to our fears to protect us, to stop us falling into the same traps and potentially hurting ourselves. It's easy to feel fear. It's much harder to let it go. But it can be done.' He kicked the water gently, making tiny splish-splosh wavelets. Fran's eyes were everywhere but on the water.

'I *do* want to let it go. After all these years of hiding it. Making excuses for not getting into water. It's quite easy, after a while. And people stop asking. But now, I see Caitlin and her girls having so much fun out there and I . . .' She ground to a halt, swallowing hard. 'I want to do it too.'

'Well, the good thing is, it's your choice now,' Wyn said, his own words landing in his brain, like boulders thrown into the deep end. Ker-splosh. *Listen to yourself!* 'You're in charge here. You decide how much we do, okay? We can stay in the shallow end, and if that turns out to be enough for you, then that's fine. Baby steps.'

'That's what my cardiac nurse keeps telling me.' She walked her feet back into the water, dipping her toes so they just dimpled the smooth surface. He watched the long muscles of her thighs. She looked like a runner.

'Yep. It's what they told me too. It's irritating, isn't it? You already feel like you've lost all your power and you're taking the tiniest possible steps as it is! Especially when you're so used to being fit and able to do whatever you want.'

'Yes! Yes, that's exactly it.' Nodding, she flashed a sudden small grin his way. 'Yes. Thank you. Let's do this. What happens next?'

He could see she was good at hiding her fears and putting on a brave face. He was doing it himself. And sometimes, fooling your body could send the right signals to trick your brain too. He was banking on it.

'First off, I'm going to teach you how to float. It's incredibly reassuring to lie on your back like a starfish and know that the water will hold you up. And it will.' Again, his words reverberated in his brain. He held out a pair of swimming goggles.

Fran stared at them, her hands bunched at her sides. 'I can't go underwater.'

'It's a lot nicer in there if you can see. Try them.'

She took them hesitantly. He could see her hands shaking as she yanked them over her hair. They rolled over, the lenses coming to land upside down over her eyes. He was unsure how close to get, how much to help. Nevertheless, he couldn't bear to see her struggle. Getting up awkwardly, he kneeled beside her to adjust them.

'Okay?'

'Are my eyeballs meant to be sucked into them?'

He laughed. 'Not ideal. Take them off and I'll loosen them.'

'You coming in too?'

'No. I'm more effective on the poolside.' He swallowed, handing her back the adjusted goggles and directing her to the shallow steps. *And I don't have to face my own fears as well as yours.*

'I . . . I don't . . . I'm not sure I . . .' Fran licked her lips, frozen on the top step of the pool. 'I'd much rather someone was in here with me. In case I—'

'I should stay on the side,' he said stiffly. 'It's not good form to be in the water with a student.'

'I'm not going to accuse you of anything nefarious, if that's what you're worried about.' Her voice was sharp, and she sniffed, dashing a hand over her eyes. 'I'm just . . . I'm . . . Look, I'm bricking it here, Wyn. I would really appreciate you being in here with me. Please.'

He swallowed. He was going to have to get into the pool. How could he help her overcome her fears if he couldn't deal with his own? He bent, sucking his stomach in to unbutton his shorts. They *were* a bit on the tight side, now he thought about it. 'I might not be able to get these back on, y'know.'

'Please tell me you're not wearing budgie smugglers that are also twenty-five years old . . .'

'Excuse me. I do have some pride.' Stepping out of his shorts and kicking them to one side, he rolled down the legs of a pair of black mid-thigh swimmers.

'Much better.' She gave him a thumbs-up. Cheered by her approval, he peeled off his rugby shirt to a short-sleeve T-shirt and saw her trying not to look at his scar. 'Ouch,' she said, her mouth downturned. 'We're survivors, you and me.' She smiled tremulously at him as he joined her on the top step. 'Thanks, Wyn. Much appreciated.'

They waded into the pool, side by side. The water was warm and inviting. Clean and clear. And shallow. He watched her closely, seeing her jaw set, shoulders and elbows rising, muscles clenched. His own anxieties retreated a little, as he focused on speaking gently and encouragingly to her. The pool shelved gently until Fran was about waist deep.

'These are called woggles.' He wobbled a long polysty-rene sausage in each hand, offering them to her and reaching for another pair. 'Or noodles. You put one around your back and one under each arm, like this. Then you lie back like you're on a reclining lounger.'

Fran's huge smile as she managed to lie back and then stand up encouraged both of them enormously.

'Well done, Fran.' He got her to repeat everything over and over until he could see her shoulders relaxing. He took the noodles away, one by one.

'Don't let go!' Her eyes were wide through the goggles.

'You're doing it yourself, Fran . . .'

'Oh. My. God.' Her face split into a huge beam. 'I never ever thought I'd be able to do this in a million years.' He grinned back, delighted for her.

'Brilliant. You're a natural.' Pushing a kick float her way, he reached onto the poolside and emptied some Ping-Pong balls into the pool.

'See if you can blow them away.' He'd used the technique with children, getting them to doggy paddle and blow bubbles in the water, the very first steps in actual swimming and breathing. He demonstrated, surprising himself by sinking into the shallow water and submerging his mouth to blow. It came easily to him, the water familiar, clear as gin. A lifetime away from the awful terror of . . .

'Easy,' Fran said, smiling. He forced his attention to the present. As the little plastic balls bobbed away he blew them back to her and she laughed.

He let her experiment, making a game of blowing the balls at each other, chasing them across the pool, until she slipped, lunging forward. Her head sank beneath the water and instantly she began to flail.

Instinct took him beside her in a flash — even then, careful about how he touched her, holding her up by her shoulders. Her muscles felt tense beneath his hands, her smooth skin warm. He used the voice he reserved for timid children on their first days at school.

'Shh, shh, Fran, you're okay, you're okay. Lie back and float. You can do this.' He reached for a noodle but Fanny the inflatable flamingo floated past and he grabbed it.

'Fanny! My lifesaver!' Fran's voice was on the edge of tears but she was still putting on a brave face. Wyn kept his voice calm, repeating the same words he'd used to teach her the moves, right at the beginning. His brain replayed her slip, over and over, and relief flooded his body. He'd faced the worst thing and hadn't let her, or himself, down. He was still in there. He could do this. Another tiny step in the right direction.

Her body was jerky and wooden, but she managed to float for a few moments, before her body folded up like a pretzel.

'I'm sorry! I'll never be able to do it. I'm useless. You've been really kind but please don't waste any more time on me. I'm hopeless.' She stood up, pulling off the goggles and holding them out to him.

'Oh Fran, of course you're not hopeless,' he said, ignoring the goggles. 'If it were that easy, you'd have cracked this years ago. Give yourself time. Your body needs to learn. You've got years of inbuilt reactions to undo. You *will* get there.'

Fran nodded, but her head hung, and the euphoria of earlier was nowhere to be seen.

'Let's finish on a good note, shall we?' Wyn kept his tone deliberately light, getting her to relax and float again and, finally, exhale with her head partially submerged.

'Now *that's* progress. Well done, Fran! I think that will do for our first lesson.' He checked his watch. 'It's been just over an hour.'

Fran stood upright, still clutching Fanny the Flamingo, who was beginning to deflate. 'Blimey. I can't believe it. It's flown by. Look at my hands! I've never been in water long enough for my fingers to go wrinkly — apart from the bath!'

'You know what they say — the longest journey begins with one small step.'

She looked over her shoulder at him with a ghost of a smile as she stepped out of the pool. His mind took a snapshot of her, her skin rosy, green-blue eyes flecked with gold, chin lifted over lean and graceful shoulders. A very far cry from the pinched, anxious expression she wore an hour ago. Climbing the wide steps out of the pool behind her, he wondered whether he looked similarly relieved, because he certainly felt it.

'Thank you.' She picked up her towel. 'I feel like I've just walked on the moon. Is it too early for an Elin-strength gin, do you think?'

'Never. Sun is over the yardarm somewhere, as Elin would say.' He grinned. 'Well done. I'm sure she's waiting for us with a couple. Want to do it again?'

'If Fanny the Flamingo can bear it, I'd like to. I hope I wasn't too awful a student.'

Fran waggled the sagging inflatable, and Wyn felt a surge of affection for her bravery. The first steps were always the hardest. He smiled at her.

'Nah. Not nearly enough snot and tears!'

CHAPTER TWENTY-ONE

Fran's hair was a damp, bedraggled mess. And she didn't care one bit. Towelling herself off, she relived the last hour, ticking the wins off in her head. She'd been in a pool, she'd floated and she'd put her head in the water!

She might even have actually enjoyed herself when she hadn't been scared shitless. Yes, okay, she *had* had a bit of a mini-meltdown, but Wyn had been there just as she'd imagined he would be. He was a genius, getting her to achieve all that.

As she emerged from the little wooden changing hut, he'd changed back into his rugby top and shorts, and was packing away his armoury of swim toys. Her mind, though, retained the afterimage of his body in the wet T-shirt and swim trunks. She fanned her face. Goodness me. Exercise made you terribly hot.

'Wyn. Why aren't you doing this full-time? You're fantastic! Thank you so much!' She reached up and planted a kiss on his cheek.

He beamed, reddened, dropped all the plastic toys he was packing away, and squeezed Fanny the Flamingo under his arm, causing her to fart lengthily. Fran laughed and Wyn looked mortified. Her lips still tasted his warm, smoothly shaven skin. His faint soap-and-chlorine scent lingered in her nostrils. She didn't feel a bit sorry for kissing him. It had meant nothing, she told herself. It had been one of those purely spontaneous moments. Despite the memory of his long, lean torso. It wasn't as if he'd kissed her back or anything.

In the passenger seat of his van, she glanced across at his huge, capable hands on the steering wheel and her legs went a bit wobbly. It was all that swimming. Obviously. It had worn her out.

'So, how do you think that went?' He braked, squeezing the van almost into the hedge as a car drove heedlessly along the middle of the road at them. He tutted gently and Fran swore.

'God's sake! Oh, I so wish I was still in the job. I'd love to have had a word with the driver.'

Wyn flashed a grin her way as he steered them back onto the tarmac. 'Hard to let go, huh?'

'No.' Fran shrugged. 'Yes.' She laughed. 'I think I'll be grinding my teeth with useless frustration for a long time.' She gazed at his lean profile, the broken nose, full mouth and strong jawline, and smiled. He was surprisingly perceptive. 'How did it go? Well, first of all, I don't remember the last time I spent that long in a swimming pool without clinging to the steps.'

He nodded thoughtfully. 'That's a good start.'

'Mm. And nobody has ever shown me how to float, so that was a revelation. I suppose I'll get over the fear of having my face in the water. It's a bit silly, really. I mean, I shower and bath and that doesn't scare me.' She watched his mouth curve up in a smile. 'So when can you fit me in for the next lesson? This afternoon? Tomorrow morning?'

'I'll have to check my—'

'Just kidding, Wyn. Whenever you can. Truly, I'm grateful for your . . .' She broke off as he swung into the side of the lane and stopped. 'What's up?'

Wyn's mouth was a straight line as he stared into his wing mirror, and Fran craned her neck to see. She didn't need to wait long. The uniformed figure of the policeman she'd only met on her first day in Llanbryn appeared at the driver's window. What was his name? AJ. Whatever that stood for.

Wyn casually let his window down, leaving the man standing glaring inside at them for a moment or two. Fran hoped her expression was neutral, although she doubted it. She wasn't renowned for her poker face. And after what Wyn had told her about him, she was very interested to witness what might be coming next.

'PC James . . . How can I help you?'

'Good afternoon, Mr Morgan. We've had a report of stolen goods being transported in a white van. I'd like to see inside, please.' The policeman's polite words were delivered in a sneering tone that was hard to miss. The back of Fran's neck prickled.

'Goodness me,' Wyn said, his own voice light and beyond reproach. 'I have been busy. You stopped me only a few days ago with the very same words. How are you getting on with finding my roof tiles?'

'*If* you would, please . . .' AJ stepped back smartly, dwarfed by Wyn as he climbed down.

Fran twisted in her seat to watch as the rear doors were opened. She hid a grin as AJ rifled through the bag of pool noodles and held up the partially deflated flamingo with a look of puzzlement. The van contained an assortment of bags of tools and he took his time inspecting each one. Wyn stood back with a long-suffering air.

'What are you looking for, PC James?' Fran asked, keeping her voice friendly and light. 'Perhaps we could help you look?'

He lifted his head slowly, his eyebrows rising at the same speed. 'I'm not at liberty to say, Miss . . . ?'

Fran ignored the request for her name. He clearly hadn't recognized her from that night she arrived. 'If we knew, we could keep an eye out for them. That would be helpful, wouldn't it? Where were they stolen from? Near here? Are you using social media to help? Could you let us have the identification numbers and makes?'

The policeman ignored her and she continued brightly, 'Because, if there is no report of theft, and this isn't the first time you have stopped Mr Morgan for the exact same reason, then you are harassing Mr Morgan and he has no option but to report the matter to Professional Standards. Or I will.'

She watched the policeman's face go purple. Scowling, he slammed a bag of tools onto the van floor and Fran said, 'I hope there was nothing breakable in that bag as Mr Morgan would have to invoice you for replacements.' She didn't dare look at Wyn. He might be furious with her. She couldn't allow behaviour like this AJ's to go on though. He made them all look bad.

'Just . . . just watch it.' AJ stepped back and glared at Wyn, who stared impassively down at him. It was a good thing that the doors were closed then as Fran opened her mouth to deliver more advice. She scooted into Wyn's seat and peered at them through the wing mirror. Wyn had his hands lifted and was shaking his head. Might it make matters worse if she got out? Had she emasculated Wyn by making it seem as though he couldn't deal with the situation? As she was deciding, Wyn strolled towards her, his easy gait belying his furious expression. She slid back into the passenger seat. Might this be the end of her swimming lessons?

As he climbed in, he flashed a broad grin at her, his deep-blue eyes twinkling. Her heartbeat leaped. 'You, Fran, are a tigress!' He barked a laugh. 'I shouldn't think anyone has read *him* the riot act before.'

They watched as the patrol car executed a messy three-point turn behind them before wheel-spinning away back up the hill.

'God help anyone who gets in his way today,' grunted Wyn. 'Pompous ass. I think we'll just make ourselves scarce, shall we?' He started the engine, still wearing the grin. 'What are your plans now?' Before Fran could answer, he carried on, 'Fancy a pub lunch? I think a celebration is in order.'

Fran's stomach growled in response and they laughed. 'It's a yes from me!' Her pulse beat a little faster at the idea of spending more time with him, until he added, 'Elin's always up for some pub grub. And I need to change. I'll be back for you in ten. Fifteen tops.'

'Great!' Fran stretched her mouth into a bright smile. How could she possibly have thought he wanted to spend more time with her exclusively? She was an idiot. 'I'm starving. I'll tell Elin, shall I?' Fran jumped out as he stopped outside her cottage. 'See you in ten. Bye!' She slammed the van door. Waving him away, she turned to see Elin at her doorway.

'How did it go?'

Fran beamed at her. 'Are you free for a pub lunch now with me and Wyn? Ten minutes.'

Elin's face lit up, and Fran berated herself for even considering that she hog Wyn to herself. Elin probably didn't go out to lunch very often. She hurried to her cottage, smoothed some leave-in conditioner through her hair and changed into jeans and a top, tying a sweater around her shoulders. At the last minute she added some lip gloss.

Wyn returned on foot nearer twenty minutes later, more appropriately dressed in knee-length khaki shorts and a navy polo shirt. He looked smart and very handsome. His smile brought the dimples to his lean and craggy face and Fran felt a bit dazzled.

'So, you both look happy. I said you'd be fine without me, didn't I?' Elin looked from one to the other with a decidedly smug expression. 'Hope those terrible shorts have gone in the bin, my lad.'

'Can't see what was wrong with them myself.' Wyn bellowed a laugh. 'Don't worry, I'm having a ceremonial bonfire later.'

Elin and Wyn chatted about a village book sale for the few minutes it took to get to the pub, and Fran was quite happy to just listen. Their easy banter made it clear that they had a long association, although Fran could hear the respect in Wyn's tone. She felt privileged that she'd been taken under the older woman's wing.

It was warm enough to eat outside, and Fran was quick to stake her claim on a table with some sunshine and shade.

'My treat, guys. As a thank you for organizing the lessons.'

'Nope.' Wyn shook his head. 'This was my idea. You're not allowed to hijack it.'

'No fighting, children.' Elin eyed them both over the menu. 'I'll buy my own. I'll have the steak and Guinness pie and chips. It's the business. And it doesn't come in one of those ridiculous little dishes. It's a proper pie, made by the redoubtable Mrs B.'

'That's me decided too then.' Wyn sat back. 'Can't beat Mrs B's pies.'

'It's that good, is it?' Fran ran her eye down the menu. Her mouth watered at the thought of succulent pieces of steak and chips. She sighed. 'I'll have the tuna salad.'

Elin spluttered. 'You'll be sorry . . .' She looked over as one of the staff came out, order pad in hand. 'Hello, Stefan. A pint of the guest bitter, please, and the pie.'

'Same for me.' Wyn nodded. 'Thanks.'

'I'm going to have order envy, aren't I?' Fran groaned. 'Go on then, same again for me.'

'Three pies, three pints,' Stefan intoned, collecting the menus and returning to the pub.

'Breaking strain of a Kit Kat, me,' Fran said with a sigh. 'I'll never be thin.'

'You look all right to me,' Elin said.

'Me too,' said Wyn. He blushed and reached for a pint that wasn't there, looking around the neat garden instead. 'Wonder how Scruff is doing?'

'Scruff? What about him?' Elin asked. Wyn's face was crimson with embarrassment by the time she'd drawn out his tale of rescuing Phil.

'You're a regular good Samaritan, you are.' Fran was impressed, quite enjoying seeing him go even redder, if it were at all possible. What an enigma he was, this colossal man with a heart to match.

'I heard about Phil going into hospital,' Elin said. 'Wasn't it the same night that Fran arrived?'

'Might've been . . .' Wyn muttered laconically. As Fran ran her mind back over the events of that evening, thinking how different her opinion of him was now, he said to Elin, 'Talking about dogs, Fran's a bit of a rottweiler. I thought she was going to jump out of the van and savage PC James earlier.'

Elin looked towards her with interest. Fran fidgeted. 'Well, I . . . I mean, he . . .'

'He's a . . .' Wyn's mouth shaped a word that he thought better of, ending with a grunt of disgust.

'He's a bully,' pronounced Elin, pursing her lips. 'He always has been. What did you do, Fran?'

Fran chewed her lip, still wondering whether she should have kept quiet, and Wyn told the tale with relish. 'I had trouble keeping a straight face,' he finished. 'I thought he was going to burst.' He laughed. 'He didn't know where to put himself.'

Their food arrived then, and Fran admired the crisp, golden chips and pastry, with its steaming, rich filling. 'This looks amazing. Good call, guys.' They ate in silence for a while until Elin said, 'So, how do you feel after your lesson?'

'I confess that I was wound up like a top to start with. I'm surprised at how relaxed I felt by the end.'

'You did good.' Wyn nodded.

'You made it easy for me. I only wish I'd done something about it sooner. I can't tell you how many excuses I've made for not swimming. And then felt miserable, watching everyone else having a good time. Not getting my hair wet, time of the month, gippy tummy — you name it, I've used it.'

'And you've never tried to get over it?' Elin tipped her head to one side, her tone kindly.

Fran shrugged. 'I tried a couple of swimming teachers, but of course, with shift work, I'd miss so many lessons, it just wasn't worth it. It sounds really stupid and cowardly, but once everyone knew me as the non-swimmer, it was easiest to go along with it. Not challenge it.' She sipped her beer.

'Hearing about you standing up to PC James, I think you like a challenge,' Elin said. She glanced at Wyn. 'What about next year's triathlon event?'

Fran spluttered into her pint. 'What? Me? No.' She laughed and coughed, and Wyn reached around to bang her on the back, nearly knocking her off her chair. 'Are you having a laugh? I've just had a heart attack! Swim in the sea? In a competition? No. Absolutely not.'

'You've got a whole year to train,' Elin said. 'And you're fit. And young.'

Fran stared at her incredulously. 'Fit? I can't even walk the length of the beach and back without having a nap halfway!'

Elin said, 'We've been discussing a newcomers' event for a while now, haven't we, Wyn?'

Wyn grunted, his mouth full — deliberately to avoid replying, Fran suspected.

Elin was like a dog with a bone though. She continued, 'A shorter swim, by itself. We've been asked often enough. That way it wouldn't interfere with the cyclists or the runners. Using the same water safety personnel and boats. We'd just need to put out some buoys to shorten the course. The tide will have gone out too. What do you think?'

Fran looked at Wyn. He shrugged. 'Mm. Doable. We can discuss it with Dylan.' Elin nodded, satisfied. Fran stared at them both. Wyn didn't seem as enthused as Elin.

'What? Don't do it on my account. It's a mad idea.' She cut a piece of steak into a thousand pieces. 'Completely mad. All I've done so far is *float*! I haven't even swum yet! I'm not doing it.'

'No,' Wyn said. What did he mean by that?

Fran narrowed her eyes at him. 'I could though. If I wanted to.'

'Yes,' Wyn said. Fran glared at him. He was no help.

'Totally.' Elin nodded encouragingly. 'You're a survivor. And a rottweiler. You can do anything.'

'I am! I can!' Fran speared a chip with her fork and waved it. 'Apart from that.'

'The thing that marks out top athletes is that they visualize themselves succeeding,' Wyn said thoughtfully. He rested his eyes on her for a long moment before returning silently to his plate. Fran glowered at him in exasperation. Not that he noticed.

It was several minutes before she said, 'This swim. Just asking for a friend. How far would it be?'

CHAPTER TWENTY-TWO

Wyn almost choked on his beer at Elin's suggestion that Fran take part in a competitive event. Luckily, Fran *did* choke and he was able to disguise his own reaction under cover of hers.

His reaction wasn't totally about *Fran* though. There was absolutely no reason why she shouldn't be able to do it. As Elin said, there were plenty of distance athletes her age and no doubt it would be age-grouped. And providing she had no further medical complications and trained, she could do it.

The pit opening up in his belly was all about himself. *His* fears. They were noisy in his brain, drowning out the conversation. What would *he* be expected to do? Would she expect him to train her in open water? If she was still living here, then she would be surprised if he didn't do it. Apart from his injury, his mind was damaged since that terrible, awful . . . He'd never manage to go out of his depth again in the sea. And as for the dark . . .

He was pretty sure she was only staying for the summer though. Even though April and Ken were planning to be away until the end of the year. Another reason not to get involved. He wasn't good at short-term flings. He didn't have the gift of the gab like some of his mates, who seemed to attract women in their droves with their quicksilver chat lines. It took him longer to warm to people, but once he'd built a relationship, he kept it for ever. And look how that had turned out . . .

He grimaced, and caught Fran glaring at him in a way that seemed to require a response. What had she said? Best to agree.

'Yes,' he said warily, having already said 'No' on auto-pilot, thinking he was agreeing with her, which seemed the safest option. Judging by her expression, that wasn't quite what she was looking for. He tried to rewind the conversation and ended up spouting some wordy dirge about visualization. Both she and Elin sent a mystified look his way and he cursed himself for not listening.

He felt weirdly protective about teaching Fran to swim. Swimming was a sport that relied on good technique. It wasn't all about how fit you were.

He'd watched lithe, fit men overtaken by overweight swimmers with better technique, to their utter mystification. It was true that the cycle and run legs evened them out, but it demonstrated clearly that technique was everything. He didn't want Fran picking up bad habits from the beginning and making life difficult for herself. He wanted it to be as easy and fun as possible.

But God, how would he fit everything in? It wasn't as if he didn't have enough going on in his life. He was barely camping in his half-finished house, had a constant list of jobs around the village and the gardening jobs would be taking over his evenings soon too, plus there was his father, and his own hobbies. Thankfully his father was as fit as a flea and had a great life. When he wasn't giving Wyn a hand with the schoolhouse, he was out on his vintage tractor with 'the lads', showing it off at village fetes and schools and having a great time.

Why had he tied himself down to so much? Was it a desperate need to be needed? To explain why he stayed in the village despite his wife leaving him? Was he that shallow? With an effort, he tuned in to Fran asking how long the newcomers' swim might be.

209

Elin had her teeth into it, putting forward various ideas. He thought a kilometre but said nothing. Elin may have other ideas, and he wasn't at all sure that he wanted to be involved.

He'd returned from paying the bill and saw a set to Fran's jaw and posture that hadn't been there before. He didn't know her that well, but damn, she looked determined.

'Could we firm up our pool dates, please, Wyn?' She had her phone calendar app ready, so what could he do? 'And I do realize how much of your time this will take, so please let me know how much I owe you.' She'd looked quite fierce, what with her sun-dried pool hair curling wildly in a froth around her head.

'Little and often is best in the beginning, if you're really keen,' he said, in an effort to claw back some authority after his inner ditherings.

'I am.' Her jaw jutted and he grinned.

'I'll have to check with Gwynedd, but we could go every morning . . . Just for half an hour or so to start off with? I can certainly manage that from tomorrow.' He looked up from his phone. 'What do you think?'

'I want to be in the sea. When my mum arrives.' She stared up at him, shoulders back, eyes piercing, and only her tell-tale swallow betrayed her inner struggles. In that moment, he wanted to gather her up, hug her, assure her that she'd be swimming like a fish, like someone born to the sea.

How could he make that promise? He didn't have a crystal ball. It would undoubtedly be uneven progress and require patience and perseverance. There would be a lot more tears and snot, he was sure of that. But she believed in him. Believed that he could banish her fears. And hadn't he just told her that visualization was the key to success?

So, how about believing in himself, for a change? He held out his hand and she placed her smaller one in his, trusting, but firm.

'In the sea, swimming. By the time your folks arrive.' He hoped it would be nearer four weeks than three. All about the tutoring, obviously, and nothing at all to do with spending time with her.

Her eyes grew bright, a tremulous smile curving the sides of her wide mouth. She nodded. 'Deal.' Her hand stayed in his for a long time and he found himself reluctant to let it go. Holding somebody's hand was such an intimate thing to do. That first touch — it was all about trust. A willingness to give. He supposed that was how shaking hands on a deal came about.

He'd made a deal with her. But in that moment, he made it with himself too. In the sea, with Fran. Before her parents arrived.

His own tell-tale swallow was more of a gulp. Waving goodbye to Elin and Fran after lunch, he jogged home. Things to do. He'd been muddling along for too long lately, fitting things in as and when, and Fran's deadline had focused his mind.

Standing before the old schoolhouse, he took in the assorted heaps of building materials and coils of cables and hosing, thankful that the thieves hadn't returned to clear him out. This project had become an excuse for his life. He was drifting through it, every day the same.

At his current rate, he'd be dead before it was finished. He went inside and found the clipboard that he'd once used to itemize everything to be done. Every job seemed to spawn another half a dozen though, and he'd abandoned his list, and any hopes of it being finished by Christmas. In any case, he couldn't visualize himself sitting alone in this vast building by candlelight, draped in tinsel, looking like a sad character from *Great Expectations*. A building that had once housed more than a hundred happy children.

Compressing his lips, he hunted down a pen that worked, and clipped a fresh sheet to his board. In a firm hand, he wrote a new list. If he was going to sell it, he'd get more money for it completed. If he decided to keep it, it needed to be finished. So whichever way he looked at it, Y Hen Ysgol needed to be done. And then he could decide where his life was going.

CHAPTER TWENTY-THREE

Fran spent the afternoon in the sheltered, sunny garden in shorts and T-shirt with her novel. In between nodding off, exhausted after her adventures that morning, she barely read a word. Despite her physical weariness, she felt euphoric. Shaking hands with Wyn — how very old-fashioned he was — on the challenge of swimming with her mum, in the sea, filled her with restless energy.

Excitement for once outweighed terror and she fizzed inside. The idea of finally learning to swim and being accomplished enough to complete an event — in the sea, no less — was nothing short of ludicrous, but she couldn't seem to dislodge the possibility.

Over lunch, they'd talked about fear and how to overcome it.

'Picturing a negative outcome can stop you trying,' Elin had said. 'You can't see into the future, so why not try being positive and brave instead?'

Fran considered herself positive and brave. She'd never shirked the dirty or scary jobs. And she supposed that was why her inability to swim had always felt shameful and cowardly.

She went inside the cottage and hunted out her laptop, typing into the search bar, *beginner training for sea swim*. The results filled several pages of articles and videos, and she was completely absorbed when she heard the familiar sound of car doors slamming and cheery calling outside. Shutting the laptop, she hurried out to greet the Sea Sisters.

'Hey, Fran!' In leggings patterned with mermaids, sheepskin boots and a vast hooded sweatshirt that looked much too warm for the weather, Caitlin waved, her face split into a huge grin. 'How's the training going? Heard you were up at the Edwards's pool this morning.' She dragged a hold-all out of her car and dumped it on the pavement. 'Coming down with us?'

Fran stared at her for a split second, conflicting emotions whirling through her brain. She was euphoric about what she'd achieved, but by their standards, it wasn't much. She didn't want her bubble bursting just yet. She wavered. 'My swimsuit is still wet . . .'

Caitlin laughed. 'Just come down for a natter then. Bring your coffee. You can tell us all about it. See you in a bit!' The other girls waved and smiled.

Fran recognized Wendy, Cora, Lila and some of the others from the village classes without remembering their names, but there always seemed to be more. Her mother, of course, would be in her element. In a matter of moments, she'd know all their names, horoscope signs and families. Fran envied that.

She herself had a great memory for Criminal Records Office numbers, dates of birth and full names for offenders she'd dealt with, including their car registration details, so she supposed she'd inherited an eye for detail. Of no use at all in social circles though.

She felt cross. Five minutes earlier, she'd been googling sea swimming, but at the first opportunity to actually go in the sea, she'd backed out. But she couldn't actually *swim* yet, she reminded herself. It would be foolish to put herself, and possibly others, at risk. She'd just been caught off guard, she told herself. She'd go next time. And she'd buy herself another swimsuit too, so one was always dry.

Feeling better now she'd made a plan, she filled her stainless-steel bottle with boiling water, popped a mug and teabags into her rucksack, plus a packet of unopened Welsh cakes, and strolled onto the beach. The blue, sparkling sea was halfway in, and the girls had left their belongings in the usual place in the dunes. Slipping off her sandals, she stuffed them into her rucksack and wandered barefoot to the sea. This time, she waded into the shallows, wincing as the cold water lapped at her shins and then her knees. Toes squishing and sinking into the soft sand, she looked down to see the tiny, lacy waves surging against her skin.

It was like being on a swing. The sea sucked her in and pushed her back, sucked and surged. Whispered and called to her. She watched, mesmerized. A memory, long forgotten, began to surface, like the bubbles in the water, and then fizzled away.

'Yay, go Fran!' the girls called out to her. 'Coming in?'

Impulsively, she lifted her arms and kicked out at the same time, watching the arcing spray catch the sunlight. Bending to scoop the fizzing whiteness of the bubbles, her fingertips stung with cold. It was so different to the pool that morning. It was alive.

The sea lapped up to the hem of her shorts. She looked down at herself in wonderment and out towards the Sea Sisters with the strangest feeling of belonging. The tide, she realized, was coming in quite quickly. Fear gripped her. She forced herself to turn and wade steadily towards the beach. She wasn't scared. She wasn't. She could float, after all. And she *would* be able to swim.

Maybe tomorrow. Maybe the next day. But definitely one day. And soon. She stared steadily ahead, willing herself not to rush headlong out in a panic like the last time. End on a good note, as Wyn said.

Kicking her feet this time landed her straight onto her bottom. Shocked, she sat in the cold, salty water for a moment before scrambling up, brushing at her soaking shorts.

'I'm okay!' she yelled, seeing Caitlin and the girls turning towards her. Not wanting them to worry about her, she did a little dance, splashing in the shallows. 'Woohoo!'

The girls called back, lifting their arms and waving. Shaking her booty at them to their laughter, Fran marched along the tide's edge to get some feeling back into her feet.

Despite the sun beating onto her upper body, her legs felt chilled as stone, and she began to understand the big coats and hoodies the girls wore after their dips. She was very glad to have brought the flask of boiling water now too.

There was a familiar tall, imposing figure at the far end of the beach, and she waved at him. He closed the gap between them at a lope, carrying a half-filled bin bag in one hand.

'Bit of a beach clean,' he said, indicating the bag. His eyes scanned her with interest, his mouth curving slowly. 'Getting a bit of extracurricular training in?'

Fran felt her cold body heat up in an instant. Clearly at her age, she was menopausal, having hot flushes. Had he seen her, goofing about, falling over?

'Yes, um, no, er . . .'

'Glad I've seen you . . .'

Fran went even hotter. 'Really? I'm glad I—'

'I've spoken to Gwynedd Edwards,' he continued without missing a beat. 'And she's happy for us to use the pool every morning from tomorrow. She swims at seven thirty, so we've agreed on eight thirty, which gives me time to crack on with jobs for the rest of the day. Not too early? We'll readdress it at the end of the week. Hope that's okay?'

'Oh. Yes, of course. That's fine by me. Thank you.'

'Right. I'll collect you tomorrow morning at eight fifteen.' He stood for a long moment, looking down at her as if he couldn't decide what to say next. Fran stared back, feeling seawater trickling down the back of her legs. She opened her mouth to say something, anything, just to keep him there, when he looked over her head and gave a decisive nod. 'Bye, then.' Turning on his heel, he strode away.

Fran plucked her damp shorts away from her skin and turned back thoughtfully towards her end of the beach, where she could see the Sea Sisters skipping and dancing across the beach towards their bags and coats. She smiled. Lunatics.

That would be her in a few weeks. It would. She filled her head with visions of herself swimming across the bay as she'd seen that swimmer the night of the full moon.

'You're supposed to take your clothes *off* for a dip, Fran.' Only Caitlin's head was visible above her voluminous coat, which seemed to have a moving, tumultuous life of its own. The other girls were similarly contorted, limbs appearing with some, all or none of their clothes on.

Fran laughed, wiggling her damp bottom. 'So, is that what they're for, those big coats?'

'They're changing robes,' said one of the girls breathlessly, wiggling into her trousers. 'Also known as Dryrobes, but there are lots of other makes now. Keep you warm, dry and apparently—' unzipping, she emerged like a chrysalis, tugging her bra into place with one hand and yanking a T-shirt over her head with the other — 'phew, apparently, maintain your modesty. Tadaaaa!'

'Dryrobe and no knickers is the way to go.' Wendy's voice was muffled beneath the depths of her clothing, and was as ever met with a volley of laughter. 'And no bra either. Impossible to put on when you're cold and wet. Unless you're flat-chested. In which case, what's the point?'

'You're a hussy, woman,' Caitlin said, stepping out of her changing robe and diving into the oversized hoodie Fran had seen her in earlier. 'I bloody love my Dryrobe. The first day I had it, I didn't want to take it off. Ooh, that's better.' She poured herself a hot drink from a flask, set it into the sand and shrugged back into her changing robe, zipping it to the neck and pulling a thick, colourful bobble hat over her head until only her eyes were visible. 'Lovely to feel the sunshine on your face.'

Fran laughed, shivering in her damp shorts. 'I always wondered what was in those enormous holdalls. They're full of clothes!'

'Damn right,' said Wendy.

'You always seem to have so much fun,' Fran said. 'But it's freezing in there, isn't it?'

'Nooo, it's . . . Yes, it is, really. It's bloody bonkers, innit.' Wendy pulled the sleeves of her knitted sweater over her hands. 'But once you're in—' she poured her drink and cupped her palms around it — 'it's as if you're wrapped in a glorious, warm duvet, and your skin feels like it's glowing.' Nods and murmurs of assent accompanied the rustling of coats, bags, holdalls and containers of biscuits and cakes.

'I get that. I feel like that TV ad for the Ready Brek kid, d'you remember?'

'No, Brenda. God, you're old,' Wendy replied with a dead straight face, although Fran judged Wendy herself to be approaching sixty.

Brenda laughed. 'I am. I'm sixty-five next year and bloody lucky to be here too, I'll have you know.'

'Sixty-five! Party time!' Caitlin's face lit up. 'On the beach? Lanterns, firepit, fresh fish, how about it?'

Fran watched as the group joined in with suggestions for food, despite not checking the date or their diaries, as she would have. Their lives were organic. Shaped by the tides, not by their calendars. It seemed as if they *made* time. If the tide was high in the morning, they swam then. If it was better in the evening, she'd see them trekking down in their changing robes at dusk instead. Her sense of belonging slipped.

No point in her checking her diary even if she knew the date. She wouldn't be there next summer. But, she thought, her mind rambling backwards as she half listened to them salivating over food ideas, what a lot she'd learned in such a short time. About herself, mostly. About slowing down, forgiving herself, letting people in, not always being in charge. Sometimes, she even managed it.

She sipped her tea, enjoying the banter as ever. She would never forget this summer, these women. Sometimes hilariously rude to one another, there was always kindness, and always, always acceptance.

The lady who never spoke unless she was in the sea was pink-cheeked, animated and nodding, offering the occasional stammered phrase. The other ladies would wait patiently until she'd painfully completed her sentence, listening intently. Fran wondered if she'd had a stroke. She didn't seem very old. There was always someone worse off than yourself.

'Ooh,' Caitlin said suddenly. 'That reminds me, there's a bunch of swimmers meeting up for the Strawberry Moon dip just along the coast here, on whatever day it is . . . Who's coming? We can share lifts. Coming, Frannie?'

'I'll come and watch . . .' Fran replied, her words almost lost in the ensuing babble of organization. She couldn't imagine herself in the sea at night as she'd seen the girls that time with Elin, the eve of the triathlon. *Give it time*, she told herself.

'So, come on, Fran, are we allowed to know how the swimming lessons are going?' Caitlin nudged her out of her reverie.

'Only one, so far,' Fran began cautiously.

'With the lovely Wyn . . .' Cora winked.

'And his shorts,' Wendy said, 'or lack of them . . .'

'What's this?' The other girls looked at Fran with interest.

'Is there some sort of bush telegraph in this village?' Fran looked round at them all. 'I mean, you don't have any internet signal, but it's not like any of you need it! Or are you all telepathic?'

'We're witches,' said Wendy, waggling her eyebrows. 'Are you scared?'

'Yes!' Fran laughed and then stopped, seeing their gazes fixed on her. 'You're not, are you?'

'What's this about Wyn's shorts?' Caitlin rolled her eyes.

'Gwynedd told me,' Wendy began, giggling. 'She said it was a wonder he could walk, and how on earth he'd managed to climb in and out of his van was a mystery to her.' Wendy snorted with helpless laughter. 'She said that there was a lot of man inside those shorts, and Fran was a lucky girl.'

The girls hooted and rocked with laughter around her.

'I'm not . . . He isn't . . . We aren't . . .' Fran tried, her voice drowned out among the mirth. She pursed her mouth in mock exasperation and waited. Honestly. They were worse than the blokes she used to work with!

'Any photos?' asked someone, her face a picture of innocence. 'Just asking for a friend . . .'

'*Aaaand*, back to the swimming,' Caitlin said, her dry voice cutting across the hilarity. 'How *did* you get on, Fran?'

'It was good,' Fran said. 'Wyn got me floating—'

'I bet he did,' sniggered Wendy. 'Sorry. Carry on.'

'And blowing out underwater. And that probably sounds like nothing to you lot, but to me it's massive.'

'Excellent.' Caitlin nodded. 'Well done. When are you going again?'

'Tomorrow morning. And every morning for the next week.'

'Wow. You don't do anything by halves.' Caitlin eyed her over her mug.

'Wyn says I'll be swimming by the time . . .' Fran hesitated and Caitlin pounced on it.

'By when?'

'By the time my parents arrive.' Fran took a deep breath. 'I want to swim in the sea, with my mum. They're coming down. In three or four weeks.'

'But you said your mum didn't go anywhere near the water, didn't you?' Caitlin's brows drew together, and Fran found herself telling the story of the phone call with her parents that had finally prompted her to take action. Her stomach lurched as her words hung in the air before her silent audience, and her determination wavered.

Did she really think she was going to be able to confidently go for an actual swim? In the sea? Her inner critic was staggering about laughing at the idea of her *competing*. She didn't mention that part.

'Good for you,' Caitlin said crisply. 'It's always good to have a project on the go. You seem like the sort of person who will succeed too. And with Wyn on hand, you won't fail.'

'And we look forward to meeting your mum,' said Wendy. 'We'll try not to mention that she stopped you swimming in the first place.'

'She doesn't seem to remember that!' Fran shook her head. 'And weirdly, fragments of a memory of something watery keep coming back to me and I can't quite recollect the whole thing. It's exasperating.' She frowned, clawing through the snatched flashback for clues.

'Maybe we should hypnotize you,' Wendy said. 'Watch this Mars bar, *veerrry* closely . . .' Cora snatched the dangling chocolate bar from her hand and ripped the wrapper off, to Wendy's cries of outrage and everyone else's laughter. The seriousness of the moment was gone, and Fran was relieved. She wasn't sure she'd enjoyed being the focus of their expectations. Her own were tricky enough to live up to.

CHAPTER TWENTY-FOUR

Fran's front door opened beneath Wyn's poised hand at eight fifteen the following morning. She stepped onto the path, carrying her rucksack, locking up behind her.

'Good morning!' He smiled at her. Her neat ponytail swung jauntily. 'You're keen.'

'I am,' she said, returning his smile and making his chest bounce in a way it hadn't in so many years. Her gaze fell on the jogging bottoms he wore over his swim shorts. 'So, did the shorts get the ceremonial burning?'

'My lucky shorts?' He snorted a laugh. 'Man and boy I've had those . . .' He sighed, shaking his head. 'They've bitten the dust. Gone to a better place. A sad day.'

'Mm — for all the old women in this village.' Fran's eyebrow twitched in an otherwise deadpan expression. 'You've been the talk of the place.'

'Oh God.' He shook his head, feeling heat climbing his face. 'Ah well. They have to have someone to talk about.'

Settling herself into the cab, she buckled her seat belt and turned towards him. 'I spent the whole evening watching YouTube videos about how to swim, so now I know *everything*.' She used both hands for emphasis and he grinned.

Yesterday she'd been a nervous wreck, and today she was a budding mermaid.

'Everything?'

'Yep. Except how to do it in real life.'

He laughed. 'Knowing what you should be doing is a good start. But—'

'Yeah, I'm not that naïve. I know how far I've got to go. But I understand now why you got me blowing Ping-Pong balls.'

'Would you like me to explain things to you as we go along?'

She nodded. 'Yes, please. I always like to know the whys and wherefores.'

'Excellent. So today, we're going to look at the body position in the water, so that it creates the least amount of resistance. The less resistance, the more efficient and less tiring it is.'

She bombarded him with questions and it seemed only minutes afterwards that they were both poolside again. He still had to help her with the goggles, her shaking hands belying the confidence she wore so thinly. Standing so closely beside her threatened to make his hands shake too.

He still wished that Elin had come along, as a chaperone. He remembered Fran herself had already acknowledged the situation the previous day, but he felt the need to make sure.

'I should have sorted this out beforehand, but if you wanted one of the swim ladies to come along, or Elin maybe, then that's perfectly fine, you know,' he said hesitantly, as they stood on the top step of the pool together. 'And if you're at all uncomfortable about, erm, this—' his arm moved back and forth between them — 'then we can stop the session straight away.'

'Yep, thanks, Wyn,' she said, in a matter-of-fact tone. 'I know you're a perfect gentleman and I'm very aware that I'm potentially putting you in an awkward position. If *you* would like them here, then I'm okay with that.'

'Uh,' Wyn began. 'Um, thanks . . . I was thinking of you, but, erm . . .' He coughed. 'Thank you.' They waded into the warm water. So distracted was he by the fact that she'd somehow taken charge and reversed his concerns about her, that he barely noticed that he was waist-deep already. She pulled the pool noodles around her, as he'd shown her, and waited for his instructions. The session passed quickly, as he reviewed and repeated the skills she'd learned the previous day, each time building up the skill level — a little more face in the water, a little less flotation assistance.

The lessons continued every morning. Each time he demonstrated what he wanted her to do, his own confidence grew.

'Well done, you've cracked the push and glide,' he told her a week later. She was so much more relaxed now and he was delighted for her. 'First steps in controlling your body position. We're going to add the strokes now. I want you to think of yourself like an arrow, long and thin. Watch me now.'

Focusing on his breathing, he went through the familiar motions, feeling the water close over his head. The water was clear and blue and nothing like that awful blackness . . .

He forced his mind into the present, staring at the cerulean pool tiles, Fran's painted magenta toenails, his heart thudding in the silence . . . He glided to a stop, regaining his footing as easily and automatically as he always had. Why couldn't he do it in the sea?

'Okay?' he said. She inclined her head, chewing at her lips. 'I'll be right here. Keep it nice and slow. Deep breath, make like an arrow.'

She put her head in the water, and pushed away from the side, emerging spluttering and coughing a few feet away. He was beside her in a moment but she faced her palms towards him.

'I'm okay. I forgot to breathe in first! Let me have another go.'

'It's a lot to remember at first. Take it slow.' He gave her space, watching carefully as she got into position again. There was nothing arrow-like about her body shape, but everyone had to start somewhere.

'Fingers together,' he instructed, as she repeated it over and over. 'Point your toes.' He checked the clock. 'Nearly time to get out, Fran!'

'Really?' Her face split with a delighted beam. 'Did I do good?'

'You did really good!'

'No tears and snot today!'

'Me neither!' Wyn laughed, only half joking. A sudden blast of cold air drew his attention. The door had opened, and a familiar figure was poised at the deep end, in shorts and a pink, sparkly cropped hoodie. What the hell was she doing there?

'Tasha! Uh, excuse me, we're . . .' Showing no sign of hearing him, she flicked off her flip-flops, stripped off and executed a perfect dive. Of course it was perfect. He'd taught her. Crossing the pool in a smooth front crawl, she duck-dived beneath the rope separating the shallow and deep ends, and popped up in the shallow end before him. Beaming.

'Hello, Wyn!' Wrapping her arms around his neck, she planted a kiss on his surprised mouth. 'Fancy meeting you here!'

He jerked backwards, her additional weight overbalancing him so that he sank instantly. Heart pounding, he fought to control his breathing. Her pale face too close to his, eyes distorted by the goggles. Her long legs coiled around him . . . Her hands reaching towards him . . .

She appeared unearthly, devouring, predatory. He shoved her away, surfacing with his hands outstretched, keeping her at arm's length.

'What are you doing here?' Chest heaving, dragging his lungs for breath, coughing and wiping his face. 'We've booked this session and we still have ten more minutes, if you don't mind.' His head whipped around, looking for Fran. She was his responsibility, while Tasha was behaving in this frankly bizarre fashion. He was relieved to see that she was safe, holding the pool edge not far away. She watched them, her expression unfathomable. He couldn't imagine what the hell she was making of this. 'Get out, Tasha,' he growled. 'You can come back later. This is a private class.'

She pouted. 'Don't be like that. There's room for all of us, honey.' Her gaze swept around, landing with pinpoint accuracy on Fran, as if she knew where her audience had been the whole time. '*Sorree*,' she called, hooking her arm around Wyn once again. She was like an octopus. Ignoring his attempts to unwind her body from his, she carried on, '*So sorry*, I didn't see you there. I'm Tasha. Wyn's wife.'

'*Ex*-wife!' Wyn was quick to correct her. 'Ex. For years now. Short memory, Tasha?'

Tasha gave a silvery titter that contained not one whit of humour. 'I was just saying,' she continued as if Wyn hadn't spoken, directing her words at Fran, 'we could share the pool, there's room for all of us. You won't be using the deep end at all from what I've heard. Even paddling in the sea is a bit too much? Aw, bless you . . .' She sang the words in a patronizing way that put Wyn's teeth on edge. Then she rounded on him in the same tone. 'And no chance of Wyn using it either these days, so I'm told . . .'

Wyn's jaw dropped. What the . . . ? What did she know? He'd told nobody about his fears. Nobody. Not even Elin knew the full extent of them, and even if she'd guessed, she'd be very unlikely to divulge them. Had Tasha seen him in the sea at night? Seen his terror, his panic-stricken clawing for safety? He felt sick.

He glanced at Fran, whose glare, directed at Tasha, could have set the pool steaming. What would she think, if she knew that her instructor was probably more scared of the water than she was? She'd lose every ounce of confidence in him. His credibility would be shot.

'Tasha, that's enough.' He cleared his throat, hearing the wobble and hating it. 'I don't know what your game is, but you're not welcome. I'm teaching here. Please. Go. Now.'

Marshalling his teacher voice for the final word, he heaved a sigh of relief as Tasha reluctantly relinquished him.

He turned away in a deliberate move calculated to deprive her of the attention he knew she craved, and heard her freestyle smoothly away down the pool. He looked over his shoulder in time to see her pick up her discarded clothes and stalk out of the door in her swimsuit, head high, wet through, limbs gleaming in the sunshine. Tash had always known how to make an entry. And an exit, evidently.

His mind whirled. What the *hell* had that been about? He knew though. Oh, he knew very well. This was the trouble with living in such a small place. There wasn't enough going on. The whole village would have been discussing him and Fran. A week of daily contact, the two of them, in swimsuits, in that pool . . . Had they, hadn't they? Will they, won't they?

Tasha was jealous. She didn't want him, but she couldn't bear the thought that someone else might. Her self-image was so fragile that she had to belittle him to maintain her superiority. Perhaps she'd forgotten that he knew her so well.

He caught himself. He was being very presumptuous about Fran. Just because he found himself increasingly attracted to her, it didn't necessarily mean that she felt the same way. He lifted his right hand and rested it on his left bicep, feeling the fissured puckering and pitting through the long-sleeved Lycra rash vest that he wore. His body was functional and still strong, despite everything, but it wasn't pretty.

Tasha had loved his body. He couldn't imagine anyone ever looking on it as she had. But she'd rejected him *before* his accident. It was almost as if he'd rejected his own body after that, brought the accident upon himself. Careless about his own safety. If she hadn't wanted him, what was the point in anything?

He slapped the water, angry with himself and furious with her. How could he have lost himself so thoroughly to Tasha? And for so long? She was a beautiful, attention-seeking, demanding, mercurial minx. Even while she was being an absolute bitch, he'd always loved her.

226

Not anymore though. His heart hardened. She'd cooked her goose as far as his goodwill. His life had to move on. He suddenly saw himself in twenty years, a sad shell of the man he used to be, grieving a failed marriage, alone and still pottering about pretending to be useful in the village. Ending his days like old Phil — crapping himself where he fell, broken. He glowered, raging. No. Time to move on.

CHAPTER TWENTY-FIVE

Clutching the pool rail, Fran watched the incident unfurl as if she were a spectator in a film. Tasha had appeared almost magically, ethereally, at the other end of the pool, in miniscule pink shorts and one of those trendy crop hoodies that seem to cost more the less material used. Her limbs were evenly and smoothly tanned. Fran decided it was fake, but no less beautiful for that.

Her own legs would never look like that in a million years. She never tanned due to her Celtic colouring — she had freckles, moles and blotches everywhere, knobbly knees, and to top it all, increasingly wobbly thighs. The older she got, the wobblier they got, and shorts like the ones Tasha wore would never make it out of Fran's wardrobe, even if they made it in.

The pool opened up with barely a ripple when Tasha dived in. Her body pierced the surface and it closed over her as if she'd never existed. Fran's entire body was hot with envy as the woman streaked across the pool in a few powerful strokes. Would she ever look like that? Would people ever watch her and sigh, wishing they could swim like she could? Even her pool exit had been graceful. Bitch.

Was she envious also of the way Tasha claimed possession of Wyn? Hell yes. The words resounded in her brain and surprised her. Not on a romantic level, of course, she scoffed. But because he was her swimming tutor, and for those hours in the morning, they were bonded. Committed. Tasha had gatecrashed that time, careless of Fran's feelings. Or was she warning Fran off?

She was still trying to decide what she thought about seeing Tasha apparently attempting to initiate sex with Wyn, in front of her, as he waded towards her in the waist-deep water. One look at his face told her that he was furious. Every feature on his lean face was a straight line.

He looked, she thought, magnificent. Like a glossy, burnished warrior, rising from the water. His triangular torso in the clinging T-shirt narrowed to the black swim shorts and muscular thighs. His shoulders bunched angrily and the sinews in his neck ran like snakes. Her thoughts flew back to the first time she'd seen him, and she wondered anew whether she'd saved PC James from a real pasting that night, whatever misdemeanour he'd committed. Lucky for them all, Wyn was a gentle giant.

He looked at her as if seeing her for the first time. Sinking onto his knees in the pool, putting himself at her eye level, he sculled his hands to hold his balance there, a few feet away.

'I am so sorry.' He held her gaze and she felt her stomach liquefy. 'I can't imagine what you must think of, of . . .' He shook his head, running a huge hand through his close crop.

His mouth opened and closed as if he were about to say something, and Fran had to fight the urge to put her own lips on his mouth. She'd seen the way he'd reacted to Tasha doing it though and doubted herself. Time stood still for a moment as their eyes met. One step each, towards each other, their bodies would touch . . . their lips would find each other, she would pull him towards her . . . But he'd never given her even a moment of encouragement. No sign that he fancied her at all. He would shove her away like he had Tasha, they'd both be horribly embarrassed and, on top of it all, she'd have lost her best chance of ever learning to swim.

'I think she must've heard about your pulling shorts,' she said, straight-faced.

His deep-sea-coloured eyes rested on her gravely, and for a horrible moment she thought she'd misjudged the moment. Then his mouth curved upwards and his shoulders shook as a laugh rumbled from his chest. She saw the tension ebb from his shoulders. Dipping his head beneath the water, he surfaced sleek as a seal, restored to his usual good humour.

'Maybe I should get them back out of the charity shop bag if they're that good.' He grinned at her. 'Right. Let's forget all that and finish our lesson. Five more minutes. End on a good note.'

The teacher had returned. Hey-ho. She hadn't wanted a relationship anyway. 'Am I getting my arm action right?'

'Keep your elbows high,' he said. 'Like this — but with both arms.' She watched him push off from the side, his body long and powerful, and a feeling of absolute desire to feel the length of that body against hers swept over her. She had to steel herself to pay attention to what he was doing with his arms.

The water streamed past her skin as she copied him. For the first time, it felt . . . right. Familiar. She stared at the ceramic-tiled floor, noticing that she was actually looking. For a moment she felt calm. Until her breath ran out and she somehow forgot which way was up. Wyn was there, as ever, a hand beneath her arm, righting her gently.

She gasped, catching her breath, cross with her incompetence. 'How long does it take before you don't have to think about everything all the time?'

'Not renowned for your patience, are you?' He raised his eyebrows. 'Lesson's over for today. You haven't swum your whole life and you want to swim like a fish in a week.'

'Oh.' She huffed. 'It never seemed like a possibility before. Now it feels so close I want to be an expert.' She made her way to the steps and he angled his head diffidently at her.

'So you do want to carry on with the lessons? I mean, I can understand if you . . . After, you know, Tasha . . .'

'Wyn, I am very happy to carry on, if you still want to,' she said firmly. She just wanted to be out of the pool and changed, so that he didn't keep looking at her body and comparing it to the lissom Tasha's in his head. 'Thank you.'

She hurried carefully to the changing shed, sucking in her stomach and attempting to walk so that nothing wobbled too much. Bloody Tasha.

He was hovering outside with a pensive expression when she emerged fully dressed. Sunshine streamed through the glass and perspiration beaded on her skin. She pulled at the neck of her T-shirt.

'God, it's hot! For the first time in my life, I feel like I actually want to get back into the pool.'

'Good to hear!' He held up a hand and she high-fived him.

'What's it like, swimming in the sea?' Fran creased her brow, thinking ahead to meeting her mother. 'I mean, as opposed to the pool? I know it'll be colder, and there will be waves, but what else?'

'Well — it's saltwater, so you're more buoyant.'

'That's a plus.'

'Yes. Well, obviously the sea is moving, never the same. The tide is the main thing. It comes in twice a day, twelve hours apart, about an hour later each day so it's never the same. Plus there are spring and neap tides and rip tides . . .'

'Stop! I mean, I know I need to know all that, but I meant — how does it *feel*?' Fran felt a ripple of panic spread in her stomach about all the things she didn't know. She knew the sea went in and out, but as for how far and when, it was a mystery. She needed to pay more attention. How could she be living with it in view and still not have understood it?

They climbed into his van and he started the engine, his face serious. He sat forward for a long moment, his arms resting on the steering wheel, chewing his bottom lip. As she watched his wide, generous mouth, Fran's stomach tightened.

'The sea,' Wyn began, his eyes focused on something far out of reach. 'She's a loving mother, a playmate, a total fiend. So vast she makes you feel tiny and insignificant. Like all your problems are nothing.' His soft, deep Welsh voice died away. His face still, his mouth and jaw set.

Fran watched him, sensing that he was lost in his thoughts. She wondered how many of them had been triggered by Tasha's appearance that day. How much was due to his injury, about which she knew practically nothing. Or perhaps his elderly father. She realized, sitting silently in his van beside him, that she knew very little about this man. He was even more buttoned-up than she was. He seemed so generous with his time and energies, and yet gave nothing of his feelings away.

He twisted towards her. 'Erm, Fran, erm, do you eat, erm . . . ?'

She narrowed her eyes quizzically at him. 'I do eat, yes.'

'Mussels?'

'Hell yeah, I adore mussels. In garlic and wine and cream? Crusty bread?'

'Perfect. The only way.' He drummed his fingers on the steering wheel. 'Are you, er, free tonight? Because it's not dark now until really late and so I wondered whether you, er, I mean, I, could, er, cook you some.'

Fran frowned. 'Do you only eat in daylight then?'

'What?' He wheezed his trademark Muttley laugh. 'Shit, I'm *so* out of practise at this. I'm so old now, I can't remember how to ask a woman to dinner.'

Her heart leaped. She kept her voice steady with an effort. She had a workshop that night on cushion making but she could send her apologies. She'd catch up later. 'Okay, I got mussels, garlic, cream, wine, but I didn't catch who's cooking it. If it's you, then yes. If it's me, then no, because I've never cooked mussels, even though I've eaten them a billion times.'

'It's me.'

'Done.'

'With a difference.'

'Am I catching my own mussels?'

232

He grinned down at her and all her resolve about not wanting a relationship dissolved like wet tissue paper. 'Not exactly. An introduction to the sea. I'll collect you about five. The sun will still be up until nine thirty. Wear your bathers, a towel and warm clothes.'

'My bathers? Not usual dinner wear . . .'

'This isn't a usual dinner.' He grinned, giving nothing away, and as her heart rate raced, her mind danced.

'I'm really sorry about Tasha,' he said, glaring at the road.

'I don't think it's for you to apologize, to be honest. Unless you knew she was coming.'

'No!' He shook his head emphatically. 'I imagine it's something to do with that knobhead husband of hers too. I wonder if he gave her a hard time after seeing us together in the van.'

Fran was confused. If her husband had been angry about being belittled, why would that make Tasha throw herself at Wyn? It made no sense to her. Did she really want to know? She was only going to be there for the summer. And she wanted Wyn all to herself for that time. Her body had decided. Whatever nonsense her head was saying. She waved him off after he dropped her at the door.

'See you at five!' he called after her.

By the time she'd pegged out her swimsuit and towel in the garden, she'd completely reversed her thinking. Wyn was too complicated with Tasha hanging about. He might have the most magnificent body, be great company, terrific with babies, make her laugh and be a brilliant swim tutor, but that was all. They would just be mates. She was good at that. Sex just complicated things.

And also, what if she had another heart attack? The doctors had been very casual about it when she'd asked about the possibility. It wouldn't be fair on him to be saddled with that. So that was that. Just mates.

Wearing a face pack and a hair pack, she took a stitching project into the garden, and spent a happy afternoon surrounded by coloured cottons and strips of fabric, painting her toenails and working on her tan, such as it was. Beneath the cloudless, blue sky, listening to the seagulls and the faint and always present sound of the waves whispering over the sand, it was like being on holiday.

And so much better than the sound of city traffic, she found herself thinking.

CHAPTER TWENTY-SIX

Wyn worked through his list of jobs for the day at top speed after dropping Fran off. Preparations for the evening ran through his head. His capacious chest freezer boasted several bags of frozen mussels but he preferred to defrost them overnight. A phone call to his favourite supplier along the coast bagged him fresh, farmed supplies, and he nipped out to make his purchases, deliberating about wines and ending up buying three different bottles. Stopping off en route, he collected several sizes of buoyancy aids from a friend, along with wetsuit boots and gloves.

All the bases were covered. The beach trolley held everything he needed. He loved cooking like this and it was so nice to have someone to cook for. He inspected his living quarters through a visitor's eyes, just in case she was to visit. His heart sank. He'd taken over the newest, most habitable part of the building, which had previously housed the offices, staffroom and toilets, knocking down walls and turning the space into a bedsit/studio.

It was warm, dry and functional, but nobody would call it homely. It was, frankly, now he looked at it through Fran's potential eyes, grim. His van was more welcoming than his living quarters. Tidying wasn't going to improve anything. He settled for cleaning the kitchen area and ensuring there were clean towels, handwash and loo rolls in the tiny bathroom.

She was as punctual as ever, and even in shorts and a T-shirt, somehow more polished than usual. A few bobbing and ridiculous false starts saw him eventually, hesitantly, bend to kiss her cheek in a hello. He hadn't kissed her before but it felt as if it were the right thing to do now. He'd asked her to 'dinner', so did that mean it was a date?

He inhaled a delicious waft of something faintly coconut-and-mango-ish. Doubts assailed him. He wasn't at all sure, suddenly, that he'd judged it right.

She beamed up at him, both of them shy in these different circumstances. Was it a date? It was just a dip in the sea and some food. He found himself wishing Elin was there. He felt old and out of touch. But it wasn't like he was planning to seduce her or anything. She'd probably black his eye if he tried anything anyway.

They'd been nothing but matey since meeting and that was fine by him. He probably shouldn't have even kissed her hello. This was just about furthering her goal, and they both had to eat, didn't they? So why not make it as interesting as possible. It wasn't about sex. Just mates.

He hefted her rucksack onto his shoulder. 'We're walking, by the way. Hope that's okay. Plenty of warm clothes? It'll be chilly later even if it's hot now.'

She shrugged, falling into step beside him along the beach path. The sun threw long, lilac shadows and he was glad of his sunglasses. 'Walking is fine. I hope I've got enough clothes. Depends what we're doing. You're being very mysterious.'

Wyn made a face. 'Hmm. Well, it seemed like a good idea at the time . . .'

'Why isn't it now?'

'Because you smell nice.'

'What?' She burst into laughter. 'It's nice of you to notice, but how has it changed your mind?'

236

'Because we're going in the sea.'

'Okay.'

He glanced down at her. Had she heard him?

'Are you okay about that?'

'It's what I said I wanted to do. And you're coming in too, aren't you? You said "we".'

'Yes.'

'Then that's okay. I trust you.'

Did he trust himself? At the end of the path, he turned towards his schoolhouse.

'I just need to pick some stuff up. You can wait for me at the beach if you like.'

'Oh, I've been dying to see your place.'

'Have you? Most people would run a mile.'

'I'm not most people.'

He laughed. 'I've noticed.' After a pause, he added, 'You know when people apologize for the mess when you go to their houses, and then it turns out their place is immaculate?' She nodded. 'Well, I'm apologizing and it really *is* a mess.' He pushed open his front door. '*Croeso*. Welcome.' He waved her in before him and watched her taking in his surroundings. Her jaw dropped. She whirled around.

'But . . . this is spectacular. So much potential. The amount of room you have — and this is only a tiny part of the building. You could hold a dance in here!'

'Yeah.' He laughed. 'I often pole dance round the acrow props . . .'

'Tell me what your plans are. Can I see the rest of it? I am so jealous of all your space. My place is tiny. I'm going to feel like I'm living in a shed when I get back there.' Her stomach catapulted at the thought of her flat.

'Whoah!' He held his hands up. 'All in good time. Tides wait for no man, and if we're going in — which we are, right?' She nodded, and he continued, 'Then we have to go now, before the tide turns. I have some stuff to make things safer and more comfortable.' He loaded her rucksack onto the beach trolley, and trundled it out and into the lee of the sand dunes beyond the houses. The beach was deserted, despite the sunshine.

'That's a nifty bit of kit,' she said, nodding towards the trolley. She'd pulled off her shoes and socks and was wrestling with the neoprene bootees.

'Awesome, isn't it? One of the physios recommended it to me. Do you need a hand with those? They need to be tight, but that makes them tricky to get on and off.'

'Yes, please.' Sitting down, she held out the neoprene boots to him together with her lifted foot and he tugged them on one at a time, managing not to let his gaze travel up her long, bare, smooth legs.

'I was struggling to carry everything, and this is collapsible, lightweight and you can get a ton of junk in it.' He stepped out of his jogging bottoms and hurled them into the trolley along with his fleece, as she neatly folded her clothes, posting them into her rucksack. 'I've even given kids rides in it. It's a festival trolley. I like to think I'm at Glastonbury when I'm using it.' Painfully aware that he was gabbling out of nerves, he shut up. As she tried the gloves on for size and peered at the settings on her watch, he inflated the tow floats.

'Okay. Ready?' Still not ready to bare all his scars, he wore his Lycra rash vest. She wore her high-neck swimsuit. A stranger looking at them would never know there was anything amiss. He lifted out a buoyancy vest and held it out to her as if he were the maître d' at a restaurant. 'Here we are, madam. One each. Plus a tow float. Safe as houses.' She pushed her arms in and stood before him as he zipped her up and pulled the waist belt snug. 'How does that feel?'

'Fine.' Her eyes were dark, huge and unblinking in a face gone pale, and he wanted to kiss her. She flapped her arms up and down and tried out a smile. He looped the tow float belt around her waist, adjusted it and handed the inflated float to her. 'Thank you.'

Putting on his own buoyancy aid and tow float, he reached towards her with the other hand and what he hoped was a confident and encouraging smile. 'Let's go then!'

As if it were the most natural thing in the world, she placed her gloved hand in his and the desiccated husk of his battered heart warmed and skipped a little. He would never betray her trust in him. He could swim, he knew the tides and the currents and he'd taken every precaution to keep them both safe. Probably to the point of overkill, but better to be safe than sorry.

He could choose whether to feel fear, he repeated to himself, turning towards the beckoning sea, bathed in golden late-afternoon sunlight. It was less than a hundred steps away — blue as a duck's egg, flat, calm, with tiny rippling wavelets. Perfect for a novice. Flat, sandy beach. Perfection. If he could do it in the pool, he could do it in the sea. It was daylight. The water would be clear. Not dark. He'd keep them in their depth. Deep breaths.

He could do this. He could.

CHAPTER TWENTY-SEVEN

The orange buoyancy jacket smelled musty. As if it had never been quite dried out between uses. It pinched beneath her arms, her hair was caught under it and she was pretty sure it added about fifty pounds to her silhouette.

It wasn't quite the look she'd been hoping for on her first date with Wyn. Somehow, she'd envisaged herself loping gracefully over the sand and splashing in the shallows with him, like a holiday advert.

And then he'd smiled that cute, dimpled smile and held out his hand, and it hadn't mattered what she looked like. She was doing the thing she'd longed to do all her life. That elusive memory finally unfurled, stopping her in her tracks.

Her birthday picnic at some beach. She'd been so looking forward to it. She was six. It said so on the big badge pinned to her frilly pink dress.

Mummy's voice was strange. High. She was laughing too much. Fran stared at her. What was she laughing at?

She was boiling hot. The dress was scratchy. Her friends wore shorts and T-shirts and swimsuits. One of the dads ran with them to the sea. The sea twinkled. It was calling Fran in soft whispers. So pretty. Fran stood up.

Mummy grabbed the bottom of her dress. 'Where are you going?' It didn't sound like Mummy.

'Pleease, *Mummy? I'm so hot and all my friends are going and I'm all on my own and it is my birthday . . .' Fran pointed towards the dancing lights on the wavelets.*

'No!' It was a shriek, and Fran's tummy jumped and hurt. 'No. What about an ice cream? Shall we make a sandcastle? You don't want to get your pretty dress all wet, do you?'

'I hate this dress!' Fran screamed at her. 'And I hate **you!***'*

She hadn't seen her mother's hand but she could still remember the shock of the slap, her cheek stinging cold then burning, her ears ringing. She'd been too shocked to cry.

'I'm sorry, my darling.' Her mother caught her into a fierce and hard hug that didn't take the pain away. 'It's only because Mummy loves you, darling . . . and after what happened . . . I couldn't bear it if . . .'

But Mummy would never talk about whatever had happened. Nobody did. There were no more beach parties after that. Or holidays by the sea.

'Okay, Fran?' Wyn's face was concerned.

She blinked. 'I've just had a horrible flashback to when I was a kid.' She shook her head. 'Why on earth would you give a child a birthday party at the beach and not let them go into the sea?'

'Is this your mum? Maybe she was trying to overcome her own fears and thought that she could let you do it, and then realized she couldn't.'

Fran stared at him, chewing her lip. 'Do you know, all these years I've hated her for giving me this fear of water. It's never once occurred to me that she was having her own battles. It's all me, me, me.' She eyed the sea. 'Dammit, you're good. Have you ever thought about doing psychotherapy? Right. Time to get my past back. Let's do this!'

They waded into the calm turquoise sea with linked hands. His sheer bulk and calm confidence made her believe in herself. Nothing bad could happen to her while he was there.

Her mind captured the sea spray, hanging in myriad sunlit bubbles in the air as they kicked and splashed. She wondered whether she could find little beads and stitch them into something for one of her textile projects as a memory of this.

'This is mad!' she yelled. 'It's freezing! Don't you feel the cold?'

'Want to get out?'

'No, I bloody don't.' She turned to him, grinning, her hand safely locked in his giant paw. 'This time, I'm doing it and nobody is telling me otherwise. I decide whether I'm scared, right?'

'Right! It's all about positive mental images.'

He waded alongside her, step by step, deeper and deeper. She looked down at her legs in the clear water, transformed into lean, long pins without a trace of wobble. It was deeper than she'd ever been in the sea. As the cold water lapped at the top of her thighs, a mischievous wave surged up to her waist and she yelped.

'Agh! Oh my God, that was ffff—' She felt him watching her and changed her mind about what she was about to say. '*Ffflipping* bracing! Really, really, *ffflipping* bracing.'

He laughed. 'Splash your face — it acclimatizes your body. And we're taking it nice and slow, to let your heart rate settle.'

She glanced at him in surprise. It was never far from *her* mind, but she hadn't expected him to be considering it too. 'Thank you for thinking of me.'

'Can't lose my star pupil this early in the day.' His craggy face dimpled in a lopsided grin. 'You're doing really well, Fran!'

Warmth spread through her body, despite the water circling her waist. Her mind captured each moment, to keep and remember afterwards. The feel of the salty, soft water against her skin, her gloved hand in his, the buoyancy jacket pushing at her chin as she waded deeper. Turning her face to the golden sunshine that warmed her face and bare arms, she inhaled the salty air.

'Brrr. Why is it so hard to put my elbows in?' She bounced on her tiptoes to stay higher than the water and he laughed.

242

'Once your shoulders are under, you'll be fine.' He was still only submerged to the bottom of his buoyancy aid. They went a little further. How far out to sea were they? She'd surely be out of her depth soon.

Twisting her head, she looked behind her. The beach seemed miles away, an expanse of water between her and safety. She reached out, gripping him with her other hand.

She gulped. 'This is far enough, Wyn. I don't want to go any further.'

'Okay, Fran, you're doing really well. Take a nice, deep breath and hold it for four, now out and count to four . . .'

His voice was calm and quiet.

'I-I . . . Too far, it's too far . . .' She couldn't get her breath.

'Breathe in and hold . . .' He sank down so that his face was at her level. 'Let's check your heart rate — it's fine. Look at me, Fran. You trust me, don't you? I won't let anything happen to you. You can do this. You *are* doing this. The water is calm, you're wearing a life jacket, you can float . . .'

His voice reached her distantly through the buzzing noise in her head, but finally she followed his patiently repeated instructions.

'Oh my.' She blinked, still holding both his hands. 'That was so weird.' She risked a look at the beach again, concentrating on her breathing. 'I felt like I was marooned out here. Miles out. And it didn't matter that I *knew* I was still in my depth, my body was telling me different.'

'Well done, Fran.' He squeezed her hands. 'You did really well to overcome your fears. Trust me, I know it's not easy. Lie back and float now, to tell your body that you're in charge. You're wearing a life jacket, so it'll be easy.'

'Okay.' She didn't want to let go of his hands. He was her only link with solidity and safety. 'Talk me through it again.' Gently disengaging one hand, he did.

'You're right,' she said eventually, as she lay like a star-fish, staring up at the soft, blue sky. 'It's so much easier to float in the sea.'

'That'll be the buoyancy aid.' He smiled down at her. 'And the saltwater. How are you feeling now?'

'Amazingly, I feel . . . okay. Better than that. Calm. And . . . sort of nothingy. In my head.'

'Sounds lovely.' He sighed.

'You okay, Wyn?' Guilt washed over her. She was so selfish. He gave up his mornings to teach her and still hadn't asked for payment, and now here he was in the sea with her, babysitting her through yet another meltdown and then feeding her afterwards. She felt humbled and grateful. 'I really do appreciate everything you've done for me, you know. It hasn't been long but, honestly, I'm feeling so much more confident in the water now. And that's all down to you. You probably think I'm being a wuss.' She righted herself, realizing that she was still holding his hand, and let out an embarrassed laugh.

He looked down at their linked hands. 'Fran, you really don't need to thank me. Believe me, I do understand about fear, and particularly fear of the water.' Looking directly into her eyes he opened his mouth as if to continue, and then shut it just as quickly. Turning towards the shore, he said in a bright voice, 'Let's head back before we get cold — and put some food on, shall we?'

She glanced at her watch as they waded. 'Oh my gosh, we've been out here for ten minutes. I would never have thought it. That's about how long Caitlin's ladies stay in for.' She grinned at him. 'I can tell them I've lost my sea cherry now.'

He bellowed a laugh. 'Indeed. And, er — not being paranoid or anything, but if you do decide to go for a dip with them, please let me know so I can loan you a tow float and stuff.'

'Aw, thank you. I think I'll wait until I can actually swim properly on my own. I couldn't have done this if you hadn't been with me, Wyn. I feel really safe with you.'

She reached up to plant a shy, thank-you kiss on his cheek. Their eyes met and his mouth sought hers. Heat surged through her body as his arms reached out to enclose her. Her buoyancy aid bounced off his and he reached out to grab her before she ricocheted away. Arms and legs entangled, their lips strained together, to complete that kiss. The inflated orange vests squeaked and farted between them and, despite her longing for his touch, Fran collapsed into helpless giggles.

'I'm not giving up that easily,' murmured Wyn, his lips close to her ear. Her heart soared.

Sinking to his knees, he unzipped his buoyancy aid, wrapped his long arms around her and scooped her against him. Their lips fused together. His hands pushed through her curls, caressing the back of her neck as her body arched towards him. She tasted his salty skin, rubbed her face against his cheek, wished she wasn't wearing gloves. Wished she wasn't wearing anything. Her bare thighs wrapped of their own accord around his and his arms encircled her more tightly.

She could have stayed like that for ever, in an endless kiss, their lips exploring exposed skin, the water swirling around their knees, the world, when she opened her eyes, bright and blue and salty and golden. His face close to hers, smiling, the deep blue of his eyes pulling her into his gaze.

'Time to get out, my little mermaid. I don't want you getting hypothermia on your first dip.'

Her body felt strangely warm and alive. 'Do we have to? I don't feel like I will ever be cold again,' she told him. Her skin glowed from his touch. She wanted more. Much more.

'Hah! It doesn't last, sadly. Come on.' He towed her in a gentle jog back to their spot in the dunes, unzipped her buoyancy aid and peeled it off her.

'Oh my God, give it back! Now I really am cold!' She wrapped her arms around herself, hopping from foot to foot.

'Put this on. I brought two.' He pulled out one of the giant fleece-lined changing robes she'd seen the ladies wear and cloaked it around her. The hem swept the sand. The feeling of warmth was instantaneous. Peeling off her gloves, she pushed her arms through the sleeves.

'This coat is like a giant hug!' He bent to tug off her boots and she stood on one foot, holding onto his strong, broad back, his skin warm beneath her fingers. 'But I know a better way to get warm.' She held the coat invitingly wide and smiled at his expression as he shrugged off his buoyancy aid and tow float in short order, reaching his arms around her once again. Lips and tongues meeting, she sighed as his warm hands lowered the zip on her swimsuit, moving over her slippery skin. As he lifted her bodily into the shelter of the sand dunes, her thighs wrapped themselves around his again and this time there was nothing between them and their urgent need for each other.

CHAPTER TWENTY-EIGHT

Cradled within his arms before the burning logs in the shelter of the dunes, they sat on a pile of cushions and blankets, their changing robes wound around them. The fragrant scent of onions and garlic rose into the twilight air from the big, old cast-iron pot that had belonged to Wyn's mother.

Fran leaned into him, inhaling with appreciation as he stirred the pot. The fire and setting sun turned her copper hair into curling licks of flame, and he watched, mesmerized, as she closed her eyes to the warmth.

She'd been right about that changing robe. It had been a giant hug. He'd managed to zip them both into it and their cold, wet naked bodies had met in a gasp of gooseflesh and giggles. Freezing skin and hot tongues. He'd never been so turned on. Sex in a Dryrobe. It was a thing and they couldn't get enough of each other. He couldn't stop looking at her now. Squeezing her fingers as her hand lay on his thigh. Knowing her nakedness now beneath the layers. Their scars — felt but not seen, in such close proximity — had meant nothing. They'd been explored, kissed and accepted.

Her eyes flashed wide as half a bottle of wine sizzled into the saucepan, and he laughed as she peered into her empty mug.

'There's plenty more,' he said, topping up her mug. 'Cheers.'

'Cheers!' Lifting her mug to him, she watched as he tipped the mussels into the boiling pan. 'This looks amazing, Wyn. I'm starving!'

He set the pan to the side of the fire until it was simmering, and put the lid on. By the time he'd hacked a fresh loaf into thick rounds and set the stoneware bowls and spoons out, the mussels were cooked. He stirred a pot of cream in and let it heat up again on the hottest part of the fire for a moment or two. A handful of chopped chives was the final flourish.

'Say when,' he instructed her, as he ladled the fragrant shellfish into the bowls.

'You've got to be joking.' Fran's eyes never left his hands. He grinned, spooning a good ladleful of the wine-and-garlic-infused cream over the gleaming indigo-and-purple shells.

They settled with their backs against the trolley, facing the sea. Fran picked up an open mussel, loaded with fragrant sauce. She held it up to the fire light.

'I feel like I should say something momentous. But I'm far too hungry for that.' She slurped the fish and closed her eyes as she chewed. Her eyes flew open and she stared at him. 'Bloody hell, Wyn. You're a genius.'

He laughed, delighted. 'Shut up and eat it then. Or I'll be—' He reached around her with his spoon and she shielded her bowl with her body, nestling into him at the same time.

'Get lost, big boy. There will be nothing left over in this bowl, muhahaha.'

The low sun dipped its golden fingers into the sea, sparkled into pinks and purples on the damp sand and sank as the sea retreated.

'Look at that.' Wyn pointed to the horizon. A deep-pink moon hovered over the sea, huge and almost unreal. 'It's a gift.'

'Oh! It's the Strawberry Moon! The Sea Sisters were talking about it the other day. They've met up with another group tonight.'

'It is indeed. I'd completely forgotten about it. Didn't you want to go with them?'

'I'd rather be here with you.' She snuggled into him. 'This is magical. It really is blood red.'

They stayed there for hours, warm, full of food and wine, wrapped in blankets, skin to skin, watching the rose-red orb rise into the sky. As the light faded into a navy sky, they made love again, gently, whispering and murmuring, lips as one. Seagulls pecked at their leftovers as the fire died. They slept until dawn. Pink and orange wisps streaked the sky. Wyn stretched and wriggled his body closer to Fran's.

'Nearly time for our swimming lessons.'

'No. I want to stay here for ever.' Her voice was sleepy and he smiled, tightening his grip around her.

'The old lady who collects driftwood will be along soon,' he said against her ear.

'She can go around us.'

'And the council man who combs the sand. And then the dog walkers, and the dogs will pee on us . . .'

'Ew.' She giggled. 'They comb the sand?'

'Yep. On a giant tractor, towing a massive sand comber.'

'You're kidding me.'

'Yeah.' He nibbled her ear. 'They come later in the summer. And only on the main beach.'

She rolled to face him, wriggling beneath him, her arms stretched above her head, her copper hair spread around her sleepy, smiling face. 'Can't I entice you to stay just a little longer?'

His body responded instantly, as it had that entire fire-warmed night. 'You're a siren, woman, luring me to my doom.' He reached into the pocket of his changing robe, squinting at the little sealed flat packet in his fingers. 'And luckily for you, one left in our sweetie box.'

Their love-making was gentle, quiet, careful of each other's hurts and flaws, where the night had been full of passion and need. He'd thought about her wired-up breastbone right from the off and she'd assured him with a vice-like grip that it was perfectly fine and not to worry. He'd still played it safe though. His injured arm didn't bear weight the way it used to, but they'd managed to be inventive with no loss of pleasure.

The tide had returned, along with the morning sunshine. Lake-flat, the sea was only metres away. Wyn sat up and looked around him. Nobody about. 'Skinny-dip before breakfast?'

She gulped. Nodded. 'Only because you said breakfast.' She sprang out of the blankets like Venus emerging from her shell and he admired her all over again. 'And because I'm desperate for a wee!'

She ran towards the bright sea, her tousled hair bouncing on her naked shoulders. He raced after her, his feet flying across the sand, hurdling the tiny waves to throw himself full length into the clear-as-gin shallows. He acknowledged how much better he was now at being in the sea in daylight, since pool training with Fran. His own psychology was working, he told himself. One day he'd manage a night swim. The very thought made him shudder and he disguised it by scooping water at Fran.

'Aah!' she squealed, holding her hands up to fend off his splashes. Beads of sunlit seawater ran from her naked breasts and over her curved hips. She was beautiful. He didn't even notice the scar. 'Get away from me, you sea monster!'

He flipped over, floating on his back in the shallows. They both looked down at his long torso as parts of it bobbed on the surface. 'Not exactly a sea monster at the moment,' he observed with a wry grin.

'I can fix that later . . .' She ran her tongue over her lips.

'Remember what Mrs Edwards said about no petting in the pool . . .'

'How could I forget?' Fran splashed him and ran away up the beach giggling, with him in hot pursuit. They didn't bother to get changed, throwing on their changing robes to keep warm. Wyn hurled everything into his trolley and they hurried towards the schoolhouse. 'Erm, Wyn . . . Do you think maybe we'd better go to the pool from yours, so I can just reappear at my front door afterwards as normal?'

'Instead of the walk of shame, you mean?' He sent her a sly look and she rolled her eyes.

'Exactly.' She groaned. 'Only, I'm starting to realize that this village has a really effective set of jungle drums, and we weren't exactly discreet last night.' Her face flamed.

'We're both free and single.' He shrugged.

'Yes. Yes, you're right, dammit.' She flapped her arms in the big coat. 'You're right! I've spent so long having to cover my tracks and avoid being the centre of the cesspit of gossip in a police station. Bah.' She turned a pair of blazing eyes his way, her cheeks pink. 'And, Wyn, I don't regret a single second of last night.'

He pushed his front door open and ushered her inside. He didn't regret it either. And the urge to confess his fears to her grew stronger. Later, he decided. He would tell her. When he considered himself fixed. He didn't want anything to spoil this moment. He pushed away the guilty feeling that he was enjoying being on the pedestal of her appreciation. It had been a very long time since he felt like this.

'Shower's there.' He pointed. 'I'll start breakfast.'

'You're really looking after me!' She reached up to kiss him, her nose cold. 'Thank you, Wyn. For everything.' She scooted into the shower. He grinned as she reappeared briefly, pink-skinned in a bath towel, scurrying away with her rucksack full of clothes. Putting the bacon in the warm oven, he stepped into the shower with her.

Afterwards, they finished the cooking together and ate ravenously.

'I'm going to swim like a brick now,' Fran announced, leaning back in her chair and rubbing her stomach. 'I know I've said it a million times, but I can't believe I actually went into the sea. Twice.' She widened her eyes at him. 'You could be monetizing this, Wyn. Overcoming fear. It's a big thing these days.'

He shook his head. 'It's empathy,' he said, mopping up his plate. 'And you'd already taken the biggest step by wanting to do it. Nothing can stop you now.'

He watched her to see if she picked up any clues as to his inner turmoil, but she took his words completely at face value and, for that moment, he felt calm and still inside. He'd also gone into the sea twice. Carefully controlled visits that avoided either of them being underwater or out of their depths. Or in the dark.

His fears mustn't become her fears. He needed to make her stronger than him. Make her as he used to be. It was the most precious gift he could give her. He could do that. By the time her parents arrived, she'd be confident enough to bob around out there with Caitlin's girls, looking like she'd been doing it all her life. Within her depth. And with a tow float.

CHAPTER TWENTY-NINE

Fran could almost see steam rising from the pool during their session that morning. Despite her lack of sleep, she felt vibrant and alive. Detached from the ordinary world. Her body somehow bypassed her brain, imitating his demonstrations, following his instructions, pushing her muscles to be longer, more streamlined, more efficient. His hands gently shaped hers to the correct positions, lifted and straightened, until right at the end of the lesson, she had a glimpse of what it felt like to swim in a coordinated way.

'It's like flying,' she told him wonderingly, 'in the water.'

'My work here is done. You *are* a mermaid.' He beamed and she reached out a finger to place it into one of the deep dimples that formed in his craggy jaw. Playfully, he pretended to bite, laughing as she mock-squealed and splashed him. 'You've come such a long way, Fran.' His face grew serious.

'Oh no. You're not getting off that easily. This—' she threw open her arms and whirled them around her — 'just being confident in the water, is more than I could ever have imagined. But I still want to be able to swim properly. And breathe at the same time. I have so many years to catch up on. So many wasted years of fear.' She shook her head. Her mouth opened about to say, *Where have you been all my life, Wyn Morgan?* and clamped shut on the words as she spotted his glance at the door.

It hadn't been the first time that morning. Her stomach dropped like a stone.

'Wyn.' Her tone nailed him. 'I'm too old to mess about.' Her words fell like pebbles into the still water. 'What's the score with you and Tasha?' His face set, and she swallowed. 'Look, I'm not known for mincing my words. I'm a grown-up, Wyn. We've had a good time. A really good time. But we can go back to the way we were. Nobody need know.' She licked her lips. 'As long as I know where I stand. Just . . . just don't make a fool of me. That's all.'

His face was carved from stone. *That's the end of that*, thought Fran. She looked away.

'Please don't try to lie to me and tell me you're not still in love with her. If there's one thing I'm good at, it's spotting a liar. Bye, Wyn. Thanks for everything.' She waded towards the steps, feeling suddenly fat, bloated, lardy, heavy, ugly. Old.

'Fran.'

She paused, one foot on the bottom rung. She didn't want to be the first to get out. To feel exposed.

Last night she'd felt beautiful. Wanted. Beneath the moonlit sky their fingers and lips gently explored those tortured fissures that had been torn apart as the only way to heal. In the daylight, their eyes had seen and accepted. Now, she felt revealed. More naked than she'd been at any time.

'Fran.' She felt the surge of water as he covered the distance in the effortless stroke of even one mighty arm. He put a warm hand on her shoulder and her entire body fizzed. She wanted to whirl around, throw herself into his arms, say, *Oh hell, it doesn't matter, let's just have a good time. I'll be gone soon anyway. Forget I said anything*.

But she couldn't. Why did she always have to find the truth in everything? Why couldn't she just lie to herself once in a while?

'I feel . . .' He grunted, correcting himself. 'I *felt* sorry for Tash.'

'What?' Fran looked over her shoulder at him, askance. The woman seemed to have everything. Fran wasn't going to mention the endless legs and tiny waist in case Wyn hadn't noticed, but what did she have to feel sorry for?

'And guilty.'

Fran's eyes narrowed. Oh, here we go. He'd been over the side during their marriage. Poor Tasha. She glared at him.

'She looked up to me,' he carried on, scrubbing at his cheek. 'And I know that sounds like I'm bigging myself up, and it's not what I mean, but I'm older than her, and my life probably seemed glamorous to her. An escape.'

'Huh?' Fran was lost. Nothing about his life seemed glamorous.

'She had rotten parents. They didn't give a shit about her. Really. I hate to psychobabble but I don't think she ever had any unconditional love, like children should have. I was a substitute parent, but it took me a long time to work that out.' He shook his head. 'Too long. I mean, my mates took the piss but, y'know, I was stupid and flattered, and who wouldn't want a pretty, young thing hanging on your every word when you're a broken-nosed rugby player with cauliflower ears?'

Fran glanced at his ears. Now he mentioned it, they did look a bit gnarly. She'd never noticed before. Cauliflowers though? Interesting analogy.

'Rugby is glamorous?'

'Wales loves their national rugby team. They're gods. Soccer is okay, but rugby?' His face split into a ruefully wonky grin. 'It's in their souls, the Welsh. Their hearts are rugby-ball-shaped.' He grunted. 'It's like a war out there, on the pitch, and then afterwards, in the bar, it's all handshakes and no bad feelings. They say it's a hooligan's game, played by gentlemen.' His eyes stared, unfocused, through the pool windows. 'You score a try, or get man of the match, you never put your hand in your pocket all night. Rugby players don't earn what the big soccer names do, but it's a good life if you're at the top. And I was. For a good while.' He shook his head. 'It suited Tash down to the ground.'

Fran listened, watching him carefully. Liars could always be nailed by their body language, and so far, everything tallied. No cover-ups that she could spot.

'So what happened?' She almost didn't want to know. Didn't want the opinion she had of him to be tarnished. But she wasn't exactly box-fresh, newly minted, untouched by life — so why did she expect him to be? Jealousy of a past life laid you firmly on the psychiatrist's couch, in her opinion.

'I gave the rugby up before my body broke too many times. And went back to my first love.'

Fran's jaw dropped. 'You did what? You *left* her and took up with someone else?'

'What? No! No — I went back to teaching!' He stared at her with a mixture of exasperation and amusement. 'You really don't have a high opinion of me, do you?'

'I do!' She rolled her index finger impatiently. 'Get on with it. I'm sorry. Just bloody say what you mean.'

'*Okaay*.' He cleared his throat, eyeing her sharply. 'Long story short, I'd trained as a teacher first, but had played club rugby since I was a *dwt*. I carried on teaching for a year but I couldn't do both. Rugby training takes up so much time, but I loved it. When I was selected for Wales I felt I had to decide between full-time rugby or teaching. I never regretted that decision. Eventually I returned to teaching and life became normal. But normal for me meant boring for Tasha. She hadn't known me as a teacher. She probably never thought I'd go back to it. And of course, the big money dried up. But I loved teaching.'

'You're good at it.'

'Thank you. I miss it.' The dimple reappeared and Fran stared, mesmerized. 'Turned out though, without the money, I wasn't enough for Tasha. We'd put off having a family, and when we started trying . . .' He lifted his shoulders, his face sad. 'I don't believe it would have saved us. Babies aren't emotional Elastoplast, in my opinion. That seemed to be all my fault though, so I did the only thing I thought I could to save us.

'I gave up teaching to go into commercial diving. I was already a qualified PADI diver, so it didn't take long to train. It gave me the big money. But . . .' He sighed, his expression troubled.

Fran didn't guess aloud. But she was beginning to see the trend. 'But . . .' she prompted.

'Tasha needs air to her fire. She needs money *and* attention. I couldn't do both. So—' he shrugged his eyebrows — 'she found the attention elsewhere.'

'AJ.'

'Uh-huh.'

'So why is she still hanging around you?' Fran frowned. 'And what is *his* beef with you? None of it makes sense.'

'I'm at fault for her still hanging around. I put my hands up to it. I feel like I let her down, mis-sold her our lives together. I should have cut the ties properly when she left. But . . .'

'But you still love her.'

'No.' He shook his head but shrugged minutely. 'You never just stop loving somebody you built a life with. It's not that simple. But it's not the same love. It's a different angle somehow. And it's more than that. He, AJ, he's a bully. He's mean.'

'You mean, he doesn't give in to her demands for more money?' She sounded cruel but she needed it in plain language.

'Well, there is that. And that isn't altogether a bad thing. She can be shockingly naïve about money.' He shook his head. 'But no. He's free with his fists.'

'What?' Fran's jaw dropped and a bubble of fury leaped in her stomach. Tasha was tiny. Not that violence would be any better had she been Amazonian. 'Do you have proof or is this another way of her winding you in?'

He swallowed. 'I do have proof, as it happens. You remember the CCTV footage from the pub, the night you arrived?'

'Yes, but I never saw it.'

'Well, it's all there. Plain to see. He fetches her a slap in the head that virtually takes her legs away, fucking coward, and—' his face twisted with fury — 'I was about to give him the pasting of his life—'

'Just as I turned up and stopped you.'

He nodded. Fran stared at him. 'I wondered, actually,' she said slowly. 'Afterwards. The way she was hanging onto your arm to stop you. I've seen that so many times in domestic abuse calls. He punches her, she rings us, we turn up to nick him for assault, she's trying to claw our eyes out for hurting him! I've never understood it.'

'I don't either. I've told her to leave him. She won't. She says it's her fault.'

'Classic.'

'I think she's punishing herself for leaving me.'

'So you make it up to her by not quite leaving her . . . ?'

He stared at her, his bottom lip caught beneath his teeth. 'Oh God. You're right. I'm enabling, aren't I? Every time I "patch up her life", she can go back for more punishment . . . And AJ never really feels that he *has* her, because she's still on speed dial to the Wyn Morgan Helpline.'

'I'm sure it's not that simple,' Fran murmured. 'And you can't blame yourself for her choices. She could do him for assault.'

'And look like a victim? Not her style. It's all about appearances for Tasha.'

Fran was getting cold. She bounced on her toes, feeling the water surge over her shoulders. 'So . . .' She almost didn't want to know.

'So where does that leave—'

'Us . . . ?' She swallowed. 'Look, we're adults, right, and I hardly know you, and last night, well, it was . . .' She took a deep breath, and tried again. 'I'm not saying it was a mistake or anything, but, you know, we can—' she whirled her index finger anticlockwise — 'reset?'

'I don't want to pretend nothing happened between us. Last night was — oh hell, it was like letting go.' He lifted his

258

arms like a tree, an adoration to the sky. 'It was wonderful! Fran, I know my life is messy and complicated. But you're the only person who's actually let me unravel the whole sorry, tangled mess and, and . . .' A deep flush spread from his battered ears across his lean cheeks. 'And I really, really like you. Oh God, I sound like a bloody teenager. How naff was that!' He put his hands over his face and sank beneath the surface of the pool.

She reached into the water and prized his fingers away. 'Oi!' she yelled into his submerged face. 'I really, really like you too!' She smiled into his eyes as he surfaced. 'And last night was wonderful for me as well.' She dipped her head and their lips met in the water. They resurfaced together. 'I'm just a suspicious old ex-copper, who likes to know where I am.'

'Fair enough.'

'And what I want to know right now . . .'

'Do you ever stop with the interrogating?'

'No.' She grinned. 'I want to know what my real chances are of swimming in a competition.'

He grinned back, finger and thumb cupping his chin, pretending to think. 'Higher than they were a week ago?'

Fran tipped her head and pursed her lips. 'Good answer,' she said, 'considering I haven't even swum a length yet. I can take that.'

'I like your optimism. Let's get that length nailed then.'

Her heart drummed. They were back to real life again. Nothing now was as simple and pure as it had been beneath the moon's eye, but there was a thread of strawberry moonlight that shimmered still between them. And as Wyn had pointed out, she was an optimist.

CHAPTER THIRTY

They enjoyed a week of scorching heat, but the weather in Wales could often be measured in pints, and the following fortnight was no exception to that rule. Wyn was kept busy fixing gutters and old windows that leaked and disintegrated beneath the relentless onslaught of rain after sunshine and salty winds.

'Tell Fran that hoodie she fancies is in stock, Wyn,' Ffion from the Surf Shack told him as he patched up the ancient window. 'I got it in another colour too, one that I think will be better with her hair.'

He could feel the heat rising up his neck as he bent over his tools. He cleared his throat. 'Thanks, lovely. You could always text her yourself. In case I forget, like . . .'

'Not much point really, is there? We all know you're joined at the hip these days. It's so sweet.'

Wyn sighed. *Sweet.* At his age. God. It had been the same at the pub, where Barty and his wife asked both of them over for dinner one evening with a faraway look on their faces at the memory of romance. The pensioners at the church hall where he was emptying the sodden attic space had made no bones about their curiosity, their sharp elbows jabbing him in the ribs as they cackled.

'Such a lovely-looking girl, you'd never think she was a copper. She seems far too nice,' they agreed loudly, grouped around their tables with tea and Welsh cakes, poker cards in hands. 'This hand is a foot! Who dealt?'

'Poor thing, so young to have a heart attack. I hope you're not wearing her out, young Wyn.' Nudge, nudge, cackle. 'Take that. Straight flush. Think she'll stay here or go back to the smoke?'

Wyn didn't know. Stolidly shovelling sodden, ancient Christmas decorations into rubble sacks and hefting them out of the building, he thought only of his and Fran's entwined fingers over the table of the tiny bistro café further along the coast the previous evening. They'd ordered crab, cracking open the vibrant shells and eating with their fingers. Tiny, salty Pembrokeshire new potatoes and locally picked samphire arrived in bowls along with chilli prawns and sourdough. It had been heaven.

His van had been parked outside Fran's cottage all night, every night for ages. Elin had ignored their red faces on the first occasion they'd emerged, blinking into the sunlight like moles, greeting them as cheerily and casually as if they'd been her neighbours since for ever. Almost as if it had been her idea all along, Fran had pointed out as Wyn died a thousand deaths inside. It was hardly surprising the entire village knew about their burgeoning relationship, and had an opinion.

Would it last? He didn't need to know, but he was nothing if not a realist. How could it last? She was a city girl. He was a country bumpkin. What did he have to offer her? Life in an endlessly unfinished doer-upper, in a village beside the sea, with one pub and a couple of shops.

Even as the thoughts scrolled across his brain, he felt ashamed for doing the village of Llanbryn a disservice. It was so much more than that. His head jerked up at the volley of laughter from one of the tables, followed by a cracked but enthusiastic rendition of 'We Are the Champions'.

Pensioners here were fitter than many. They hiked across the fields and beaches in animated groups, did Tai

Chi on the sand, and held regular Zoom quizzes to keep any housebound members involved.

Phil, recovering his mobility nicely at his daughter's, visited the village often to see Scruff, and to meet up with this bunch. Wyn's own dad, in his eighties, thought himself too young to join in with the over-sixties clubs, preferring to continue his hobbies and lifestyle with scant regard to his age. Wyn remembered that Elin, who also seemed ageless, maintained friendships with people of all ages.

If anything, it was hardest for the much younger here. Everything had become further away. Schools, doctors, hospitals — they'd all been pulled away from the communities and reassembled into sprawling concrete buildings under the umbrella term of 'super'.

Wyn pushed a stinking bag of oozing, handmade paper-chains, dissolved into multicoloured papier mâché, into the back of his van, reflecting that the village's loss in respect of the school had been his gain. He still felt guilty about it. He'd gone to school there, along with his entire village generation and several beyond. It was a beautiful building though, and he remembered with a glow Fran's reaction to it.

The weeks since he started teaching her seemed simultaneously to have lasted for ever and to have passed in the wink of an eye. Time sped up and then yawned. It had been four weeks since her parents had told her they were visiting. Fran had made terrific progress and he was so proud of her. And, he acknowledged with a wry nod at his lack of modesty, of his teaching.

Fran was capable now of swimming lengths, treading water and floating. They'd made several forays into the sea — always during the day and carefully managed by him for tides and weather — since that first, wonderful time, and each time her confidence grew.

His own confidence in the sea grew in smaller increments than hers. He'd made her promise to take a tow float if she went in with anyone else and never to swim alone, and then worried that he'd sounded paranoid. He'd never heeded his own advice and pre-accident regularly swam alone, particularly at night. He missed and longed for the peaceful calm of his old night swims. The regularity of his breathing, the soft, salty cold water as it lifted him over the moonlit sea, the strength and rhythm of two equally strong arms that he'd taken for granted. Gone now. Replaced by the withered arm, and a damaged and terrified mind.

He'd trusted himself. And now, flawed, weakened and scared, he didn't. But Fran did. And her trust in him pulled him along with her. He wouldn't, couldn't let her down.

Despite these pockets of squally weather, the long school summer holidays were imminent. The ever-popular campsite would be bursting at the seams, the beach would be packed with families and windbreaks, and even the secret hideaway in the dunes at his end of the beach would be invaded.

The villages were mostly equable about the summer invasion. It meant that the council kept the roads and car park in good order, the beach was clean and they had a lifeguard service. Geraint from the shop did well. Opening from morning till night, he, along with the pub and the coffee shop, employed the uni youngsters that returned home for the holidays.

It wouldn't be long before there wouldn't be any youngsters though. There was nothing year-round and sustainable for them there. Prices had risen now that the internet had enabled working from home, beyond the reach of most young couples.

He remembered Tasha's face as they'd been shown around that house on an inland estate. The slight but unmistakeable curl of her lip.

'Easy to maintain,' he'd said brightly, as they peered through the identikit patio doors into the pocket-hanky garden. How had she never understood that the money for exotic holidays, trips, designer clothes had all come from the same pot that would provide a home? It had been his fault. He obviously hadn't explained it properly. Made her believe it was a bottomless pit. Their savings had been frittered away. The excuses for her resounded hollowly these days.

He shook himself mentally. She hadn't contacted him since that day she'd showed up at the pool. He still couldn't decide whether he was relieved or worried. He consoled himself that she had to report for work, so if her knobhead husband bashed her about, somebody would notice if she was absent. Or damaged. It was awful to have to worry about that, no matter what relationship they did or didn't have. She was still a person. And he cared about her.

'My parents arrive tomorrow.'

The sun reappeared the following week, and Fran was helping him in the garden. 'Coming to me first and we're walking over to the pub.'

'Yes.'

'They've driven a coach and horses through my plans for them, as ever.' She jabbed the hand fork into the soft, damp soil and flicked earth into the air.

'Oh?'

'Mum is on Facebook.'

'Uh-huh.'

'So she's found the village hub, and posted that she's coming down, that we'll be in the pub and it would be lovely to meet the Sea Sisters.' She plunged the fork viciously into the ground. 'Why couldn't she just ask *me* about the girls? Why does she have to make a drama out of it? Isn't having a meal with me — *us* — not enough for her?' She waggled the fork, now stuck fast into the turf. 'She always makes me feel as if I'm twelve!' She sat back on her haunches and pushed the curly hair off her forehead, leaving a muddy smear.

In the new green dungarees that she'd proudly made herself in one of her classes, striped T-shirt and mutinous glare, Wyn thought she looked about twelve too. He suppressed a smile.

'Have many taken her up on it?'

'I have no idea. I didn't know anything about it until Caitlin sent me a message saying she'd see me at the pub and how nice it would be to meet my folks.'

'I expect it will be.'

'That's not the point!'

'*O-kaay* . . .'

'Shouldn't *I* have been inviting the Sea Sisters? I feel guilty about not even thinking of it!'

'How long will your parents be here?'

'God knows. I bet *they* don't know. Probably not that long, as they're having to pay for it.'

'You'll have plenty of time to be with just them.'

'Yeah. And that's something else I'm worried about. Oh, just ignore me. I'm being a proper grouch.' She yanked the fork from the ground and used it to exhume a plant with a delicate stem and yellow flower. 'Is this a weed?'

'No. Put it back in, poor thing.' He watched her as she carefully poked the straggling Welsh poppy back into its home.

'Sorry, buttercup. You're coming to the pub, aren't you, Wyn? I need the moral support.' She laughed quickly, trying to dismiss it as a joke.

'Poppy,' he corrected her. 'Welsh poppies are yellow. Moral support? About the swimming? Because I don't know you well enough yet to offer insights into any other areas of your life.'

She opened her mouth and shut it. He loved that she never even tried to fake her answers.

'Yes, the swimming. Do I need it?' She tipped her head and huffed with irritation. 'I don't, do I? I know what you're going to say. *I can decide when to feel fear.*'

'Very true.'

'Bah. You're no help.'

'So, do you want me there tomorrow or not?'

'No.' She grinned up at him. 'Yes.'

'You just want to show me off, don't you?' He'd said it flippantly, looking down at his stained and ancient overalls and holding out his battered ears, and then watched with astonishment as a bright-red stain flushed her cheeks. Her eyes slid away from him and she prodded the poppy she'd just replanted. 'I've seen these in the hedges. How come they're not weeds, then?'

'A weed is just a flower growing in the wrong place.'

'Elin says that.' She sighed. 'Because they always go on about me never having been married.' She bedded the soil more firmly around the poppy and sat back on her heels. 'Poor Fran. Married to her awful job. Time someone stood up to her, took her in hand.' She glowered at the ground. 'And just before I came down here, this *sort of* ex—' she coughed to disguise the words — 'told me, when I threw him out, that I would always be single. "Cop all the way through", he said. Nothing womanly about me.'

He looked at her for a long moment, deciding on his words. 'You know, that's not fact. That's just an opinion. You can choose whether or not to believe it.'

She glared at him and he stared impassively back.

'Bloody *hell*, Wyn.' She sighed gustily. 'You do make it hard for me to feel sorry for myself.'

He laughed, shuffling closer on his knees to fold her in an embrace and not caring who saw. 'Trust me, Fran. There is *nothing* unwomanly about you. Whoever said that is covering up for his own shortcomings.'

She took a deep breath and said into his neck, 'Thank you. You're completely right. Isn't it weird how people can say all sorts of nice things to you, like how good you are at your job, and those words all land on the same pile in your brain to be pushed away and forgotten, but it's the one nasty barb that stays with you for ever?'

He hugged her tightly. She was such a tough cookie on the outside, with her carefully nurtured hard shell. 'I'll be there.'

'Okay. Just warning you that they're a bit . . .' She paused, scuffing her hand fork over the grass before adding, 'Different. Not . . . normal. Not like me.'

'Normal is overrated.' He laughed, reaching over to nudge her with an elbow. 'And who on earth said you were normal?'

Her jaw dropped. 'I *am* normal! Mainstream, then. I should've said mainstream. Establishment? Law-abiding. Do as I'm told.' He laughed even harder and she tutted. 'Mostly. Look! I'm wearing khaki! How much more normal could I be? You won't catch my mum in khaki.'

'I'm looking forward to meeting them,' he assured her, once he'd wiped the tears of laughter from his eyes. He was.

CHAPTER THIRTY-ONE

Fran's parents texted to say they'd been held up and would see her at the pub. The fluttering in her stomach signalled either disappointment or relief, she couldn't decide which. The sun had returned with a vengeance after the apocalyptic rain, and she decided to enjoy it in the garden, watching video tutorials about swimming.

Geraint from the shop appeared from the path through the dunes, pulling a trolley laden with boxes.

'A'right, Fran?' he greeted her. She hadn't even realized he knew her name. 'Delivery for you. From Jean and James.'

'My parents?' Beneath her astonished gaze, he offloaded wine, gin with an assortment of tonics, salty snacks, pasties and loaves, and a variety of deli-type foods. As if, she thought crossly, she hadn't been able to cater for her own parents? Or had she missed a party invitation? Or maybe it was for them?

Geraint obligingly carried the boxes up the stairs for her, and Fran stowed away anything that needed chilling. She texted her parents.

A ton of stuff delivered! Are we expecting more people?

It's always good to be prepared, came the reply.

Fran typed: *I am perfectly able to shop, if you'd let me know what you wanted. I'm not a child, in case you hadn't noticed, and I am sick to death of you treating me like one. And I have plenty of money.*

She deleted it. After all, she reasoned, it hadn't occurred to her to buy in party supplies. She thought about not replying, then typed, eventually: *Okay X.* Even she thought it looked churlish. All that stuff must have cost a fortune. They were just being helpful, and she was being a cow. She added, *See you soon XX*, because she was nothing if not a grown-up. Occasionally.

Her afternoon in the garden had lost its appeal. Needing to walk, she wandered barefoot to the sea, enjoying the feeling of sand between her toes. Wading in, she admired her toenail polish in the clear water as it lapped over her knees. The sunlight sparkled on the fringes of the waves. She wondered what she would use to create that sparkle in her latest textile art project. A metallic thread, maybe. She'd see if Elin fancied another trip to Mumbles to have a poke around the charity shops, see what they could find.

As she waded along the shallows, she thought what a difference the summer had made. She'd arrived broken, bruised and angry with the world. She couldn't have dreamed of even paddling like this when she'd arrived here. Now she was fitter, calmer and enjoying her life.

She'd made friends all over the village. And there was Wyn. Her skin remembered his touch as she thought about him and a delicious glow crept over her. She firmly pushed away thoughts of what would happen at the end of the summer. It was wonderful for now. Nothing was for ever, was it? You had to live in the moment. Seize the day. That was what all those frankly irritating mugs and cushions said, anyway. Life was good. She could surely afford to be nicer to her parents.

* * *

Her parents were sipping wine at a table in the pub garden when Fran and Wyn arrived that evening. Despite her earlier admonitions to herself, Fran wondered how long they'd been there and why they couldn't have made it the few hundred yards around the corner to the cottage.

'Darling!' Leaping to her feet, Jean threw her arms around Fran in a typically exuberant embrace. She wore a long, tie-dyed jersey skirt with pink combat boots, a vibrant scarf artfully draped around her neck, topped off with a denim jacket. Her previously salt-and-pepper curly hair was now silver and tumbled onto her shoulders in a perfect cut. She looked annoyingly half her age.

'How lovely — you're looking well!' she said. 'The sea air obviously agrees with you. Good to get out of stuffy old London, isn't it? What a super place, and the campsite is fabulous, even if it is a bit pricey. Still — location, location, location. What a lovely village! You've really fallen on your feet here. You must give us the tour tomorrow.'

Fran hugged back, doing her best to stick to her 'be nice' resolution and trying not to jump to the conclusion that 'looking well' meant 'looking fat'.

'Hello, darling.' Her dad hugged her gently. 'How's the old ticker?'

'Still going!' Fran patted her scar, trying not to let her fingers notice the furrowed dip in her breastbone. It still freaked her out, although she thought about it a lot less since becoming involved with Wyn. She turned to him now.

'Wyn, this is Jean and James,' she said. 'And this is Wyn. He's my . . .' Fran stopped dead. Boyfriend? *Eww.* Did you have boyfriends at fifty? Significant other? That sounded very established. What then? She flicked a glance at Wyn for help.

'Lover,' he supplied with a grin, wrapping an arm around her and pulling her close. Fran felt her face heat up as if she were a teenager.

'Pleased to meet you,' Jean said. Fran noticed that she avoided his outstretched hand and went straight in for the cheek kiss. God, her mother was such a flirt. 'Fran has told us absolutely nothing about you.'

'Mum!' Fran felt her brow lower and smiled with an effort. 'I'll go and get some menus, shall I?'

'I'll go,' Wyn said, 'you catch up with your folks. What are we all drinking?'

They decided to share a bottle of wine. Fran watched him stride across the garden, dipping his head beneath the doorway of the pub.

'I do hope I haven't scared him away,' her mother said, following her gaze. 'It's so nice to actually meet your boy-friends for a change.'

Fran tutted. It was like being fifteen again. 'So, how are you both?'

The talk turned to the Sea Sisters.

'Lovely girls,' said Jean. 'We've had quite a chat online.'

'Yes. I saw that you'd invited them here later.' Fran heard the waspish note in her voice and cringed inwardly.

'Problem, darling?'

'I just wondered why you didn't ask me to do it.'

'Oh, you know, I was on social media, and before I knew it, I'd done it.' Jean peered at her over her glass. 'So you must be on Facebook now? You used to be so anti. I didn't see you there.'

'No. That's kind of the point.' Fran shrugged. 'I have a fake identity, thanks to my lovely neighbour, Elin.'

'You must ask to friend me. You can keep up with our adventures then! See where we are in the world, what we're up to.'

Fran felt suddenly furious with her mother. So, she didn't merit any special attention. She had to read about her parents with everyone else in the world. Why did her own life seem tame and dull by comparison? The future stretched out before her. Empty. She wished Wyn was still there, with his kind, effortless charm, to provide a balance to her grumpiness. He was so nice. What did he see in her? He'd been gone for ages. She was such a grouch though. He'd probably found a million people to chat to rather than go back to her.

'Did we tell you?' Jean didn't seem to notice Fran's sullen silence. 'We're off to Ireland after we do Wales. So close to the ferries, and it's somewhere else we've overlooked. So much to see!'

Fran wanted to say, *What happened to stop me swimming? Why have you never told me?* But she didn't want Wyn to return to a family drama. And she wasn't at all sure she wanted to resurrect the memory that lurked in the distant corners of her mind, in case it brought all her fears to the surface again. Let sleeping dogs lie, she decided.

She was heartily relieved when Wyn returned with a wine bucket, bottle and glasses, the menus tucked beneath his arm, and a smiling Elin.

'Sorry to be so long,' he said, after the introductions. 'It's heaving in there. The sunshine brings them all out. Elin was looking for you, so I brought her out to meet you.'

James and Jean stood to shake Elin's hand as Fran made the introductions. 'Elin is my wonderful neighbour. She's taught me some Welsh, how to make pizza and a proper G and T, and was responsible for finally getting me on Facebook.'

'It's been a treat having Fran next door,' said Elin, 'and I'm delighted to meet you both.'

'Please,' James beckoned her into a place around the table, 'you will join us for dinner, won't you?'

'If you're sure . . .' Elin began. Fran listened to their conversation, feeling as if she'd stepped into an old-fashioned radio play. Wyn cleared his throat.

'The specials are . . .' He read them from his phone. 'I took a photo of the board.'

'How clever of you,' Jean said. Fran rolled her eyes, and then caught Wyn's raised eyebrow and felt a blush creeping up her face. She was behaving abominably. Elin would be bound to notice. She felt ashamed.

'I'm having the sea bass,' she decided quickly. 'I can recommend the pies, Dad. And the chips.'

'You've obviously tried them all, darling,' said her mother.

'What's that supposed to mean?' Fran felt her body stiffen.

'Why would it mean anything? You are funny, darling.' Jean squinted at the menu and Fran realized that she wasn't wearing her glasses. 'Read out the specials again, Wyn, darling.'

Someone came out to take their order and Wyn ordered another bottle of wine as he emptied the last of the first bottle into Fran's glass. She felt a rush of affection for him. He chatted easily with her dad, and Elin asked them both relevant and interesting questions about their lives in a motor home, full-time.

'How do you get your post?'

'We have a mail-forwarding service and either collect it from an old neighbour, or they forward it to us if it's something we need, like passports or driving licences,' James told her. 'But there's not really much mail these days. It's all email.'

'Do you take it in turns to empty the toilet?' Elin leaned forward, interested.

'Eww.' Fran snorted in disgust and her parents laughed.

'Depends who's filled most of it,' her mum said. 'It's not so bad these days. The biological loo stuff smells quite nice.'

'Do you miss having a house?' Wyn wanted to know.

This was met with an emphatic no, although her dad was quick to add, 'We do sometimes house- and animal-sit. We're always keen to get back to the van afterwards.'

'What happens if you need a doctor?' Elin again.

'You can use any surgery as a temporary visitor. Touch wood—' her dad tapped the table — 'we're healthy as horses.'

'Long may that continue.' Wyn lifted a glass to them both with a smile.

Fran listened with mixed feelings. She had long seen her parents' lifestyle as self-indulgent escapism. She regarded her firm adherence to a mortgage, rates and bills as her contribution to society. A working lifetime dealing with dropouts, tenant shirkers and scammers who made their landlords' or neighbours' lives hell meant she strived always to be a responsible member of the community.

Now, though, doubt pierced her previously unswerving belief in her lifestyle. Had it compromised her health, resulting in a heart attack before her fiftieth birthday? She contemplated her parents now, both slim, active, healthy and looking younger than their years, despite their apparent fondness for wine and salty snacks. And still, evidently, having fun. How was it fair?

They were now in their seventies. Would they carry on their nomadic lifestyle as they became older and possibly infirm? Would they, God forbid, become dependent on her?

She realized with a shock that she had no idea about their health, about how they accessed medical services if they needed them. What did they do about dental check-ups, for example? How did they cope when they were abroad and sick? How had she got to nearly fifty without ever thinking about this?

Fran looked towards her parents, chatting animatedly to Wyn and Elin. She recalled guiltily that she'd told Wyn that her parents weren't 'normal'. Perhaps it was her that was out of step.

Their meal arrived and Fran was relieved that it was as delicious as she'd promised. Somehow she felt responsible for the village putting on its best face. As if by magic, as they folded their knives and forks together, Caitlin and several of the Sea Sisters arrived in the garden. Fran hailed them.

'Hey, ladies! Come and meet my folks.'

'So nice to meet you in real life!' Caitlin and the other girls were big on hugging and her parents were in their element.

'I would have gone in for a dip when we arrived but I'd left my costume in the van,' her mother said. 'Not that it usually stops me.'

Fran couldn't decide whether she was impressed or appalled at the idea of her mother jogging naked down to the sea. After all, she and Wyn had, that dawn after the Strawberry Moon.

'Sounds like you're one of us!' Wendy looked chic in white jeans and a navy shirt. 'All ready for tomorrow!'

'What's happening tomorrow?' she said, trying not to feel left out of yet more information sharing.

'Tomorrow night, it's a . . .' Her mother paused for dramatic emphasis.

'What? It's a what?'

'Full moon!' the Sea Sisters and her mother chorused. Fran had an urge to slap them. In a line, one after the other. How could she be feeling so sidelined?

'A time to visualize your goals . . .' Jean intoned, eyeing Fran and Wyn in turn.

'Mum!' Fran rolled her eyes. 'Sorry, Wyn. I have no control over her.' Wyn, deep in conversation with her father, showed no signs of having heard, to her relief.

'Fire on the beach, wine, cake, hot dogs, the works,' Wendy said, waggling her head at Fran's apparent inability to keep up. 'Skinny-dipping.' She looked around at everyone with a wolfish grin. 'All very pagan.'

'We'll be there, won't we, Wyn?' Fran said brightly, as if she'd known about it all along.

Wyn's head jerked up from his conversation with James. 'What's that?'

'Moonlight dip, tomorrow night.' It would be Fran's first swim beneath the moon. The Strawberry Moon held a special place in her heart, but they'd admired it from their Dryrobe cocoon, on the beach. The idea of venturing into that dark sea had been scary as hell. Who knew what was in there? She was excited at the prospect, but she couldn't do it without him. He was her rock.

'Me?' He cleared his throat. 'You don't want me there, it's a girl thing, isn't it.'

'The Lads 'n' Dads are coming over from the Three Bells at Penwaun, so there'll be plenty of blokes,' Caitlin said.

'Ah.' Wyn's smile had frozen on his face. 'I'll do the barbecue, if you like.'

'Lads 'n Dads have it covered,' Caitlin said. 'Besides, you always do the barbie. You can come and enjoy yourself for a change.'

'Oh. Thanks.'

Distracted by the girls and her mother discussing who would bring what, Fran didn't notice that Wyn had fallen completely silent until the pub called time.

CHAPTER THIRTY-TWO

He hadn't thought this through at all. How had he not considered that Fran would want to do a moonlight dip? He couldn't do it. He couldn't go into the sea in the dark. He felt as if the air had been punched out of him, just thinking about it. How could he excuse himself? He wouldn't lie to her. She'd know anyway.

The thought of telling her that he was scared was awful. What would she think of him? She'd spent a career with men whose lives were about taking decisive and sometimes split-second action. He fell far short of that ideal right now. His insides turned to mush. He'd assured her that he would keep her safe in the water. That she could trust him. She did, and he had. But that had been in daylight, with careful attention to sea conditions, never in the dark. Never in pitch-black water. The sea in daytime was a challenge that he was getting better at, but at least the water was clear . . . He gulped, his brain overwhelmed again by the heart-pounding horror — the terrible pain, wanting to die, afraid to die . . . the black, pitch, empty void of that appalling place. *He couldn't.*

What would her reaction be if she knew that all the time they were in the sea, even during the day, his heart was beating in the same panic as hers? That he faked his calmness?

She might go right back to where she'd started and reject all his teaching. She was so thrilled to be swimming now, he couldn't take that away from her.

And in the dark recesses of his brain was the belief that Tasha had left him because she'd stopped looking up to him. When he became a teacher, he became a nobody in her eyes. He couldn't bear the thought that Fran might feel disappointed in him. She already referred to him as her rock. A rock, only he knew, made of papier mâché, which would disintegrate in dark water . . .

'So, Wyn,' James said, in his unhurried way, 'you started telling me about your schoolhouse. How far along is it now?'

Relieved at the distraction, Wyn dragged his attention back to the present.

'Come over and have a look round, if you're interested,' he said. 'The building is up to first fix — so the structure is there. It seems to have taken for ever.'

James chatted in a surprisingly knowledgeable way, considering, thought Wyn, that he didn't even live in a house. He laughed when Wyn pointed it out.

'Oh, we've lived in some terrific places over the years. We've babysat old buildings mid-renovation when the owners have been ill or called away. Sometimes they're almost habitable!' He smiled into the distance. 'It does make me think sometimes about stopping in one place. Jean loves the van life though. She does like to collect people.' They both looked to where Jean was chatting animatedly, surrounded by the Sea Sisters, Elin and Fran. 'Especially young people. When you get to our age, all your friends seem to be dying or complaining about their ailments. You don't get that when you're a van-lifer. People are still out there, looking for the next adventure. I'm all for that. Excitement till we die, that's what I say.'

The party fizzled out fairly early. The Sea Sisters all had plans to get up for a dawn swim, and Jean was keen to join them. Wyn could have gone along with that, no problem. He sighed. The five of them walked back to James and Jean's motorhome via Elin's cottage, where they shared goodnight hugs. Wyn was taken aback to see that the motorhome was extremely large and very plush inside. He'd somehow been expecting something much smaller.

'I take my hat off to you, squeezing down our lanes,' he said to James.

'You should hear the language.' James smiled at Jean. 'And I'm no better.' He and Jean laughed together. Wyn thought how in sync they were. They'd been excellent company that evening. They were opening cupboards now and offering nightcaps.

'Not for me, thanks!' Wyn held up his hand.

Fran patted her chest. 'Had my quota. See you in the morning for the dip!' They left after a barrage of hugs. He took Fran's hand as they crossed the beach, and they walked in silence. He told himself they were enjoying the peace and warmth of the evening, but in reality, he was waiting for her to speak first. Eventually, as she was almost home, she did.

'Turned out okay tonight. Despite my misgivings.'

'Yes,' he said cautiously. 'Your parents are interesting people.'

'Ever the diplomat.' She laughed and then exhaled a sigh. 'Was it okay, though? Honestly, Wyn, I felt like it was me that was out of step the whole evening. I'm sure I got grouchier as the evening went on.'

Wyn squeezed her hand and changed the subject. 'Your dad has said he'd like to see round the schoolhouse. I said I'd show him tomorrow. They've had fascinating lives, your folks.'

'So I *was* grouchy then.' Fran huffed.

Wyn turned to wrap her in a huge embrace, kissing her grumpy face. 'Let me take you to bed and see if I can cheer you up.'

'It's going to be a tough challenge.'

'I'm up to it.' He swept her up in his arms and tried not to stagger too noticeably to Fran's front door. She giggled helplessly.

'You idiot, put me down!'

As she hunted for her door key, he said, 'All that swimming has done me good. I don't think I could have done that a month ago.'

'Make it sound like you've just won the World Weightlifting Championships, why don't you?' She rolled her eyes and then grinned wolfishly at him. 'Let's see if you can manage the next challenge.'

Afterwards, lying wrapped in each other's limbs, he thought about the moonlight dip. He couldn't let Fran down. She was relying on him. And he didn't want to let himself down either. Was he never going to be able to swim in a night sea again? It was the same sea that he and Fran had swum in already. But always daylight, and within their depth, the clear water bringing with it no nightmares . . .

He repeated the mantras he'd told to Fran, visualizing himself out there, succeeding. He could do it.

He slept fitfully until Fran slid out of bed the following morning, leaving a cold spot. The sun was up already.

'Going for my swim.' She kissed his neck and whispered into his ear, 'Won't be long. You can stay there and warm me up when I get back.'

'Take a tow float,' he said, resisting the urge to pull her back into bed. *Please be careful.* 'Enjoy!' he called, as he felt her warm lips leave him.

'I will!' She let herself quietly out of the front door, and he heard the sounds of the other girls arriving, just as Fran had described them when she'd first met him. It was quarter to six.

'Woohoo, get you, Frannie, virgin dawn swimmer!' He recognized Caitlin's voice and Fran's laugh in response. The other voices blended into an anonymous chorus.

'Great party last night.'

'New bathers, I see — are those the recycled ones?'

'Yeah. They're giving me a bit of a wedgie but maybe they'll stretch in the water.'

'Too many buns, Wendy . . .'

'Shut it, you.' There was raucous laughter as the voices drifted away, and Wyn smiled to himself. He was sure Fran was in good hands, and he almost wished he was going with them, but it was such a comfortable bed. He snuggled back down. His body twitched as he drifted off.

The blackness was more than black. It was hell. Thick, impenetrable darkness. Things floated past. Were they inside his face mask or outside? Were his eyes open or not? He couldn't even tell which way up he was.

Trying to breathe slowly. Failing. Oxygen tank emptying fast. Too fast. Heart pounding like a boot against a door. The pain. The terrible, visceral, awful pain. Crushing, squeezing, pinning him like a butterfly in a frame. Helpless.

His groans, on every outward breath, like an animal. He'd once heard a cow in distress bellowing like this. It had been shot. Its life over in a moment. He wanted to die. Be out of pain.

No! He didn't want to die! Not there, not—

He jerked awake, sweating and panting. He checked his watch — eight minutes. It had felt like a terrible eternity. Body and brain shuddering, he dragged himself out of bed, pummelling the blood back into his tired face, scared to close his eyes.

Switching on the radio and turning the volume up loud, he stood in a hot shower and scrubbed at himself. By the time Fran returned, he'd made the bed and had bacon sizzling in a pan. Pink-cheeked and bright-eyed, she came upstairs to find him. He kissed her cold, salty cheek.

'How was it?'

'Awesome!' She was fizzing with energy, jigging from foot to foot. Her damp hair curled around her shoulders. 'I stayed in for ten minutes. I even swam a bit, but I stayed in my depth. And I had my tow float, of course.' She put her arms around his waist and squeezed him. 'Mum was in for longer — but Caitlin said nobody gave you a trophy for staying in too long, so I was a good girl and got out as soon as I started to feel cold.'

'Well done.' He kissed her. 'I've created a monster!'

'I'll just go and hang my stuff up so it's all dry for tonight. I'm so looking forward to it! In a sort of apprehensive way, if you know what I mean. I'm so glad you'll be there. I can't do it without you, Wyn. The thought of not being able to see what you're swimming in. There might be jellyfish! Or even real fish . . . Eww!' She shuddered, scurrying down the stairs. 'Smells amazing,' she called up. 'I'm starving. You're my hero, Wyn!'

Not being able to see what you're swimming in . . . Wyn stared at the bacon curling in the pan, trying to think about anything but the moonlight swim, and how much of a hero he absolutely wasn't.

Between bites of her bacon sandwich, she continued her excited chatting.

'There's going to be street food! And music! A double dip *and* my first moonlight swim. You are coming, aren't you?'

Wyn collected their plates and stacked them in the dishwasher. 'I'll go down to the shop and get some fresh pastries, for your folks to have with coffee when they arrive.'

'Oh, that's a good idea, why didn't I think of that? You are an angel, Wyn.' She jumped up and wrapped her arms around him. He stooped to kiss her forehead.

'Jump in the shower and warm up. You're still cold.'

He caught her slight frown as she went downstairs and he heard the shower running. Pushing his wallet into his jeans pocket, he let himself out. The sun was already hot. It was going to be another glorious day. And all he could think about was what was going to happen at the end of it.

CHAPTER THIRTY-THREE

Fran wasn't too worried when, an hour later, her parents arrived and Wyn hadn't. He'd probably been lassoed into some plumbing emergency or other, she thought. And with no signal in the village, he wouldn't have been able to let her know. She set the coffee machine to work and rummaged through the goodies her parents had sent.

'You really didn't have to,' she said, loading coffee mugs, milk and sugar onto a tray for her dad to take down to the garden. 'I can shop.'

'It's nice to be able to spoil you once in a while,' he said. 'You don't make it easy, you know.'

Fran followed his tall, thin frame down the stairs with a packet of Welsh cakes. It was very unlike her dad to make judgements. She'd been horrible, hadn't she? She mentally rewound the last twenty-four hours. And probably to Wyn too. Which was why he still hadn't come back.

She showed her parents around the house and was wondering what to do with them next when Wyn returned. Without the pastries. He looked pale and slightly sweaty.

'Are you okay?' She reached up to kiss him, alarmed when he barely dipped his head. Her lips slid off his cheek. There were patches of sweat on his T-shirt, she noticed, and his skin smelled somehow sour, after the freshness of his morning shower. She substituted *Where have you been?* for 'Has something happened?'

'I'm fine,' he said, his face taut. 'Are we going for this walk then?'

'Yes.' Fran tried not to react to his unaccustomed brusque tone. She'd never heard him like this. Was it her fault? What had happened? What wasn't he telling her?

* * *

Wyn hated himself. From somewhere outside himself, he watched Fran recoil from his coldness and yet he couldn't seem to do anything about it. If the world would just go away, he'd be fine. But it was hurtling towards him and he felt as if he were frozen in the path of a speeding truck.

Once she was in the shower, he'd hurried away from the cottage, bathed in relief to be away from her relentless chatter about the moonlight swim. He'd marched straight out of the village, with no clear idea where he was going, until he'd found himself at the Edwards's farm. Staring at the swimming pool where he'd been teaching Fran.

He'd stood there for a long time, his mind drifting over the weeks since she'd arrived, all gung-ho and officious. How she'd worked on her fitness, integrated into the village and finally conquered her secret fear. How proud he was of her. And now, how big a part of his life she'd become, in a relatively short space of time. He felt winded at the thought of how much he would miss her.

And for all that, she'd surely be gone at the end of the summer. Back to the big city, with so much to distract her. If she remembered him at all, he would no doubt be consigned to a holiday romance. A hopefully nice memory of a summer spent learning to swim.

If, he reasoned, he confessed his fears now, and their relationship fizzled out, did it matter? He could just say, *Sorry, not going, had a terrible experience and I don't do dark water. But you'll be fine. Off you go. Have a nice time.*

He felt sick just rehearsing the words through his brain. He couldn't even admit them to himself. It had been so much worse than a terrible experience. It had been the stuff of nightmares. It still was. And saying it aloud meant that it had really happened. And wouldn't it infect Fran with his fears?

He wasn't stupid. Oh, he knew it had happened. But he'd separated the incident from his familiar life in the village, so that he never had to speak about it. No danger of bumping into somebody and having a conversation about it, which would bring it all back to him. Could consign it to the past, where it belonged.

Fran was lucky. She had no memory of what had caused her fear of the water. Nothing to draw on, no night terrors, no waking bathed in sweat. Reliving it every time he looked at his scars. Reduced to half his strength. Half his power. Pitied.

Furious at himself and the feeble turn his brain was taking, he stomped up the road. He remembered Fran feeling faint that day he'd scared her in the garden, how she'd made a joke about it. How brave she was. How much she'd overcome. She'd think him a coward right now, for the way he was thinking. He was better than this.

Pivoting on his heel, he pounded back down the hill. If she could do it, he could. If their relationship didn't last beyond the summer, he could at least make the most of knowing this extraordinary, strong woman. She had done more than anyone to make him feel whole again. To make him proud of himself.

Surely he could do this dip. *Think how good it will feel to finally nail that fear*, he told himself. He didn't want to lose her. Whatever happened at the end of the summer, he wanted her to still be in his life. Somehow.

So why he behaved like an absolute pig when he returned to the cottage, without either explanation or the pastries he'd gone for, he had no idea.

He caught himself, thundering along the beach path to his schoolhouse, his long legs taking him further and further away from Fran and her parents. It felt good to move, to push himself. It silenced the tingling pins and needles in his hands and feet.

'You're behaving like an ass,' he said aloud, forcing himself to turn around and go back to them. He was shocked at how far away they were. He wrapped Fran in a hug. 'I'm sorry,' he murmured in her ear. 'I don't know what's the matter with me today.'

The relief in her expression made him hate himself more. He gazed at the sea with longing. Now would be a good time to throw himself in. How he missed the embrace of the saltwater, the simultaneous chill and warmth that drove scratchy thoughts from your head, and left you calm and smoothed out. Apart from the world but at one with nature.

If he conquered his fear tonight, he'd be able to swim whenever he wanted to. He pulled his shoulders back and strode away, only to have to wait a hundred yards further on.

Like the Tortoise and the Hare, they reached the schoolhouse.

'Sorry, the scaffolding makes it hard to see the real shape of it.' He waved a hand towards the building.

'It's a handsome building.' James nodded. 'I love the gabled hall.'

'Me too.' Wyn nodded, happier to be talking about something close to his heart that wasn't the moonlight swim. 'I'd thought that would make a fabulous pool house. Now I'm wondering if it might be a waste of all that wonderful double-height space.'

'It would be lovely if you galleried it and made the most of the views over the sea.' James looked thoughtfully at the building. Fran and Wyn stared at James.

'That's a brilliant idea,' Wyn said. 'Why didn't I think of that? I've been thinking that it's a shame that I can't see the sea, despite being so close.'

'Or make it into an upside-down house, like the one Fran's in.'

'And another cracking idea!' Wyn stepped back, looking up at the building. 'If I really want a pool, there's plenty of room to put it somewhere else.'

'Or one of those resistance pools,' said James. 'Good for fitness and takes up less space.'

'Blimey, Dad.' Fran stared at her father in surprise. 'When did you become an interior designer?'

'We've house-sat places we could never have afforded to buy.' James smiled. 'You pick things up.'

Wyn walked them around the outside of the property, pointing out what had been done and what he planned to do next, with a growing sense of anticipation. By the time that he was showing them around the inside, he was itching to crack on with his list of jobs and heard himself blurt it aloud.

'Why don't you all go back and enjoy Fran's sunny garden?' In the corner of his eye he saw her jaw drop, and hurried on, 'The girls in the coffee shop do a takeaway cream tea. If you ring them, they'll deliver it.' He held his breath as they exchanged glances.

'Cream tea sounds like a plan,' said Jean. 'Come on, darling.'

Wyn tried not to look too relieved as they left. He gave Fran a long hug to make up for being such an arse.

'Are you sure you'll be okay on your own?'

'Of course.' His jaw was so tight he could barely get the words out. 'Go and spend some time with your folks. They're good people.'

'See you later?' She said it with a hopeful lift at the end, fixing her eyes on his. He couldn't bear it.

'Enjoy your cream tea!' Releasing her, he faced her towards the door. He couldn't miss her puzzled, hurt expression as she walked away from him. He shut the door and leaned on it before his legs gave out.

CHAPTER THIRTY-FOUR

Fran pinned a bright smile on her face as she caught up with her parents. What had happened to everyone today? They'd all had personality transplants. Her dad had suddenly turned into a talkative expert on old buildings, her mum seemed, well, *nice*, and Wyn had become — frankly — completely weird. What the hell had happened to make him behave like this?

'Have we upset him?' Her dad looked at her enquiringly.

'I have no idea.' Fran shrugged. 'I've never seen him like this before.'

'He seems like a nice bloke.'

'He *is* nice.' Fran heard the defensive tone in her voice. He was. Apart from the last few hours. 'Perhaps he's got something on his mind.'

'I'm sure you would know,' said her mum. 'We don't know anything about him.'

Fran was silent. She wasn't sure that she knew as much about him as she thought she had.

'Looking forward to this cream tea,' she finally said. 'I had no idea they did deliveries.'

'Did you put the prosecco in the fridge?' Jean said. 'And we don't need a cream tea. Didn't your little shop deliver a huge box of goodies yesterday? Let's go and investigate. I hear the pasties are excellent.'

Fran laughed. 'Good call.'

Suddenly, she was very glad to have her parents there. Whatever was going on with Wyn, he was right about one thing: they were good people. She yawned, wondering if they felt as tired as she did after her early start. They'd all be asleep in the garden chairs with a glass of prosecco inside them and the sunshine. She'd better get the sun cream out. And the parasol that she'd seen in the shed. The shed where she'd screamed at Wyn that first morning, unnerved by her new vulnerability. How wrong she'd been about him. Everything here reminded her of Wyn . . .

They decided to take their pasties onto the beach and have a picnic. Taking mugs instead of glasses, they ferried the parasol, folding chairs and a little folding table along the path between the dunes, along with a cool box containing the bubbly, snacks, water and suntan lotion.

'This feels terribly decadent,' Fran said, as the cork from the prosecco bottle flew into the air. No prospect of her driving her parents anywhere later then.

She felt nicely lazy. She'd had a swim and a walk and her smartwatch told her she'd almost completed her exercise quota, so she felt entitled to some downtime. 'I can't believe I haven't actually done this before.' She dipped her pasty into a puddle of brown sauce and took a bite. 'Apart from eating cake here with the Sea Sisters. And Wyn's amazing mussels . . .' Her voice petered out as the memory returned. 'I've only just got used to having a garden.'

'You're going to miss all this when you're back in the flat.'

Fran's stomach ricocheted. Trust her mother to point out the obvious.

'I suppose,' she began, 'that at least it gives me a decent capital to work with if I wanted to move. Or something.' Her parents eyed her.

'You've had a life-changing experience, darling,' said her mum. 'Don't make any decisions until you're fully on your feet.'

'You surprise me, Mum.' They'd been surprising her all day. 'I thought you'd be urging me to sell up and buy a camper van.'

'It's not for everyone.' Her mum picked the pastry off the top of her pasty and ate the filling only. Which was clearly how she stayed so thin. 'It's a great life, but you have to compromise. There's no space for anything nice to wear. Everything has to do double duty.'

'I don't have a lot of clothes, so I'd be okay.' Fran thought about her minimalist wardrobe back in the flat. 'I don't even really know what to wear these days.'

'We could go shopping while we're here,' her mum said. Fran couldn't remember the last time they'd shopped together. 'Get you a decent haircut.' Soothed by the twin effects of sunshine and prosecco, Fran laughed.

'Cheers, Mum.' Some things never changed.

The afternoon wore into evening. All three of them snoozed in the sunshine, lulled by the sound of the sea and their earlier exertions. The sun was still high but the heat was going out of it. They took the picnic things back to her garden and thought about dinner. In the end, Fran bought them fish and chips and tea in cardboard cups from the takeaway.

'This is a Welsh salad, apparently,' she told them with a grin, almost expecting her mother to refuse it.

'Shall we sit here?' her mum said, colonizing one of the benches that looked out across the bay. 'It's too nice to go inside. You'd never think this was Wales.'

Fran sat between them. She would have liked to go back to the cottage in case Wyn was there and looking for her. She'd checked her phone a dozen times in the last half an hour. Nothing. Given that the Wi-Fi in the village was non-existent, she told herself not to worry.

She texted the details of the swim, with times and what would be there. No reply. He hadn't even opened her message.

'Expecting a call?' Her mum caught her checking her mobile for the millionth time. Fran jumped.

'Uh, no, just, um, haven't heard from Wyn. About tonight.'

'Maybe he's just got busy on all those jobs,' her mum said. 'Does it matter if he doesn't come? We'll be there.' She glanced at James, dozing sitting upright, sun hat low over his face, hands clasped on his stomach, snoring gently. She rolled her eyes. 'Or at least, I will be. Your father is going to have a crick in his neck falling asleep like that.'

Fran said, in a rush, 'I've never done a moonlight swim. I've watched the girls swim but I was on the beach. I can't do it without him.'

'Of course you can. We'll all be there.'

'You don't understand. Wyn has been teaching me to swim this last month. He's been brilliant. It's only because he has that I came out with you and the girls this morning. It was my very first swim with them!' Fran could feel her fish and chips sitting like a stone in her stomach.

Her mother narrowed her eyes. 'You only learned to swim in the last month?'

'Yes!' Fran's voice was shrill. She took a deep breath and forced herself to be calm. This was it. 'How do you not realize that I've been terrified of water my whole life? And the worst of it is, I don't even know why!' She faced her mother. 'Why, Mum? What happened?'

Her mother's eyes swivelled to where her dad slumped, still asleep. She pursed her lips, shaking her head. 'You've obviously moved on now. So you don't really need to know.'

'You have no idea how hard I worked to be out in the sea with you this morning.' Fran fought to keep control of her voice. 'I've wanted to ask you so many times. It's driven me mad. I have this hazy memory of being in a swimming pool and being so glad that I'd swum a width and I'd have a badge and then—'

Her mother caught her breath with a sob and slapped her hand over her mouth.

'Oh, Mum . . .' Fran was shocked to see a tear rolling down her cheek. She reached out but her mother held up her hand, pulling away slightly.

'I told myself you wouldn't have remembered anything. All these years. I've felt so guilty.' She blew her nose in one of the chip shop serviettes. 'I was never very happy in the water, but I didn't want to make you scared, so I made myself go swimming with you.' Her voice was low and Fran had to strain to hear. 'And you were so cute, with your little, chubby legs and curly red hair. You had a turquoise swimsuit with spotty dogs on it.'

'I haven't changed much . . . apart from the swimsuit,' Fran said. Her mother gave a wan smile.

'You were off that day, like a little wind-up toy. And you were fine, bobbing along. I was so proud of you.' She took a long breath, her eyes in the distance. 'I'd got in with you, but it was crowded and the noise, the smell of chlorine, the pressure to look happy — I wasn't coping at all well. I remember just hanging on to the side of the pool, waiting for you. Counting the minutes until we could get out. I was supposed to be watching you. Calling encouragement. I felt guilty for being such a bad mother.' She tore at the cardboard packaging from her fish and chips. 'Somehow, to get away from all the kids jumping in and shouting and everything, I'd gone right around the pool holding the rail. I was in the deep end and hadn't realized. And then you jumped on my back, for a piggyback, like you did with your dad.

'I went down like a stone. I looked up and saw this little pair of legs kicking on the surface.' She covered her face. 'And I reached up and grabbed them.' She rocked in distress. 'To save myself. I pulled *you* under, to save myself.'

Fran stared at her sightlessly, piecing her memory together with her mother's. 'Oh my God. It was me that nearly drowned you!'

'It wasn't your fault. You were so little. The lifeguard was brilliant. He was straight in to get you.' Her mum's voice was cracked and small. 'But I left you in there, drowning. I've had nightmares about it for years. How could I have just left you in there?'

'Jean?' Her father was awake, frowning at them both in turn. 'What's happened?'

'I've told her.' Her mother's expression was bleak. James clambered to his feet, rubbing his neck. Fran shifted along the bench and he dropped onto the bench beside her mother, shoulder to shoulder. She leaned her head against him. 'I'm so ashamed.'

Fran was silent, thinking and staring out at the sea. She remembered Wyn's words when she'd told him about the beach birthday party that first day she'd gone into the sea with him. That it had been more about her mother trying to overcome her fears than about her. She missed him keenly at that moment. What a lot he'd done for her. And what mental burden was he carrying right now?

'Oh, Mum.' She edged closer to her mother. 'You've carried this around for so long. You couldn't help it. Fear is a terrible thing. I know you wouldn't have hurt me deliberately. Time to let it go.'

Her mother reached out and took her hand. Fran could barely remember a time when she'd done this. Her mother was big on the effusive welcome and goodbye hugs but short on the day-to-day physical gestures. Fran clung on now, feeling the birdlike thinness of the bones in her hand. Her mother had always been whip-thin. But strong. Now she seemed wraithlike and insubstantial and Fran felt a nudge of fear at the thought of losing her.

'I never did get my width badge,' she said, with a rueful smile. Her mother squeezed her hand.

'I'll sew one on for you now, if you like.' She made a wobbly smile.

'Not at the price of bathers these days!' Fran gently bumped her mother's shoulder. 'So, how did you conquer your fear of water?'

'Same as you. Found a good teacher. Eventually. After many false starts. But being in the van, in the heat, and by the sea or a pool — I realized I had to do something about

292

it. Took me a lot longer than a month though. Your Wyn must be good.'

'He is.' *Her* Wyn. Was he hers? 'We're meeting on the beach for nine. What do you want to do for the next couple of hours?'

'We'll go and sort out our kit for tonight, and see you at yours for eight thirty, how's that?'

'Okay.' Fran was relieved. She needed some time to process her mum's revelation. She wished Wyn was there to talk it over with. She could go back to the cottage and try contacting him on the Wi-Fi . . . On the other hand, he knew where she was. She refused to pursue him. She had some pride. He could be weird all by himself.

They put their takeaway packaging in the recycling bins and hugged a goodbye. Fran watched them go with an unaccustomed feeling of sadness. All these wasted years. How much longer did she have with them? She trailed back to the cottage. Her skin felt tight and hot, despite slathering on the sun cream and sitting in the shade. She needed a cool shower, a decent cup of tea, some downtime with one of her textile projects and, possibly, a bit of shuteye. It would have been perfect if Wyn had been there, curled up with her in the bed.

He made her feel secure. For years she'd stepped up to the role of being in charge, and although it had taken her a while, it was lovely to relinquish it. Even in a small way.

She was a realist. Were either of them really likely to give up their lives and move to be with the other, on opposite sides of the country? She couldn't bear the thought of him giving up his life by the sea, his schoolhouse. And did she want to sell her flat? It had been home for so long. But their relationship was so special to her. This lovely, generous man, who shared his kindness and expertise with her, giving her the gift of confidence and swimming. She would miss him terribly. She squeezed her eyes shut, trying not to think about going back to the city. What would she do there? Did she have to go back? Would Wyn even want her to stay here?

It hadn't sounded like he wanted her around for even the afternoon, today.

She couldn't stay out here for ever. Hiding from the world. Wasn't that what her parents did, moving from place to place and never settling? Or were they the ones getting out there and experiencing the world and what it could offer? She'd never had to think about these things when she was working. There'd been too much else to think about.

She wondered for the millionth time what Wyn was doing and whether she ought to go over and find out.

CHAPTER THIRTY-FIVE

Wyn tortured himself all afternoon and evening. Working himself into a sweaty lather, he cleared the weeds and brambles threatening to engulf what had once been the playground and sports pitch. The industrial shredder wolfed down the dried-out branches he'd previously hacked back. Both he and the compost heap steamed in the sunshine.

His mobile remained out of sight, indoors. When he went inside for a drink of water, he saw Fran's messages stacked up on the screen and swallowed.

Coward, his brain shrieked at him as he turned the phone over without unlocking it. *All that stuff you told Fran about choosing to feel fear. That was a lie then, was it?*

He couldn't bear it. His bad arm ached to the bone from going at it like a bull at a gate all day. He hesitated over his stronger painkillers before shaking a couple of paracetamol from a packet. The strong tablets sent him to sleep. He didn't want to be let off the hook that easily. Because he was going to be at that swim. He just needed to get his head in the right place, that was all. He could do it.

He couldn't do it. Propping his arms either side of the toilet bowl after vomiting copiously, he stared down at the foaming flush and only saw the black, hideous depths of that terrible jetty. His legs trembled like a newborn foal. Anger engulfed him.

Why couldn't he shake this off? It was getting worse as the swim drew closer. Fran had overcome a childhood fear that she didn't even remember. A fear that had dogged her entire life, without a firm basis, but a fear that had been very much present. She was now confident in the water. Because of him. So why couldn't he heal himself? He punched the wall and winced at the pain. It was almost satisfying to have something else to occupy his brain.

He couldn't stay here. Fran would come looking for him. He picked up his phone several times but his mind was a blank. He could lie and say something had come up, but lies never came easily to him and she'd know. Running away wouldn't help either, but the clawing, churning sensation in his stomach couldn't let him stay a minute longer.

He threw a random selection of clothes into a holdall and almost ran from the house, pausing only to lock the door.

* * *

At eight thirty, the Sea Sisters arrived outside Fran's with the familiar banging of car doors, along with her parents — all of them in the voluminous changing robes — but no sign of Wyn. Fran joined them outside, dispensing hugs all round. *I've turned into my mum*, she thought.

'Is Wyn coming?' Caitlin looked behind her as if she expected to see him hiding there.

'No idea,' Fran said, trying for a nonchalant smile. She picked up her bag and her inflated tow float, in which was the cycle light that she'd bought from the corner shop, and joined the gentle glows of the other tow float lanterns as they trekked through the dunes. There were crowds of people on the beach. The sun had just sunk below the sea and the clear sky was streaked with turquoise, pinks and lilacs. There was no sign of the moon yet. Unbroken lines of pale surf rolled in right across the darkening beach.

'Yay, waves to play in!' one of the girls shouted.

'I have my camera,' said Fran's dad, patting the bag at his hip.

'Don't you be pointing that my way when I'm in the sea.' Wendy laughed. 'I don't want photos of my arse all over social media, thank you!'

Fran eyed her dad, but he remained his usual, urbane self. 'Different kind of full moon,' was all he said, to a round of laughter.

They set up their camp as usual, as the lilac twilight gave way to a deeper blue dusk. This time, there were other groups nearby, setting up barbeques and firepits, along with chairs, blankets and ice boxes. Everyone wore the ubiquitous changing robes, like the multicoloured uniform of a club.

'I need one of those,' Fran said.

'They're so useful,' said her mum. 'If we're on a site with showers, we just walk over wearing one, shower, and come back to the van to get changed.'

Fran tried not to think about her parents wandering around a campsite naked beneath their changing robes. And worse, what if they'd done what she and Wyn had done in theirs?

'I wonder if I'd ever wear it when I get back to my flat. It's a long way from the sea.' A feeling of dread overcame her at the thought of her flat, the fumes and noise of the city. If Wyn had gone off her, would she stay? She thought of the pitying looks from the villagers and decided she wouldn't.

As the firepit was coaxed into life, Elin materialized at her side. Fran was cheered to see her. 'Hello, are you coming in for a dip?'

'No. I thought I'd come down and watch, as it's your inaugural moonlight swim. I've brought cake.' She put a tin with the other offerings. 'Wyn tells me you've done really well. He's very proud of you.'

'When did he tell you that? Tonight?' Fran looked around, hopeful that he might be there.

'Last week sometime.'

'He's a brilliant teacher.' Fran hesitated. 'But he's been acting really weird today. I thought he'd be here tonight and I haven't heard from him all afternoon.'

Elin put her hand on Fran's arm. 'Wyn is his own man. There'll be a good reason why he hasn't been in touch. And men lose all sense of time, you know. Don't worry, he never lets anyone down. It's a wonderful evening, and look, the moon is just peeping over the horizon.'

She pointed to where a giant orb was shimmering, rising out of the sea and a sharp recollection returned of their night of love on the beach, beneath the deep-pink Strawberry Moon. Where *was* Wyn now? Beacons of flame licked into the night from the assortment of fires along the beach, and naked figures were silhouetted against them on their dash to the sea. Pink and orange tow float lanterns already bobbed on the darkening water. Her mind took a snapshot of the scene. She hoped her dad's camera was up to the task.

'Time to get into that sea!' yelled Caitlin, shrugging off her outer layers. Fran averted her eyes, sure that Caitlin would be naked, relieved to find that she still wore her bathers and ashamed to discover that she was such a prude.

Wendy, though, was not so shy, hurtling naked down to the water's edge with a shriek, accompanied by Cora and, to Fran's horror, her mother.

'Dad!' She spotted him with his camera held to his eye. 'You can't!'

'Don't worry.' He carried on clicking. 'They asked me to. It's good to have memories like this to look back on when you're old and grey, you know. What about you?'

'What about me?' There was no way Fran was stripping off in front of her dad at her age. 'I'm keeping my kit on!'

'Come *on*!' Caitlin urged her.

Fran looked around one more time for Wyn. He wasn't coming. She'd known that, really. All day. Her stomach lurched and she felt nauseous.

'Come on, sweetheart. I want some photos of you in the sea,' Dad said, beckoning her with his head. 'Momentous achievement, tonight. Good for you.'

Fran's legs seemed to have turned to jelly. Caitlin, perhaps sensing how scared she felt, stayed with her as she edged into the water.

'Splash your face,' she reminded Fran, doing it herself and then throwing herself headlong into the indigo water and swimming out to the other girls. Fran set her smartwatch to Outdoor Swim and checked her pulse. Around her, people of all ages, sizes and shapes ran into the sea, many naked. There were shrieked swear words as the cold hit their tender areas, and laughter. Fran remembered the time she'd walked along the beach with Elin and watched enviously as the girls played in the night sea. Now, a pair of moonlit legs shot into the air, waggling for a moment before cartwheeling with a splash. She smiled. Wendy. She wondered if her dad had caught the moment.

The waves frothed around her, rushing up to her armpits, and she gasped, regulating her breathing. The girls cheered as she reached them.

'Well done, Fran!' Caitlin grinned at her as she bobbed towards her. 'That's three boxes ticked today! Your first dawn dip, first moonlight dip, first double dip! You're officially awesome, girl!'

'I bloody am!' Fran grinned back, her heart soaring with pride. 'Thank you, ladies. I would never have done this without you.' Silently, she added, *Or you, Wyn. Wherever you are tonight.*

CHAPTER THIRTY-SIX

'Hi, Dad.' Wyn stooped to enter his father's cottage. 'Sorry to surprise you like this. I, er . . .' He lifted his arms and dropped them again, shoving his hands in his pockets and then taking them out again. His father, Lew, almost as tall as Wyn but stooped by continual bending over tractor engines, held the door wide. 'Would it be okay for me to stop over tonight?'

Lew raised his eyebrows and nodded, but said nothing more than 'All right,' and 'Tea?'

'Aye, please, Dad.'

'Got time to have a gander at the latest project?' Lew asked as he boiled the kettle.

Wyn nodded, feeling his pulse slow as the world receded. 'Course,' he said. 'Does this one have wheels? Or is it a box of bits like the last one?'

'It has wheels.' Lew handed him a mug and led the way into a huge, extended workshop, twice the size of the house. 'They're in the box with the rest of it . . .'

They both laughed the same wheezy laugh and Wyn felt relief wash over him. Guilt filled his mouth with sour bile. He sipped his scalding tea and forced himself to concentrate on his dad's voice.

They were on their third cup of tea and still in the garage when his mobile rang. He fished it out to look at it before he had time to think about who it was.

* * *

Fran and her parents sat around the firepit with the Sea Sisters after the swim, sharing wine, cake, hot dogs and marshmallows, listening to music and sometimes getting up to dance too. She checked her mobile endlessly. Nothing. Barely concentrating on the chat, she thought back over the last couple of days.

What had gone wrong between her and Wyn? Had it been meeting her parents? He'd been fine until then. But he'd been so determined to get rid of them at his house. He'd practically put her outside the door. And no contact at all was very strange. All her senses told her that something was wrong.

She'd had enough of men who kept secrets from her. Secrets that turned out to be wives, in her bitter experience. She was better off on her own. And hadn't that been the whole concept of this stay? No men, she'd said. This was exactly why.

Her parents rose to their feet, brushing sand off themselves. Fran got up too. Elin had retired to bed an hour or so earlier.

'Darling, it's been wonderful, but we'll say goodnight.' Her mum wrapped her in an embrace that felt so much realer than her usual kissy-faced showbiz hug. 'And we're going to move on tomorrow morning. We've had an invitation from some old friends to stay just up the coast, just for a couple of nights, but they're moving on then too, so . . .'

Fran felt abandoned. She tried to swallow past the lump in her throat. 'Okay,' she said brightly. 'Thanks for coming. It's been lovely to see you both.' This time she meant it.

'So we'll be coming back,' her father said, throwing his long arms around the two of them. 'We're only going for a few days, and we'll be back, if that's okay?'

'Oh, yes!' Fran nodded, dashing at the tears that brimmed over her bottom lashes. God, how soppy was she? In the past, she'd always been relieved to see her parents go. 'Have a good trip!'

The Sea Sisters clambered to their feet and gave her parents a hug, waving their goodbyes. Fran fought the urge to burst into tears, like a child.

'All right, Frannie?' Caitlin knuckled her in the arm.

'Mm.' Fran nodded, draining her glass.

'Your folks are awesome,' Wendy said, lifting her glass in a toast. 'And congrats again, Fran, for getting into the sea today. You're bloody awesome too.'

Fran really did cry then.

'Mum told me,' she said, checking that her parents were out of sight and earshot. 'She told me what happened.' The girls leaned forward into the circle of fire as she explained. The sight of one or two of them wiping their own eyes made her throat constrict and tears dribble down her neck.

'Bloody hell,' she said, wiping her eyes as the girls topped up her glass and found something for her to blow her nose on. 'You'd never think I'd been a rufty-tufty police sergeant. I feel like I've missed out on a lifetime of getting to know my parents, and now I have, they're off somewhere else.'

'Aw, *cariad*.' Caitlin's voice was soft. 'They'll be back. And at least you've built those bridges — and you've both conquered your fears. A happy ending, really.'

Nobody mentioned Wyn. He was the elephant in the room, Fran thought. She wrapped her arms around her knees and tried to focus on the conversations going on around her.

* * *

Wyn was thoroughly ashamed to feel relief at not seeing Fran's name on the phone. His disquiet wasn't much alleviated by the caller being Tasha though. As soon as he answered, her sobs reached him.

'Wyn! Where are you? You're not at your place, and I don't know where else to go. I can't stay here, he'll find me—'

'Tash — what's happened?'

'He h-hit me and . . .' Her breath came in a ragged sob. 'I hit him back.'

Wyn put his hand over the receiver and raised his eyebrows at Lew, who shrugged. 'Tash, I'm at Dad's, are you okay to drive? Come straight over.'

'Okay. Th-thank you . . . I'm sorry to be a nuisance.' She sniffed.

'Don't worry about that. Drive carefully. See you in a bit.' Wyn hung up. 'Bugger.'

'What's up?'

Wyn brought him up to speed. 'I'm sorry to land this on you, Dad. I should have gone back home, but I, er . . .' He swallowed, the thought of going to the schoolhouse tonight triggering his fears instantly. He hadn't spoken about his accident to anyone. Nobody. He didn't even know where to start even if he wanted to. His mouth opened and closed.

Lew grunted. 'Mm. You can tell me when you're good and ready, lad. Are you staying over?'

'Thanks, Dad. I think so — but I think it's also time that Tasha made a complaint of assault.'

'Sounds like you could use the advice of that nice policewoman you've taken up with.'

Wyn stared at him. Of course, Fran would know exactly what to do. Could he ring her? After ghosting her all day and behaving like an absolute arse . . . what would she say? Had she done the swim? He'd thought about her all evening.

Tasha's car pulled up outside, interrupting his train of thought. She almost fell through the door as he opened it.

'I'm sorry,' she wailed. Her hands shook. Wyn led her into the kitchen, where Lew already had the kettle on.

'No sugar and no milk for you, is it still, Tasha, love?' he said, as if her visit were perfectly routine and run of the mill. Wyn wanted to hug him. He took his dad for granted, wrapped up in himself as he was. Tasha nodded.

'Thanks, Dad,' she said. Wyn was jolted. She'd always called him Dad. His parents had become her parents, he

303

remembered. He looked at her now, hunched and small on the kitchen chair, her legs knitted together in that way she always had, her make-up smeared and her nose running, and he realized that the love he felt for her was that of a brother. He would never just abandon her. But he didn't love her as a husband. Not the way he loved Fran.

The knowledge skewered him. He loved Fran. If anyone deserved to know what was happening in his life, it was her. If he couldn't tell her about his deepest fears, there was nothing between them.

Tasha rolled up her sleeves and showed them the deepening bruises. The finger marks were livid and turning purple. Worse, though, were those same finger marks around her neck, and the huge bruises on her ribs and back. Wyn felt his fury mount at the sight of her ribs, clearly visible, and the dark linear weals on her back that had broken the skin. When had she got so thin? How had he let this happen?

He picked up his phone and dialled Fran. He'd cope with the fallout of his behaviour later. There were more important things to deal with here.

CHAPTER THIRTY-SEVEN

By one in the morning, the Sea Sisters' firepit was a mere glow. They'd listened to music, played some terribly inappropriate card game by the lights of head torches and laughed until wine came out of their noses, chatted and sung. Confidences were exchanged, relationships were examined and reassembled.

Fran said nothing about Wyn. She refused to believe that they were over. Surely it was a glitch. Something must have come up. Although his strange behaviour belied that, no matter which way she looked at it. Why hadn't he contacted her? She yawned hugely.

'I'm off to bed. You ladies have more stamina than me.' She looked round at them all with affection before scrambling to her feet. 'Love you, ladies. I'm so glad I met you all. Night night.' She blew them a kiss, and Caitlin got up and hugged her fiercely.

'We're glad we met you too. Don't be up all night worrying about Wyn either,' she said quietly into Fran's ear. 'He's a good bloke. Everything will be okay. *Nos da, cariad,* night night.'

Fran's eyes filled again and she fumbled for her already sodden tissue as Caitlin released her.

Her mobile rang. She pulled it out and read the screen. 'It's Wyn.' She stared at Caitlin.

'Well, answer it! Isn't it what you've been waiting for all night?' Caitlin rolled her eyes. After a moment's hesitation, Fran pressed *Accept*.

'Fran — I've got a lot to explain, I know, and I know it's really late, but I, we, really need you right now, so could you possibly come over to . . .' He broke off, and she heard him clearly speaking to someone else. 'No! Don't wash it! I'm pretty sure that's evidence . . .'

'Wyn — I've been drinking. I can't drive anywhere. What's happened?' Fran stared at the girls around the fire, all of them looking back at her. Evidence? She shrugged in bemusement.

'Can I come and get you? It's Tasha . . .' Fran rolled her eyes. *Tasha. Again. Of course it was.* 'She's black and blue and we've persuaded her to make a complaint about him. But I'm out of my depth here . . .' She heard his sharp, frustrated intake of breath. 'Please. If you could, can you help? I'm sorry I've been an arse. I can explain. I'll be there in fifteen, twenty tops.'

Fran slipped straight into police mode. 'Don't let her change or wash. Not even her hands. I'll be ready when you come over.'

'Thanks, Fran, I—' He hung up.

'Gotta go, ladies,' she said to the group. 'Seems that at least I have some uses.' She flashed them a rueful smile and hurried into the cottage to their chorus of 'Good luck, whatever it is!'

There was just time for her to wash the salt off herself and change into clean jeans and a sweatshirt before he turned up. Her heart jumped at the sight of him until she looked more closely. He looked grey and stricken, his cheeks somehow sunken. What the hell had been happening?

He bent to kiss her, and although every cell of her wanted his lips on hers, she turned a cool cheek and walked out of the cottage towards his van, locking the door behind her.

'Thank you, Fran,' he began, sitting beside her in his familiar seat. 'I have a lot to explain.'

Fran gritted her teeth. *Yes, you can explain why you've ignored my calls all day and night and yet Tasha seems to have a direct line to you.* 'It can wait until later. What's happened with Tasha?'

Wyn filled her in and she compressed her lips. 'You said she hit him back?'

'Yes, I don't know anything about that. I thought you'd be the best person to . . .' He glanced at her. 'I'm really sorry, Fran. I—'

Fran lifted a hand and cut him off mid-flow. She didn't want to hear his apologies. Tasha was an all too prominent part in his life. She couldn't think of any of the men she worked with who had anything much to do with their ex-wives, unless there were children involved. There had to be more to it. All she could think was that he'd blown her off in favour of Tasha and now expected her to rock up and help. Well, she was a professional, and she'd do it. After that though . . .

She glanced at his lean, serious profile and her throat closed. Was this the end? The journey continued in an uncomfortable silence. His father's cottage was between Llanbryn and the next hamlet, and occupied a considerable piece of land.

In the dark, Fran made out a large workshop, garage, greenhouse and those tall sticks in a tepee shape that indicated things growing up them. The tall, lean man in the doorway looked like a slightly shorter version of Wyn, but with white hair. Same deep-blue eyes, same generous smile. Wyn made the introductions quickly as they went inside.

'Nice to meet you, Fran.' Lew held out a warm, dry hand. 'Tasha is in the kitchen.' He led the way through the small but cosy sitting room, which opened out into a large kitchen with a scrubbed pine table in the centre, at which sat a dejected Tasha. Any animosity against Tasha dissolved at the sight of her. One side of her face was puffing up before her.

'Hello, Tasha.' Fran kneeled before her and looked up into her miserable eyes. 'You haven't washed or changed your clothes, have you?'

'No.' Tasha's voice was low and thick with tears. 'Wyn told me you said not to.'

'Good girl. Let's get you to the police station and get a doctor to see you. They'll want photos and that sort of thing, okay?'

Tasha nodded. 'Thank you. I'm sorry to be a nuisance.'

Fran stood up and smiled at her. 'You don't have to be sorry. You've been very brave, and it's time to be a little bit braver. But we'll be there for you. Can you walk okay?'

They put Tasha between them on the bench seat of the van, like a child. Fran explained in a quiet, calm voice what she could expect to happen when they arrived.

She looked around her with interest as they helped Tasha into the police station. It felt like déjà vu. Apart from all the bilingual notices and posters, it was just like her own nick. The officers were kind and courteous with Tasha, and procedure swung into action beneath her approving eyes. She was quietly thrilled when Wyn produced the CCTV file from the Mermaid Inn on the night Fran had arrived, providing evidence of another of AJ's assaults on Tasha.

Eventually, Fran and Wyn were left to their own devices. They promised Tasha they'd wait for her and sat in the car park in Wyn's van with a takeaway coffee. The first faint hints of dawn streaked the sky with lilac. Fran felt wide awake.

'Fran, I . . . God, I don't even know where to start here.' Wyn braced his arms against the steering wheel and took a deep breath. Fran froze, clutching the coffee in both hands. This was it, wasn't it? He was going to tell her that he and Tasha were back together. She couldn't really blame him. Tasha was so vulnerable, and they had a long history together. He would look after her, just as he always had. Because he was a good man. And Fran could look after herself. Just as she always had.

'Thank you, first of all.' He turned to her and reached for her hand. She looked down at it and didn't respond. She understood what he was doing, but she didn't have to like it. His hand trailed back to his side, returning to rest on the steering wheel. She wanted to cry. 'I've never told anyone this. Not a soul.' He scrubbed a hand through his hair, leaving it sticking up. 'I should have told you—'

'Look, Wyn, shall I make it easy for you? You and Tasha, back together, yes?'

'What?' His jaw dropped and his head whipped round to face her. 'Me and—? No! God, no.' He slapped the steering wheel and turned his whole body towards her, his knees rammed up awkwardly against the gear stick. 'No, Fran.' He shook his head, vehemently. 'No.'

'That's a no then, is it?' Fran smiled faintly. She didn't dare breathe.

'Yes! It's a no.' He laughed and reached for her hand again. This time she met it halfway. 'I'm sorry you even thought that. Fran, I love you. And I know it's not been that long but — when you know, you know. But listen . . .' He held his hand up as she opened her mouth to speak. 'I have to tell you something. About why I've been a total arse the last couple of days. And you've been utterly wonderful.'

She contented herself with nodding to show that she was listening. His hand felt just right round hers. He loved her!

'My accident. I told you it was—'

'A crane fell on you . . .'

'Yes. What I didn't tell you was that—' he inhaled raggedly — 'I was underwater at the time . . .'

'*Uuuh* . . .' Fran digested this news with growing horror.

'A tanker had overturned in this dock. They brought a crane in to lift it, but someone had to go down and attach hooks to the tanker so it could be lifted. That was me and another bloke. We'd done the job and I was swimming away . . . The stupid bastards didn't wait for me to come up before they started lifting. They'd miscalculated the weights and . . .' He gulped. 'The tanker pulled the crane into the dock. I was trapped between it and, well, it was either the dock wall or some other structure that was down there, I never did find out.' He rubbed at his scar.

'Oh my God, Wyn.' Fran could barely breathe. 'How did they . . . ?'

'How did they get me out?'

She nodded. 'You don't have to tell me if . . .'

'No. It's helping. Weirdly. I never thought it would.' He drained his coffee. 'I was alone down there. It's pitch black in the docks. The water is always filthy with crap from the boats, and all the muck had been stirred up from this tanker. I didn't even know which way up I was.' His fingers gripped hers convulsively. 'It was terrifying. And I was in so much pain.' He turned his deep-blue eyes on her. 'I wanted to die. To be out of pain. Away from the fear. I never thought I would ever say something like that.'

Fran caught the sob in her throat and shuffled across the bench seat towards him, folding him into an awkward embrace. 'I'm so glad you're still here.'

'So they called out the fire brigade and those guys came down with inflatable air bags.' He shook his head. 'Amazing. I was almost out of air by then. I'd sucked that tank dry in my panic. They pulled me out of there half dead. I owe them my life.' He was silent for a long moment. Fran was lost, visualizing what he'd been through.

'I spent a long time in hospital, being rebuilt. Plastic surgery and all that. They thought I would lose the arm. There were times when I thought it might have been preferable.'

'You've come a long way since then. You're amazing.'

He shook his head. 'I survived. But . . .' He swallowed. 'I can't . . . I can't be in the water the way I used to.'

Fran frowned. 'But you went into the pool with me.' She thought back. 'And you took me into the sea!'

'Carefully controlled.' He looked out of the windscreen. 'Always in daylight. Never out of our depth.' He glanced at her and then away. 'I did not want to get into the pool, that first time. I was terrified that I wouldn't be able to save you if you drowned.'

'But . . . You were always so calm! You made me calm!'

He huffed a laugh. 'I used my own psychology on myself. And, of course, the water in the pool was clean, and clear and blue, so it didn't remind me of . . . And I controlled the sea swims really carefully. That first swim, late afternoon, in the sunshine, remember? The Strawberry Moon came up that night . . .' He smiled at her. She'd never forget that night. 'The other swims, always in the daylight, never out of our depth. Perfect tides. Tow floats, buoyancy jackets, as much safety as I could manage.'

'Wow.'

'And it worked. But I couldn't make it work tonight.'

'You've been having the terrors since that night at the pub,' Fran realized, piecing it all together. 'Oh God. You poor thing. And I went on and on about it . . . and you were probably screaming inside for me to shut up. I wish you'd told me.'

Wyn hung his head. 'I couldn't.' He sighed gustily. 'I couldn't even come to terms with it in my own head. I felt — *feel* — like such a failure.'

'Didn't you get counselling in hospital?'

'I was offered it. I turned it down. I've never believed in all that crap. Least said, soonest mended, my gran used to say.'

'All this time — you've carried this terrible fear? And still taught me to swim? Oh, Wyn . . . You're so brave!'

'I thought I could do it. I didn't want to disappoint you.' He cleared his throat. 'I was more scared about losing you than about the water, in a way. But my body wouldn't let me.' His head drooped. 'I was physically sick — uncontrollably. I couldn't handle it at all. And then I felt so angry with myself that I couldn't fix myself the way I'd helped to fix you. All I could think about was how disappointed you'd be in me. In the end—' he averted his eyes — 'I ran away. To my dad's. He doesn't know how badly the accident affected me either. I don't know if he guesses. He never asks questions. Just lets me be.'

Fran's heart broke for him. She sat in silence, holding him, feeling how tense his muscles were.

'I'm glad you told me.' She nestled closer to him — uncomfortable as it was, it was preferable to being apart. 'And I hope you know that I could never be disappointed in you. Thinking back now, it's all making sense. Why you wouldn't get in the pool with me . . .'

Wyn nodded, relief flooding his face. 'I was terrified that I wouldn't be able to save you if you got into trouble.'

'But you did. My first tears-and-snot episode, and you were straight there. I remember thinking how awesome you were.'

'*Your* bravery helped *me* to conquer my fears. I wasn't awesome. I was relieved.' They sat in silence for a long moment. Wyn said, into her hair, 'I haven't even asked you. Did you swim tonight?'

'I did!' Fran sat up and faced him. 'I'm not going to tell you how much I missed you or you'll get bigheaded, but I did it, and it was amazing.'

'I was there in spirit.'

'Like hell you were.' Fran grinned at him, cheekily. 'You were mentally in the next county, as far away from a moonlight swim as it was possible to be . . .'

His mouth lifted. 'I can't deny it.'

'It's okay though,' she said, peeping at him from under her lashes. 'Because I love you too.' Their lips met in a fusion of longing and realization. 'I've been wondering about renting out my flat and moving down here . . .'

'The sea is quite a pull, isn't it?' In the bleak lights of the car park, she saw a smile flit across his face and she knuckled him gently on the thigh.

'Only if you're there with it,' she told him, reaching up to smooth the bristles that were showing on his firm jaw.

'I was thinking about selling Y Hen Ysgol and moving to the city,' he said, as her lips lingered over his. 'I don't want to let you go now I've found you. You mean everything to me.'

By the time Tasha rang them to collect her, the windows of the van were completely steamed up.

EPILOGUE

The strings of bunting flapped in time with Fran's heart-beat. The Sea Sisters clustered around her, clutching their early-morning coffees and blondies, just as they had at the same time last year. Only this year, everything had changed.

'Save me one of those for when I get out,' Fran said. She stood on the beach in a wetsuit and changing robe, surveying the flat, calm sea.

'You'd better swim quick then,' Caitlin told her. 'These blondies are hard to resist . . .'

'I do love that changing robe, Frannie.' Wendy reached out to touch it. 'I'll look after it for you while you're in the water . . . It'll really suit me . . .'

'It's gorgeous, isn't it?' Fran looked down at the brilliantly colourful pattern adorning the changing robe that her parents had given her for her birthday — another wonderful day on the beach with all her favourite Llanbryn friends and family. 'It's got my name in it, by the way, Wendy.' Laughing at her friend's pretend pout, she gazed in wonderment at the tall feather flags and the barriers. 'I still can't believe I'm actually here.'

Her memory replayed the months. AJ had been arrested and charged, and eventually resigned after the court case. He and Tasha divorced and sold their house, and rumour had it he'd moved to England. Tasha had moved in with a newly single girlfriend and seemed much more settled.

In a wonderful turn of goodwill, Tasha told Wyn that one of their teams of builders was at a loose end after a contract fell through, and suggested they could be available to push on with work on his schoolhouse.

'Fran can't live with you in that mess,' Tasha had said matter-of-factly. 'She deserves better.' Fran had returned her ghost of a wink with a smile. It hadn't taken Wyn long to accept, and the building was finally habitable.

When April and Ken emailed to tell Fran that they were extending their visit and staying with a couple they'd met on their travels, and would she consider staying on, Fran was only too overjoyed to accept, and Gavin and Ally were delighted to remain in her flat.

Her parents hurried across the beach towards her, wrapping her in a hug. She couldn't wait to show them Y Hen Ysgol now. It even included a separate, self-contained property which could be rented out. Or which her parents could live in, if they ever needed to stop travelling.

'Break a leg, sweetheart,' said her father. 'I'll get lots of photos.' He tapped the ever-present camera slung round his neck.

'You look *faaabulous* in that changing robe, darling!' her mother said. 'I'm so proud of you. Where's Wyn?'

'He's out there, on one of the rescue boats.' Fran pointed. 'That way he can yell at me as I go past.'

'How sweet.' Her mum smiled. 'Words of encouragement.'

'More likely: *keep your elbows high*! Or, *look where you're bloody going*!' Fran grinned. Wyn had trained and prepared her for this first newcomers' swim event to be held at the Llanbryn Triathlon. Although her heart thudded crazily, it was with anticipation and not fear, or another heart attack. She could do this.

'Good luck, and enjoy!' said another competitor, passing her with his small children in tow.

'Thanks, you too!' Fran called back, feeling tingly at the thought of belonging to this expanding field of black neoprene gathered at the sea's edge. She checked that she had her goggles, that her race number was securely fixed to her fluorescent-pink bib for the millionth time, and that her hair was tucked inside her bright-pink competition swim hat.

'Yo, Sarge!'

She whirled around at the familiar voice. Gavin and Ally, burdened with beach chairs and blankets, pushed through the soft sand towards her.

'Hi, guys! What a lovely surprise! *Bore da*!' She wished them good morning in Welsh, enjoying Gavin's huge grin.

'*Bore da* to you too! *Da iawn*, well done!'

'Steady, Gav, there's a limit to my language skills!' Fran smiled. 'You've come to welcome your folks home? I've virtually moved out ready for them!'

'Tell you later. Lots to catch up on, we won't distract you now. Good luck!' Gavin nodded towards the officials, marshalling the competitors towards the start, and Fran felt her stomach cartwheel.

'Start at the sides or the back,' Wyn had reminded her that morning, as he applied lube to the back of her neck to prevent her wetsuit chafing. 'And go in at your own pace. You're aiming to get round, that's a huge achievement. You know you can do it. I'll be watching!' He'd kissed her, given her a solid hug and rushed off to man one of the rescue boats. She'd smiled to see his tall form loping away.

'Good luck, Frannie!' chorused the Sea Sisters as she joined the rest of the wetsuited throng. She could still hear them shouting, 'Go, Frannie, go, Frannie, go!' as she waited for the klaxon to sound. In that moment, she took stock of herself.

Over a year ago, lying in a hospital bed after a shock heart attack, she could never have imagined that she'd be swimming in the sea, let alone in a competition. That she'd find new, wonderful friends, a new lifestyle, a new passion — swimming had become so much more than a hobby — and love. And that her terrible scar would fade to a thin, silvery line that was barely noticeable.

She'd become immersed in her textile art, reawakening her love of art alongside Elin, who had embarked on yet another art course. She'd worked several times at the Art Hotel — she and Wyn finding much common ground with Lucy and Ash. She'd learned to garden, forged a relationship with her parents at last, and found a soulmate to share her life with. Whatever shape their lives together took, she and Wyn would shape it together. It was an adventure. And wherever it would take them, it had only just begun.

She barely noticed her feet skimming across the damp sand with everyone else when the starter horn hooted. She was aware of nothing but the moment as she settled her goggles into position. She even remembered to set her watch as she waded into the sea, feeling the water creeping up her wetsuit in a way that was now wholly familiar to her. Her heart thumped away, doing its job. Her routine cardiac check-up had been at the local hospital, where she'd been thoroughly scanned and tested, and pronounced fit to go. They'd nodded wisely when she told them she swam daily.

'Best exercise there is,' they said. 'Just be sensible now. Go and enjoy your life.' She really was.

The first buoy appeared through a haze of swimmers' arms and flailing legs and she was glad she'd hung back. She couldn't imagine the responsibility of having to check your course at the front of the race. Wyn had taught her the quick way around the buoy and she'd practised it over and over. She hoped it wouldn't desert her now. Flipping over and back as she imagined herself skidding around the corner, she was rewarded with Wyn's yell of joy. She smiled, remembering that he'd told her to do that too.

'Relax and smile at the water,' he'd said. 'If your jaw is relaxed, then you are too. Enjoy it!' She was astounded to find that she was. The water was calm and she settled into her stroke and her breathing, reassured by the presence of so many other swimmers around her. She glimpsed the crowd on the shore during her breaths, wondering if they were cheering, remembering the guy swimming across the bay on that first moonlit night. That would be next on her agenda. Maybe with Wyn, maybe not. What would be, would be. She was in nature's arms, in the sea, at one with the world. A tiny speck afloat on life's ocean.

The second buoy came into view, with a swimmer holding on to it. Another competitor was being hauled onto the RIB and larger gaps had appeared between swimmers. Fran lined herself up and managed her fast turn, patting herself on the back as the beach drew closer and closer.

She had no idea where she was in the field. She didn't care if she was last as long as she got to that beach. Her arms seemed to have a life of their own, churning over and over like a living paddle steamer. The waves gave her a much-needed push and she felt her hands brush the sand even as she watched the swimmers in front stand and run out of the sea. She felt as if she could just lie there, in the water, heavy and waterlogged.

'Come on, Fran!' her friends shrieked at her, and she pushed herself upright. She felt a hundred stone. How the people in front were jogging out, she had no idea. She'd seen the triathlon competitors running out and jumping on their pedal cycles the year before. How did they do it? At least she didn't have to do that. But . . . *Maybe next year*, she was shocked to hear her brain whisper.

Pinning a smile to her face as she spotted her father and his camera, she waded and skipped over the shallows, managing a little jog to the finish line before flopping forward, her hands braced on her knees. Seawater poured out of her nose.

'You're a proper mermaid now, missus,' Caitlin said, throwing her changing robe over her and patting her back. 'Well done, you.'

'Well. I suppose we'll all have to do it next year, now you've showed us up,' said Wendy. 'I nearly ate your blondie in all the excitement.'

'Congratulations, Fran,' said Elin, binoculars around her neck. 'Textbook race, excellent job, well done. Obviously, I picked the perfect teacher for you.'

Fran stood up straight and beamed at them all. She turned to face the sea. For a lifetime, she'd been terrified to even paddle in it.

'I couldn't have done it without you all,' she said.

'God. Is it the Oscars?' Wendy grinned and reached out to hug her, followed by all the other Sea Sisters, then her parents, Elin and Gavin and Ally. Just as Fran thought the hugfest was over, she was assailed by Lucy and Ash from the Art Hotel, Ash's tall and willowy teenage daughter Daisy, and their cute-as-a-button baby girl, Lowri, in an all-terrain buggy.

'We saw you!' Lucy said, wiping tears from her face. 'You're amazing! It was such a long way, however did you do it? We would have been earlier but Lowri had a poo-nami . . .'

They all looked at the baby, who gurgled a laugh and waved her chubby fists at them.

Fran laughed. 'Aw, she's so cute!'

'Excuse me, I think it's my turn now,' said a familiar voice, as she was enveloped by a giant bear of a man and lifted off the sand. 'Fran, you're an absolute marvel, you are. Fantastic swim. I love you!'

'Only cos I make your teaching look good,' Fran said in a muffled squeak as she was squashed against him. He released her a little, but not much, grinning down at her with pride in his eyes. 'And I love you too!' She looked around at them all. 'You're all coming to the beach party tonight, aren't you? I'm looking forward to it even more now — can't wait to try the street food!'

'Too right!' they choroused.

'Can we?' Daisy looked pleadingly at her parents.

'Of course, sweetie!' Lucy nodded. Daisy opened her mouth, and Fran smothered her grin as Lucy added quickly, 'We'll discuss timings later, darling, shall we?' Like all teenagers, Daisy was keen to push her boundaries, but Lucy was no pushover.

Tasha stepped over the sand towards them, tanned in tiny pink shorts, sheepskin boots and an oversized white cotton sweater. She looked like a Neapolitan ice cream. She beamed at them, reaching out to hug Fran first.

'Congratulations, Fran! You did really well!' Fran grinned, accepting the almost condescending tone. Tasha was trying hard. They would never be mates but that was okay now. They respected each other.

'Thanks, Tasha. How's things?'

'I just wanted you both to know that I'm leaving.' Tasha looked up at them. 'For the city lights!'

'Wow!' Wyn said. 'London?'

'Cardiff!' She shook her head without a trace of irony and Fran hid a grin. 'My company have a big project there and—' she lifted her pointed chin in a smile — 'my new boss has taken a bit of a shine to me. We're getting on really well, so . . .' She met Wyn's eye. 'And don't worry, we're taking it slow, and he's really good to me, so there'll be no late-night calls to be rescued anymore.'

'I'm pleased to hear it.' Wyn reached out and shook her hand. Fran reached out to hug her again, genuinely happy for her.

'Good luck, Tasha.'

Much later, sitting around the familiar firepit with her parents, the Sea Sisters, Gavin and Ally, and of course, Elin, music thumping into the soft indigo night, they toasted one another in wine and beer and hot chocolate, danced and ate hot dogs and street food. The organizers certainly knew how to stage an end-of-event festival. Even Wyn's father joined them, after staging a vintage tractor procession through the village with all his tractor mates.

'I've missed this,' Gavin said to Fran, as she sat alongside. 'And your constant updates haven't helped at all.'

'Mm?' Fran eyed him. She knew him well enough to know that he had something to tell her. Ally sat close to him, warm and pretty in a colourful knitted bobble hat.

'So, I've applied for a transfer.' He tipped his head towards her. 'Here.'

'Yes?' She focused on him intently.

'And I've been accepted!'

'Sergeant?' She held her breath.

'Yes!'

'Gav, that's brilliant news!' She pumped his hand and Wyn reached out a long arm to shake hands too. 'Your parents will be thrilled!'

'I haven't finished.' Gavin glanced at Ally with a shy smile, and Fran knew what was coming next. 'We're pregnant!'

'Aw, congratulations, both of you.' Fran felt tears pricking at her eyes and squeezed Wyn's hand. 'I'm thrilled for you.'

'We're not at the public stage yet, but we wanted to let you know, and when we heard about the swim, we couldn't not come,' Ally said, her cheeks flushed by the firelight. 'And I think this is a very good place for children to grow up.'

'Congratulations.' Wyn got up to hug them both. 'You know where to come for babysitting. Fran is a dab hand with a nappy.'

'Really?' Gavin's eyebrows rose into his hair.

'No.' Fran laughed. 'But Wyn is, and I can learn.' She grinned. 'And as it happens, I have some news too.'

'You're staying in Wales. Aren't you?'

'I am, yes! Top detective work!' She looked up at the solid, reassuring bulk of Wyn, listening quietly to the conversation with a smile. 'I didn't want to throw you out of the flat, but I'm going to rent it out.' She took a breath. 'It'll be lovely to meet your parents at last.'

'It will be good to see April and Ken again,' Elin said, 'but I will miss you as a neighbour, Fran. I've enjoyed our art appreciation sessions!'

'Oh, me too, Elin! I've learned so much about gardening from you. And gin,' she added, to laughter. 'And I'm not going far . . .' She smiled up at Wyn, a little shy. 'Pity you didn't let me know, Gav, you could have stayed at Seagull Cottage tonight.'

'Where?' Gavin raised an eyebrow.

'I never did master that Welsh name.' Fran laughed. 'It will always be Seagull Cottage to me!'

'If we get married, you'll have to learn a bit more Welsh . . .' Wyn said.

'If?' Fran sat upright, her heart pounding. 'Is that a proposal?'

He turned towards her. 'Do you want it to be a proposal?'

Fran swallowed. 'I have thought about it . . .' She studied him. 'Is it a proposal?' She frowned slightly. Was he being serious? 'It's not very romantic.'

A smile flitted across his handsome, craggy face. 'What do you mean, not romantic? There's a fire. And nearly a full moon, look!' He nodded firmly. 'Yes. It's a proposal. But only if you're going to say yes. I don't want to embarrass myself any further.'

Fran was aware of everyone holding their breath and listening intently. She ran her tongue around her lips. Was this for real?

'I'm only teasing you. Of course I'm going to say yes. I want a real proposal though. And a ring. Or it doesn't count.'

'I knew you wouldn't let me off the hook.' Wyn kneeled down before her, and her father raised his camera. To her astonishment, Gavin produced a small velvet box and passed it to Wyn. The Sea Sisters and Elin linked hands with her mum and Ally, beaming.

'Fran, will you marry me?' Wyn held out the opened box to her. A beautiful ring winked at her, with a blue sapphire in the centre.

'Yes! Of course, yes! Yes, please! Erm, *ydy wir*! Of course! Did I say that right?' Tears sprang to her eyes. There was a cheer from her friends and parents.

'It's stunning,' Fran breathed. 'I'm not taking it out of the box, on the sand.' She stared at the lovely ring before closing up the box carefully and throwing her arms around Wyn.

322

'I guessed your size, so it probably won't fit. We can have it altered though.'

'It's so beautiful . . .' Fran tore her eyes from Wyn's and stared around at family and friends, as they grinned back at her. 'And you all knew!'

'Yeah. Call yourself a copper?' Caitlin laughed.

'Not anymore,' Fran said with a smile.

'No, you're honorary Welsh now!' Wyn said. 'And we're keeping you!'

THE END

ACKNOWLEDGEMENTS

Those wise words, 'write what you know', ring very true for this story. I'd originally planned for poor Fran to be assaulted on duty, but when I found myself in hospital for six weeks following a surprise heart attack, I decided that it was useful research and gave her a heart attack instead.

My first thank you is to the wonderful staff at the University Hospital of Wales in Cardiff, particularly the Cardiac Units. It's a tribute to them that I'm here to tell the tale, particularly as I thought I was just having a bad bout of indigestion and would be kicked out pronto with a big bottle of Gaviscon . . .

My thanks also, as ever, to my friend Pippa, who runs the fabulous Coco&Co chocolate shop opposite my studio. She patiently reads every one of my books in their raw, draft version, and has a unique ability to oversee clunky grammar and punctuation and get right to the nitty gritty of what makes the characters tick.

I trained as a swimming instructor when I left the police, and always ended up teaching the youngest children — mainly as I had no qualms about standing on the poolside barking like a dog and making like a frog as my charges copied me. Thanks to my lovely friend Annie, for letting me practise the swimming tuition that Wyn does with Fran. I'm pleased to say I improved her stroke technique no end, but I let her off the barking like a dog.

The swimming group I belong to on the South Wales coast has been the primary inspiration for the friendship and support that hopefully shines through in the book. None of my characters are based on any one person, but rather a flavour of them all. They're fabulous.

I have a Facebook author page, with a terrific bunch of lovely and involved readers, who sprang into action when I needed to rename a couple of characters. One was the dog, whose name was too similar to the landlord, and caused confusion. After a gazillion posts, I chose Scruff from Kaye Hewins, and it turned out that the original Scruff had been a rescue dog from Spain. He also looked a lot like my beloved border terrier, so that sealed the deal.

I also needed a name beginning with T, and fellow Choc Lit author Kirsty Ferry suggested Tasha, which fitted the bill nicely. We had a lot of fun with that and I will definitely be doing it again.

Lastly, thanks to the Choc Lit panel for their lovely comments on that first read, and to my editors for their tireless inspection of my occasionally wonky timelines, argh!

THE CHOC LIT STORY

Established in 2009, Choc Lit is an independent, award-winning publisher dedicated to creating a delicious selection of quality women's fiction.

We have won 18 awards, including Publisher of the Year and the Romantic Novel of the Year, and have been shortlisted for countless others.

All our novels are selected by genuine readers. We are proud to publish talented first-time authors, as well as established writers whose books we love introducing to a new generation of readers.

In 2023, we became a Joffe Books company. Best known for publishing a wide range of commercial fiction, Joffe Books has its roots in women's fiction. Today it is one of the largest independent publishers in the UK.

We love to hear from you, so please email us about absolutely anything bookish at: choc-lit@joffebooks.com

If you want to hear about all our bargain new releases, join our mailing list: www.choc-lit.com

Printed in the USA
CPSIA information can be obtained
at www.ICGtesting.com
LVHW091251050124
767941LV00069B/2781